WORLDS COLLIDE

THE MAFIA WEAPON

By

Paula Ellison Franklin

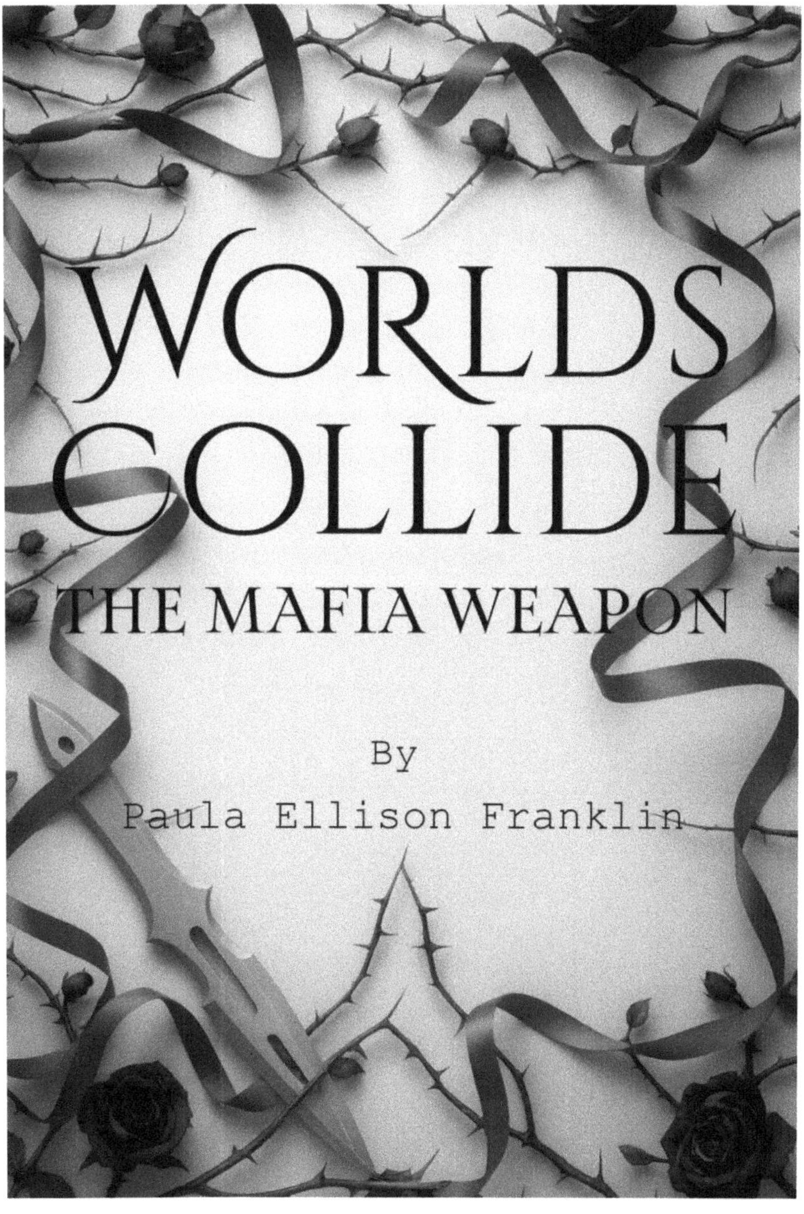

ISBN:979-8-9994056-1-6

Book cover and design by:
Paula Ellison Franklin

Illustration- All images were originally designed or photographed by: Paula Ellison Franklin

Author Website:
https://doc.gus.mybluehost.me/website_3e1e9279

Author email:

prettypaulaspages@yahoo.com

Table of Contents

CHAPTER 1

Conner's heart was crushed. Even with Riley's approval to seek a way to win Tennly back, he couldn't muster the energy to believe it would actually happen. Instead, he spent every day of Thanksgiving break lounging on the couch until his eyes grew too heavy to stay open. His friends urged him to go out with them several times, but he remained unmoved, moping around his house and avoiding reality.

Dougy, on the other hand, enjoyed having Conner home. It allowed him to spend time with his brother without outside distractions. Aside from Thanksgiving Day, when Conner went to Riley's, something he had done every year since middle school, the two Marks brothers spent every day together. They watched movies, played video games, and Conner even taught Dougy how to cook a few things. It was the closest Dougy had felt to his brother in years.

"I'm going to grab a beer," Conner said, sliding off the recliner. "Want one?"

"Sure."

Conner placed his plate in the sink and got two cans of beer from the refrigerator while Dougy enthusiastically shouted over an amazing football play. Conner quickly walked back over in hopes of catching the replay, but as he sat down, he noticed Dougy was looking at his phone, worry lines forming across his forehead.

"What's Rick want?" Conner assumed.

"It's Josie," Dougy corrected hesitantly.

"What does she want?"

Dougy took a deep breath before explaining, "Tennly's coming back. She should be here later tonight."

Conner felt as though his soul had been sucked out of his chest. The thought of seeing Tennly filled him with a mix of emotions, making it difficult to pinpoint exactly how he was feeling. Not wanting his brother to see how much the news affected him, he leaned back and pretended to focus on the football game.

"Come on! Where's the line at?"

Dougy glanced at his brother; his body language suggested he was fine, but his sorrowful eyes and the way he bit his lower lip told a different story. "What are you doing?"

"Watching a football game."

"No, you're ignoring what I said."

"Yep," Conner replied, signaling that he wanted Dougy to drop it, which he did. However, after a couple of minutes of stewing on the thought of Tennly's return, Conner unexpectedly asked, "Does she know if she'll be at school tomorrow?"

"Her dad is taking her first thing in the morning to re-enroll her," Dougy answered, relieved that his brother was finally discussing it. "What are you going to do?"

"I don't know."

Tennly woke up earlier than usual, having tossed and turned all night due to the uncertainty of what would happen when she saw Conner. The feeling of anxiety intensified as she sat in the school office waiting to get re-enrolled. She almost told her father that she wanted to leave; however, as she watched student after student come in and cast looks that ranged from contemptuous to pitying, her nervousness turned into anger. Seeing them reminded her of Conner's reputation, which she despised. So, by the time she met her friends at their lockers, she was ready to face anything.

"Hey," Tennly said, poking Josie on the back as she was organizing her locker.

Josie and Abby simultaneously squealed, "Tennly," as they took turns giving her hugs.

"Are you okay?" Josie asked as Tina approached.

"I'm fine," Tennly replied, "I just needed a mental health vacation."

"I'm glad it helped," Josie said.

"And we're so glad you're back," Abby added.

"Thanks," Tennly responded, leaning back against the lockers while her friends continued to get their books ready. "It's nice to see that nothing has changed around here," she sarcastically grunted.

"The stares?" Josie asked.

"Yeah," Tennly answered.

Abby shut her locker and muttered, "You didn't tell her?"

"Tell me what?" Tennly inquired.

"There's a rumor," Josie disclosed, playing it off as nothing. "You know how it gets around here."

"What rumor, Josie?" Tennly pressed, just as Tina finished locking her locker.

Josie hesitated before replying, "They still think you got pregnant and went away to have an abortion."

Tennly let out a boisterous laugh with a sarcastic undertone. Of all the things she had been through over the last several weeks, the last thing she needed was for everyone to think she was pregnant. She leaned her head back against the lockers to gather her thoughts and then looked back at her friends.

"I needed to get away from here," Tennly admitted. "From him. I went back to my old boarding school to think. It gave me a new outlook on things: what's important and what isn't. These rumors are not important."

"What about Conner?" Abby shuddered. "I only ask because... he's walking this way."

Tennly looked in the direction Abby had pointed and saw Conner approaching. The sight of him reignited the fire she had over him taking the money, making her want to punch him in the face. She had thought she felt better after her father told her that he had returned it, but she didn't.

Despite how she felt, she couldn't bring herself to hurt him. Seeing him again rekindled every emotion she ever had for him, and it was as if her feet were glued to the floor. She could feel her body trying to move, to walk away, but, like a magnet, the closer he got to her, the stronger the pull became.

"Hi," he said, causing everyone to stop what they were doing to watch.

"Hi," Tennly replied in a terse tone.

"We need to talk," he sighed, with pleading eyes.

"There's nothing to talk about," Tennly retorted. "I need to go to class."

Her words helped her break free from the emotional pull she felt, giving her the strength to turn away from him. She slipped her arm through Josie's, as if using her as a tugboat, and then started to walk away.

"Stop!" Conner yelled.

He understood her intentions; she was trying to demonstrate to him and everyone else that she wouldn't easily accept him back. Although he agreed with her stance, he felt the need to explain himself. She paused but didn't turn around, not wanting him to think she was conceding so easily.

"Tennly, please." Sensing the sadness in his voice and hated knowing she was the cause; she turned to face him. "I need to show you something."

Tennly's rational thought urged her to do what her mind suggested: walk away. But as Victoria's words telling her not to give up on him echoed in her mind, her heart won over. She glanced at her friends, who clearly didn't want her to go with him, and said, "I'll see you guys later."

"Tennly," Josie pleaded, concern etched on her face.

"I'll call you later," Tennly reassured and turned back toward Conner.

Both were nervous, wanting to say something, but remained silent as they left the school and got into Conner's car. It wasn't until she noticed they were driving out of town that Tennly spoke up.

"Conner, I can't do this. I have to get back."

He swerved the car over and looked at her. "I'll take you back if that's really what you want. I know I don't deserve anything from you, but if you could just let me show you something, I promise I'll never bother you again."

His admission that he didn't deserve anything from her reminded her of how he always felt about himself, and tears welled in her eyes. She placed her hand over her mouth to hide the quiver of her lips and looked out the side window.

"I just don't want to hurt you anymore, Ten."

"Okay," was all she could manage to say without revealing that she was crying.

They drove for twenty minutes out of town before turning onto an old two-lane dirt road that eventually forked. He took the left path and drove for another mile before turning onto a narrow gravel road that ended a quarter of a mile later at the top of a slight hill. Without a word, he got out, and walked to the front of the car, leaning back against the hood.

Knowing this was his way of telling her to follow, she walked up beside him, immediately captivated by the view. The sun shone down on the rolling hills, making the long blades of grass glisten as they swayed in the wind. In the middle of the field stood a dilapidated, unfinished wooden barn, flanked by two tall oak trees that had already shed their leaves for the season. A portion of the large pond behind the barn was visible, peeking out from the left side. Beyond the pond lay a vast forest stretching for miles, and in the background, a majestic mountain range was visible, painted in dark blues and purples.

"It's beautiful," she marveled.

"It's mine," he divulged.

"What do you mean?"

"Well, mine and Dougy's." She looked at him with curiosity, waiting for him to continue. "My mother's father owned it. I never knew him. He didn't approve of my father," he chuckled as he spoke. "He must have had good taste... When my mom married my dad, her father refused to speak to her. So, the story goes... A couple of years ago, I received a visit from a lawyer. My grandfather had passed away and left the land to me and Dougy, but only after proof of my mom's death... It specifically stated that."

"My father doesn't know about it," he continued as Tennly listened intently. "I suppose he specified in his will that my dad shouldn't be informed. When I told the lawyer that my mom had left and we didn't know where she was, he mentioned that if she doesn't claim it by the time Dougy turns twenty-five, it will go to us."

"Wow... That's amazing, Conner."

"Come on," he said, extending his hand. "I need to show you something."

She took his hand, and he led her down a path to the barn. The worn trail through the tall grass showed signs of being frequently traveled. The lower level of the barn was empty; only a dusty dirt floor with a few patches of grass sprouting throughout.

The loft measured 30 feet by 40 feet, about half the size of the barn, and was completely open, providing an overview of the ground below. Close to the left wall beside the ladder was a lounge chair covered with a blanket, along with two crates filled with several magazines and books. Next to the chair was a medium-sized kitchen trash can with a fast-food bag sticking out of it. In the center of the loft lay a thin futon mattress, equipped with one pillow, a sheet, and another blanket. On the wall opposite the ladder was a large opening, ten feet wide, that stretched from the ceiling to the floor of the loft. At the top of this opening, there was an adjustable shower rod with two long curtains hanging from it. Conner used the curtains to shield the space from the elements, especially the cold. They were pulled back to each side and draped over wooden hooks that Conner had made and attached to the wall.

"You stay here?" she asked, imagining him being afraid to go home.

"Sometimes," he replied. "When the weather isn't too bad." He walked over to the opening and waited for her to join him. As they gazed out over the property, he pointed to the left of the pond and described, "One of these days, I want to build a house right there. I want to have a couple of horses and maybe some other animals. I'd like to stock the pond with fish, build a large dock, and have a small boat. I want to be able to fish and go swimming..."

He then paused, noticing tears in her eyes. "Five hundred thousand dollars means nothing to you. But to me, it could change my life. With that much money, I could build my house and finally get away from my dad. I could pay for Dougy to go to college... I knew the moment I took the money that I wasn't going to keep it; I just wanted to know what it felt like to have it. I wouldn't have taken it, but when your dad said he would do whatever it took to keep me away from you... I..."

She placed her hand on his right cheek before he could say anything else and pulled him closer. She started kissing him, wanting him to know that she understood and didn't blame him, but he pushed her away.

"Stop!" he yelled. "Whether I took the money or not, your dad is right. I'm not good for you. You have so much potential, and being with me will only bring you down." Then he started walking back toward the ladder, muttering, "I shouldn't have brought you here."

Before she could think about what she was doing, she pulled out the throwing knife from her belt and threw it in front of his feet as she yelled, "Don't!" The knife barely missed his right foot and kept him from taking another step.

"Shit!" He screeched, being startled by her action. He turned around to look at her and saw the tears strolling down her cheeks.

"Don't," she repeated. "Don't you dare bring me here and tell me all that and then walk away. You're so afraid you'll hurt me that that's exactly what you end up doing. You broke my heart three years ago. And every day that you stay away from me, my heart continues to break. The only way you won't hurt me is to just stop... Be with me, Conner."

He didn't know what had come over him. All he knew was that he had to have her. He quickly scooped her up and carried her to the mattress. Their lips met, and as the kiss deepened, he lowered her gently, her hands sliding away her sweater before helping him pull off his shirt. His touch felt like feathers tickling her shoulders, her body shivering, not from the cold but from the softness of his caress. He traced his fingers along the strap of her bra down one shoulder, then the other, his fingers gliding softly down her arms before landing behind her back seeking the clasp as if following a secret path. When her bra fell to the floor and he paused, gazing at her, she longed to confess her love, but fear kept her silent.

She remained still, surrendering to his slow, deliberate touch, as his lips brushed hers before wandering to the curve of her neck. Placing his right hand on her lower back, he pulled her closer while gently cupping her left breast, causing her to feel a delightful tingle. She ran her hands over his shoulders, clinging to him as his kisses deepened, their closeness pulling them gently down onto the mattress. Every movement felt unhurried, deliberate, and full of unspoken longing, as he unbuttoned her jeans, finding her pink lacey boy-cut panties to be extremely sexy.

She went to unbutton his jeans, but he stopped her and said, "I just want to look at you."

He lifted her hands above her head, putting her in a vulnerable position. Gently brushing her hair back from her face, he lightly ran his fingers down her arm and across the front of her body. Conner had had sex many times with many girls and never cared once about looking at them or pleasing them, and he didn't want that with Tennly. If she was going to give herself to him, he wanted it to be all about her.

As she felt his hand glide between her legs, she instinctively arched her back, licked her lips, and let out a moan that he found to be so erotic that he wasn't sure if he would be able to make it through. Giving her a look to ask if she was sure she was ready to go further, she nodded and kissed his neck as she squeezed him tighter.

He maneuvered his body in between her legs and then gingerly slid himself inside her, causing her to let out another moan, half in pain and half in pleasure. Gently, he moved slowly to avoid hurting her, taking his time to ensure that with every movement, she felt more sexual gratification. When he felt her body begin to tremble, he finished in a restrained, tearful groan as if it were not only her first time, but his.

He collapsed on top of her, holding her as if he were afraid to let go, and whispered in her ear, "I love you. I've always loved you."

She closed her eyes in relief upon hearing those words, a warmth radiating throughout her whole body as tears of joy ran down her face. He rolled over beside her, brushed her hair back behind her ears and then wiped the tears with his thumb.

Feeling slightly guilty about what they just did, he asked, "Are you okay?"

"Yeah," she replied, sensing that although what they had just experienced was beautiful, he had mixed feelings about it. "Are you?"

"I just..." he began to say, upset with himself for giving in to his desire. "I can't believe I did this."

"Why do you always do that?" she asked, frustrated.

He sat up, grabbing his jeans. "I'm not a good guy, Ten... If you stay with me..."

As she watched him put on his jeans, she deliberated whether to tell him about her family. She knew it was risky, but it was the only way to show him that he didn't have to worry about hurting her.

She pulled the blanket around herself and annoyingly demanded, "Shut up! Just... shut up... What I'm about to tell you, you can't tell anyone else. No one." Taking a deep breath, she told him everything about her family, finishing with, "You're not the bad one, Conner. I am... Eventually, you'll inherit this beautiful land... But I... when I turn 18, I'll take over a whole syndicate. I'll become the boss."

He listened intently, absorbing everything she told him. It was as if a huge weight had been lifted from his shoulders. Knowing that their worlds were not as apart as he had once believed, along with the security her family would provide her, all his reservations about them being together disappeared.

He crawled over to her and kissed her softly. Then he laughed and joked, "So, your dad really is going to kill me."

"Yeah," she laughed. "But... I'm the boss... so..." She nestled beside him and then looked up to ask, "Does it bother you... my family... what I am?"

"Not at all. The opposite actually."

They lingered in each other's arms, savoring the quiet comfort that followed, neither wanting to let go. The chill in the air eventually became too much for her, so they made their way to the yacht. Still shivering as they stepped aboard, she smiled seductively and led him to the bathroom, where they proceeded to take a hot shower. Out of everything he had done, Conner had never showered with a girl before, and he was glad that his first time was with the one he loved.

He had noticed the scar on her side at the barn but hadn't asked about it in the heat of the moment. However, as he washed her body and saw the one on her back as well, he couldn't help but inquire about it.

She explained how she got the scars during her training in Prague with Duncan, revealing who Duncan ultimately turned out to be. As she spoke about her experiences and capabilities, she became even more irresistible to him, and he couldn't get enough of her.

"What are you going to tell everyone when they see this?" he asked, tracing his finger over the scar on her side.

"I don't know."

"Looks like a cat stitched you up," he teased.

She chuckled as she explained, "Well, I did three of them myself, so..."

"Are you serious?"

"Yeah... One of my lessons... Got in three and then passed out."

"I don't think you can get any sexier than you are right now," he said as he gave tiny little kisses all over her stomach.

They spent the rest of the afternoon on the yacht, and since her father had driven her to school that morning, Conner drove her home. Having told her father that she would ride home with Josie, they parked around the bend at the end of her street. It never crossed her mind that the school would call her father when she didn't show up for class.

Daniel was furious when he learned that Tennly had been seen leaving the school with Conner Marks. His anger intensified further when Thomas reported that she was in the car with Conner at the end of the street. As Daniel approached the bend in the road and spotted Tennly kissing Conner inside the car, he realized that nothing would stop him from finding a way to dispose of him.

Surprisingly, his rapid pace didn't alert them; they were too focused on each other and didn't notice Daniel until he pounded on the driver's side window.

"Get out of the car, Tennly!" Daniel yelled, startling them both.

"No," Tennly refused, knowing her father's intentions.

"Get out of the car, now!" Daniel demanded.

Tennly glanced at Conner and assured, "I'll take care of this, I promise." Then she kissed him and ran over to her father. "Do not hurt him!"

"Get inside the mansion," Daniel ordered.

Conner knew that if he wanted to earn any respect from a man like Daniel, he couldn't run. So, he rolled down his window and told Tennly it would be alright. She shot her father a warning look before running home, knowing he wasn't foolish enough to do anything to Conner right there on the street.

"I thought we had an agreement," Daniel reminded, giving Conner a disappointed look.

"Well," Conner replied, "I'm going to have to break it."

"Then you leave me no choice," Daniel threatened.

"Do what you have to do," Conner countered, making direct eye contact.

Daniel nodded, both understanding what that meant. As soon as Daniel walked away, Conner realized he had been holding his breath to hide his fear. Although he always found Daniel intimidating, knowing what he had recently discovered about him made him even more frightening.

As Daniel walked back through the gate and into the mansion, he mentally rehearsed different scenarios for killing Conner, knowing it had to be something Tennly wouldn't suspect as foul play. The moment he stepped into the foyer, he was confronted by Tennly, who sat three steps up on the stairwell on the right.

"You will not harm him," Tennly commanded.

"I warned him," Daniel responded.

"You will not harm him," she reiterated, her eyes conveying a clear threat.

"Tennly, you're too young to know what's best for you. It's my job to keep you safe."

Smiling maniacally, she sarcastically giggled, "You keep me safe? Really? How do you keep me safe? Training me to be a weapon? Sending me away to boarding school? Bringing me here? I thank you for all of it. But your hypocrisy is astounding. You place me in more danger than Conner ever could. I don't need you to protect me. I can protect myself. You made sure of that. And in less than two years, I will be your boss. So... I'm going to say it one more time. You will not harm him."

"Okay," he said, hoping she didn't suspect that he was lying. He was sure he could appease her and still find a legitimate way to kill Conner that wouldn't look suspicious.

However, he had forgotten how well she could read people; she could see right through him. Without saying another word, she pulled out the pistol she had been hiding behind her back and shot him. Daniel screamed as the bullet grazed his left arm, ripping his shirt and creating a centimeter-wide wound. After the initial shock, he glared at his daughter, not sure if he should be angry that she shot him or proud that she could.

"I'm not playing," she apathetically said. "Promise me you won't hurt him."

"Okay," he responded, to which she noticed he didn't promise.

As if something dark within her was surfacing, her response was to shoot him again, grazing his upper right arm. At that moment, both Thomas and Marie ran into the foyer. Marie screamed at the sight of blood streaming down Daniel's arms, terrified that someone had broken into the mansion.

Thomas aimed his gun at Tennly and yelled for her to put the gun down. The whole event caused Marie's legs to give way, and she had to hold on to the banister to avoid falling.

Ignoring both Thomas and Marie, Tennly continued to stare at her father. "Promise me."

"Put the gun..." Thomas started.

"Lower your gun, Thomas," Daniel interrupted.

"But Dan...," Thomas refuted.

"I said, lower your gun," Daniel ordered.

Thomas lowered his gun, feeling relieved because he truly didn't want to shoot Tennly. He cared for her deeply and didn't want to be the cause of her pain.

The tense stare down between father and daughter felt like it lasted for hours. Both were stubborn, and neither was willing to give in. It wasn't until Tennly noticed her father blink and look down, as if defeated, that the intense moment finally ended.

"I love him," Tennly said, revealing to him for the first time just how much she cared for Conner, hoping that her father would finally understand.

Daniel nodded while processing her words. "Okay... Thomas, Marie, please leave us."

Once alone, he continued, "I'll give you a month. I promise during that time, I won't harm him. But I want to meet him."

Tennly agreed, placing the gun beside her on the steps. She felt relieved by the one-month timeline and believed it would give her enough time to convince her father that she could date Conner while still prioritizing her responsibilities.

Daniel sat down beside her and inquired, "You love him that much?"

"I do."

"I have to go out of town on Wednesday and will be back Saturday. I want to meet him before I go."

"That only leaves tomorrow," she expressed, knowing how difficult it was going to be to get Conner to agree to the stipulation.

"I know. I expect him to be here for dinner tomorrow night."

"Okay," she agreed, worried.

"Okay."

Then, as he stood, she admitted, "For the record, I wasn't going to kill you."

With a stern look, he confessed, "For the record, I was going to kill him. You have a month."

Tennly woke up the next morning, feeling as though her heart was being torn in two different directions. The day before she had experienced the best day of her life, only to come home and have to shoot her father twice. Even more nerve-racking was when she checked her phone and noticed that there was still no word from Conner. Her mind repeatedly returned to the rumors she had heard about him; that once he slept with someone, he never spoke to them again. Although deep down she didn't believe he would treat her that way, the lingering thought created a knot in her stomach.

The child in her wanted to stay home and avoid all the stares, and the possibility that Conner would snub her. But as she sat at her vanity, she realized that she no longer had the luxury of being a child. If she was going to be running the Irish syndicate, she would have to learn to face her adversities head-on.

She made it to school and arrived at her locker, where her four friends were already waiting for her, eager to hear everything that had happened with Conner the day before. As Tennly approached, their eyes expanded twice as big, expecting an exciting story.

"Okay," Tennly said, leaning back against her locker. "I had the best day of my life."

"That's it?" Abby asked, disappointment evident by the pouting expression. "That's all you're going to tell us?"

"If things go the way I'm hoping today, that should tell you everything you need to know."

"What does that mean?" Abby inquired, getting even more excited.

"I guess you're just going to have to wait," Tennly responded.

"Maybe not," Tina chimed in, motioning with her head toward the direction down the hall.

The girls braced themselves as Conner approached Tennly, gently placed his hands on her face, and kissed her. He then pressed his forehead against hers and said, "See you at lunch?"

"Yeah," Tennly replied, feeling a thrill as he ran his thumb over her lips.

He smiled at her, then turned to Tennly's friends. "Ladies," he said with a wink, before walking away.

As soon as he was out of earshot, Abby started jumping up and down, exclaiming, "Oh my gosh, oh my gosh..."

"Well," Josie remarked, "I guess that gives us our answer."

"Are you all forgetting who we're talking about?" Lucy interjected. "I mean, I won't lie, I'm just as shocked as the rest of you, but you have to be a little scared."

"Why?" Tennly asked, noticing the concerned expressions on the other girls' faces, which indicated they understood Lucy's implication.

"It's all well and good now, Ten," Lucy informed, "but just don't sleep with him."

Tennly gave a half smile, curling up the left side of her mouth as she tilted her head, indicating she had already done just that.

"Are you saying," Josie asked, perplexed, as the others jaws dropped to the floor, "that you slept with Conner Marks?"

Tennly nodded just as the bell rang for class. As she walked away, her friends followed closely behind, hounding her for details.

At lunch, as Tennly sat at the cafeteria table with Josie, Tina, Dougy, and Rick, she noticed the girls were looking at her differently. Dougy and Rick were clueless about what was happening, and amid the awkward silence, Rick finally asked, "What's going on?"

After an enthusiastic explanation from Josie about what had happened, Dougy became ecstatic. He believed that Tennly was good for his brother, and the thought of them finally being together gave him a sense of calm.

Tennly didn't wait around to discuss it; as soon as Riley emerged from the path, she excused herself to go to the landing to be with Conner. When she arrived and saw him standing there, smoking a cigarette, her heart began to flutter. Everything about him was perfect: the way he stood, the way he inhaled and exhaled the smoke, his hair, his clothes, and the smile that spread across his face as he noticed her approaching.

"You don't have to wait for him to leave anymore," he mentioned after giving her a kiss. "He's ok with it... with you."

"Okay," she said, relieved that Riley had accepted her.

"So... Is your dad going to kill me?"

"Not for a month... at least."

"Well," he chuckled. "I guess that's good. How did you get him to hold off?"

"I shot him," she giggled, with a look that told him she was telling the truth. "Twice."

"You really shot your dad?"

"More of a couple of nicks, really."

"I don't know whether to be amazed at you or scared of you," he teased.

She put her arms around him and suggested, "Maybe both." She took a deep breath and added, "There is one stipulation, though."

"What is it?" He asked, brushing the strand of hair behind her ear.

"He's insisting that you eat dinner with us... tonight... six sharp."

"Ten, you know I don't do parents very well."

"I know," she acknowledged as she wavered her hands up and down. "But I figured meet with a parent or death..."

CHAPTER 2

Tennly was extremely nervous about Conner and her father being in the same room. As she sat at the dining room table, watching the clock tick away, she realized she should have picked him up. The thought struck her as she noticed the pursed lips on her father's face, a clear indication that he was not happy. She knew Conner would come up with some excuse for not being there, and as soon as she could, she planned to find out what it was.

"He probably forgot," she claimed, hoping to minimize how bad the situation was.

"Since lunchtime today?" Daniel asked rhetorically.

"He has a lot on his mind," she defended.

Daniel put down his fork, took a drink of wine, and then wiped his mouth with a napkin. "He's not off to a good start, Tennly."

"I know."

Daniel stood up and reminded her, "I'm heading out this evening. I'll see you on Saturday."

Tennly sat in silence, her thoughts tangling into knots as she pondered why Conner hadn't shown up? He knew how much this moment mattered and how important it was. She couldn't decide if her frustration was directed at Conner for letting her down or at herself for not realizing it wouldn't be as simple as just asking him to meet her father for him to do so.

After taking a drink of wine, she poured herself another glass, gulped it down, drove off to search for him. She didn't have to go far, seeing his car parked in Riley's driveway. She sat there for a moment to regain her composure; however, before she could get to the point of being so angry she would want to punch him, she walked up to the door and knocked.

"Is he here?" she hissed as Riley opened the door.

"Yeah," Riley replied as she wedged herself past him and entered the house.

As soon as she stepped into the living room, she spotted Conner sitting on the couch, drinking a beer, and watching television. If that wasn't enough, she could smell fresh bacon, evidence that he had eaten dinner with Riley. She sauntered angrily through the room, trying to look calm, although she knew she wouldn't be able to pull it off, especially when he looked up at her and acted as if nothing was wrong.

He sat up straight, sensing her anger, and gave her a smile in hopes of smoothing things over. "Hi," he greeted, giving her puppy dog eyes.

Tennly didn't respond. Instead, she sat down in the chair to the right of the couch and gave Riley a look that signaled he needed to find somewhere else to be. Riley shook his head in disgust but walked into the kitchen.

"Forget something?" Tennly scolded.

"Yeah, sorry about that," Conner replied, brushing it off as if it weren't a big deal.

"I know how you felt about coming to dinner tonight," she whispered, trying to sound as serious as possible. "But my father isn't a normal parent. You clearly don't understand the gravity of your decision not to show up. Don't you realize you are playing with your life?"

"I'm not going to let him scare me," Conner said defiantly.

"You're not going to have to worry about it," she replied, raising her voice and no longer whispering. "You'll be dead!"

She stood up and looked back over at Riley, who had taken a couple steps closer to the living room. Then she looked back at Conner and cautioned, "If you don't care about your life, you should care about his. When my father decides to finally kill you, he won't care who you're with."

Then she gave Riley an evil look as she threatened, "If you say one word to anyone about what you've heard... I'll kill you myself." Then she stormed out of the house.

Riley gave Conner a scared yet confused look as he sat down in the recliner. "I'm just going to say this: either she's psycho, or there's a lot more about her that I don't know."

"She's not psycho," Conner replied, struggling to find the right words. From what he knew about Tennly and her family, he believed she was telling the truth. So, with that and given the fact that he knew Riley would remain suspicious of what Tennly said, he felt he had no choice but to tell him about her secret.

He pulled out his phone, googled the Connolly family of New York, and handed it to Riley. That was Conner's way of passing along the information without directly saying anything.

As Riley read the article, he occasionally glanced up at Conner, as if to ask about its purpose. Conner simply gestured for him to keep reading. Once Riley finished, he handed the phone back to Conner and asked, "Okay...? So, what was that for?"

"That's Tennly's family. They're like... mobsters..."

"So... when she said kill you, she really meant... kill you?"

"Yeah."

Riley started nodding his head as he tried to let it all sink in. "Okay... I can see why you're nervous about meeting her father."

"Yeah. I already know he doesn't like me... What if I can't change his mind?"

"I guess he'll kill you," Riley chuckled, which caused Conner to laugh as well. After their laughter died down, Riley became serious. "Conner, I love you, man. So, I need you to listen to me. I've seen you stand up to the scariest people without blinking an eye. You're resourceful and extremely intimidating. You have this confidence that exudes out of every pore in your body. And if there is any family that you fit perfectly into, it's Tennly's. It all makes sense now. Like the two of you were born for each other. So... go apologize to her... before you get yourself... and me... killed."

Conner wasn't sure if what his friend said was true, but he did know he had to apologize to Tennly. He walked out of the house and was surprised when he saw her sitting on Riley's front porch steps. She had full intention of going home when she walked out of the house, but she wanted him to know she was wrong to push him.

He sat down and immediately apologized, "I'm sorry."

When he looked over at her, he could see tears in her eyes. "It's funny... ironic." She turned, so he could see how serious she was as she continued. "How all these years you stayed away from me for fear you would hurt me. When, in reality, my selfishness and need to be with you can actually get you killed. I should stay away from you... I love you. But if you can't..."

"Sh," he soothed, taking ahold of her hand. "There is nothing you can do to keep me away from you. I'd risk my life just to be near you."

She buried her head onto his shoulder as he wrapped his arm around her. "He will kill you. And as much as I threaten him, he knows I'll never turn on the family."

"You won't have to," Conner reassured. "I'll meet your father. I can't promise he'll like me, but I'll meet him."

She looked up at him and said, "Just be you, and he'll love you. I know it."

Despite everyone knowing that Conner and Tennly were dating, riding to school together for the first time made their relationship feel official. They walked hand in hand into the school, and Conner gave her a kiss at her locker before heading off to their first period classes. It was also the first day that Conner met Tennly in between classes to walk her to the next one.

Though Conner's behavior with Tennly seemed strange to everyone, it was nothing compared to the sight of Conner and Riley walking back from the landing at lunch and sitting at the same table with Tennly and her friends. The Untouchables never sat at a table in the cafeteria, let alone associated with anyone outside their group. Even though Josie and Tina had spent one night with Conner and Riley, it felt unnerving to see them so close. Dougy and Rick did most of the talking with Conner and Riley while the girls listened, hearts racing and nerves on fire.

After last period, Conner waited outside Tennly's classroom to walk her to his car. He drove to their neighborhood, and instead of dropping her off, he pulled up to the gate. She had no idea he planned to drive her all the way to the front of the mansion, and she smiled at his chivalrous gesture, giving him the code.

When they stopped in front of the main door, she said, "Come inside."

"I didn't think your father was home," he replied.

"He's not."

"Won't that be risky?... Being seen together?"

"That's a little too late," she informed, pointing to the camera above the front door. "Come in. You can meet Marie."

He groaned as he rested his head on the steering wheel. Believing he might find an excuse to avoid going inside, she was surprised when he finally sat back up, let out a fearful growl, and turned off the car. Leaning over the center console, she gave him a reassuring kiss before they both got out.

As they walked through the front door, she felt his grip on her hand tighten. The only other time he had been inside, he had been too hungover, drugged up on pain medications, and in a hurry to leave. Although he remembered it being large, he didn't recall it being so grand. The vastness of the first room he entered was overwhelming. The foyer alone was bigger than his entire house, and he began to second-guess his decision to go inside with her.

"You, okay?" She asked as she felt his hesitation about going further.

He took a deep breath and said, "Yeah."

"Come on... It'll be fine... I promise."

She guided him up the right stairwell to her bedroom, where she placed her bookbag on the desk as he explored the room. She watched him move from corner to corner, examining everything, and then he peeked into her bathroom but didn't go inside. She found it adorable that he was acting like a child visiting an amusement park for the very first time.

"What?" He asked, smiling at her.

"You sure you're okay."

"No," he replied, even though he was nodding his head.

She gave him a hug as he turned back to investigate her bathroom again. "You have a shower... that doesn't look like a shower."

"Yeah," she seductively flirted. "Plenty of room for..."

"Grr," he moaned as he laid his head on hers, squeezing her tighter. "You're truly going to drive me crazy."

"That's the plan... You hungry?"

"I'm always hungry."

Conner found the kitchen fascinating. Unlike a typical kitchen, its architecture, decorations, and color scheme gave it the feel of a living room, creating a warm and inviting atmosphere.

Two crystal chandeliers hung above the two countertop islands, and the brown and tan marble flooring added to the elegance. Crown molding adorned the edges, extending from the corners to the center of the ceiling. A large smoker designed to resemble a fireplace, a triple sink on the back wall, and the most unusual refrigerator he had ever seen completed the space. The refrigerator was transparent, and when he looked inside, he saw everything neatly arranged, resembling a piece of art.

The kitchen was shaped like a pentagon. One wall contained the door through which Tennly and Conner had just entered from the hallway that led to the foyer. Two walls were lined with kitchen appliances with one of the walls featuring a scalloped opening that led to the breakfast nook, Marie's bedroom, and the laundry room. A fourth wall had storage cabinets and included the door that lead to the garage and the fifth wall had a large French door that opened to the dining room.

As soon as they entered, Marie noticed them. She stopped stirring and looked up at Tennly and then at Conner, saying, "You must be Conner?"

"Yeah," he said.

"I'm Marie." Without another word, she walked over to the oven, reached inside, and pulled out a dish.

Conner looked at Tennly with confusion, and she shrugged her shoulders in response. They both watched as Marie carried the dish back and set it down on the counter in front of Conner. Inside the dish was a small whole chicken. She then placed a large bowl beside it and grabbed a set of tongs, a knife, and a large fork.

Handing the utensils to Conner, she said, "Be a dear and get all the meat off the bird. I really dislike doing that."

Conner looked at Tennly again, still confused, but this time she started to laugh. "She really hates doing that."

He didn't mind helping; in fact, he always enjoyed cooking but had never had the money or tools to do it properly. While Conner focused on removing all the meat, Marie deep-fried the tortillas just enough to soften them. Once they were both finished, Marie seasoned the chicken, and then they set up an assembly line to stuff the enchiladas.

While they waited for dinner, Tennly showed Conner around the rest of the mansion. By the time they had reached the atrium, the angle of the sun's rays made it feel as if they had just stepped outside on a warm summer day. Conner froze, his wide eyes and parted lips showing his astonishment. He took a few more steps inside and spun around to take in the stunning scenery from every angle.

"You have a forest... in your house?" She smiled at him as he asked, "What's that noise?"

Although the waterfall was visible, the sound it produced was unlike anything he had ever heard before. The steady, low white noise was accompanied by tiny pinging sounds as the water struck the various surfaces and splashed against the surrounding rocks and ponds.

"It's the waterfall. Come on."

She guided him along the winding paths, over the streams, and past the gazebo until they reached a bench directly across from the largest waterfall. They settled onto the bench and watched as water cascaded down a twenty-foot-high rock formation. It flowed from a makeshift cliff into a stream, eventually arriving at a small pond filled with colorful Koi fish and other aquatic life.

"This is amazing," he professed.

"Yeah. I love it in here. My father created it to look like the inside of the Opryland Hotel. Have you ever been?"

"No, I've never been anywhere."

She laid her head on his shoulder and vowed, "We're going to have to change that."

Over the next three nights, Conner and Tennly had established a routine. After school, they would drive to the mansion, watch some television, and help Marie cook dinner. Conner found that he really enjoyed cooking in the mansion, where the nice utensils, appliances, and exotic ingredients allowed him to do much more than he ever could at home. While preparing the evening meals, Marie shared stories about life in Ireland, entertaining them with humorous tales. Conner found Marie to be extremely funny, and they often teamed up to tease Tennly just to get a reaction out of her.

Conner never imagined he would feel comfortable in the mansion. He wasn't sure if it was because of his connection with Tennly, the inviting ambiance of each room in the mansion that made him feel safe, or

Marie, who treated him as if he were part of the family. Whatever the reason, by the time Friday night arrived, he felt like he truly belonged there.

After finishing dinner, they returned to the upstairs living room to watch television before Conner was scheduled to leave. Usually, he would leave the mansion by 9:00 PM to give Tennly time to get ready for bed and get enough sleep for school the next morning. However, since it was Friday night, he decided to stay a bit longer. Before they knew it, they both had fallen asleep, only to be awakened by Marie gently tapping their shoulders.

"Oh shoot," Conner sprung up and rubbed his eyes.

"What time is it?" Tennly yawned, sitting up next to him.

"A little after midnight," Marie answered.

"I'm sorry," Conner apologized, preparing to leave.

"Come," Marie pressed, gesturing for them to follow her.

Although they were confused and unsure of her intentions, they followed her out of the room and in the opposite direction of the foyer. She led them down the hall, around the corner, and to the first guest room on the left.

"It's too late for you to find a place to sleep tonight," Marie said as they stepped inside the bedroom. "You can sleep here." She then pointed out some extra blankets, the attached bathroom, and where the towels were stored in case he wanted to shower. Finally, she showed him a set of pajamas, clean underwear, sweatpants, and a hoodie that she had placed on the bed.

Before she left, she patted him on the shoulder. "Don't make me regret this decision." Tennly smiled peacefully as they watched Marie leave.

"Do you think I should stay?"

"If Marie went out of her way to do this, then yes." She could tell that, even though he had gotten used to being in the mansion, he was a little nervous about staying overnight. "Are you okay with it?"

"I don't know."

"I can stay in here with you if you want."

"I'm pretty sure when she said, not to make her regret letting me stay, she meant... you know."

Tennly licked her lips and purred, "Yeah, but..."

He gave her a look that told her he wanted to respect Marie's wishes. "Okay," she accepted as she thought of what her friends and everyone else would say about him turning down sex.

Once he was alone, he began to wander around the bedroom, nerves creeping in, despite having spent the week in the mansion feeling at ease. Staying the night felt different; it blurred the line between being a guest in a luxurious hotel and a strange sense of belonging.

The walls were adorned with tapestries, and crown molding stretched from the corners to the center of the ceiling. Each piece of furniture was intricately carved, and there was the biggest area rug he had ever seen. The attached bathroom was slightly smaller than Tennly's but just as beautiful, filled with the same scents, though with a more pronounced woodsy aroma. The dressing room/closet resembled Tennly's, but it contained absolutely no clothes: only several hangers for guests to use during their stays.

He approached the bed and examined the stack of clothes that Marie had laid out for him. It had been years since he last wore pajamas; even as a toddler, it was rare. His father believed spending money on such frivolities was wasteful, so he typically slept in just his underwear or street clothes. He moved the sweatpants and hoodie to the nightstand beside the bed and ran his fingers over the pajamas. They were a cream color, made from the softest silk he had ever felt, with buttons crafted from pearl.

He sat down on the bed, contemplating whether to put them on. A part of him longed to wear them, curious about the comfort they offered. However, the louder voice, the one that feared he was already changing, warned him that wearing something so luxurious would push him over the edge, blurring the last thread that tied him to his roots. In the end, he pushed the pajamas aside and settled into bed wearing nothing but his underwear.

It took him a few minutes to get comfortable with the bedding. There were two sheets, two thin blankets, a large comforter, and a big fluffy quilted throw that he had to figure out how to maneuver beneath. Unsure which pillow he should use for sleeping, for the king-sized bed had four regular-sized pillows atop two king-sized ones, along with several decorative pillows: three square, two round, and two long bolsters, he moved all but one pillow to the side of the bed opposite the door. He then pulled back the covers and tossed the quilt and comforter to the side with the pillows. Lying on his back, under the remaining sheets, he stared at the ceiling in disbelief. Even the ceiling was ornate, featuring elaborate moldings and a variety of colors.

It was hard for him to fall asleep; harder than usual, and the nightlight plugged in under the large window wasn't helping. As he reached the nightlight to unplug it, he noticed that the window offered a view. Each bedroom lining the atrium opened to its own balcony, providing a sweeping view of the beauty below.

Tara chose a window that opened into the atrium, but Tennly did not. Despite the atrium being her favorite spot in the mansion, Tennly believed that if she had a window facing it, she would eventually take it for granted. Besides, she liked the idea of having a window that opened to the outside so she could hear the comings and goings.

Conner sat at the window seat, looking down at the exquisite foliage and streams, debating whether he should leave, but the atmosphere was peaceful, and he didn't want to go. When he finally grew too tired to stay awake, he left the window open so he could hear the sounds and laid back down.

It was 7:00 AM the next morning when he woke, and he couldn't get back to sleep. His mind was racing with thoughts, the main one being that he had stayed overnight at Tennly's house without her father knowing and wondered what he would do about it.

Remembering that Marie had given him permission to take a shower, he removed his clothes and stepped inside. It took him a few minutes to figure out how to operate all the spouts and handles as he experimented with every possible combination. Eventually, he turned on all the shower heads and set them to the soft spray option. It felt like standing outside during a summer rain.

He noticed that the showerhead on the wall to the right of the sliding door had a long cord attached to it. Curiosity piqued; he examined it more closely and discovered it was removable. Carefully, he detached it from the hook and ran the water over his body, laughing to himself at the luxuries enjoyed by the wealthy.

To his dismay, there wasn't a bar of soap anywhere. As he examined the four-compartment dispenser, he noticed each compartment was labeled: soap, shampoo, conditioner, and hair mask. The label made him chuckle as he wondered what a hair mask even was. He positioned his hand under the compartment labeled 'soap' and watched as a tablespoon-sized amount of liquid soap was dispensed. He smiled as he washed his body and then repeated the process for the shampoo.

He took great satisfaction in the entire experience, finding it to be the most amazing shower he had ever had. He finally understood how people could stay in the shower for longer than the five minutes he usually managed. It turned out to be the longest shower he could remember, and it was invigorating.

Once finished, he went back to the bed to retrieve his clothes, remembering placing them on the side table next to the sweatpants, but when he went to get them, they were gone. When he couldn't find his clothes anywhere, he resigned himself to wearing the sweatpants and hoodie.

Poking his head into Tennly's room, he saw that she was still asleep. Not wanting to disturb her, he proceeded downstairs for a drink of water. He wasn't expecting to see anyone, so when he stepped into the kitchen and saw Marie sitting at the bar, sipping a cup of coffee, he was startled.

"Don't you ever sleep?" He asked as he sat down next to her.

"I could say the same of you," she responded.

"New place," he implied.

"I understand. I see those sweats fit. I figured they would. I have your clothes in the wash."

"Thanks," he said in a tone that told her he was feeling a little off.

"I bet this is all so overwhelming for you."

"You have no idea."

"Oh, but I do. I grew up in a small village in a very small cottage. Both my parents worked, so my siblings and I were alone quite often. They were very strict, but fair and loving."

Conner listened as Marie stood and began to gather the ingredients she needed to make breakfast. She pulled out some flour and butter, placing them on the bar in front of him. "Cut the butter into half-inch sections," she instructed. Then she retrieved some other ingredients and kitchen utensils and continued, "One day, my mother decided to take me to work with her. I never knew what she did before that day. I was nine years old, and I was mesmerized when we pulled up to this grand castle. I thought maybe she had taken a wrong turn."

She opened the refrigerator to grab some sausage and milk, placing them next to the stovetop. "She hadn't, of course," she went on, retrieving a large pan from under the other island and taking it to the stove. Turning back to Conner, she shared, "I remember how I felt the first time I walked into that castle. I was overwhelmed with emotions. I was excited to be in such a grand place, yet I was scared to touch anything, even though I wanted to. I felt happy for my mother because she got to be in a place like that every day, but I was also extremely angry that she had to come home to our humble place. But she never complained... always had a smile on her face... the same person no matter where she was... she was happy."

When she patted his hand, Conner thought she might ask him how he felt or continue her story. Instead, she said, "Now help me make some homemade biscuits and sausage gravy."

He appreciated her discretion and understood her message: he could stay true to himself while learning to navigate the world of the wealthy. He smiled to show her he understood and then followed her culinary instructions.

Daniel and Thomas arrived home earlier than Daniel had expected. Instead of getting back just before dinner, they reached the mansion shortly after Conner and Tennly had finished lunch. As he walked into the kitchen and spotted Marie cleaning up, he immediately started sharing stories about his trip. However, he paused mid-sentence when he noticed the suspicious expression on Marie's face. "What's wrong?"

"He's here."

"Conner?" he said, as he felt the heat of anger boil inside him.

"Aye. He's been here every day since Wednesday."

"I told Tennly she wasn't allowed to see him until I met him," he huffed as he started to walk away.

"Daniel, they're young and in love... Cut them some slack."

"You like him," he speculated.

"He reminds me of a young boy I used to know," she admitted, referring to him.

"*That* doesn't help," he grimaced. "Where are they?"

"In the girls' living room." Then, before he walked too far away, she advised, "Daniel, go with an open mind. You might be surprised."

The girls' living room didn't have a door. Instead, there was an opening flanked by two marble pillars. Daniel entered cautiously, clearing his throat as a warning in case he was interrupting something private. To his relief, they were simply lounging on the couch, watching television. Upon hearing him, they both sat up; Tennly twisting around to face him while Conner subtly shifted, putting space between them. A nervousness washed over Conner, the same uneasy flutter he hadn't felt since his very first day in the mansion.

"You're home early," Tennly mentioned as Daniel walked around the couch and sat down.

"Yeah," Daniel replied. He glanced at Conner before returning his gaze to Tennly and adding, "I thought we had an agreement."

"Not my fault you weren't here," she retorted.

"Well, I'm here now, so..." He turned to Conner and asked, "Why should I let you date my daughter?"

"Dad," Tennly interjected, upset that her father was starting the interrogation so abruptly.

"It's okay," Conner assured. "It's a fair question. If I were you, I wouldn't."

That answer not only surprised Daniel but intrigued him. "Because...?"

"I know my reputation," Conner admitted.

"So," Daniel pressed, "does that mean it's all true?"

"Most rumors stem from some form of truth," Conner informed.

"Knowing that," Daniel continued, "I'll ask again: why should I let you date my daughter?"

"And I'll answer again... You shouldn't."

"Yet here we are," Daniel pointed out.

"Yeah," Conner agreed.

"How do I know you won't involve her in drugs or whatever your lifestyle entails?"

Conner smiled confidently, a glint in his eye that reminded him of what Riley said. "I've never brought her into my world, unlike you. With all due respect, she's more likely to get caught up in your world than in mine."

A part of Daniel wanted to lash out at him right then, especially since it was clear that Tennly had shared details about their family. He shot his daughter an angry glance before turning back to Conner.

"It's not the same," Daniel insisted.

"Why?" Conner replied rhetorically. "Because you're rich and I'm not? The only difference between what you do for a living and what I do is that I do it to survive, not to buy a second yacht."

"You're not afraid of me?"

"No," Conner replied, surprised by the surge of confidence he hadn't expected to feel.

"You should be," Daniel warned.

"I've seen worse," Conner said matter-of-factly.

"I doubt that," Daniel boasted, trying to sound more intimidating.

"Well," Conner said, maintaining his relaxed demeanor, "you've never put out cigarettes on me or beaten me with a baseball bat while I slept. So..."

Daniel recalled the night Conner had arrived at the mansion, bruised and broken and couldn't believe that Conner was suggesting his own father had been the one responsible.

"We all have our crosses to bear," Daniel said evenly, masking the hurt those words caused. He fixed his gaze on Conner. "Do you feel sorry for yourself?"

"No. As much as I hate some parts of my life, they've made me who I am."

"And you like who you are?"

"Does anyone like who they are all the time?" Conner responded.

"I suppose not. As long as we try to be the best person we can be, making decisions that will help us reach our potential, filling at peace at the end of the day."

"If you're talking about self-actualization, I find it hard to believe that even you have achieved it. So, asking someone my age if I feel fulfilled in my potential seems a bit absurd."

"How do you know what self-actualization is?" Daniel asked, surprised that someone like Conner not only knew about such a philosophy but also had a good vocabulary.

"I read," Conner answered tersely, annoyed by the implication that someone like him couldn't be intelligent.

Intrigued, Daniel asked, "Does that mean you have expectations for when you graduate?"

"No, I have no idea what I want to do."

"So, let me get this straight," Daniel reviewed. "I'm supposed to let a juvenile delinquent, who not only sells drugs but also uses them, has a smart mouth and no respect for authority, along with no intentions of planning for the future, date my daughter?"

"Yeah," Conner answered, assertively.

"Why?"

"Because if there's anyone who knows about the dangers out there, it's me... And I promise you, I will do everything in my power to keep her safe."

Daniel was impressed by Conner's responses throughout the entire conversation, but nothing resonated more than his promise to keep Tennly safe. It was also reassuring to hear Conner acknowledge the dangers of his lifestyle and how to navigate them. He felt that someone with Conner's abilities could be useful. It was also refreshing to talk with one of his daughter's boyfriends and receive honest answers instead of pre-scripted ones that they thought he wanted to hear. He appreciated Conner's honesty, feeling it demonstrated integrity, unlike many others he encountered daily who seemed fake or insincere.

"Okay," Daniel said, letting out a deep sigh of resignation. "But I'm going to hold you to that."

Conner nodded, signaling that he understood what Daniel meant: if he couldn't keep his promise or ended up hurting her, Daniel wouldn't hesitate to kill him. Tennly watched in confusion as the two men stared at each other, almost as if they were establishing a hierarchy.

"So," Tennly intervened, not understanding the male social order, "does that mean...?"

"We'll give it a shot," Daniel said, his eyes narrowing as he turned to Conner. "This is your one chance, don't screw it up."

"Thank you," Tennly replied with a bright smile, while Conner nodded solemnly.

"Now," Daniel said, his demeanor turning serious again, "we need to talk about what you know regarding this family."

CHAPTER 3

Christmas was a significant celebration for the O'Brien and Connolly families, and Tennly couldn't wait to share it with Conner. She knew that the Marks family did not celebrate Christmas, which caused Conner to have some resentment toward it. She wanted to show him the kind of Christmas she had grown up with; a Christmas filled with lights, decorations, gifts, giving, and family.

The mansion was beautifully adorned with Christmas decorations, both inside and out. Crews hung wreaths adorned with red bows on every window, door, and gate, and strung white lights across the trees, bushes, and perimeter wall. A 30-foot tree stood in the cul-de-sac, while the atrium showcased a magnificent 40-foot tree surrounded by lights, spotlit waterfalls, floating candles, and life-size holiday figures.

Inside, candles flickered in the windows, and garlands and poinsettias filled every corner. Each room featured at least one Christmas tree: smaller ones in the bedrooms, 10-foot trees in the main areas, and impressive 20-foot tree in the foyer, pool house, and one 30-foot tree and 20-foot tree in the great room, leaving the 20-foot tree bare until Christmas Eve, when the entire family would decorate it together.

Marie usually decorated the girls' trees with cherished keepsakes and ornaments, but since Conner hadn't had a Christmas tree since he was four years old, Tennly insisted that she and Conner decorate the tree in her bedroom that year. Marie brought out all the boxes of Tennly's ornaments and baubles, placing them on the floor beside the tree. She then left to get cookies and eggnog while Tennly played old-fashioned Christmas songs, hoping to capture the essence of a real Christmas experience.

Conner enjoyed watching Tennly's eyes light up as she placed the ornaments on the tree and danced to the music. He found more joy in observing her than in decorating the tree, though he didn't want her to know that. The delight she expressed in thinking she was giving him an experience he hadn't had was far more valuable to him.

When they were finished putting up all the decorations on the tree, they sat back against the bed and admired their work. Even though it was the same set of ornaments they used every year, Tennly found the tree to be more beautiful than ever. She wasn't sure if it was because it had been three years since she last saw it or if it was the fact that she got to experience it with Conner.

After he left for the night, Tennly lay on her bed, gazing at the tree and thinking about all the firsts she would be sharing with him. One of those experiences was celebrating with a big family. Suddenly, she sat straight up, realizing that she had been so caught up in everything happening to her that she hadn't told her sister about her relationship with Conner.

Tara was arriving the next morning for her Christmas break, and her flight was expected to land in Marinsburg at 7:30

AM, which meant she would reach the mansion by 8:00 AM. Conner was expected to return to the mansion around 11:00 AM to spend the afternoon with Tennly before going out with his friends later that night. This meant that Tennly needed to get up early enough to have time to talk with her sister before Conner arrived.

With the anticipation of having to talk with her sister, she woke up just in time to take a quick shower and get dressed for the day. She found Tara in her closet unpacking a suitcase, finding it odd since she had plenty of clothes left behind and shouldn't have needed to carry anything back and forth.

"Got some favorites, do ya?" Tennly asked, which startled Tara, causing her to shriek.

"Oh my gosh. You scared me." Then she walked over to Tennly and gave her a hug. "I thought you would still be asleep."

"Ahhh," Tennly explained. "I missed you."

"I know. I missed you too," Tara said as she walked back over to her suitcase. "So, how's it been?"

"Well," Tennly said, trying to think of a way to tell her sister about Conner, but finding it extremely difficult. "A lot has happened since being back."

"I bet," Tara acknowledged as Tennly sat down on the ottoman. "What was it like coming back here? Going back to school? Were your friends happy to see you?"

"Yeah," Tennly answered, dreading what she was about to bring up. "I'm so sorry I haven't called. Like I said, a lot has happened."

"Okay...?" Tara questioned, sensing that something was off.

"Well," Tennly inhaled, taking a deep breath. "I'm just going to come right out and say it... I'm dating Conner."

"What?" Tara gasped, not believing what she heard.

"Yeah."

"Like... what do you mean?"

"Like... dating."

"Conner doesn't date."

"Tara," Tennly said, trying to get her to be serious.

Tara paused in silence, contemplating what it would be like to date an Untouchable, as she sat down beside her sister to keep from falling. The idea frightened her more than it intrigued her, and she couldn't shake off her worry.

"How did it happen?" Tara asked as if there was an accident.

"You sound like there was a death or something," Tennly remarked.

"Does Daddy know?"

"He does."

"And...?" Tara asked, trying to picture their father corresponding with an Untouchable.

"So far, so good. Actually... at times, I look at dad, and I think I can sense that he likes him."

"Daddy doesn't like anyone."

"I know. And Marie adores him." Tennly changed her demeanor to a more excited one as she turned and crossed her legs toward Tara. "Get this, Conner and Marie spend hours cooking and baking together."

"Conner bakes?" Tara pondered, finding it hard to picture Conner in the kitchen.

"He does. And he's really good at it."

"This is so surreal," Tara sighed, running her hands through her hair. "What are you going to do when he wants to... What happens after you two... you know... He's not known for staying around."

Tennly was exhausted from having to defend her relationship to everyone, but she understood that her sister was only concerned for her. Taking a deep breath, she grasped her sister's hands and held them tightly. Tara felt a wave of nervousness as she wondered what her sister was about to say, so she sat quietly, bracing herself for potentially bad news.

Tennly looked at Tara directly in the eyes and confessed, "We've already..."

Tara wore a confused expression, unsure if she was understanding her sister correctly. She released her hands from Tennly's and sat up straight, trying to articulate her thoughts but struggling to find the words.

"It was my first day back at school," Tennly divulged, a smile spreading across her face as she reminisced about that beautiful day. "It was perfect, and he was so gentle."

While Tara was struggling to accept her sister's relationship with Conner, Tennly was grappling with her own issues with him. Despite her efforts to be alluring, he never showed any signs that he was interested in having sex with her again. She attempted to be seductive multiple times, but he did not respond.

She wanted to ask him about it many times, but the fear of pushing him away kept creeping up on her, so she never did. It wasn't until they were on their way back to the mansion from a party with their friends that she finally gathered the courage to bring it up.

"Is your father home?" She asked.

"No," he answered.

She scooted over closer to him as she started to kiss his neck. "Then let's go to your house."

"Won't your dad and sister wonder where you are?" He asked with more fear than curiosity.

She leaned back in her seat, unsure how to respond. Her racing heart was overpowered by a strong urge to slap him across the face. However, the further they drove, the more worried she became, and as tears began to form in her eyes, she mumbled, "Was I not any good?"

"What?" He asked, confused as to why she would ask that.

"It's been almost two weeks since we..."

He knew precisely how long it had been because the urge was growing stronger each day. However, since their first time, he had been striving to remain celibate with her, though he wasn't entirely sure why, other than fear.

He pulled the car off onto a rural, one-lane road, put it in park, and gave her a sincere look. "You scare me. I mean... not you, but... when we... it was the best I'd ever felt in my life. Being with you is all I think about. But it scares me."

"Why?"

He reached over, put the strand of hair behind her ear, and then ran his hand over her shoulder. "Because sex to me was always a way to not feel... to forget. I never cared about the girl after I got what I wanted. I didn't care if I hurt her or any consequences. When I got home that night after we... all I thought about was if I hurt you or what if..."

Feeling a lump form in his throat, he leaned back against his seat and looked up at the ceiling. Then he turned his head to look at her and admitted, "I've never been afraid to have sex. Ever... And even though I've never wanted it more than I do with you... having sex with you scares me."

"The consequences never scared you before?" She asked as she leaned the side of her head against the back of her seat and stared at him.

"No, like I said, I didn't care."

"You weren't afraid of getting a disease or someone pregnant?"

"No. I didn't care what happened. Which is why this is all scary to me. Because I lack self-control, I could have put you into a situation that..."

"Stop," she interrupted, understanding where he was heading. "I'm not stupid. And although it would have been extremely difficult to say no, I would have if I wasn't already protected. So, unless you have some sort of funky disease, I'm fine. I've been on birth control for two years... to regulate my periods. So..."

He smiled at her, feeling the weight being lifted off his shoulders, relieved that she was protected. Then, to lighten up the mood, he teased, "You calling me stupid?"

"If the shoe fits," she teased back with a seductive glare as she licked her lips.

"No, my dad isn't home," he replied, leaning in and giving her a kiss. "And I'm disease-free... so..."

She kissed him back and playfully responded, "That's very romantic."

"I try," he said with a smile that melted her.

Their desire was too powerful to wait to get to Conner's house. Their kissing led to undressing, which motivated Tennly to climb over to him and straddle his legs. He put his seat back to give them more room as her body moved up and down on his. When they got into a rhythm, she stretched her arms upward and braced her hands on the ceiling. He loved watching her, and it made him want to please her more than she was pleasing him. So, he grabbed her and rolled her over to be on the bottom, but the center console jabbed her back, and she let out a small scream. He was about to apologize when she started to laugh as she scooted into the back seat.

Tennly lay on her stomach while Conner gently ran his fingers up and down her bare back. He brushed her hair to the side, revealing the scar between her shoulder blades. Although it was healing, it was still pink and quite noticeable.

"Have you ever thought about what excuse you're going to give for these?" he asked, tracing his finger over the scar on her side.

She rolled over to face him and replied, "My plan is just to keep them covered."

"Even in the summer?"

She buried her head in the pillow, then looked back at him and teasingly said, "So you don't think, 'Hey guys, I'm a trained assassin who's going to take over my family's illegal organized crime syndicate' would work?"

He shrugged and said, "Which brings me back to my original question."

"I don't know... I should really get home," she said, sitting up.

"I know."

"I had fun tonight."

"Me too," he agreed as he started kissing her. "I think we should do this every night."

"Play your cards right, Marks, and that might be a possibility."

He gave her another kiss, and then after they got dressed, he drove her to the mansion. She watched him drive off and then paused just outside the front door, taking a moment to compose herself before going in. She suspected that her father had been watching the monitors and would be waiting for her as soon as she stepped inside. So, when she heard his voice as she walked through the foyer, just before reaching the stairs, she wasn't surprised.

"You do remember your sister is home," Daniel reminded, stopping Tennly from going up any further.

She turned around, and as she took a couple steps back down toward him, she countered with, "You do remember that she goes to sleep at 10 o'clock."

"While your sister is here, you need to be extra careful. She will not understand why you have different rules than she did."

"Okay," Tennly conceded and then turned to continue to walk up the stairs.

"Tennly," Daniel called, stopping her again. "I have made our lives as safe as I possibly could over the years. But it doesn't keep me from worrying when my girls are out. So... just let me know that you're safe when you're going to be late. Okay?"

"Okay. I'm sorry."

Tennly never worried about any dangers of living in Marinsburg. But as she walked up the stairs and down the hallway toward her bedroom, she couldn't help but wonder about the importance of

the cameras lining her path. Had they kept
her family safe all those years because of
the precautions her father had put in place,
or was Marinsburg simply so remote that no
one could find them there?

Lying in bed, she pondered all the
potential dangers she might one day face.
Strangely, none of those possibilities
seemed to threaten her in Marinsburg.
Exhausted, she drifted off to sleep
without being able to imagine any scenario
in which she could be harmed in such a
small town.

Tara was still struggling to
understand what kind of relationship
her sister could possibly have with
someone like Conner Marks. She worried
that her sister's choices would damage not
only her reputation but, even more
importantly, her heart. She met her
friends for breakfast, and although she
was glad to see them, her mind couldn't
focus on anything they were saying. She

was preoccupied with thoughts of Conner ruining her sister. She stayed as long as she could but eventually, she apologized and excused herself to head home.

Marie noticed the concern etched on Tara's face, as Tara took a seat at the bar. Not wanting to press her she simply waited, knowing exactly what weighed on Tara's mind as she quietly continued cutting pieces of beef for that evening's dinner.

To avoid the subject, Tara began talking about college, but her drifting focus made it clear that she needed help facing what was really troubling her.

"Why don't you just ask the real question, Tara."

"Tennly says you like Conner," Tara blurted out.

"I suppose I do."

"Why?"

Marie put down the knife, picked up her coffee mug, and took a drink. She sat it back down and then, with a nostalgic smile, said, "He reminds me of your father when he was that age."

"So, you're saying my father was a juvenile delinquent?" Tara asked half teasingly.

Marie smiled as she informed, "There's more to people than what they show."

"What did Daddy do?"

"I wasn't talking about your father."

"Oh," Tara sighed.

Marie picked up the knife and started cutting the meat again, as she suggested, "Give him a chance, Tara. He surprised your father... he might surprise you, too."

Tara didn't have to wait long for her chance to get to know Conner better. Before she could respond to Marie, Conner walked into the kitchen. She felt as if she were back in high school. Her heart began to race, her palms grew clammy, and her tongue felt twisted, making her worry that she wouldn't be able to speak properly in front of him.

"Hello, Conner," Marie greeted.

Tara felt herself tense as she debated whether to look at him or to walk out of the kitchen. She realized that if her legs would cooperate, she would choose the latter. While she struggled to muster the courage, he walked around the bar toward Marie.

"Marie," he said, reaching into the cabinet to the left of the sink and pulling out a glass. It struck Tara as strange to see him acting as if he lived there, and she wasn't sure if she liked it or not.

"Tennly up yet?" he asked, opening the refrigerator to pull out a pitcher of sweet tea.

"She's in the gym," Marie replied.

Conner poured a glass, placed the pitcher back in the refrigerator, and then turned to look at Tara. She watched him take a large gulp of tea before putting the glass down on the island. He was just as gorgeous as she remembered, and his presence was still intimidating, but there was something different about him. He didn't seem as angry as he always had before, and she sensed a feeling of contentment within him.

"Hey Tara," he said, which sent shivers up her spine.

"Hey," she quietly replied after she took a deep breath.

Marie slid over the cutting board with the meat on it to Conner, handed him the knife, and said, "Be a dear and finish cutting this into squares for me. I forgot I had some laundry in the wash."

Conner and Tara watched as Marie walked out of the kitchen, then exchanged glances. They both knew that not only did Marie never forgot anything, but she also never did the laundry on Sundays. Tara smiled, trying to come up with something to say, while Conner started to cut the meat in the manner that Marie had instructed, occasionally looking up at Tara, waiting for her to speak.

"Tennly said you enjoy cooking," she finally was able to get out.

"I guess," he admitted.

"You know Marie doesn't have laundry to do."

"I know."

"She lied because..."

"I know," he interrupted with a wink and a smile.

Somehow, the gestures that had always made her feel a lump in her throat became the tools for her to understand what Marie had said about Conner. Once she let go of her guard concerning him, she was able to see her father more clearly. She realized that Daniel had used the exact smile and wink with others when he wanted them to see the real him.

"How did you get in here?" she asked. Tara knew that Thomas was with Daniel, so he couldn't have let him in. There hadn't been any interruption from the intercom in the kitchen, leaving her puzzled about how he managed to get through the main gate.

"I know the code, and Daniel gave me a key to the front door... So..."

"Oh," Tara sighed as if she hadn't fully understood what he said.

"Just ask me what you want to know."

She was face-to-face with the most popular boy in Marinsburg, and he was giving her permission to ask him anything. She had so many things that she wanted to know about him, but she had to focus on the problem at hand.

"Why my sister?" She asked.

"Why not?"

"Conner," she pleaded, giving him a look that told him to tell her.

He cut the last piece of meat, placed the knife on the counter, and then turned to get a large bowl from a cabinet. As he turned back around, she began to wonder if he was going to answer her question. She watched him scrape the meat into the bowl, then cover it with foil. He put the bowl in the refrigerator, placed the knife in the sink, and used a bleach wipe to clean the counter. She found it strange that someone like Conner, given his upbringing, was so tidy. It made her think that perhaps he wasn't what everyone believed him to be.

After he put the cutting board in the sink, he turned around and asked, "Do you want something to drink?"

"I'll take a coke," she answered, not only impressed that he cleaned up but that he was kind enough to think about if she was needing anything.

After he poured her a glass of Coke, he said, "I'm sure whatever answer I give you won't be good enough."

"Try me."

"I can say the obvious, like she's beautiful, I love her personality, she makes me laugh, we have a lot in common... but even though all those things are true, they're not the reasons... Before she came back, I couldn't see the future. I didn't care if I lived or died... Shit, sometimes

I think I did things in hopes that it would kill me... I can't breathe without her. But more importantly... I like who I am when I'm with her."

"She does have a way of bringing out the best in people," Tara agreed with a smile.

"Yeah," he said, with a slight chuckle. "She was even able to get my friends to enjoy hanging out with hers. And they don't like hanging out with anyone."

"So, I've been told," she replied teasingly.

"I think she's a witch," he responded with a wink.

"Who's a witch?" Tennly asked after she stepped into the kitchen and heard what Conner said.

Conner looked at Tara and whispered, "See?" Then the two of them started laughing.

Tennly walked over to them, feeling elated that they were getting along, and gave Conner a kiss. Tara lingered for a moment, watching the two of them together. They moved around the kitchen, acting like

a married couple who had settled into a
morning routine.

CHAPTER 4

The ranking of the Irish mafia was like that of the military. The highest individual, who oversaw all the clans, was referred to as the captain or head boss. Below him were the bosses leading their respective clans, known as either boss or skipper. Directly under each skipper were the underbosses, also called clan chiefs, who served as the second in command within their individual clans.

Warlords acted as the enforcers of the organization. Their role was to ensure that employees, associates, and soldiers adhered to the rules. Reapers were the hitmen, and cleaners were responsible for handling any messes that arose and disposing of any incriminating evidence.

Quartermasters were non-family members who were leaders in their communities and acted as mediators between the families and the common people. Associates were also non-family members for whom the clans had made arrangements that could involve the purchase of a product or property or simply turning a blind eye when necessary.

The lowest-ranking members of the clans were the soldiers. They walked the streets, kept their eyes and ears open, ran errands, and performed various tasks as needed. Despite their rank, soldiers had to be intelligent and skilled fighters and marksmen.

Counselors typically held psychology degrees or had expertise in other fields, allowing them to serve as advisors to the heads of the clans. They were sometimes permitted to attend meetings with the bosses when others were not.

In addition, each clan also had a secretary, who gathered information, conducted background checks, and maintained records of every family member, employee, and anyone who had dealings with them.

Before Tennly's grandfather took over as boss, the Connolly family adhered strictly to this hierarchy. However, as the Bianchi feud escalated, James Connolly became increasingly suspicious of anyone who wasn't family; his growing distrust alienated his lower-level employees. When James died, Daniel faced the daunting task of mending the fractured relationships. He was determined that his daughter would not inherit control of a syndicate on the verge of collapse or, worse, a mutiny. Although he didn't return entirely to the traditional Irish hierarchy, he reinstated several important positions and raised their salaries.

Daniel especially liked the idea of having quartermasters and used them to improve relationships between the communities and the Connolly clans. For the most part, this approach worked brilliantly. The quartermasters allowed the clans to hide in plain sight, and since the Connollys paid them a substantial sum of money, the quartermasters always redirected any legal troubles away from the clan. That was why it was hard for Daniel to believe when he heard that one of his quartermasters was turning state's evidence against the family.

William Standford was a quartermaster for the Connollys in one of the larger neighborhoods in Columbus, Ohio. He had worked for them as a devoted and loyal employee for fifteen years, so when news of his betrayal emerged, it was a total surprise. William's son, Lucas, had been arrested for possession with intent to sell an illegal substance and was set to stand trial the day after Christmas. After talking to Lucas's attorney, William realized he had to do something to protect his son.

This was Lucas's third drug possession offense, and the attorney stated there was no way he would get off without at least two years in prison. To keep his son out of jail, William told the attorney that he knew of a crime family running most illegal operations in Columbus. He proposed that if they could negotiate a deal to drop his son's case, he would reveal the crime family and provide plenty of evidence against them.

When a soldier overheard this news, he reported it to the warlord, who realized it was already too late to coerce William into silence. The warlord informed a prosecuting attorney who also worked for the Connollys. This attorney reported what she was told to Jimmy before the courts had a chance to act.

Jimmy immediately contacted his brother, and the two of them took the earliest flight to Marinsburg to discuss what needed to be done. Daniel met his brothers-in-law in the bar at a hotel owned by the O'Briens downtown. Daniel had just ordered a drink and an appetizer when Jimmy and John walked in and took a seat across from him.

"How long do we have?" Daniel asked.

"His son's hearing is for the day after Christmas," Jimmy answered. "That's when the prosecution is supposed to drop all the charges."

"Any way of getting to William before then?" Daniel inquired.

"Not a chance," John replied. "He's not only under protection, but he's being held in an undisclosed location."

"We've tried, but we can't find out where," Jimmy added.

"And the son?" Daniel asked.

"He's being held in jail until the hearing," Jimmy disclosed.

"I'm sure we have a prisoner that can take care of..." John suggested.

"The son isn't the problem," Jimmy interrupted.

"So, what else do we have?" Daniel asked, knowing that if William could be turned that easy, he would always be a liability.

"He also has a daughter," Jimmy mentioned. "She lives by herself in a downtown penthouse."

"The bad thing is," John continued. "Ever since William decided to go to the authorities, he's placed a security detail on her."

"They follow her around everywhere," John finished.

"Is there anywhere she goes on a regular basis?" Daniel asked.

"She also goes to school at the university, a friend's apartment, and a nightclub downtown."

"The university is too crowded," Daniel noted. "Also, too risky. Is she seeing anyone?"

"Not that we've seen," Jimmy responded.

They stopped talking as the waitress approached with their drinks and took their lunch orders. After she left, Daniel asked, "Can the bodyguards be paid off?"

"Not sure," Jimmy answered. "If we try and the answer is no..."

"Yeah," Daniel interjected before he could finish. "So, we have to take her before she gets to her penthouse. What nightclub?"

"The Music Note," John answered.

"We've thought about that," Jimmy continued. "But The Music Note is very exclusive. Not to mention it wouldn't be a good idea for us to be seen in Columbus right now."

"Exclusive how?" Daniel inquired.

"It's a young person's club," Jimmy described.

"With a bouncer," John added. "That only lets young, beautiful people inside."

"Then," Daniel concluded. "We need to find someone that can get into an exclusive nightclub that only lets in young and attractive people and is charismatic and manipulative enough to get her to ride in a car with him."

"We can ask Toby," Jimmy suggested.

"No," John refuted. "Toby is too well known in Columbus. What about Jacob?"

While James and John reviewed a list of young men who worked for them and matched the description of what they needed, Daniel already had the perfect candidate in mind. He listened to his brothers-in-law, hoping one of them would suggest a good choice, but deep down, he knew the best option. He just didn't want to admit it.

After five minutes of failed suggestions, Daniel finally declared, "I have someone in mind... meet me at the mansion tonight at six."

Daniel called for Conner as soon as he got home. He wanted to speak to him before his brothers-in-law arrived, so he would have an idea of what they needed to do regarding the situation with William. When Conner reached the office, Daniel led him through the foyer, out the front door, and up to Conner's car.

"Get in," Daniel ordered as Conner wondered what it was that Daniel wanted from him.

"This isn't the day you finally decide to take me out and kill me, is it?" Conner joked.

Daniel shrugged his shoulders, gave him a smile, and repeated, "Get in."

Daniel ordered him to start the car, and then instead of directing him down the driveway toward the gate, he told him to take a right around the high hedges and go to the side of the mansion where the garage was located.

"You're a strange man, you know that?" Conner teased after he stopped outside the furthest garage door from the mansion, where Daniel had told him to park.

Despite all the times Conner had visited the mansion, he had never been inside the garage. It was unlike any Conner had ever seen. It featured eight stalls, each with two double doors: four at the front and four at the back, and one stairwell in the back left corner, leading up to Thomas's apartment.

The garage walls displayed neatly arranged stacks of totes and tools hung in designated locations. There was no grease or clutter, unlike the other garages he had encountered, and it smelled different too. While there was a slight engine odor, the predominant scent was that of citrus.

Starting from the door closest to the kitchen, the black Mercedes sedan that

Thomas and Daniel drove most often was parked. Directly across from it was the black limousine. Next to the sedan was Tennly's Scout, with Tara's Bentley parked across from it. Between the two girls' cars were Tennly's motorcycle and a Harley-Davidson Cosmic Starship. Beside Tennly's Scout was a bright red 1965 Buick Riviera, while across from that sat a dark green 1968 Chevrolet C3 Corvette Stingray.

Next to the Stingray was the shell of an unpainted 1970 Pontiac Trans Am, raised on lifts for restoration. In their free time, Daniel and Thomas enjoyed purchasing classic cars and restoring them to their original condition.

As Conner explored the garage and admired the cars, Daniel walked over to the left wall. He opened a 12-inch box that had eight buttons, laid out like the garage doors. He instructed Conner to stand in the middle of the garage before pushing the first button. Suddenly, a thumping sound was followed by a low hum as the Mercedes began to rise into the air. It was then that Conner noticed each car was parked on a platform that elevated to reveal another car beneath it.

Daniel pressed each button until every platform had risen, showcasing the six cars underneath: a silver 1994 Jaguar XJ220, a silver 1970 Lamborghini Miura, a 1969 blue Ford Mustang Boss, a black 1970 Plymouth Barracuda, a yellow 1970 Ferrari Dino 246 GT, and a dark blue 1967 Shelby GT500 Mustang. All the cars were in mint condition, impeccably polished to a soft shine.

"Remind me to tell Tennly she needs to work on her tour of the grounds," Conner noted as he walked around, admiring all the cars.

"Yeah," Daniel agreed. "She has a tendency to forget about the garage when she shows people around."

"I have a friend who would die in here," Conner mentioned, referring to Sam.

"Oh?"

"Yeah. He loves cars. Wants to be an auto mechanic when he graduates."

"You should bring him by sometime."

Sensing a hesitation in Daniel's voice, Conner could tell something was on his mind. "We're not in here to look at your cars, are we?"

"No," Daniel answered. "How far would you be willing to go for this family?"

"I think you know the answer to that."

"I'm in some trouble," Daniel said, gesturing for him to sit down at the patio table outside the back of the garage. "If we don't fix it, I can end up going to prison for a very long time... and it will cause Tennly to be in danger." He then went on to explain to Conner the reason the family was in peril.

"So, what do you need me to do?" Conner asked.

"Seduce his daughter enough to get her alone."

Seduction was always easy for Conner. He never had any trouble getting any girl to do what he wanted, so doing what Daniel was asking would be easy. The hard part was going through with it. Ever since he had gotten with Tennly, he hadn't thought of being with another girl and was afraid to be put in that predicament.

"I can't."

"That's not what I hear."

"Not that I can't, can't, because I could do it in my sleep. I can't hurt Tennly like that."

"You're dating my daughter, Conner. I'm not going to agree with you sleeping with another girl. Before it gets that far, you'll drug her. We're not sure of the logistics of it all yet. We'll discuss it when Tennly's uncles get here."

"Okay," Conner accepted. "But Tennly has to agree to it."

"There are going to be times when you have to make a decision quickly and you won't have the opportunity to ask for permission."

"With all due respect... With this specific decision, I have plenty of time. And I'm not asking for permission." Conner got quiet, looked down, and took a deep breath before he continued. "Before Tennly... I had a reputation..."

"I'm aware," Daniel replied in a tone that suggested he get to the point.

Conner gave him a look that told him to hear him out and then explained, "I don't want Tennly to ever question my loyalty to her. That's all."

"My brothers-in-law will be here for dinner tonight. We're planning on meeting afterward to discuss what we need to do. Your first job is to find a way to get Tennly there... without Tara knowing."

"I accept the challenge," Conner confirmed, smiling.

"Now on to the next reason I brought you to the garage."

Daniel instructed Conner to follow him to a locked box on the wall beside the kitchen door. Using a key, he opened the box and retrieved a remote garage opener and a key fob. Conner was confused about what was happening, especially when Daniel handed him the garage door opener.

"If you're going to be around here as often as you are, you need to stop parking out front. That's the remote to that garage door. You'll park in here from now on." Then he handed Conner the key fob. "This opens the kitchen door."

Daniel led Conner through the garage as Conner contemplated the idea of having his own parking space. It was a relief that Daniel had accepted him, but it also felt like he was betraying everything he believed in. Visiting a mansion was one thing, but having a parking spot in its garage was something entirely different. He placed his hand on Daniel's shoulder to stop him before they reached the kitchen door.

"I don't know if I can... I mean...
This is a big..."

"Are you questioning your beliefs?"
Daniel interrupted.

"I don't know. Maybe... yeah...
Sometimes I'm afraid I'll forget who I am...
where I came from."

"And where is that?"

"I know what you're thinking," Conner
assumed. "You're thinking I came from
trash and should be thankful someone like
you has taken me in."

"Don't you ever put words in my mouth,"
Daniel firmly stated. "Do I make myself
clear?"

Conner wasn't scared of Daniel; in
fact, he was enamored by him and held a
great deal of respect. Because of this, he
didn't take offense at Daniel's words or
tone. Instead, recognizing that Daniel
wasn't finished speaking, Conner nodded to
show that he understood.

"It's insulting that you assume I
meant a literal where," Daniel continued.
"When it was obvious, you meant a
figurative one. Now, tell me where you came
from."

Conner remained silent as he searched for an answer. He had always believed that he was supposed to hate rich people and that poor individuals were inherently better human beings. However, as he pondered this belief, he realized that being poor did not automatically make him a good person.

"I don't know," Conner replied.

"Do you like who you are?" Daniel asked.

"I don't know," Conner repeated.

"Then it sounds like you have more to think about than a parking spot." Daniel put his hand on Conner's shoulder, consoling him as he gave some inspiration. "It doesn't matter whether you have money or not, where you live, or what you do for a living. Find out what kind of man you want to be and be it."

Upon arriving in Thomas's apartment, Tennly noticed her father and two uncles sitting in the living room with worried expressions on their faces.

"What's going on?" Tennly demanded as she and Conner took seats beside the men.

"There's a situation going on," Daniel mentioned. "And if we aren't successful on this next job, there's a very good chance I might be sent to prison."

"What?" Tennly gasped. She hadn't seen her father that serious since the night she snuck into his car after her mother was killed. "Why?"

As she listened to her father explain what was happening, a painful ache gripped her chest with each heartbeat. She clenched her hands together to stop shaking and began to rock back and forth.

"I'm coming with you," she offered out of shear fear. "I'm a better shot than any of you, and I can..."

"As much as I would love to have you with us," Daniel interrupted. "I can't. Tara is here, and she will question where you are. It could possibly take us a few days before we'll be back."

"Then, what's the plan?" She asked.

Daniel explained that they needed Conner's help to get into an exclusive nightclub, where he would track down Amelia, the daughter of the man who was turning state's evidence against them. Their plan was to kidnap her and use her life as leverage to keep William from speaking. They spent hours brainstorming and refining each step until their scheme seemed foolproof. Yet one problem remained unsolved: how to take Amelia without the bodyguards knowing.

"Wait a minute," Tennly said looking at Jimmy. "Did I hear you say she's been going to the university campus?"

"Yeah," Jimmy answered. "She goes to school there."

"When was the last time she was seen there?" Tennly asked.

"I do believe two days ago," answered John.

Tennly smiled as she informed, "I know for a fact that school has been out for over a week for winter break. I heard Tara talking to one of her friends who goes there."

Daniel and Conner smiled, understanding what Tennly was saying as

Jimmy suggested, "So, maybe she's studying or has a project to finish."

"No," Tennly refuted. "But that's what she's telling her security detail."

"She's using the college to lose the bodyguards. Why didn't I see it? That's perfect." Then he looked at Conner and said, "You need to find a way to get her to meet you secretly. Do you think you can do that?"

"Oh yeah," Conner responded confidently. "Still have a problem, though... It won't work if I go in alone."

"Why?" Jimmy asked.

Conner smiled because he thought it was fun that he knew something that they didn't. "The whole concept of an exclusive nightclub is being able to get into it. The rich and famous go to them. Alone, I would be just another pretty boy waiting in line, desperate to get in. And if you know anything about these types of nightclubs, they don't let desperate in."

"Then what do you suggest?" Daniel asked.

"I need a wingman," Conner answered. "Someone to go with me so we just look like we are out for a good time, and we belong there. And not like I'm some sad sack trying to get laid."

Conner and Tennly sat quietly as the three men once again reviewed all the young men who worked for them, searching for the perfect match to be Conner's sidekick. Just as Daniel had listened to his brothers-in-law earlier, knowing that Conner was their best option, Tennly and Conner listened as they discussed potential candidates, already aware of who the ideal choice was.

They waited until the men paused, then Conner stated, "If you don't mind, I'd like to pick my own."

"Not gonna happen," Jimmy replied at the same time John said, "No way."

"Then I'm not going to do it," Conner insisted.

"Conner," Daniel replied, trying to remain open-minded. "You won't say anything because of your love for Tennly. How can we trust anyone else?"

"Before Tennly," Conner explained, "all I had were my friends. We would kill for each other and die for each other... we nearly did a couple of times. They're my family, much like yours. If you trust me, you can trust them."

Daniel looked at Tennly with a questioning look, and Tennly nodded in agreement. Taking a deep breath, Daniel finally said, "Only one..."

"Dan," Jimmy interrupted. "I don't think that's a good idea."

Daniel raised his hand to signal Jimmy to be quiet while he continued. "You can only pick one. Explain the entire situation to him, and make sure he understands that if we even suspect he might betray us, we will take action. He needs to be certain he wants to do this. Understood?"

"Yeah," Conner replied.

"If he agrees," Daniel said, "bring him back here to the apartment tonight. We want to meet him."

Conner nodded and immediately set out to find Riley. Before leaving the estate, he texted Riley to ask where he was. When Riley replied that he was at a party with Sam and Joel, Conner instructed him to find a way to leave and meet him at his house without the other two following him.

When Riley arrived home, he found Conner waiting for him in his car. Sensing that whatever Conner wanted to discuss was important, despite feeling uneasy, he didn't hesitate to get in the passenger seat.

"Are you okay?" Riley asked as soon as he shut the door.

"You remember what I told you about Tennly's family?" Conner mentioned, ignoring his question.

"Yeah."

"Well, I need your help. But if you do this with me, Daniel and Tennly's uncles will know you know, and that means your life will forever be in danger."

Riley took a deep breath before saying, "Whatever you need. I'm in." Riley didn't have to think too long. He spent the last several years protecting Conner and wasn't going to stop just because he was dating a mafia boss's daughter.

Riley had never been inside the walls of the O'Brien estate. From the road, the mansion was hidden from view, allowing him and the other neighborhood kids to grow up imagining what it looked like. When Conner began spending time with Tennly inside the mansion, he tried to describe it to Riley, but as they drove down the long driveway and the mansion came into sight, Riley realized that no words could truly capture its splendor.

His jaw dropped at the extraordinary beauty of the grounds. He never could have imagined its grandeur and eagerly anticipated seeing the inside. His excitement grew as Conner drove around the hedges toward the garage. The outside of the garage impressed Riley just as much as the exterior of the mansion, but when Conner pressed the garage door opener, Riley was taken aback.

"You have a garage door opener?" Riley asked, astonished.

Conner smiled as he drove inside. Riley was about to ask about the garage door opener again when he noticed the cars parked within. In the flurry of everything happening, Daniel had left all the platforms raised, except for the two holding Conner's car and the Mercedes.

"Holy shit," Riley marveled as he got out and started looking around.

"I know," Conner agreed, following his friend. "Sorry, but we'll have to look at them later."

When they reached Thomas's apartment, they found Thomas still perched on a bar stool in the kitchen. The open-air design of the space reminded Riley of the apartments he imagined existed in big cities, and he couldn't believe such a beautiful dwelling was situated above a garage in Marinsburg.

As they walked into the living room, Daniel, Jimmy, and John stood up to greet them and immediately began quizzing Riley on his character and loyalty before discussing their plan.

"I assume you two have fake IDs?" Daniel asked, after Jimmy and John felt comfortable about Riley being involved.

"Yeah," Conner replied.

Riley was shocked that Tennly's father seemed okay with her boyfriend having a fake ID. He hesitated to take out his own until he saw Conner do it first.

"Let me see them," Daniel said, gesturing for the boys to pass them to him. Daniel looked over the IDs as if he were grading a diamond. Then, after a few seconds, he shook his head. "These might work around here, but they will not get you into an exclusive club in a big city." He handed the IDs to Jimmy and questioned, "Do we have time?"

"We have someone in Columbus that can get them done in a couple hours for a fair price."

"Give them a call," Daniel commanded. "Let them know we'll be there tomorrow. Make Conner's name Mark Riley and Riley's name Will Conner. Be easy to remember that way." Then he looked back at the boys. "We'll have the IDs and the proper clothing ready for you when you get there."

"Okay," Conner said.

"Oh," Daniel added. "One more thing. You won't be driving your car. Drive here a half hour before you need to get on the road. Thomas will have a car for you. It's late. Go home. Spend tomorrow as you would, but make sure you leave here by 5:00 PM."

After Conner arrived at Riley's house, they sat quietly in the driveway for a few moments, both reflecting on the situation they were about to face. Neither of them was scared; instead, it was a mix of excitement and respect. However, when Conner noticed a hint of confusion on Riley's face, he realized that something was bothering him.

"You, okay?"

"Yeah," Riley answered. "I just... I mean... I saw the yacht and had heard the numbers of how much she's worth... but I guess it didn't truly register until I saw it..."

"Yeah," Conner understood, thinking back on the first time he saw the mansion.

"Does it bother you?"

"Sometimes, but it's more than the money that scares me."

"What do you mean?"

"Do you see the power that Daniel has?"

"Yeah."

"He can get anything he wants with just a phone call. People respect him yet fear him. And with a snap of his finger, he can make someone disappear.

"Cool, though," Riley admired.

"Yeah," Conner agreed. "But how can I compete with that? How can I ever be able to live up to it?"

"What are you talking about? You are that. And if Tennly is supposed to take over some day, there would be no better person to stand beside her than you."

CHAPTER 5

The Music Note was an upscale nightclub featuring laser lights, disco balls, and a DJ booth positioned to the right. Musical notes suspended from the ceiling were enhanced by vibrant fabrics, while four large pedestals shaped like notes framed the corners around a brightly illuminated dance floor. Plush couches with small side tables lined the walls, and larger round tables filled the back area beneath a loft that overlooked the dance floor.

At the back of the loft, there was a neon-lit bar with twelve black stools, while the center had small tables and couches. The highlight of the loft was five private sections at the front, each featuring semi-circle sofas around a table, enclosed by floor-to-ceiling curtains each in a different color: dark purple, yellow, red, blue, or dark green.

On their first night at The Music Note, Conner and Riley arrived at 11:00 PM and had no trouble getting inside. The outfits that Daniel had chosen for them were perfect and highlighted their lavish personas. Conner wore black skinny jeans with rolled cuffs, a black undershirt, a casual black suit jacket, and black loafers. Riley opted for form-fitting gray dress pants, a lighter gray button-up shirt, a black suit jacket, and black dress shoes. They were both impressed by Daniel's ability to choose outfits that matched their personalities so well. Even though they had never worn such luxurious clothes before, they felt completely comfortable in them.

They were at the nightclub until two in the morning but had no luck finding anyone who resembled the girl in the picture Daniel had shown them. On the positive side, it allowed them to familiarize themselves with the club and how things operated before they had to introduce themselves to anyone.

They woke up before 8:00 AM, and with no plans until the evening, spent the day exploring Columbus. After enjoying lunch at the lively North Market, they walked to COSI, the Center of Science and Industry Museum. As children, they had always dreamed of visiting but never could afford it, so they explored every exhibit until closing. Afterward, they headed to the German Village, sampling local beers at various taverns before having dinner. Finally, they returned to the hotel where they snuck Daniel, Jimmy, and John through the side entrance and up to their room.

Since they still had two hours before the boys had to be at The Music Note, Daniel thought it would be interesting to see how the boys would fare at poker. The game started with a quarter ante, but as they continued, it became more heated. Conner and Riley found themselves in the highest-stakes poker game they had ever played. Daniel noticed the concern on their faces about possibly not having enough money to cover any losses, so he assured them it wasn't a big deal and offered to cover them. Although neither of them liked the idea of owing money to a mafia boss, they were having too much fun to decline, so they took the risk.

In the end, Daniel was the big winner of the night. Conner won some money and didn't end up owing Daniel anything when they were done. Unfortunately, Riley ended the evening with a debt of $2,080.

As the boys left their hotel room for The Music Note, they repeated the same routine as the night before. They drove the silver Porsche 911 that Thomas had arranged for them after their arrival in Columbus. This wasn't the car they had used to get to Columbus; they had ditched that vehicle for something more luxurious to avoid drawing attention by using the same cars repeatedly.

As they emerged from the Porsche, dressed in different outfits than the night before, the bouncer at the entrance gestured for them to bypass the line and were granted immediate entry. Once inside, they walked around the lower level to ensure that Amelia wasn't present before heading up to the loft.

At the bar, Conner informed the bartender that they had reserved a private section. The bartender checked the ledger, noted their name, and returned to collect the fee.

Conner handed the bartender double the amount and said, "Keep a tab open for our table, and give yourself $500."

"Will do," the bartender replied. "Whatever you need, just let me know. Thanks!"

The bartender then directed them to their table behind the dark green curtain, just to the right of center. When they sat down on the sofas, they were relieved they could still see most of the first floor and the lower half of each staircase.

"You're really good at this," Riley commented.

"What?" Conner asked.

"Being rich," Riley stated.

"Shut up," Conner replied.

"No," Riley insisted. "It fits you."

Conner shot Riley a disapproving look, although he couldn't deny that what Riley said was true. Being rich did fit him, and he was good at it. That was what made it so conflicting for him. He shook his head and then motioned for Riley to keep an eye on the dance floor.

Just as they began to think the night would pass without seeing Ameila, Conner spotted her entering with another girl, trailed by her security detail.

Amelia was tall and thin, with long, wavy, bleached-blonde hair and brown eyes framed by heavy lashes and thick mascara. Her puffy, filler-plumped lips shone bright red, underneath high cheekbones and a pointed nose that was pierced with a diamond stud. She carried herself with an air of arrogance rather than confidence, treating her security like servants as she ordered them to stand against the wall.

"She's pretty," Riley noted.

"She's plastic," Conner retorted.

"So," Riley said. "Now what?"

"We do what we know how to do," Conner said.

The boys instinctively understood this part of the plan. They watched Amelia like predators stalking their prey, waiting for the perfect moment to strike. Amelia and her friend joined two other girls on the dance floor while her two bodyguards stood against the wall, keeping a watchful eye on her. Shortly after, two of the girls made their way up the stairs and to the bar, giving the boys their first opportunity to set their plan in motion.

Conner nodded at Riley, signaling that it was time. Riley walked over to the bar next to the girls and ordered two beers.

While he waited for the drinks, he glanced at them and smiled. They smiled back, and the girl closest to him slowly licked her lips. Taking it as interest, Riley decided to turn on his charm as the drinks arrived.

"Put whatever these ladies want on our tab," Riley said. Then he winked at the girls and walked back to Conner.

"Well?" Conner asked as he took the bottle of beer from Riley.

"The seed's been sewn," Riley responded.

Conner caught the girls' gaze and responded with a slow nod, accompanied by his most seductive smile. To maintain an air of mystery, he leaned back on the sofa and allowed his eyes to wander over the dance floor. The boys resisted looking back, playing hard to get, until they noticed Amelia and her friend ascending the stairs to the loft.

"They must have a private table," Conner whispered. "Watch where they go."

Riley nodded and then did as Conner told him. After the girls got drinks and started walking toward the front of the loft, Riley reported, "Looks like they're two behind you. The one on the end. What do you want to do?"

"Wait."

"We wait too long," Riley worried. "We might lose her."

"We appear too desperate," Conner countered. "We lose her anyway."

It seemed as if Conner was not only born to lead but also instinctively knew how to handle any situation he faced. It came naturally to him, and at that moment, waiting was the best option. Before long, Amelia and her friend stood beside their table, displaying a level of boisterous cheer that neither of the boys appreciated.

"Our friends said you bought them drinks," Amelia said, not knowing which one to look at. "Is that the same for us?"

"Depends," Conner replied in an alluring yet distant tone.

"On what?" Amelia asked flirtatiously.

"On what you can offer us," Conner said with a wicked grin, the smile that always got him exactly what he wanted.

"Hm," Amelia responded. "My friends didn't have to offer you anything."

"I didn't want anything from them," Conner claimed with a wink.

Amelia blushed as she tried to hide her embarrassment and brushed the right side of her hair back. "And what do you want from me?"

"Sit," Conner ordered as he patted beside him on the sofa.

Amelia glanced past the crowd toward the first floor, where her bodyguards stood watch. She asked for the boys for their names, and after they shared their aliases, Amelia squeezed her friend's hand, a silent cue to dig into their identities.

"I don't want any trouble," Conner muttered, feigning frustration. "If it's that important, just forget it."

He pushed back from the sofa and headed for the bar, leaving Riley to seal the deal. Riley leaned in closer with an easy smile. "He's a good guy; he just has trouble trusting people."

"Neither do I," Amelia responded.

"Look, I'll deny it if you say anything, but I made him come out here tonight. His girlfriend of three years just broke up with him, and it broke his heart. So, if he appears disgruntled, that's why."

"Ah," Amelia heartbreakingly sighed.

She glanced at the bar and noticed Conner, beer in hand, casually leaning on his elbow. Handsome and fresh from a breakup, he drew her sympathy, and she found herself staring until her friend whispered that the names were good.

Amelia introduced herself and her friend to Riley, and as Jane took a seat, Amelia's gaze returned to Conner. Her heart fluttered; he was the most gorgeous guy she had ever seen. Excusing herself, she approached the bar and slid onto the stool beside him.

"I'm Amelia."

"What are you drinking?" Conner asked, continuing to play it cool, even though he was relieved that their false names worked.

"Moscow mule," Amelia answered. Conner gestured for the bartender and then told him to get Amelia a Moscow mule but said nothing else.

"I have to be careful when I meet new people."

"You walked up to me," Conner reminded.

"True."

Conner tilted his head in that disarming way that left girls breathless. "It's been a while since I've had to do this. So..."

"Your friend told me," Amelia confessed. "I'm sorry."

"Remind me to kill him," Conner replied, playing along that he didn't want his friend to let her know.

Amelia laughed, and their playful conversation carried them back to where Riley and Jane sat. Shortly after, the other two friends of the girls, who had been at the private table behind the boys, announced that they were leaving, prompting Conner to signal Riley, asking him to take Jane with him to the table, leaving Conner alone with Amelia.

Though hesitant, he knew this was his chance. Within half an hour, their talk gave way to kissing. Guilt tugged at him, but he recognized it was a necessary step.

When Amelia pressed further, sliding her hand across his lap, he guided it upward with deliberate restraint. She drew the curtains, climbed onto his lap, and kissed him again, her skirt riding high to reveal pink lace.

Conner's body responded instantly, and he knew if he didn't stop now, he wouldn't be able to. He grabbed her shoulders, looked in her eyes, and said, "I can't."

"Why?" Amelia asked.

"I mean... I really... really want to... but not like this." He then lifted her up and gently placed her beside him. "I'm sorry. I thought I was ready, but..."

"I understand,' Amelia sighed.

Conner turned to her and lied smoothly, "With my last girlfriend, we just were. We started dating immediately, before we even really knew each other. I promised myself I would get to know the next one first." Amelia couldn't help but feel admiration toward Conner. He made her feel special and wanted, and it made him completely irresistible. "I know that sounds stupid..."

"No, it's nice."

"I'll understand if you want to leave," he said, hoping he hadn't pushed her away too much.

"I don't."

Conner felt relieved that his act was working, despite Jane's loud, shallow chatter grating on his nerves. For an hour, he pretended to be interested, smiling through her trivial complaints and irrational concerns. At one point, he even imagined slapping her just to silence her. The torture finally came to an end when Jane whispered Amelia's name outside the curtain. Amelia pulled the curtain aside, told Jane she would be right there, and then turned back to Conner.

"I had fun tonight," Amelia said.

"Me too," Conner lied. "Do you have to go?"

"Yeah."

"You wouldn't be..." Conner started but stopped to make sure he continued to not look too desperate. "Never mind."

"No... What?"

"You wouldn't be interested in meeting for coffee tomorrow morning?"

"I can't," Amelia said, which scared Conner. For a moment he thought he had failed. But then she added, "If you want, though, I will be on campus at three. I can break away for a few hours if you want to pick me up."

"I'd love to," Conner said, relieved.

Amelia smiled and then asked for his phone. Conner handed her the burner phone and watched as she typed. "This is my phone number. Pick me up behind the library on campus. Text me when you get there."

"I will."

They drove back to the hotel, where Daniel, Jimmy, and John were waiting for them in their room. Jimmy and John were impressed and couldn't believe the boys had actually pulled it off. They looked at Daniel with disbelief on their faces, to which he nodded as if to say, 'I told you so.'

The next morning Daniel called Thomas to let him know they were ready for the car that Conner was to use to pick up Amelia. To avoid anything being traced back to Conner, he and Riley drove a black Honda Accord from Marinsburg to a safehouse located on a farm in a small town outside of Columbus. They left the Honda there and picked up the Porsche that had been left in an abandoned parking lot.

From there, Conner and Riley followed Daniel, Jimmy, and John, who were driving Daniel's Mercedes with fake tags on the back. They used the Porsche as Mark Riley's car while he was staying in Columbus. The Porsche would only be seen at the hotel and the nightclub. To prevent the same car from being spotted at the library, Thomas had one of their soldiers pick up a different vehicle, a black Chevrolet Camaro with tinted windows, and park it two blocks away from the hotel.

It was a brand-new Camaro, and Conner desperately wanted to race it around the city, but he knew he couldn't risk attracting any unwanted attention. Instead he drove slowly to the campus library, texted Amelia and waited.

As soon as they left campus, Conner realized he didn't have much time before she noticed he wasn't following her directions to wherever it was she was taking him. When they came to a red light, he leaned over to her while they waited for it to turn green. He placed his left hand on her right cheek and looked into her eyes as if he were about to kiss her.

"You better keep your eyes on the lights," she suggested with a smile.

"They can go around," he replied with a mischievous grin.

He reached down with his right hand, grabbed a syringe hidden beneath his leg, and slowly moved it toward her shoulder. Just when it seemed he was going to run his hand behind her back, he jabbed the needle into her neck. She let out a scream and tried to back away, but before she could grasp the door handle, she lost consciousness.

After they arrived at the safehouse, Conner carried Amelia inside and laid her down on the couch. Jimmy took a zip tie and secured her hands together in front of her body. Then he placed a chain around her waist and fastened it to the base of the couch, ensuring she couldn't escape.

"It's time for you to go home," Daniel ordered, pointing at Riley. Then he turned to Conner and gave him precise instructions.

Conner and Riley drove the Camaro north for an hour until they reached the designated town. There, they proceeded to an abandoned farm, where they were instructed to wipe down the car to remove fingerprints. They were fine with everything until they got to the next step: to douse the car with gasoline and set it on fire. They stood there for a moment, as if saying goodbye to a loved one, before continuing their remaining orders.

They watched the car go up in flames as Riley mumbled, "What a waste of a nice car."

"Yeah," Conner agreed.

Once the car was fully ablaze, they walked twenty minutes into town and found the lone parking garage. On the second level sat their new ride, a dark blue Ford Focus, keys tucked under the driver's seat. They left in silence, not speaking until they got onto the highway that led to Marinsburg.

"They're going to kill her, aren't they?" Riley asked.

"Yep," Conner answered nonchalantly.

"Does that bother you?"

"She saw our faces. Even if they get to her father, there's no guarantee she won't talk."

"Her friend did too."

Conner gave him a look that told him they would find the friend as well.

Riley nodded and then pointed out, "You didn't answer my question."

"No," Conner replied without thinking about it. "Does it bother you?"

"No, the way I look at it, that's two less rich people in the world."

"Are you going to feel the same way when I become one?"

"A rich person?" Riley chuckled.

"Yeah."

"No matter how much money you get," Riley assured. "You'll never be an entitled plastic piece of shit." Conner didn't respond. "Where do you suppose they get all those cars they just throw away?"

"I don't know."

"Seems like a big waste of money."

"Yeah."

"Yeah. You know who would love those cars?"

"Yeah."

"He sure could do wonders with 'em."

"Yeah," Conner agreed. "Are you thinking what I think you're thinking?"

"What are you thinking?"

"Chop shop?" Conner asked.

"Chop shop," Riley repeated.

Conner loved the idea and knew that Sam would feel the same way. The only challenge was convincing Daniel to trust Sam enough to involve him in the family business. He pondered this on the way home, arriving a little after 8:00 PM. After dropping Riley off at his house, he drove to the O'Brien estate. Although he wanted to race to Tennly, he knew he had to speak with Thomas first.

"Come in," Thomas said after he opened the door.

Conner walked into the apartment as he said, "The car is in front of the garage."

"Everything go well?"

"Yeah."

"Good," Thomas said and then handed him his phone. "Here. You can have it for the night. Daniel wants you staying here. Leave it with Marie before you leave tomorrow. Do not take it with you. And remind Tennly to do the same."

Conner turned to leave when Thomas stopped him. "He likes you, you know."

Conner had started to sense that Daniel was becoming comfortable with his presence, but hearing Thomas say that Daniel liked him filled him with warmth. It had only been a few weeks since he started dating Tennly, and he had never paused to consider his feelings for Daniel. The thought that Daniel might actually like him made him feel at home, and he realized he saw him as a father figure.

When he reached Tennly's room, the door was open, but she was not inside. He stepped further in and heard water running. Walking into the bathroom, he saw her standing in the shower; her back turned to him as she washed her hair. He took two steps closer and paused to watch her.

He smiled as she finally turned to face him and noticed his presence. She ran her hands over her stomach while he approached the shower door and opened it. Placing his hands on her face, he immediately began kissing her. She reached under his shirt and lifted it over his head to help him take it off. He picked her up, causing her to wrap her legs around his body, and pushed her back against the wall. As the water sprayed down over them, it unleashed something within him, and he couldn't help but feel an intense sense of guilt.

He rested his head on her chest as he wept, "I'm so sorry. I didn't have sex with her, but..."

She knew what he was talking about, so she lifted his head by his chin to look into his eyes. "There's nothing to be sorry about... Do you hear me? Nothing. You did what you had to do for my father, for this family... for me."

"I love you so much," he proclaimed.

Amelia woke up half an hour after Conner and Riley left the safehouse. Shaking with fear, she looked around at the three men surrounding her and repeatedly asked what they wanted and whether they were going to hurt her. She darted her gaze between them, silently pleading for one of them to respond, hardly pausing to give them a chance to answer.

"Where's Mark?" she cried, trying to catch her breath after giving up on escaping.

"There is no Mark," Daniel replied sternly. "If you would just be quiet for a minute, I will explain what's happening." She took a few deep breaths, wiped her eyes, and remained silent, though her legs couldn't help but bounce up and down. "Now, do you think you can stay quiet long enough for me to talk?" Daniel asked. Amelia nodded, so he continued. "If you want to make it out of here, you'll call your father."

After a couple heavy breaths, she shuddered, "I don't... I can't..."

Jimmy came up from behind her and punched her in the back of the head, causing her to let out a loud scream as she shrieked, "Okay, Okay... But... Oh my God... Please don't..."

"Can you get a hold of him?" Daniel repeated.

"I'm not allowed."

Jimmy pulled out a gun and held it to her head. "Oh my god... please..." she panted. "Please... I don't want to die..." Then, as Jimmy cocked the gun, Daniel asked her again. She was shaking so violently that Jimmy rolled his eyes at Daniel, who asked her again. "Yeah... yeah... Yes. I can... I can get a hold of him."

"Good," Daniel said, gesturing for Jimmy to lower the gun. "I'm going to need you to call him."

After Jimmy handed her phone back to her, she scrolled through her contacts and called a number with an alias as a contact name. It rang four times before William answered.

"Daddy," Amelia said with an obviously distressed voice.

"Honey," William replied on the other end. "You sound upset. Are you okay?"

"No, Daddy. I'm so sor..."

Daniel grabbed the phone out of her hand before she could finish. "Hello William."

"Who is this?" William fretted.

"As soon as you recognize my voice, do not say my name or anyone else's," Daniel demanded. "Do you understand?"

"Yes," William said.

"If you do," Daniel threatened. "They'll be finding pieces of your daughter all over the country for years to come. Do you understand?"

"Yes," William responded as Ameila began to cry louder.

"If you want to see her again, you'll find a way to get away and meet me. Alone. No cops. Understand?"

"Yes."

"Do you know where the old, abandoned railroad station is on the west side of Columbus?"

"Yes."

"There's a row of park benches on platform five," Daniel explained. "Meet me there tomorrow... 3:00 PM."

"Okay."

"Remember, if you don't show. I'll kill your daughter. If you involve the police, I'll kill your daughter. Do I make myself clear?"

"Yes."

Daniel knew they couldn't stay at the safehouse—if William called the police, they'd soon arrive. He ordered John to drug Amelia, smash her phone, and take her to the car. Meanwhile, he and Jimmy doused the farmhouse with gasoline, setting each room ablaze until flames consumed the living room and smoke poured from every crack. Only after the house was fully engulfed did they leave for another safehouse nearby.

By 10:00 AM the next morning, Conner and Tennly arrived. Daniel wanted her there early enough to scout the abandoned railroad station five hours before meeting William, informing her it would be similar to the job she had done at the old airfield.

The station had eight platforms around a six-story building. Once a hub sending trains across Columbus and neighboring towns, it now lay in ruin: tracks unused, windows shattered, debris scattered. Between the platforms ran narrow truck roads, with a two-lane drop-off by platform 5 and a parking lot opposite.

The bell tower rose ten by ten feet in the center of the six-story building, its staircase climbing two flights to the vacant chamber where the bell once hung. Four thick pillars framed six-foot openings on each wall, overlooking the decay below.

Upon spotting platform number five, Daniel pointed to it and instructed, "He should show up there. What we need you to do is watch for any signs of police. If you see any, let us know."

"Where will you be?" Tennly asked.

"Depends," Daniel replied. "If there's no sign of police, I'll be here to meet with William. If there is, I'll be back at the safehouse. Conner, stay with her." He then handed Tennly a rifle and said, "Do not use this unless you have to, or I tell you to."

She nodded, and then Daniel handed Conner a handgun as he said, "Keep her safe."

"On my life," Conner promised.

Knowing that Conner was present made it much easier for Daniel to leave his daughter behind than it had been during her first job at the airfield. He was grateful for Conner's support and patted him on the shoulder to tell him so. He then gave Tennly a hug and left with Jimmy and John.

Conner scanned the area with binoculars while Tennly used the rifle scope, trading shifts every fifteen minutes to rest between watches.

The abandoned station revealed its details gradually; sunlight glinting off broken glass and the bottles and cans scattered across the snow. The untouched drifts on the platforms looked almost picturesque, resembling a scene from an old English Christmas paining, disturbed only by a rabbit on Platform 6. It would have been a beautiful scene if not for the occasional whiff of oil, carbon paper, and creosote, the solvent used to soak railroad ties to prevent infestation and decay.

At 1:30 PM, the first sign of trouble appeared: a hobo was circling Platform 4, repeating the same odd routine at a nearby dumpster. Thirty minutes later, two young men wandered along the tracks, pretending to drink and kick rocks, but it was clear they were following a pattern. By 2:30 PM, the ruse became unmistakable; an unmarked car rolled into the parking lot a hundred yards away, just as Daniel checked in with Tennly.

"See anything?" Daniel asked.

"Afraid so," Tennly responded. "There's a cop pretending to be a hobo, two more pretending to be kids vandalizing, and a police car just pulled up at the end of the parking lot."

Daniel was silent as he tried to control his anger at yet another betrayal.

"Okay," he said. "Let me know when William gets there."

"Will do."

William arrived by taxi at 2:55 PM. Tennly reported his movements as he crossed the road, climbed to Platform 5, and paced. Daniel then dialed the number from Amelia's phone. William answered instantly, asking if his daughter was safe.

Daniel held the phone to Amelia and after his nod, she whispered, "Daddy."

Daniel took it back and said, "She's alive, for now. Whether she stays that way is up to you."

"Whatever I have to do," William pleaded. "Just don't hurt her."

Daniel ordered him to sit on the fourth bench from the station. Once Tennly confirmed he obeyed, Daniel asked coldly, "Did you think I wouldn't find out?"

"It's my son," William said, hoping to play on a father's heartstrings. "I had to protect him."

"I understand," Daniel responded. "And to be honest, I'm glad to hear you say you would do anything to protect your children. How far will you go to keep them safe?"

"Anything," William pleaded.

"Good. Reach under the bench. There's a gun. You have three choices. Two of them can keep your children safe. You should feel lucky; most don't get that."

William felt under the bench until he found the gun taped under the seat. He didn't want to take it, for he knew what Daniel wanted him to do with it.

"Your first option," Daniel instructed. "Take the gun and kill yourself. Second option: shoot at the police that are walking around the station. I know there are three, plus however many are in the unmarked car at the end of the parking lot. Tsk tsk, not smart, William. And your third, I kill your daughter, and then my daughter kills you. You're a dead man, William. Don't kill your family along with you."

"How do I know you won't kill them anyway?" William whined, shaking as he was thinking of what he should do.

"You don't. But at least you would die with the hope that there is a possibility they are alive. Tick tock, William."

William began hyperventilating as he reached down under the bench and removed the gun from the tape. "He's got the gun," Tennly informed. "He's holding it to his head. It's back down on his lap... in his mouth... back down."

"Can you at least tell my family everything I did, I did for them?" William cried.

"Of course," Daniel lied.

"It's at his h..." Tennly said, and then Daniel heard a loud gunshot through the com system.

"Tennly?" Daniel asked.

"He did it," Tennly reported.

"Is he dead?" Daniel inquired.

"It looks like, but... from here I can't tell," Tennly answered.

"Are the police running toward him?"

"They are... One police officer is calling someone."

"Probably an ambulance," Daniel noted.

Tennly and Conner stayed just long enough to see the ambulance arrive and confirm William was dead. They watched as the EMTs checked his vitals and attempted CPR before covering his body with a sheet.

After placing him onto a stretcher and into the ambulance, Tennly informed her father.

Daniel breathed a sigh of relief, looked at Amelia, and without a word, shot her in the head. Then he called Thomas, who in turn set in motion the death of William's son, Lucas, who ended up dead in prison due to a shanking in the bathroom. Two days later, Jane was dead from an overdose, and Amelia vanished without a trace except for the postcards her mother received from faraway places.

The Connolly family friend who worked in the court system ensured that all documents related to Daniel and the Connollys were destroyed. Since William hadn't provided their names yet, there was no evidence linking them to the situation. The threat was eliminated, and they could relax again, at least for a little while.

CHAPTER 6

When Daniel asked Conner to meet him in his office after their trip to Columbus, Conner already had a hunch why. He'd been paid handsomely for the first job, and he suspected this would be no different.

"As you know, I pay everyone who works for me," Daniel began. "Sales earn a percentage. Otherwise, it's two thousand an hour. But because you saved my life, as well as many others, we've decided to pay you $5000 an hour for this job."

"What?" Conner blurted, stunned before Daniel even finished.

Daniel only smiled and handed him two drawstring bags, each tagged with a name: one for Conner, one for Riley.

"We can't accept that much," Conner protested.

"It's not up for negotiation," Daniel replied.

"But that's thirty-five grand each."

"Correction," Daniel said. "Riley gets thirty-five for his seven hours, minus the $2080 he owes me from poker. You worked five more hours than he did."

Conner loosened the string on his own bag and froze at the sight of stacked bills. "There's no talking you out of this?"

Daniel grinned. "No. You're free to do what you want with it, as long as you follow the rules."

"I remember them," Conner said, recalling the note that came with the $50,000 from his last job.

"I'm sure you do. Clever response, by the way."

"Yeah," Conner muttered, squinting slightly. "Sorry about that."

"Don't be," Daniel said with a wry smile. "I probably deserved it."

Three days before Christmas Eve, Conner still hadn't found a gift for Tennly. What could he give a girl who seemed to have everything? When the answer finally came to him, making a promise to love her forever, there was one obstacle standing in his way: he needed Daniel's permission, not wanting to risk the trust he had earned.

The walk from the garage to Daniel's office felt unusually long. Nerves churned in his stomach as he tried to find the right words. Once at the doorway, Daniel spotted him and waved him in. "What can I do for you, Conner?"

I never thought in a million years I would ever be in this position," Conner said, biting his lower lip. "So... I'm... Can I... shit... This isn't going how I envisioned it in my head."

"What is it?"

Conner took a deep breath and admitted, "I told you once that I didn't care about what you thought... But I do. I not only care about what you think of me; I find myself needing you to like me. Which makes this even harder."

Daniel remained silent. He didn't want to add any more pressure on Conner than he already seemed to be under. So, he offered Conner a look of support and gestured for him to continue.

"I think you know I love your daughter. I love her more than I've ever loved anyone. And I know we haven't been dating that long... but I can't see my future without her. But... here's the weird part... and the part that even baffles me... I not only love your daughter, I love her family... and I love this life I'm building here... with her... with you. I never pictured myself living like this... but... I guess what I'm saying is... I... I would love your permission to ask Tennly to marry me."

Daniel sat in silence, grateful that he didn't have to kill Conner but completely unprepared for his unexpected proposal. His neutral expression gave no indication of his thoughts, leaving Conner unsure if Daniel was accepting of the situation or if he might suddenly pull out a gun and shoot him. To break the uncomfortable silence and reassure Daniel that he respected any concerns he might have, Conner stumbled over his words, searching for something to say.

"Of course," Conner rambled, getting even more nervous. "We would wait to get married until after she finishes school, whether it's high school or college... or whatever. I just need her to know. I need everyone to know. Kids at school, your family... Look... I've spent the last few years with a reputation that I can't love... and to be honest... I wanted people to think that..."

"Stop," Daniel interrupted, letting him off the hook. "Even though you never thought you would find yourself in this position, I knew one day I would. Albeit, I didn't think it would be this soon. And I often worried who it would be with. Would they be some pretentious asshole who just liked her for her money? Or worse, a man that would treat her poorly... although I would like to see someone try that. She would probably kill them."

They both laughed, easing the tension in the room as Daniel continued, "To be honest, Conner, all I hope for my daughters is to find someone who loves them. I just want them to be happy. And you make her happy. Tennly has always had a good head on her shoulders and a great sense for bullshit. I should have listened to her when I was being a dick to you. If I had, you two would have started dating sooner. She loves you, and you have become an intricate member of this family. So... I give you my blessing."

"Are you serious?" Conner asked as if he was expecting him to say no.

Daniel chuckled as he said, "Yes. You have my blessing to get engaged to my daughter. With that said, however, the marriage part will wait until after she graduates from high school, and preferably college... but we'll reconvene when that time comes, deal?"

"Deal."

"Despite the short amount of time you've been with us, we all already see you as part of this family. So, welcome."

"Thank you. That means more to me than you will ever know." Conner hadn't had a real family since his mother left when he was four, and he had no idea how much he craved it. His friends were decent substitutes that he considered family, but it wasn't the same. Being a part of Tennly's family, celebrating holidays together, being accepted by her uncles, and even participating in the mundane daily activities finally gave him what he longed for.

"I have one more question." Daniel nodded to tell him to go ahead. "Where can I go to buy her the best ring I can?"

"You're in luck," Daniel informed. "If you can be ready in three hours, the jet leaves to take Jimmy and John back to New York. I can call our jewelers to help you pick out a ring."

This was the first time Conner had ever flown, and his enthusiasm was evident on his face. As soon as he stepped onto the O'Brien's plane, Jimmy and John began laughing at him as Jimmy asked him if it was his first time flying.

"Is it that obvious?" Conner replied.

"No, not at all," Jimmy sarcastically said.

"Oh, shut up," Conner teased, only making the men's laughter stronger.

Conner fastened his seatbelt, startled by the roar of the engines. The plane moved more smoothly than he expected, but as it accelerated, the force pinned him to his seat. The runway blurred past, and then, as if the floor had dropped out from under them, his stomach churned when he realized they were airborne. The rocking motion thrilled and terrified him until turbulence set in, making each jolt feel worse. His unease drew laughter from the three men, whose teasing banter provided a welcome distraction until the plane finally landed. Relieved to be on solid ground, he barely had time to recover before they crossed the airfield to board the Connolly jet.

The Boeing 787 VIP Dreamliner felt more like a luxury hotel than an aircraft. Its main cabin resembled a lavish living room, complete with ivory couches, recliners, a faux fireplace, and a dining table for eight. The rear of the jet offered five bedrooms, including a master suite, a kitchen, an office, and elegant gold-trimmed décor throughout.

Seated on an inward-facing couch, Conner was caught off guard again as the jet began to roll. The takeoff felt steadier this time, smoother and less jarring. As soon as the jet leveled out, the seatbelt light blinked off, and a flight attendant approached. Daniel requested a charcuterie board and then she took their drink orders.

When Conner asked for a Coke, the men busted out in laughter as Daniel said, "Get the boy a whiskey."

"I have a question," John taunted after the flight attendant left. "What did you tell Tennly to get her to let you leave for a night?"

"Let me?" Conner asked. The three men burst out, grinning and making 'bull-whipping' gestures as if he were under Tennly's rule. "I told her that my friends and I were spending the night at Sam's and then heading out in the morning to go hunting."

Their amusement only grew as Daniel smirked, "You hunt?"

"No," Conner admitted, which only drew louder roars of laughter from the group.

"Does she know that?" Jimmy added, unable to contain his chuckles.

"Yeah," Conner confessed. "I told her we're more or less just... getting drunk in the woods."

"Good call," John acknowledged.

They spent the next couple of hours joking and laughing, playfully teasing Conner. This was their way of initiating him into the family, and he loved every minute of it, even managing to deliver some good comebacks of his own. When they arrived in New York City, they were slightly intoxicated as Phillip dropped Daniel and Conner off at Daniel's penthouse before driving Jimmy and John to their homes.

The penthouse foyer sparkled with white and gold marble. A slender gold table, adorned with a vase of flowers and a bowl for Daniel's keys, stood against the wall. Beyond it, Conner's eyes widened as he took in the living room, plush ivory couches accented with yellow rested on a matching rug, while an open kitchen and dining area followed the same warm color scheme. Ivory appliances, cushioned barstools, and a ten-seat dining table completed the space.

Floor-to-ceiling windows filled the room with light and opened onto a balcony stretching the length of the hotel. Stepping outside, Conner was struck by the height and the crisp air. The city below was a vibrant chaos; horns, engines, birds, and the wind blended into an almost musical symphony.

Inside, Daniel showed him the bedrooms; Tara's in purple, Tennly's in pink with violet accents. Conner dropped his suitcase onto Tennly's bed before returning to the living room to wait for Phillip to pick him up.

The jewelry store was vast and intimidating, with rows of glass cases showcasing hundreds of glittering pieces. Conner had barely stepped inside when a tall woman with waist-length black hair and striking brown eyes approached him from behind the counter.

"How can I help you?" she asked.

"I'm looking for an engagement ring for my girlfriend," Conner answered, finding it strange how he had never had any trouble talking to a woman before, but for some reason he felt quite intimidated by her presence.

"You must be Conner? I'm McKenna. Daniel told me you were coming. Is there any certain design that you're looking for?"

"I don't know any designs."

McKenna found Conner's ignorance endearing and pulled out a cheat sheet on engagement ring cuts. Even after her explanations, his confused expression remained, so she brought out two display cases. After looking through the options, Conner narrowed it down to three rings, each one close but not quite right. With McKenna's help, he refined his preferences until they finally designed the perfect ring for Tennly.

The chosen design was crafted in a vintage style; it featured a full-carat rectangular radiant white diamond in the center, surrounded by a halo of eighteen small pink diamonds. The ring also had three smaller diamonds arranged in a triangular pattern at the top and bottom, with additional diamonds in a scalloped design along the sides. The band was made of rose gold and consisted of two smaller bands running side by side, each adorned with ten smaller diamonds on both sides. In total, the ring contained four white carat diamonds and a one-carat worth of pink diamonds.

After McKenna told him it would be ready the next day in time for their fly home, Conner explored the city before returning to the hotel for the night. He settled in next to Daniel in the living room, picking a chair that faced the windows. Usually, they had only a couple of hours at a time together, in the garage, working on cars, or sitting around the mansion while they ate. However, as they sat there drinking and talking, they finally had a chance to genuinely get to know each other. By the end of the night, Conner felt so comfortable that he opened up about his entire childhood. He shared stories about his mother, explained how he earned his reputation, and, most importantly, talked about his love for Tennly and the moments they shared that led to it.

Listening to Conner made Daniel appreciate him even more. What Tennly lacked, Conner more than compensated for with his understanding of how the real world operated. The fact that Conner had risen from a difficult upbringing to a position of power and influence made him the perfect match for the future mafia boss.

Early Christmas Eve, Conner and his friends gathered at Sam's house for their annual gaming tradition, something they had started years earlier when Conner had run to Riley's house to escape his father's wrath. What once filled entire days had, over the years, dwindled to just an hour before dinner at Riley's, where his mother always welcomed them and quietly sent food home with Conner for his brother.

After dropping off the meal to Dougy, Conner arrived at the O'Brien Estate. Marie was in the kitchen with Tennly's aunts, finishing the Christmas Eve dinner. She stopped Conner as he walked through the kitchen and introduced him to the six women. From the Connolly side, there was Jimmy's wife, Valerie, and John's wife, Stella. On the O'Brien side, there were Daniel's sisters-in-law, Sheila and Anna, and Daniel's two sisters, Cara and Janette.

After Conner left the kitchen, the women smiled at Marie. They were all thinking the same thing, but it was Cara who voiced it. "He's too cute. A face like that can only mean trouble."

Dinner in the great room was festive, with red tablecloths, poinsettias, and candelabras adorning the tables, which were overflowing with ham, vegetables, seafood, and desserts. Conner admired the spread and later suggested donating the leftovers to the warehouse. Daniel embraced the idea, and the family eagerly boxed everything up, with Conner setting aside a few bags for his friends.

Soon after, they began decorating the bare Christmas tree in the great room. Daniel played some classic holiday songs while everyone added ornament after ornament until the tree was completely covered. Next, Conner was introduced to a special tradition he had never encountered before: a Christmas Eve box for all the kids. Inside each box were pajamas, books, socks, underwear, school supplies, and a unique Christmas ornament designed specifically for each child.

Conner was surprised when Victoria's brother walked over and handed him one of the boxes. He thanked him and looked at Tennly with a questioning expression. She smiled and gestured for him to open it. Inside was one Christmas ornament inscribed with, 'Conner's 1st Ornament' with the year on the other side.

"Every child in this family has received an ornament every year since they were born," Tennly explained. "It seems my dad thought you deserved your first one."

Conner glanced at Daniel, who nodded with a welcoming grin. He then looked back down at the ornament. Having never

received an ornament in his entire life,
he felt a comforting warmth wash over him
as he placed it back into the box.

By the end of the night, Tennly
noticed that the younger boys were
gathering around Conner, seemingly
enamored with him. Conner treated the boys
with respect and demonstrated genuine
interest in what they had to say or show
him. He even took the time to play some
video games with them when all the kids
headed to the game room.

Conner finally got a moment alone
with Tennly once everyone was settled in
their designated guest rooms and the two
of them placed their ornaments on her tree
in her bedroom. She could tell that he was
up to something after he gave her a kiss
and led her over to her bed.

"What are you doing?" She asked
suspiciously as he gestured for her to sit
down.

She began to get nervous that
something was wrong when he grabbed her
hands into his. "Conner? You're scaring
me."

"I'm sorry... but can you just be
quiet and let me get this out?" Seeing that
his hands were slightly shaking, she

smiled and nodded. He took a deep breath and began. "Tennly, I love you more than anything. And this past month has been the best month of my entire life. I never thought in a million years that your family would accept me the way they have. And even more than that, I never thought I would care as much as I do for them. For the first time in my life, I feel like I fit somewhere. Which is why..." He reached under the pillow that was behind his back and pulled out a small, wrapped box. It was still wrapped in brown paper, only it wasn't from the normal grocery bag. It was designer paper, light brown with white snowflakes all over it, that McKenna helped him pick out. "I... here..." he said handing the gift to her.

Tennly looked down at the gift and slowly began to unwrap it while Conner observed, heart racing as he contemplated how he would propose. Once she removed all the wrapping and opened the outer box, she discovered a smaller pink velvet container, which she recognized as a ring box. Shocked, she glanced up at Conner, her eyes questioning. He nodded encouragingly for her to continue.

Carefully, she opened it, revealing the engagement ring nestled inside. Her heartbeat quickened, and it felt as though her breath had momentarily escaped her, reminding herself to breathe as she gazed up at him.

"You are the only person I want to spend the rest of my life with," he professed. "You are my breath, my life, my heart, my everything, and I can't see a future without you in it." When she became momentarily tongue-tied, he held his breath in anticipation, worried that she was about to say no. "I've already asked your father, and he gave me his blessing, and it doesn't mean that we're going to get married right away. I mean, if you need to wait years, I don't ca..."

"Shut up," she cooed.

"What?"

"Just ask me," she pleaded as happy tears formed in her eyes.

He smiled, took the box, and held the ring in front of her. "Tennly O'Brien, will you marry me?"

It was a tradition for everyone to gather for a huge breakfast on Christmas morning. Even the O'Briens came over, having told their children that Santa delivered their gifts to Uncle Daniel's house.

Conner didn't make it to breakfast. He had a few things he needed to do before heading back to the mansion. Every Christmas Eve, Riley's mother insisted that Conner stay with them since his father was often home for the holidays. They woke up early, had breakfast, and then opened gifts. Even Dougy managed to sneak out of the house and spent a couple of hours with his brother and Riley before Conner left for the mansion.

Conner enjoyed watching as everyone scattered about as the young kids delivered presents to their recipients. He loved the positive atmosphere that filled the room; the laughter and love were palpable and warmed his heart to the point that he didn't even think about the fact that he might not receive any gifts. So, when Daniel brought him over six presents, he was genuinely shocked.

"What is this?" Conner asked.

"Santa," Daniel said with a wink.

Tennly smiled, knowing about the gifts and who they were from. The first gift Conner opened was from Daniel: a passport. Daniel had used Conner's ID picture to apply for a rushed passport for him. Along with the passport was a note that read, 'In case you need it. – Daniel.'

The second present was from Marie. She had gifted him his own set of baking pans and cooking pots, along with a recipe book from her family in Ireland. Conner looked over at Marie and saw her smiling at him. He had grown to love her, and he mouthed 'thank you' as he nodded in her direction.

The third gift was from Thomas: a heavy-duty, reliable pocketknife. The fourth and fifth gifts came from Jimmy and John's families. After asking Tennly and Tara what their boyfriends would like, Conner received two black T-shirts, a leather belt he had always wanted, and a new wallet. Secretly, they also added one shoulder and one ankle holster.

Tennly's gift was an envelope filled with receipts for supplies she had bought: 20 queen-sized mattresses and box springs, 20 area rugs, sheets, blankets, tables, room dividers, curtains, and enough hygiene products to care for a hundred people.

With confusion on his face, Conner looked at Tennly, who clarified, "Donated to the warehouse."

He put his hands on her face and said, "You are amazing." Then he gave her a kiss and asked, "When will they get it?"

"It was delivered first thing this morning, but that's not all." She reached into her pocket and pulled out a smaller box and handed it to him.

He opened the box and found two more receipts inside. The first one was from a furniture store, where a recliner, a table that seated ten people, a chest of drawers, and a king-sized bed with a mattress, box spring, sheets, blankets, and matching curtains were purchased. The second receipt was from a carpet store, listing two large area rugs.

"This is for your barn," she explained, "or whenever you get to build your house."

"I don't know what to say," he responded. In the past, he would have viewed her gesture as charity. However, for some reason, he was now able to see her gifts for what they truly were: a sign of love. "Thank you."

After lunch, the O'Briens left the estate, and while the Connollys dispersed into different rooms around the mansion, Tennly and Conner received a text from Daniel instructing them to sneak up to Thomas's apartment as soon as they could.

To avoid raising any suspicion, Tennly told Tara and Victoria that she had promised Conner that if he spent some time with her family, in return, she would go with him to see his friends in the afternoon.

Once they entered the garage apartment, they found Thomas in his usual spot at the kitchen island, while Daniel, Jimmy, and John were sitting in the living room across from Duncan. Tennly was excited to see her cousin, but she could tell by the look on his face that he wasn't there for a cordial visit.

"I hate to come here for this reason," Duncan said, "but I didn't have a choice. I was sent here by the family. Looks like the MacFaddens and O'Gradys aren't happy with Tennly becoming the boss. They went to the leadership in Ireland over it and have good reasons. The biggest one being there's never been a female boss."

"So," Daniel said, "what do they want?"

"Both families have sons," Duncan answered. "And they have requested a Donnybrook."

Conner could tell from the long faces and loud sighs that whatever a Donnybrook was, wasn't good. Tennly only recognized the term because it was an Irish word. She understood it meant, but that was all she knew, and she didn't grasp what it would entail.

"What is that?" Conner asked.

"A fight," Duncan replied.

"They want to fight Tennly?" Conner inquired.

"Aye."

Tennly could see that although Conner looked worried, it was nothing compared to the fear visible on the men's faces. To reassure them that she had learned a lot from Duncan, she stated, "I can fight."

The men exchanged glances, seemingly uncertain about who would be the one to speak up. Finally, Duncan added, "To the death."

"What?" Conner gasped, diverting his attention from Tennly to Daniel. Surely Daniel wouldn't allow his daughter to take part in a fight to the death. But when Conner looked at Daniel, he couldn't decipher his thoughts. He saw worry on Daniel's face, but there was also a sense of defeat.

"They are willing to risk their sons to keep tradition," Duncan continued. Then he looked at Tennly. "You have three weeks to get ready."

"She's not going through with this," Conner exclaimed, looking at Daniel pleading for him to say something.

"We give up our position," Jimmy stated, finally saying what the men knew but didn't want to admit, "it'll show weakness."

"Are you serious?" Conner fumed. "This is crazy. Daniel, you're surely not considering this."

"Conner," Daniel replied. "I told you, there are things about this family that go beyond what I want. But with that said, I understand your concerns. She's my daughter..."

"And my fiancée," Conner interjected, which caused the uncles to shake their heads because the news made things messier.

"You're not married yet." Daniel looked at Duncan and asked, "Are they willing to wait until Jimmy's oldest son is old enough?"

"No," Duncan answered. "To them the gauntlet has been thrown."

"If it's this simple to take over, why doesn't anyone request a Donnybrook with Keenan?" Tennly asked.

"A Donnybrook has a hierarchy," Duncan explained. "They have to beat you first, then one of the original five bosses before they could even get to Keenan."

"And most would never risk that," Jimmy added. "Even if they won and worked up the hierarchy, the thought of requesting a Donnybrook with someone as beloved and old as Keenan wouldn't be honorable."

"But requesting one of a 16-year-old girl is?" Conner asked, his tone laced with both fury and disbelief.

"Unfortunately," Duncan replied, "she hasn't earned that right, yet. Many don't."

"Do you believe I can beat them?" Tennly asked, her focus fixed solely on Duncan.

"You would be fighting them both at once," Duncan informed. "And they will not play fair. They will go after you first; get you out of the way before they turn on each other."

"You didn't answer my question," Tennly pressed.

"Aye," Duncan imparted. "I think you can beat 'em."

"You've got to be kidding me," Conner protested, feeling as if his heart was being yanked out of his chest. "Daniel, please..."

Daniel looked at Conner and disclosed, "This tradition goes back hundreds of years. If she doesn't fight, it'll be like wolves to a kill. You may not understand this world yet, but if you want to stay in it, you will learn to abide by our laws."

Conner couldn't bear to listen any longer. Frustrated, he stormed out, leaving the others to exchange worried glances. The men turned to Tennly, telling her she was responsible for Conner. They insisted that as soon as the meeting was over, she needed to find him and ensure he wouldn't, in desperation, go to the police. She nodded to confirm that she would take care of it, and then Duncan resumed explaining the details of the duel.

The Donnybrook was scheduled to take place in three weeks on a property designated in Ireland. The hardest part to hear was that the MacFadden and O'Grady families requested that there not be any throwing knives allowed.

"Evidently they were so impressed with your knife skills that they consider it an advantage and thus not fair in a fight," Duncan said.

"If she's better than them, then she's better than them. Doesn't matter how," Jimmy stated.

Duncan looked at Tennly and mentioned, "You can't have knives, but nowhere did they say you can't throw other things. Do you remember your training?"

"I do," she answered. Not being able to have her knives did make her more scared to fight, but it didn't change her decision.

"Then you know what you need to do," Duncan replied. "You have three weeks to prepare. I want you training at least an hour, preferably two, every day until then."

"Will you be here to train me?" She asked.

"Unfortunately, I have to get back to Ireland. But it's my understanding that you have the best trainer right here."

"Who?" Tennly asked.

"Conner," Duncan responded. "It won't look suspicious when Tara sees you two together, and other than your father, there's no one more determined to make sure you're ready. You just have to talk him into it." Tennly nodded, knowing that was going to be the hard part. "I'll need the two of you in the gym tomorrow at 8:00 AM."

Frustrated and worried, Conner left the mansion and headed to the warehouse to wish Dante a Merry Christmas and check on Tennly's anonymous donation. Watching Dante's excitement over the new furniture provided a pleasant distraction, but Conner's thoughts kept circling back to his concerns. He needed to get to Riley's house and vent about what Tennly was planning to do.

While Conner explained to Riley why he was upset, Tennly spotted Conner's car in Riley's driveway. She stopped in front of the house and hesitated about whether to go inside. She knew she had to speak to him, but when it came down to it, she was more scared about the situation than she wanted to admit and realized that if the roles were reversed, she would feel just as angry and frightened.

She closed her eyes, took a deep breath, and held it. As she slowly exhaled through her mouth, she felt calm enough to approach the front door.

"Can I help you?" Lexie asked, surprising Tennly.

"Is Conner here?"

"Yeah," Lexie said not offering for her to go inside.

"I'm Tennly O..."

"I know who you are," Lexie interrupted with a short tone.

Tennly had never met Riley's mother before and found it appalling that an adult would judge her simply for being herself. Standing in the doorway facing Lexie reminded her of how Bridget had treated her. She thought those days of having to defend herself were behind her and was determined not to be intimidated.

"I need to speak with him," Tennly politely said as she put on the best smile she could. "Would it be ok if I came in?"

Lexie finally stepped aside as she said, "They're in Riley's room. It's the second door on the left down the hall."

"Thank you." Tennly started to walk away but couldn't go without saying something about how Riley's mom had spoken to her. She turned back around and said, "I know you don't know me... and that you have assumptions about my family... but remember the assumptions you have about us because we have money can be the same assumptions that we have toward you because you don't."

Tennly had never found it difficult to stand up for herself or express her thoughts, but for some reason, facing Riley's mother made her anxious. It wasn't just that Lexie was the mother of Conner's best friend; it was also because Conner had mentioned that Lexie had become like a

mother to him: wanting to make a good first
impression.

"I knew your family," Lexie confessed.
"Janette. She was my best friend in
elementary school, but as we got older,
she started hanging out with richer kids,
and by the time we were in high school,
she wouldn't talk to me anymore. The only
times she did was when she was saying
something cruel or pulling some prank on
me."

"I'm so sorry." Tennly knew her Aunt
Janette and found her to be haughty,
behaving as if she was better than everyone
else. So, she smiled at Lexie and said,
"She's not a very nice person."

Lexie smiled back at her and
apologized. "I shouldn't have judged you.
I'm sorry."

Tennly shrugged her shoulders as if
to tell her she had a right and then
admitted, "That's okay. Most of us are big
turds."

They both chuckled, while Lexie
nodded in agreement and then asked, "How's
your dad?"

"He's good. I think he's lonely
sometimes. Misses my mom."

"I know what that feels like. I miss my husband every day."

"I'm sorry."

"It's okay. It's funny. When I was younger and used to spend the night with your aunt, I would do anything I could to find an excuse to see your dad."

"Your secret is safe with me."

"It's not really a big secret. Janette... she threatened to make my life a living hell... it doesn't matter now."

Tennly was relieved to finally see Lexie's point of view on why she raised her son and Conner the way she did. They nodded at each other, a mutual understanding, and then Tennly walked to Riley's room.

"What do you want?" Conner lashed out.

"Seriously?" Tennly asked, not believing that he was being so abrupt with her.

In a much softer voice, he repeated, "What do you want, Ten?"

"I tried texting you and calling, bu..."

"I turned off my phone."

"I'm going to assume you talked to Riley about this?"

"Yeah, and he thinks you're all insane."

"You know," she said with a sarcastic look on her face, "sometimes you can be a real ass."

"Because I don't want you to die?... Yeah, that makes me terrible."

"Because you never stop to think how many times I've had to sit back and wait... hoping that you come back alive from wherever and whatever predicament you were in. I stood by you every time you made a decision that could possibly send you away, get you beat up, or worse. And for what? Drugs? Your dad? Or just because you were pissed and wanted to beat up on someone? Well, it's good to know you live by double standards. The only difference is, I'm fighting for something bigger than myself. It may mean nothing to you. But not fighting puts my whole family in danger. That means I will die anyway. And not only me, but Tara, Vicki, the boys. They could all end up dead. So, get off your pedestal and try to understand what it's like to be in this family. Because I'm going to need you to be by my side... if you plan on being in it."

Conner wasn't sure what to say or if he even wanted to. "My training starts tomorrow morning at 8. I would love to have your support." Then she turned and stormed out of the room.

Conner's emotions clouded his rational thought, debating whether he should follow her or not. He wanted to, but he felt he needed some time to think. He had just gotten her back, and the idea of losing her was too much to bear.

"She really knows how to make a speech, doesn't she?" Riley asked, breaking the silence.

"Yeah."

"Not gonna lie, she's scary."

"Yeah."

"Do you think she can win?"

"Duncan does."

"Then maybe you should trust her."

Conner didn't want her to have to fight to the death, and he felt angry that her family had put her in such a position. However, he knew he couldn't stay away from her. She was right; if he wanted to be a part of her life, no matter how long that

might last, he needed to be fully
committed.

Conner's 1st
Ornament

CHAPTER 7

Conner had been sparring with Tennly for a little over fifteen minutes, yet nothing he did pleased Duncan. The thought of hurting her made him sick to his stomach, but it seemed that's what Duncan wanted. Not even when he tripped Tennly, causing her to fall to the floor, or when he punched her in the shoulder to dodge one of her attacks sufficed.

"Stop!" Duncan screamed with the angriest voice Tennly had ever heard from him. "Do you want her to die?"

"You know I don't."

"How would I know that?" Duncan responded. He could see the turmoil in Conner's face and knew he was being harsh on him. "Look, I know how hard this is. I

185

hated it when I had to train her in Prague. But if she can't beat you one on one, when you're at your best, then she will not be able to beat two fully trained men. You are not doing her any justice."

"Fine," Conner said, giving in.

"Good. Now let's try this... come after me."

Tennly had never seen Duncan fight, but she had heard that he was the best. Watching Conner throw the first punch, she grimaced as Duncan skillfully dodged the attack and landed a powerful blow to Conner's back, knocking him to the floor. The pain that shot through his ribs made him realize how serious Duncan was. When he stood up, he wasn't sure he was angry or determined to impress him.

They fought hard for a few minutes, and Conner was able to hold his own. However, when Duncan punched Conner across the lip and nose with such force that it knocked him down. Conner felt his head spin as stars danced in front of his eyes. Blood dripped from the cuts on his face, and he struggled to stay focused enough to stand back up. He raised his hand to signal Duncan to stop and slowly made his way back to his feet.

"That," Duncan pointed out as he ran his tongue over his busted lower lip. "That is how you need to train her. Anything less and she will die."

Tennly and Conner squeezed in training sessions around Tara's winter break, meeting early in the morning or late in the evening to keep her from finding out. In between, they tried to spend as much time with her as possible. Although Tara had become more accustomed to Conner's presence, she never expected The Untouchables to show up at her New Year's Eve party. She had invited her friends with the expectation of having a girls' night, and the idea of Conner and his friends joining them felt overwhelming. Should she warn her friends or let it be a surprise? If she told them, they might decide to back out. As she pondered the whole ordeal, her gaze drifted to Conner, who, even after spending days with him, still seemed impossibly untouchable.

"What?" Conner asked, noticing her stare.

"Do you think they'll come?" Tara responded, fear in her eyes.

"You don't want me to ask them?" Conner chuckled.

"I don't know them," Tara replied.

"They're harmless," he claimed.

"They're terrifying," Tara stated.

"You used to think that of me," he reminded. She gave him a look that told him she still did. "Oh, come on... You still don't think that, do you?"

Tara shrugged her shoulders and admitted, "You guys are very frightening."

"Well, in that case," he said with a mischievous grin. "I'll definitely have to make sure they come."

He and Tennly laughed when they saw Tara's eyes widen. "Shut up," Tara teased as she threw a throw pillow at her sister.

After finalizing their New Year's Eve plans, Conner headed over to Riley's. They hadn't spoken since Conner mentioned Tennly's upcoming fight, and now he needed a favor. Riley was anxious to ask about the training but wasn't sure if Conner would be willing to open up, so they both sat in silence, watching a movie and stalling.

Finally, knowing he had no choice, Conner broke the silence. "When Tara goes back to college, we're going to need your help."

Riley's pulse quickened. Certain that Daniel had another job for him, he felt a rush of excitement, the same thrill he'd experienced from the last job. Not to mention, he really liked the money.

"Cool," Riley said. "What's the job?"

"It's not a job. I need you to help me train Tennly. Duncan thinks it would be good for her to practice with both of us so she can get used to different scenarios of how to fight two guys at once."

"She's still going through with it, huh?"

"Yeah."

"She's got balls."

"So, you'll help?"

"Sure. You said after Tara leaves?"

"Yeah, Tara doesn't know about the family. So, that only gives us a little under two weeks."

"Then I guess we'll have to make the most of it," Riley said giving his best friend a look that told him he was there for him and anything that he needed him to do.

Conner nodded in appreciation and casually mentioned the New Year's Eve party that Tennly and Tara were hosting at the mansion. Since his friends had attended the same house party for five years, and Sam disliked change, he assumed they wouldn't be interested and let the subject drop. Instead, his thoughts were elsewhere as he tried to find a way to tell Riley that he had proposed to Tennly.

"How do you feel about Ten?" Conner asked.

Riley took a drink of beer and then admitted, "She's growing on me."

"That's good... Because I got her an engagement ring for Christmas."

"Wow," Riley exclaimed, not sure how he felt about it. "That's what you really want? To spend the rest of your life with one girl?"

"I love her."

"I know. Sam's never going to let you live this down."

"I know."

Then Riley got a smile on his face, held up the bottle of beer, and toasted, "Congrats, man. I'm happy for you."

Tara had invited her boyfriend, Joey, to spend Christmas with her, but he already had plans with his family. He promised to try to join her for New Year's Eve, and when he called the day before to say he could come, Tara was thrilled. She rushed to tell her sister the good news, excited for the four of them to spend time together.

Tennly pretended to be happy about Joey's visit, but she dreaded the idea of Conner meeting him. She knew it would be difficult to make them spend time together.

Joey arrived earlier than expected, just after dinner. After unpacking, Tara took him to the gym, where they found Conner and Tennly training. From the doorway, they watched as Conner slammed Tennly to the floor, knocking the breath out of her. She quickly rolled to avoid a kick, scrambled back to her feet, and landed a punch right on Conner's chin, one that stung her fist as much as it did his jaw.

"No down time, Ten," Conner coached, and then hit her softly in the stomach just to show her that just because she was in pain, the fight would not stop.

"Grr," Tennly grunted. Then they got in a stance to start the fight again.

Tara hadn't seen Tennly and Conner fight in the gym before; she had assumed they went there just to work out. While she knew her sister practiced martial arts and had competed in the past, she didn't realize that Tennly was still actively participating. Tara felt conflicted about seeing Conner Marks hitting her sister so hard. She had heard that members of The Untouchables were known to hit girls, but there had never been any rumors suggesting they were genuinely abusive. It was clear that his hit was hard enough to cause

Tennly pain, and Tara was left questioning how Conner could love her sister if he was willing to hurt her.

"Who is that?" Joey whispered as they both continued watching the fighting.

"That's Conner. Tennly's boyfriend."

"And your dad approves of them dating?"

"Yeah."

"He must not know about this, then. If I had a daughter and her boyfriend was hitting her that hard, I would not only not allow it, but someone would have to hold me back to keep me from killing him."

Tara flinched as Tennly took another punch, wondering if their father knew about the fighting, and how he'd react if he didn't. Then she remembered this was just who Tennly was: all in, no matter the risk. Back at their boarding school in Prague, Tennly had practiced knife-throwing until her fingertips were slit, knocked herself out learning backflips off the diving boards, and often showed up to dinner covered in fresh bruises and scrapes.

"Tennly... she's a different bird," Tara explained. "She pushes herself so hard sometimes she doesn't know when to stop."

"Why?"

"I don't know. I've thought about that for years. It's just the way she's made."

"So, it doesn't bother you that her boyfriend is beating up on her?"

It bothered her, especially considering Conner's reputation, but she didn't want to jump to any conclusions about him, knowing her sister. "Come on," she motioned.

After informing her sister that Joey had arrived, Tara and Joey settled into the girls' living room while Tennly and Conner took showers. Conner lingered in the bathroom, taking his time; he wasn't eager to spend the evening with Joey. By the time he finally joined them, he was more than forty minutes behind Tennly. The three of them were already snacking on Marie's spread of cookies, brownies, fruit, and a white chocolate cream cheese dip.

It took less than an hour for Joey's constant eating and endless chatter to grate on Conner's nerves. He shot Tennly a look that clearly indicated if Joey kept it up, he might not be able to hold back.

Tennly, sensing his frustration, gave him a reassuring pat on the leg, subtly signaling that it was okay if he wanted to leave. Before spending time with the Tennly's family, Conner would have simply punched Joey and walked away. However, thanks to the etiquette and restraint he was learning, he was able to politely stand up and say goodbye before leaving.

Navigating through the crowd toward the kitchen to grab beers at their usual New Year's Eve spot, Conner and his friends mingled with others before settling into the living room. As soon as they arrived, three girls stood up to greet them and offered them the couch. One of the girls squealed when Joel pulled her onto his lap, while the other two perched themselves on the coffee table.

The girls were seniors from their high school that the boys knew and had partied with on several occassions. Conner had hooked up with one of them over the past summer. Normally, that wouldn't have bothered him, but with Tennly at home trusting him, he felt uneasy. He downed his beer in one gulp and then walked to the kitchen for a refill, and quickly finished two more beers. When he returned to the living room, he felt relieved to find that the girls had left.

Sensing that Conner wasn't really interested in being at the party, Riley pulled a flask of whiskey from his pocket and poured some into Conner's cup. An hour, three beers, and two shots later, Conner finally felt more relaxed.

However, that sense of calm was short-lived when Shelby arrived. Not seeing Tennly, she assumed they had broken up or that Conner simply hadn't wanted Tennly there. Seeing her chance, she tried to sit on Conner's lap, but he shoved her off, causing her to stumble onto the coffee table.

"What the hell?" Shelby snapped as she regained her balance. Conner just shook his head, stood up, and walked toward the door. She ran after him, blocking his path and pressing her palms against his chest. "You're just going to ignore me?"

Conner's patience snapped. He gripped her wrists tightly. "Go away, Shelby!" he growled, shoving past her.

Tears welled in her eyes. Desperate, she darted in front of him again, her voice trembling. "Why don't you love me? What does she have that I don't? Please, Conner… please."

Feeling empathy for her for the first time, Conner did something that startled everyone; he apologized. "I'm sorry," he said quietly. "I don't love you, Shelby. I never loved you. I used you, and I shouldn't have. I'm sorry."

Shelby froze, speechless, as Conner walked back to Riley and Joel. "Get Sam," he ordered. "I'll be in the car."

It was evident when his three friends got in the car that Sam was not happy that they had left the party so soon. Joel and Riley remained silent, worried that speaking up might ignite a disagreement between Sam and Conner. As they drove through town, it became clear they weren't heading downtown and were instead making their way toward Conner and Riley's neighborhood. Unable to hold back any longer, Sam finally broke the silence.

"I like Tennly," Sam said. "I do. But I never thought I would see the day that you would ever let a girl put you on a leash."

Conner slammed the brake, stopping the car in the middle of the road, and turned around. "Don't!" He yelled, pointing his finger at Sam in the backseat.

"Con," Riley said trying to calm them both down.

Conner gave Riley a look that told him he should understand why he had to leave the party and then started driving again. Understanding what Conner meant, Riley explained, "Shelby confronted him, Sam."

"Shit," Sam sighed. "I'm sorry."

"I just didn't want to deal with that," Conner explained.

"So now what?" Joel asked.

"Well," Conner hesitated. "If you guys want, we can go to Tennly's. She and Tara are having a big party at the mansion."

"The mansion?" Sam asked, intrigued.

"Yeah," Conner answered.

"Through the gate, mansion?" Sam asked playfully.

"Yes," Conner said smiling, unable to withhold his delight at his friend's childlike excitement. "And her dad isn't home. He and Thomas, the chauffeur guy I told you about, are at a formal party downtown somewhere."

"Why the hell didn't you bring this up earlier?" Sam asked, enthusiastically. "Fitchett or the mansion," Sam said shaking his head. "You're an idiot..."

Tennly and Tara's New Year's Eve party turned out to be larger than expected. Attendees included, their friends, along with cousins Prudence and Patience, who each brought two guests, and Tara's boyfriend, Joey.

Marie hired caterers to decorate. Silver and gold balloons adorned the floors and pool, while balloon bouquets decorated the tables and corners. Streamers draped from the ceilings, and party favors lined every table. Dinner in the great room featured an array of dishes: chicken wings, cheesy mashed potatoes, pasta with three sauces, steak skewers, cheese and veggie trays, and rolls. After dinner, everyone moved to the pool house for desserts, which included cookies, tarts, petit fours, cake pops, parfaits, and a towering croquembouche.

Tennly took on the role of bartender to avoid swimming, not wanting anyone to question her bruises and scars. After an hour in the pool, the girls went upstairs to clean up while the guys gathered in the game room. Around 11:00 PM, Marie refreshed the spread with finger foods, fruit, and vegetable trays.

Games filled the evening, with Tennly mixing drinks and keeping a wary eye on the clock, worried that Conner might not show up. Relief washed over her half an hour before midnight when Conner and his friends entered the game room. Conversation halted as everyone turned to watch the four boys stroll in with effortless confidence.

Prudence and Patience, unfamiliar with the boys beyond rumors, suddenly grasped the stories they had heard. Tara's friends, who had briefly encountered The Untouchables at school or local hangouts, had never been this close to all four of them at once. Sitting in the O'Brien mansion alongside them felt surreal. Tennly's friends, still intimidated, had gradually grown more accustomed to their presence since she started dating Conner.

Sam was the first to say something as Tennly walked around the bar to greet them. Before she could say anything, he lifted her up, swung her around, and screamed, "Tennly!"

"Sam," Tennly said after he put her down.

"This place is insane," Sam noted while Conner leaned over and gave her a kiss.

"Thank you," Tennly said.

"We would have been in here sooner," Conner mentioned. "But we couldn't get Sam out of the garage."

"Understandable," she acknowledged, winking at Sam.

"What the..." Sam marveled as he walked down to the end of the bar and pointed to a stack of champagne glasses.

"It's a champagne tower," Tennly explained. "Five minutes before midnight, I'm going to pour champagne over it."

"No way," Sam gasped as his eyes widened in delight. "I've seen that on movies and always wanted to see one in real life."

"Want to help me with it?" Tennly asked.

"Do I?" Sam enthusiastically said.

Tennly walked behind the bar, handed the boys a cocktail menu, and asked what they would like to drink. Sam shot Riley a look that suggested frustration for keeping them from getting there sooner, then placed his order with Tennly. Since it was New Year's Eve and everyone was planning to spend the night, Daniel informed his daughters that they could have alcohol only if they promised not to break anything.

After Tennly prepared Conner and his friends' drinks, she retrieved the champagne and handed it to Sam so he could pour it over the champagne tower. The tower was constructed using glasses arranged in layers of 4x4, 3x3, 2x2, and 1. It was placed on an antique white tray to catch any champagne that overflowed. As everyone watched, Sam poured the champagne over the single glass at the top of the tower, and the liquid elegantly cascaded down into the glasses below.

With one minute left until midnight, Tennly instructed everyone to grab a glass. When the countdown got to ten seconds, the group counted down in unison, and then everyone shouted, "Happy New Year!"

Conner put his hands on Tennly's face, feeling at peace, and gave her a huge kiss. "I love you."

"I know."

Happy New Year's

CHAPTER 8

Riley watched as Tennly and Conner delivered a terrifying performance. As she took a punch and got back up, only to take down one of the toughest guys he knew, Riley finally saw her for who she really was. She wasn't just a girl who would hurt Conner; she was Conner. And she was stunningly beautiful, which petrified him.

As he prepared to enter the ring, he felt a mix of excitement and dread. He had fought his fair share of fights and had won many, but facing a girl with Conner's skills made him uneasy. It didn't feel fair to fight a girl, and going against his best friend seemed even more wrong. Grappling with the notion filled him with a sense of dishonorable immorality.

"So..." Riley asked, not sure what to do as he and Conner stood in adjacent corners while Tennly was set in the middle of the opposite ropes. "We're just going to go at her?"

Conner and Tennly started laughing as Conner replied, "Yep."

"Like... how hard?"

"As hard as you can," Conner answered. "You saw how I was. Nothing less than that will work."

Tennly could see the reluctancy on Riley's face and knew she needed to reassure him. "It's okay, Riley. I can take it."

"I have no doubt," Riley acknowledged, still feeling apprehensive.

Tennly found it easier to fight two opponents instead of one. This tactic allowed her to use one as leverage to strike the other harder than she normally could. She rolled over their backs, swept their legs out from under them, and leaped off one onto the other. Her best move came when Riley got behind her and placed his arm around her neck. As she saw Conner's fist coming toward her, she placed her hands on Riley's arm, strategically twisting to avoid the punch. Riley's face connected with Conner's fist, giving her time to swing her leg around and kick Riley across the side of the head. He fell to the floor and held his hand up in defeat as blood dripped from his mouth and nose: a slight ringing in his right ear.

"Are you okay?" Conner asked as he extended his hand to help his friend back to his feet.

"Yeah," Riley replied, wiping the blood from his brow. He looked at Tennly in disbelief, wondering how she had managed to take him down while Conner was coming at her. "Let's go again," he said with a slight smile before walking back to his starting corner.

They fought for over half an hour, stopping only when they noticed that the boxing ring floor was nearly as red as its originally white. They didn't discuss it until after they each took a shower and then met in the kitchen at the breakfast nook for dinner. Marie served them creamy spinach-stuffed salmon steaks in garlic sauce, accompanied by a bed of white rice, roasted asparagus, and French bread.

"There's chocolate chip cookie sundaes for dessert," Marie mentioned. "Just let me know when you're ready for them."

"Thanks," the three of them said.

As they sat and ate, with Riley facing Tennly, it became apparent to him just how badly she looked. The more he focused on her, examining her more closely, a particular fear began to surface in his mind.

"You look like shit," Riley answered.

"Thanks," Tennly giggled.

"No," Riley explained. "I'm serious. If we're supposed to fight like we did just now every day for the next two weeks, there might be a slight problem."

Conner looked over at Tennly and saw what he meant. "Shit."

"What?" Tennly repeated.

"School starts back up tomorrow," Riley reminded.

Seeing Conner and Riley bruised and battered wouldn't raise any suspicion, but seeing Tennly with a black eye, a cut on her upper lip, a bruise around her neck, and several scratches on her hands and upper arms was another matter.

"And this is just our first day," Riley added. "After two weeks, there won't be any unmarked skin left on her at all." Tennly gave him a look that said she still had no idea what he was talking about. "They'll think Conner is beating you."

It hadn't crossed her mind that everyone might assume her bruises and cuts were the result of Conner's actions. She set her fork down, grabbed a napkin, and wiped her face. Looking down at the fabric, she noticed a bit of blood on it from where her lip was still bleeding slightly.

"If there was ever a time where the two of you skipped school," she mentioned. "Now's the time."

Tennly used makeup to conceal her bruises and lesions that her clothes didn't cover and continued to attend school. Conner and Riley told Sam and Joel that they had gotten into a fight with two of Ty's associates, which explained their injuries.

Following Tennly's suggestion, they decided to skip school for the entire week and meet her in the gym every day after dinner. Although they understood the purpose of their training with her, they never discussed it openly. The fear of the potential outcome was too overwhelming. Nevertheless, none of them could stop trying to figure out how they could improve her chances of winning.

"You're not allowed to use throwing knives, right?" Riley asked.

"Right," Tennly answered.

"Can you use anything else?"

"They're not allowed to bring any weapons," Conner informed.

"Who said anything about weapons?" Riley replied with a mischievous grin. "Where's your bedroom?"

As soon as they entered her bedroom, Conner asked Riley again what he was doing, but Riley didn't answer. Instead, he walked over to her vanity and rummaged through her hair accessories until he found what he was looking for. He turned around and held up a long, red silk ribbon.

Tennly smiled and glanced at Conner, who seemed to understand Riley's idea. "That's brilliant!" She exclaimed. "Why didn't I think of that?" She approached Riley and took the ribbon from his hand. "Help me find some more."

After they gathered all the accessories they could find, she practiced using them while they fought. She pretended to slice, stab, or strangle the boys as they attacked her, and it worked perfectly. She was able to take down both boys with much greater ease than she had without the items.

It was late when the boys left, and since it was a school night, she needed to take a shower and get to bed. The hot water felt wonderful, soothing her aching muscles, so she stayed in until she noticed her fingertips looking like prunes.

She had just stepped into her bedroom when Marie came rushing in frantically. "There are men breaching the perimeter. We've got to go." Tennly felt Marie shaking as Marie grabbed her arm and dragged her back into the closet.

"Where are we going?" Tennly asked, heart racing, as Marie opened the secret door and then stepped inside.

"There's a panic room on the back side of the mansion," Marie said. "We need to hide in there."

Marie moved so quickly that Tennly didn't have time to grab her weapons from the vanity. She felt torn between going back to retrieve them and following Marie to safety. Ultimately, her curiosity about where Marie was taking her, combined with her concern for Marie, kept her from going back.

The panic room wasn't just a small one-room space; it was another apartment located behind the upstairs bedrooms, nestled between the atrium and the pool house. Its design was so discreet that, from anywhere inside or outside the mansion, it was almost unnoticeable.

The main area was a living room and kitchen combo, similar to Thomas's apartment but filled with far more family pictures, which Tennly found odd. Along the hallway, there were three small bedrooms and a bathroom/utility room. At the far end of the hall was a locked room with the same controls that were in the secret room connected to her father's office. The room resembled a control center at NASA: two walls were lined with several monitors displaying every corner of the mansion, both inside and out, while the third wall was covered with surveillance equipment and listening devices.

Just as Tennly grabbed some weapons and was about to leave to find out why the intruders were there, Marie shouted, "Stop! Look... it seems like they're just surveying the place."

Tennly turned back to see what Marie was pointing at and observed the men walking around the mansion without making any attempt to enter. "What do you think they're doing?" she asked.

"I don't know. But it looks like they're leaving."

"Call my father!"

After Jimmy reassured Daniel that no one from any of the families would have taken such a risk, he felt frustrated that there was nothing more they could do to identify the men involved and believed that his only option was to enhance the security of the mansion. He increased the number of cameras and surveillance equipment throughout the property. He also permitted Tennly to keep a couple of pistols in her bedroom for added protection.

Conner felt powerless, so he spent every possible moment by her side. He arrived at the mansion first thing in the morning, drove her to and from school, and stayed until it was time for bed. Though his father was at home, Conner chose to sleep there, wanting to be close to the mansion in case he was needed.

For two nights, he snuck in and out of his bedroom window to avoid his father's wrath. However, on the third night, luck was not on his side. Just as he slipped into his room and began to take off his jeans to prepare for bed, his father burst in, clearly furious and having been drinking. He accused Conner of drinking all his beer, even though Conner hadn't been there long enough to do so.

Expecting to swing his bat and strike Conner before he could react, his father was caught off guard. Thanks to the training Conner had received from Tennly, he managed to dodge out of the way just in time, grabbed the bat, and yanked it away from his father. Without hesitation, he swung it, striking Kenneth on the left shoulder. Although Kenneth stumbled backward, he managed to stay on his feet as he received another impact on his right ribs. Consumed by anger, Conner began to scream as he blacked out, hitting his father repeatedly until Dougy heard the commotion and rushed into Conner's room. Dougy quickly seized Conner's arm with one hand and the bat with the other, managing to stop him.

"You're okay," Dougy assured. "You're okay. Look at me. It's okay. Breathe..."

Dougy kept talking, trying to calm Conner down as Conner looked around and noticed the bat on the floor beside Dougy. It was more red than brown, stained with their father's blood, which had also splattered across Conner's face. He rubbed his hands over his cheeks and then glanced behind Dougy at their father, who was lying motionless. Conner realized he had beat him so badly that he wasn't moving at all. He sat down on the bed, stared at his hands, and then looked back up at Dougy, a frightened look in his eyes.

"What did I do?" Conner panted.

"It's going to be okay," Dougy consoled, despite not believing his own words.

He left his brother on the bed and then went over to their father. While he was checking to see if he was alive, Conner told Dougy to call Tennly.

"We need to call an ambulance."

"I'll go to jail... Call Tennly."

Not sure what Tennly could do, Dougy did as his brother requested while Conner went to the bathroom to wash the blood from his hands and face. He removed his bloody shirt and placed it in the bathtub before staring at himself in the mirror. After splashing his face with cold water and taking in slow breaths to calm himself down, he headed back to his room.

By the time he returned, Tennly was running in and went straight to him, placing her hands on his face. "Are you okay?"

"I don't know," Conner shuddered.

Daniel and Thomas walked in shortly after, and Daniel asked, "Is he alive?"

"He's still breathing," Dougy answered, sitting beside his father on the floor.

Daniel ordered Dougy to get towels, both wet and dry, as he walked over to Kenneth. While Dougy was out of the room, Daniel looked at Conner and asked him what he wanted him to do. "I have Dr. Pratt coming; he can save him, or he can end him."

Conner thought before answering. Even though he wanted him dead, he was still his father. "Save him."

Daniel nodded just as Dougy returned with the towels. He instructed Dougy to clean his father up as best as he could while they waited for Dr. Pratt. It took the doctor half an hour to arrive, and when he saw Conner, the boy he had treated twice before, sitting on the couch in the living room, he finally understood what had happened. Noticing Dougy's presence, the doctor said nothing to Conner and began tending to Kenneth.

After a couple of hours, Dr. Pratt told them that Kenneth had two broken ribs, a broken wrist, a broken jaw, a concussion, and several lacerations that needed stitches. He stayed overnight with everyone to change his IV bags and make sure Kenneth was going to be alright. While he waited in the living room with Daniel and Thomas, Tennly and Conner went to lay down in his bed, and Dougy went to sleep in his.

"This is the father of the young man I worked on at your place?" Dr. Pratt asked.

"It is," Daniel answered.

"Well then... If you don't mind me saying so... It would probably be a good idea if the two boys don't stay here with him anymore. I have a feeling this wasn't the first time, and it won't be the last. Won't end well, if you know what I'm saying."

Daniel watched as Dr. Pratt walked back to Kenneth's room and then looked over at Thomas, who was sitting on the couch. Thomas could tell that Daniel was planning something, so he asked, "What's on your mind?"

Daniel thought for a moment and then looked at Thomas and said, "Get Conner."

Conner got out of bed without waking Tennly and made his way to the living room. He sat down in the recliner and looked at Daniel, feeling incredibly embarrassed, bracing himself for Daniel to yell at him for lacking restraint. He also worried that Daniel might think he was too aggressive and could order him to stop dating Tennly, fearing he might hurt her. As he sat there, he said nothing, waiting for a reprimand from the man he had grown to love and respect.

"The night you came to our house the first time," Daniel brought up. "That was your father, wasn't it?"

"Yeah."

"How long has this been going on?"

"Since I was four." It felt strange to tell an adult about the abuse. He had hidden it for so many years that saying it out loud nearly caused him to meltdown.

"Tennly knew?"

"Yeah."

"Your brother?"

"He doesn't touch him... just me."

Daniel was particularly angered by a few things, with child abuse topping the list. He had to conceal his sympathy for Conner, aware that Conner despised such feelings. Moreover, if he intended to train Conner in the family business, he couldn't afford to show any weakness.

"Do you have any trash bags around here?" Daniel asked.

"Yeah, under the kitchen sink."

Daniel gestured for Thomas to get them and then looked back at Conner. "It's a shame you didn't kill him," Daniel said causing Conner to become confused. He took in a big sigh and continued. "If you had, this would have been easier." Thomas brought over the box of trash bags and handed them to Daniel. "Hiding a body isn't as hard."

Before he could say anything else, Dr. Pratt came back into the living room, pulling a large suitcase full of medical equipment. "He's awake," Dr. Pratt informed. "Sore and an asshole. Started to yell, but realized his jaw is broken and can't move it. Be thankful I wired it."

"Thank you," Daniel said.

"If you don't need me..."

"No, you're free to go. Thank you."

After the doctor left, Conner looked at Daniel and said, "I just want you to know that I'm sorry. I know I failed you, and there's nothing I can do about that... You don't have to worry about me anymore. As soon as he is able, he'll call the police on me, and I'll be sent away... So..."

"Stop," Daniel interrupted. It saddened Daniel to think that Conner still believed that he didn't belong in the O'Brien/Connolly family. "You're not the one who needs to apologize. I sat here all night trying to think about what we should do. There were a couple of times I almost got up, went to your father's room, and placed two bullets in his head. If your brother wasn't here, I probably would have... So... here's what we're going to do. You're going to pack up all your clothing and move into the mansion."

Conner's eyes widened as he struggled to respond to the unexpected request. While he had grown accustomed to spending nearly every day at the mansion, the idea of moving in brought a whirlwind of mixed emotions. He felt embarrassed at the thought of appearing weak to Daniel, as if he needed someone to save him. At the same time, a sense of joy washed over him at the prospect of living with Tennly. The most challenging aspect was the finality of leaving behind his old life and the person he had been: not sure he could do so without losing himself.

"I appreciate it," Conner uttered. "But that's not necessary. I'll be fine."

"Do you think I'm asking you to move in just for you?" Daniel asked rhetorically. "My daughter was there with Marie alone when those men... they could have broken in, and... I need someone there full time when I can't be, and you'll do everything in your power to keep them safe."

"You know I would," Conner said, a sense of relief washing over him as he realized that Daniel didn't see him as weak. However, there was still the reality that he was in trouble. "It doesn't matter anyway. Like I said, I'm going to be sent away, so..."

"You let me take care of that. Go with Thomas; get your clothes packed."

With one final task to complete, Daniel approached Kenneth. As Daniel drew near, Kenneth started to fidget, his eyes darting around as if he were trying to escape something sinister.

"Do you know who I am?" Daniel asked as he walked up beside him.

Kenneth nodded.

"Good," Daniel said. "Then I need you to listen very carefully. If you report what happened here last night to anyone, and I mean anyone, I will come back here

and... well, let's just put it this way,
you won't be saying anything to anyone ever
again. Do you understand?"

Kenneth's eyes furrowed as the fear
he once had was replaced with anger at the
thought that his son had won. Daniel
quickly pulled out a knife and held it to
Kenneth's throat. He pushed down just
enough to draw some blood and then growled
as the thought of Dougy being across the
hallway came into his mind.

"You're only alive right now because
of your sons. I wanted to kill you. Don't
test me. So, let me repeat myself. If you
tell anyone what Conner did to you or touch
your other son in any way, I will come back
here and finish what Conner started. And
know this: if you think that you can get
away with reporting any of this, I will
find out. I own this town... the police...
and now I own you. Your life is in my hands.
Do you understand?"

Kenneth nodded.

onner initially thought that moving into the mansion would feel strange or out of place, but it turned out to be quite the opposite. He not only felt like he belonged there, but he also felt safe and finally at home. Although he was unaware that being at home in the mansion came with a monetary value.

"I know what you're going to say before you even say it," Daniel said, after calling Conner into his office. "Although it doesn't matter... What I say goes, anyway." Conner chuckled and nodded to let Daniel know he was right. "As you know, I give my girls an allowance. And now..."

"Dan..." Conner started to say as he interrupted him.

"Ah," Daniel said stopping him. "What I say goes, remember?" Conner nodded, prompting Daniel to continue. "Since you're living here now, you will also be given an allowance or a monthly salary if that makes you feel better about it. You will be on call to do whatever is needed. You will also continue to be paid for each individual job you do as well."

Daniel pulled out a small bag from inside the right drawer in his desk and handed it to Conner. "Here's the first month's payment; it's $10,000. Unlike when you do jobs, it's okay to put this in the bank. I'm putting you on my books as an employee, so it's okay to open an account. You still can't put the money you get from a job in there. However, from time to time, if you want to deposit smaller amounts from the jobs, that'll be alright. Understand?"

"Yeah."

"The final thing I want to talk to you about is what we know is coming in three days."

Despite the daily training sessions with Tennly, Conner had hoped that Daniel would find a way to stop the Donnybrook. As he anticipated what Daniel was going to say, he felt a tightening in his chest. He was secretly wishing that, with the invasion and his recent move-in, Daniel had reconsidered and would attempt to persuade her to back out of the fight.

"I want to thank you for doing everything you can to help her prepare. And I know you still don't understand how a father could allow their daughter to go through with this, and you don't need to understand."

The tightness in Conner's chest intensified as he heard Daniel's words. He wanted to scream, punch the desk, or throw the chair across the room, but he remained still. As he became aware of his heart pounding so hard that he could feel it in his throat, he clenched his fists to keep himself from reacting to his anger: or sadness.

"Our families have been able to hide in plain sight for years because of the way we do things, the rules we follow. And a big part of that is keeping the hierarchy intact and respected. The Irish mafia is different than other organized crime syndicates, who go around killing each other on the streets whenever there is suspicion or a power struggle. That's not just unnecessarily risky, it undermines the whole idea of family structure. Donnybrooks have been done for centuries. It's not a fight in the streets, where all it takes is brute strength... or a bullet... to win. It's done in an arena where brains are more important. The Donnybrook gives every family the opportunity to question any position if they feel they aren't doing a good job. Does that make sense?"

"I don't like it, but yeah."

"I don't like it either, but it's the way of our people."

"Does it ever happen that once a fight is over, a family still doesn't accept it?"

"Sure. But very seldom. The punishment is death... for their whole family. In a way, it's the same thing for once a Donnybrook has been demanded. If the person being questioned doesn't fight, it's the only time the other families turn a blind eye... It can lead to their entire family being killed. Tennly's strong, smart, and can think quickly when she has to. And I've never seen anyone take a punch like she can. She can do this."

"Yeah," Conner said as if he was trying to convince himself that she would be fine. "She's amazing."

"I know it'll be tough to watch, but if you want to go with us, you..."

"Yes," Conner interrupted without having to even think about it. "I want to go."

When Conner left the office, he went up to Tennly's room, where she was reading a book. He took a moment to gather his composure as he looked at her, not wanting her to see his worry, then he entered the room and laid down beside her. She set her book on the nightstand and curled up in his arms. They lay there, holding each other, both aware of the thoughts they were sharing. Tennly ran her hand over the gargoyle tattoo on his arm before looking up at him.

"I'm sorry I'm putting you through this," she sighed.

"Don't," he said as he put his hand under her chin. "I wouldn't trade my life for anyone else's. This is the life I was meant to have... with you... with your family. And we're going to have a long, long life together; do you understand that? You're going to win."

When they went to school, Tennly, Conner, and Riley pretended to be like any other teenagers going through their day, but whenever they glanced at each other, it felt as if they were counting down the hours they had left together.

As the three of them spent their days contemplating ways to help Tennly, Riley noticed their nervousness increasing, which pained him to see. He felt that everything that came to mind seemed trivial and superficial, but he was determined not to give up. It wasn't until his afternoon classes that he finally had an idea that might provide a solution.

During his EMT class, they took a field trip to a nursing home in a neighboring town to practice working with real patients. On their way back, Riley was gazing out the window, still pondering how to support his friends, when they passed an old, abandoned church by the roadside. Remembering that Tennly had mentioned the Donnybrook would be held in a deserted cathedral sparked an idea in him, and he couldn't wait to share what he had discovered.

He provided Conner with directions to the abandoned church but wouldn't reveal their destination, as he was so excited about his discovery and wanted it to be a surprise for them. Unsure of the best route to the road leading to the church, he had to redirect Conner a few times, causing Tennly to tease him.

"Do you even know where you're going?"

"I have an idea," Riley laughed with her. "Shut up."

They finally found the right road and pulled into a cracked parking lot behind the church. Conner and Tennly knew what Riley was thinking the moment they saw it. After Tennly hugged him in thanks, the three explored the area until they found a basement window pried open enough to slip through.

The basement had a musty smell of mold and dirt, and they could see rats scurrying about. Vines were growing through the cracks in the concrete block walls, and the floor was littered with debris and boxes of packed materials.

The upstairs floor once had burgundy carpet, but it had been ripped up in small pieces. In the far corner, there was a reception desk with four large bookshelves behind it. The only books still on the shelves were a few Bibles, some self-help books, and four shelves full of hymnals. Cobwebs and dust covered everything, making it difficult to differentiate between the books.

Through the swinging doors was the sanctuary where there were rows of pews perfect for leverage or cover, Bibles and hymnals ready to be thrown, candelabras that could double as weapons, and curtains, tiebacks, and crucifixes that could all be turned against an opponent.

As they surveyed everything that Tennly could utilize, they started their nightly training session. They positioned themselves evenly apart, counted down, and then began. They practiced repeatedly until they finally discovered the right sequence that would allow her to take down one assailant, giving her enough time to confront the other. Although they understood it wouldn't be exactly the same as the real arena, they felt confident knowing that she was prepared.

CHAPTER 9

The sanctuary in the church that Keenan O'Ceallaigh, the head boss, established as the venue for the Donnybrook featured three-foot-tall round pillars that divided the seating area from the walkways on both sides. A spiral staircase was located on the left back corner that led to a loft, which was inaccessible due to a break at the top. On either side of the altar stood two organs, both covered in cobwebs filled with trapped insects. Behind the pulpit were three step levels that once served as a choir section.

A newly installed rope marked off the old choir section from the rest of the arena, where onlookers sat in new folding chairs to watch the fight. Daniel and

Conner occupied the right side of the stage alongside Jimmy, John, Thomas, and Phillip. To their left were Duncan and Tennly's uncles, Seamus and Grady Connolly. On the left side of the choir seats sat Peter O'Grady and Mikey MacFadden, whose sons were fighting in the Donnybrook. Additionally, to the left of Peter and Mikey was Tyler Sweeny, the family head who didn't have a son in the battle.

Keenan O'Ceallaigh settled into a padded chair at the center, gazing out over the sanctuary. He was a distinguished-looking man in his late seventies with short white hair, a perfectly trimmed white beard and mustache, and light blue eyes. Remarkably fit for his age, he had visible muscles beneath his light gray dress shirt, which was neatly tucked into tailored black suit pants. A sense of reverence surrounded him as he sat quietly, observing the others as they conversed and moved about.

Petey, in his early twenties, had a powerful build that commanded attention. He had broad shoulders, strong arms, and wavy blond hair slicked back, which framed a face that looked older due to the stubble on his chin. His nearly gray, dark blue eyes held a sharp intensity that mirrored his physical strength.

Mitchell, who stood just shy of six feet, was leaner but equally strong. He had short dark hair, thick brows, and clear blue eyes. His clean-shaven face gave him a smoother, younger appearance, making him look more similar in age to Conner than to Petey.

Without making any movement, Keenan gestured to two of his employees, who were standing off to the side, to approach the competitors. They were instructed to pat them down before the fight began.

Tennly watched Conner intently as the employee ran their hands over her, carefully feeling every part of her body. Pins and needles went throughout her as she hoped they couldn't find her makeshift weapons. They overlooked her hair comb, bobby pins, two ribbons wrapped around a ponytail, and the ring on her finger, but they insisted she remove her belt and brooch.

Conner could see the worry she felt as she swayed her body back and forth, breathing in through her nose and out her mouth. She put on a smile to reassure him everything would be okay, then closed her eyes. She needed to shift her focus away from Conner and concentrate on what she had to do.

The three competitors were spaced evenly away from each other in a triangle formation to make the start of the fight as fair as possible. Tennly started out on the right side of the sanctuary. Petey was to her left and Mitchell to her right, closest to where the onlookers were sitting.

While Keenan was going over the rules and recounting the history of the Donnybrook fights, Tennly was observing her surroundings, noting the locations of everything in the room. As Keenan wrapped up his speech, she recalled how she managed to take down Conner and Riley during their practice sessions. She then prepared herself, waiting for Keenan to start the countdown.

"May the best fighter win," Keenan said, and then in old Irish he yelled, "Dul!"

Tennly's heartbeat quickened with every step they took, but she resisted the urge to run until they reached the right moment. Once she noticed they had gotten to a spot where it would be difficult for them to navigate through the pews to reach her, she quickly ran toward Mitchell. She jumped onto a pew, took a couple of steps, and leapt toward him. As she soared through the air, she grabbed the longest ribbon out of her hair. As soon as she landed on his back, she wrapped the ribbon around his neck and quickly slammed his head against the back of a pew as she jumped off.

Mitchell fell between the two pews as Tennly landed in the seat, giving her time to run straight toward Petey. She took the ribbon and wrapped it around his arm as he went to punch her, twisting it as she jumped off the pew and behind him. It was exactly how she had practiced when she defeated Conner and Riley. She felt confident about the direction of the fight until Petey managed to get hold of her hair and pull her toward him. She grunted as he picked her up and threw her a few feet away, slamming her into a pillar and knocking the breath out of her.

Before she knew it, he flipped her over his head and slammed her down onto the floor. Her shortness of breath silenced her scream as he kicked her in the stomach. But when he tried to kick her a second time, she had gained her bearings and grabbed his foot and pulled, which gave her the opportunity to crawl away from him. She didn't get very far when she felt him take hold of her right ankle and pull her back toward him. She twisted onto her back, and as Petey tried to get her closer to him, she kicked him in the leg and was able to get away again.

She managed to get onto her feet and jumped up onto the end of the nearest pew as she turned around toward Petey. When he approached her, she jumped and kicked him in the chest, causing him to fall to the floor. Flipping into the air, she landed behind him before he could get up, as she took out the last ribbon from her hair and wrapped it around his neck and squeezed as hard as she could.

While Petey squirmed to get free, Mitchell ran over to them. Seeing that if she stayed in the position she was in, she would be easily accessible to Mitchell, she eased up on the ribbon at the same time she kicked Petey in the back, causing the two men to slam into each other.

She ran between two pews, grabbing a hymnal along the way. As she ran back toward the two guys, she reared her hands back as far as she could, and then when she got close enough to Mitchell, she swung the hymnal and smacked him across the face. When she landed on the seat of the next pew, Petey was there and pushed her off. He grabbed her ankles and pulled, but before he could get her out into the open, she twisted her ring around and grabbed his wrists, digging the V-shaped gem into his skin. He screamed and let go of her, giving her the chance to kick his kneecap. She expected him to scream again and was surprised when he started laughing at the same time Mitchell had placed his hands around her neck. While Mitchell continued to squeeze, Petey walked slowly up to her.

"In what world did you ever think you would be a boss?" Petey taunted.

Tennly pretended to try and find Mitchell's hands or face to get him to let go but was secretly pulling out one of her bobby pins. While she listened to Petey speak, she reared a pin back into the right side of Mitchell's neck. He squealed out a loud moan as he let go of her. She jumped on the pew and ran down the seat to give herself some time to catch her breath.

As Petey rushed over toward her, she stood her ground and waited to see what he was going to do. She dodged his first strike but was punched in the nose on the second. While she was catching her balance, Petey grabbed her and threw her, once again as far as he could back toward the center of the sanctuary.

She hit her back against the corner of one of the pews, so hard, it caused her vision to become blurry. While she was down on her knees, Mitchell came up behind her, and held her arms behind her back, so Petey could have an easy target. Once she was able to see again, she stomped her heel into Mitchell's foot and then pushed herself back into him, causing him to hit the side of a pew. The force resulted in him releasing her just enough that she was able to duck while Petey threw a hard right punch, hitting Mitchell in the chest.

Petey got so angry that he swung his arm around and ended up hitting her in the back of the neck. She stumbled a few feet forward while he kicked her in the back, making her fall to her knees. He quickly ran over to her and picked her up by the ponytail. Feeling the pain of having her hair pulled so tightly that it felt like she was being scalped, she immediately placed her hand on top of his, making it harder for him to pull up. Then she spun around and punched him in the pressure point of the elbow crease of the arm. As soon as he let go of her, she kneed him in the groin.

While he was still bent over, she jumped on his back and used him as leverage to jump on Mitchell, who had run over to them. She was able to get her legs around Mitchell's neck, pulling him down with her onto the floor. She squeezed her thighs so tight that it started to cut off Mitchell's airway. He managed to get enough air to punch her in the side until she released him. He stood up to catch his breath while she rolled under a pew to two rows down.

When she stood up, she saw Petey running toward her. She jumped on the pew seat and ran as fast as she could toward the spiral staircase. Along the way, she grabbed a six-tier candelabra and then ran up three of the steps, spun around, jumped off, and swung the candelabra at Petey's head, hitting him hard enough that it knocked him out as he fell.

By then Mitchell had gotten close enough to her that she was able to use the candelabra to hit him. She got in two hits before Mitchell grabbed it from her and used it to hit her on the left shoulder. The force of the blow pushed her back a few steps, but she was able to stay standing. By the time she got her bearings together, Petey had come to and met up with Mitchell. Her position wasn't the best, as she noticed that she was cornered. She looked everywhere to try and find something to use or a way out of the predicament as the two men walked slowly toward her, maniacal looks on both their faces, but there was nothing. She knew there was only one way she was going to get herself out of it, and that was to purposely put herself in danger.

She took a deep breath and ran toward Mitchell. Instead of attacking him at full force, she pretended to falter, allowing him to grab her to where her back was against his chest. Then, as soon as Petey came to within a foot of her, she put her hands on Mitchell's wrists and fell to the ground.

Her fall was so powerful that it slammed Mitchell's and Petey's heads together. Before the boys realized what had happened, Tennly kicked Petey so hard across the right knee that a loud pop was heard. Petey bellowed in pain as he fell to the floor. Tennly rolled over onto her back and did a kip up onto her feet. In one smooth motion, she punched Mitchell in the left ear and then swung around and kicked Petey across the face.

She then ran to a long prayer table with rows of old candles that were placed in red, tall, thin votive glasses. She grabbed one votive glass after another and threw them at Mitchell. They broke over his head, arms, and body as he pushed on toward her. She picked up one of the votive glasses and slammed it onto the table, creating a sharp, jagged edge just in time to slash it across his right cheek.

While he was worried about the gash on his face, she took the broken glass and shoved it into his stomach. Twisting the shard, pushing it further into his body, she looked him in the eyes. She was going to remove the glass from his stomach and slice it across his throat, but the look on his face made her realize that he was scared.

She pulled the glass shard from his stomach and screamed, "Don't come after me!"

Then she shoved him to the ground and turned around to go after Petey. When she looked at where she had last seen him, Petey wasn't there. She looked in between the pews until she found him crawling out from behind the last row.

Running over in hopes that she would get there before he got up, she paused as she saw him pull out a knife with a five-inch blade from under the pew. It was obvious that he knew it was there, which meant that someone had planted it in the case that they were losing.

She could see on his face that he was nervous, which told her that he had no idea what he was going to do with it. She tilted her head, giving him a smile that told him she dared him to throw it, hoping that he would and then she would have a knife at her disposal. Due to shear fright, he threw the knife, and to Tennly's surprise, it landed in her right thigh, ten inches up from her knee. The pain brought about a loud moan that was more anger than fear. She took a couple of deep breaths as she stared him in the eye and pulled out the knife.

"Bad mistake," she threatened.

She could have easily killed him by throwing the knife at his chest, but she didn't want to risk breaking the rules set for her. Instead, she threw the knife and hit him in the left shoulder. Catching him off guard, she was able to run over to him and pull the knife out as she kicked him in the bad knee. While he was writhing in pain, she got behind him and placed the knife to the front of his throat.

"Get up!" Tennly commanded as she pushed the knife harder. He reluctantly stood, having trouble putting pressure on his bad knee. "Move."

She led him to the front of the sanctuary, stopping a few feet from the choir section. When she saw Mitchell's father, Mikey, look to her right, she knew Mitchell had not heeded her warning. She shook her head, giving them a look that told them it was a bad decision to continue to fight her, and then pushed Petey away. As soon as Petey hit the floor, she threw the knife into Petey's bad knee and then went after Mitchell. Seeing that he was stumbling from pain, she knew it wouldn't take much; a hard kick to the stomach did the trick.

"She threw a knife!" Peter O'Grady yelled. "She's disqualified!"

Tennly ran over to Petey, and as he lay on the ground moaning in agony, she pulled the knife out from his knee, and before anyone knew what was happening, she threw the knife across the rope, directly at Peter. It lodged into the right side of his chest in between his clavicle and shoulder. Then, with shear adrenaline running through her body, she ran over to Peter, pulled out the knife, and held it against his throat. Everyone, except Conner and her family, backed up in their seats, not sure what she was going to do. She was behaving like a feral beast, causing the onlookers to become scared of her.

"See," Peter heaved, trying to speak through the pain. "She isn't following the rules."

"She bested two men, at least five plus years older than her, and twice her size," Daniel mentioned.

"She cheated," Mikey protested, agreeing with Peter.

Tennly remained quiet as the men shouted what to do with her. Finally, having heard enough, Keenan yelled, "Quiet! Release him."

Tennly hesitated and looked over at Duncan, who nodded to tell her to do as she was told. She slowly removed the knife from Peter's throat and backed away to the side.

"She wasn't allowed to have knives," Peter reminded. "She should be disqualified."

"You could have killed Mitchell," Keenan noted. "Why didn't you?"

"I could have killed them both," Tennly confessed.

"So, why didn't you?" Keenan pressed.

"I understand the rules of the Donnybrook, and if I had to, I would have fought to the death. But why kill potential allies when I can prove I could win without doing so?"

"Why are they so afraid of you with knives?" Keenan asked, liking what she had just said. He knew it took more skill and restraint to win a Donnybrook without killing than it did with it.

"Because of this..." Then, before anyone knew what she was going to do, she threw the knife at Mikey. He jumped as it landed in the back of the chair, right beside his left shoulder.

"How do I know you didn't miss?" Keenan questioned as the other men shuffled around in fear.

Tennly smiled and answered confidently, "I don't miss."

"Ever?" Keenan asked.

"No," she answered with a self-assurance that he wasn't expecting a sixteen-year-old would have. "If I would have been able to use my throwing knives, I could have killed them within the first ten seconds of this fight. So, I understand why I wasn't allowed to use them. It would have been no different than using a gun."

"Then why, after you got a hold of one, did you end up throwing it?" Keenan asked. "Knowing the rule."

"What's good for the goose," Tennly replied with a maniacal expression on her face.

Keenan found her to be extremely intriguing. "I've seen many things over the years that catch my attention. Things that shock me or impress me. And I'm not easily impressed... I knew your mother. She impressed me, but not nearly as impressive as you are. Your strength, wisdom, and compassion are exactly what we need to move the next generation into the new world. Do not ever lose that."

She nodded at him, her chest tightening in anticipation, knowing what he was about to say, yet not sure if she truly believed it was going to happen. "This is a milestone for us. Times are changing. Traditions are our foundations and have kept us alive and kept order among us, but some traditions are outdated, and it's time we embrace some new ones. It is my pleasure to ordain the first female boss ever to rule over the Irish families. On her 18th birthday, Tennly *will* become the skipper over all the clans in the United States."

Peter, Mikey, and their companions grunted at the announcement, aware that they had no choice in the matter. They understood that if they went against Keenan's orders or tried to kill Tennly, they and their entire families would be killed.

Through the cheers, Keenan announced, "Tonight, we gather at the O'Ceallaigh estate for a feast. All is welcome." He then looked at the doctor sitting to his left and gave him permission to check on the fighters before walking through the sanctuary and exiting the church.

As soon as he could, Conner ran over to Tennly, nearly collapsing at her feet. He put his hands on her blood-drenched cheeks and kissed her, repeatedly as tears rolled down his face. Relieved and full of emotions, all he could get out was, "I love you," as he rested his forehead onto hers.

Tennly escaped with a deep bruise on her back the doctor warned her to monitor, stitches in her thigh and temple, a butterfly strip on her shoulder where the candelabra had cut her, and a shoulder that had to be forced back into place.

Initially she thought the fight hadn't bothered that much, however, as she stood in the shower, the water pouring over her, the truth hit as to how dangerously close to death she had gotten. Her body started to shake as all the emotions she had kept bottled up during the ordeal began to surface. She was unaware of how weak she had become until her legs felt wobbly, and she collapsed onto the floor. Folding her knees into her chest, she wrapped her arms around her legs and buried her head between her elbows, allowing herself to cry.

Throughout the gathering at the O'Ceallaigh Estate, Tennly was introduced to numerous people eager to meet the first female boss. She found herself listening to countless comments about how unbelievable it was that someone so young and female had managed to survive a Donnybrook.

What she enjoyed most about the evening was observing the youth. She watched the younger children play around the room, blissfully unaware of their parents' business and behaving like children, opposite of how they were made to act in the States.

As strange as the whole night felt to her, the most unusual part was when Petey and Mitchell's mothers approached her together. She had met them a couple of times at events in New York over the years, so she recognized them but had never engaged in a real conversation.

Out of the blue, the women hugged her, as Petey's mother said, "We hear you could have killed our sons, but let them live. For that, we will forever be in your debt."

Mitchell's mother put her hand on Tennly's shoulder and added, "We do thank you. But the fact that you, a girl, will be the boss over not only our sons, but our husbands... is scary for us."

"We fear," Mrs. O'Grady continued. "That the men will not like having to report to or be told what to do by a woman... and because they have no choice to follow you, they may come home and take it out on us."

"What are you saying?" Tennly asked.

The two women looked at each other, questioning if they could trust Tennly enough to tell her. Then Mrs. O'Grady declared, "There are many wives who fear that their husbands abuse will get worse in order to feel a sense of masculinity... once it is taken from them."

Tennly put her hands on the two women's shoulders and said, "I give you my word... I will not let that happen."

"But," Mrs. MacFadden said, "how can you stop it?"

"You may not even be aware it's happening," Mrs. O'Grady added.

"I'm sorry, I know who you are, but I'm not familiar with your names."

"I'm Katherine O'Grady."

"Fiona MacFadden."

"Nice to meet you, Katherine, Fiona. As of today, I'm secretly calling upon the two of you to be my first soldiers. They are the eyes and ears... the ones the bosses rely on to know what's happening. I need you to be my eyes and ears when it comes to the women in this organization. Can you do that?"

Fiona and Katherine looked at each other, shrugged their shoulders as if to say they should trust her, and then turned to Tennly and nodded.

"Good. Keep it quiet and tell no one. Thank you for coming to me... trusting me. So... I'm trusting you."

The women took Tennly's hand one at a time, kissed the back of it, as if she were already a boss, and then walked away. Tennly paused for a moment, contemplating whether she had made the right decision or done something that could endanger her life. She realized she was placing her trust in the women, knowing it would be easy for them to turn against her. However, she also knew that she had to try to help them. If everything went as she envisioned, she could potentially gain the support of at least half the people in the organization.

The next day Thomas drove them to several tourist locations that Conner wanted to see, specifically the Guinness Storehouse. Conner enjoyed learning about the history of Ireland's most famous beer. He appreciated the fact that the company had humble beginnings.

After they had lunch at the Guiness Storehouse, Tennly took him to several lesser-known spots around Dublin. Over the course of two days, she showed him the Oscar Wilde Statue, the Doors of Dublin, the Huguenot Cemetery, Smithfield Tower, and took a stroll through the Iveagh Gardens. They also visited the Famine Memorial and had dinner at one of Dublin's most famous cocktail bars, which had once been a speakeasy.

On the fourth day, Tennly had requested a meeting with Keenan at noon. She wanted to speak with him about the women before making any promises she couldn't keep. If she was going to prove that she could lead an empire in the United States, she needed to demonstrate her ability to hold a conference with her superior.

As the butler led her through the mansion and to the great room, her legs grew weak, and her palms became clammy. Once inside she saw Keenan lounging on a sofa with a cocktail in his hand. The space was twice the size of the great room in her Marinsburg mansion, and infinitely more elaborate. Centuries-old moldings and fixtures gleamed as if newly crafted, with every corner adorned in gold and ivory. Portraits hung from the walls, while the classical music that carried through the intercom, swelled so beautifully that it felt as though a live orchestra was playing just feet away.

Keenan instructed her to take a seat across from him and asked if she would like a drink. After the butler took their orders, Keenan prompted her to explain the reason for the meeting.

"I'm sure you are aware... that there will be some men that won't like being told what to do by a woman."

"I am," Keenan acknowledged.

"Those men could go home and take it out on their wives."

"Ah," Keenan understood. "And you don't agree with that?"

"Do you?" She asked as the butler came back over and handed her the drink.

"How a man wants to treat his wife is his business."

Tennly sat quietly for a moment, taking a sip of her drink to buy some time as she contemplated what to say. If he supported the abuse of a wife and she spoke out, she could jeopardize her chances of becoming the first female boss right then and there. But why would he allow a woman to take on a leadership role if he had issues with women?

She mustered up as much courage as she could and suggested, "With all due respect, Captain... If we are really going to embrace the modern world and make new traditions, we have to start with allowing the women to have a voice. For hundreds of years, they have stood loyal to their husbands and the men in our families. They deserve to be heard. They deserve to be respected and treated equally."

"Go on."

"I would like to have a couple women work for me. Of course, I would keep the clan chiefs that are already established...

but it would be nice to have a couple women as employees as well. If we truly want to move forward, it's necessary to have all voices... opinions... heard. That way we can make educated decisions based on all parties and not just one side."

Keenan sat there for a moment, which made Tennly think she may have crossed a line. Then he got this look on his face as if telling her that it was about time and said, "America has always been a thorn in my side. Men there have a cockiness that gets in my crawl... I'm going to tell you a little secret. Women in Ireland have been running these families for centuries... behind the scenes, of course, but none the less, we have always listened to our wives. Come by tonight... around 7:00 PM for dinner... you can meet my wife, Nora. She'll love you, and we can discuss this further."

"Thank you. I'll do that."

"Bring that boyfriend of yours," he added.

Conner was excited about meeting the boss of the entire Irish mafia, and that was all he talked about for the rest of the afternoon. Daniel was proud of his daughter for taking the initiative to secure an invitation from Keenan. It was well known that, apart from formal gatherings, Keenan rarely invited anyone to have a private meeting with him, and no one had ever been an American.

Upon arriving at the O'Ceallaigh Estate, Tennly and Conner were escorted to the drawing room. The room was adorned with turquoise blue wallpaper, featuring a gold flower pattern embroidered throughout. Large gold-framed portraits hung on the walls above a white wooden chair rail.

A fireplace with two blue-cushioned chairs stood to the left, a pale blue couch with gold pillows anchored the center, and another couch faced floor-to-ceiling bookshelves on the right. Opposite the door were four tall windows with matching blue curtains that went from the ceiling to the floor.

Upon hearing the butler tell them to make themselves at home before leaving, Tennly automatically assumed that Keenan was like her father and other bosses, thinking the room might have cameras to monitor them. Initially, her instinct was to follow her etiquette training and sit down to wait patiently. However, something told her that Keenan was expecting something different from her. Instead of taking a seat, she guided Conner to the

liquor cabinet, poured each of them a glass
of whiskey, and began to explore the room,
examining the pictures on the walls and
the books on the shelves, while secretly
looking for small little holes that housed
cameras.

Keenan was indeed watching her, and
he was not alone: Duncan was with him. As
soon as Tennly agreed to have dinner with
him and his wife, Keenan called Duncan over
to get his opinion of her.

"Why do you suppose she didn't sit?
Going against everything a young affluent
lady is taught?"

"For one thing," Duncan explained.
"You'll find out that Tennly isn't your
normal debutant. But in this specific
situation... I'd say she knows we're
watching her, and she's looking for
cameras."

"How?"

"She recently found out that the
O'Brian mansion in the states has
cameras... she ripped out the one that was
in her bedroom."

Keenan remembered Seamus telling him
that Duncan had done the same thing when
he found out about the cameras in his
bedroom when he was around Tennly's age.

259

"Well," Keenan laughed as he stood up, "in that case. I must get to this girl before you corrupt her even more."

Keenan went to the kitchen to find Nora to let her know he was ready to introduce her to their guests. Instead of going to the drawing room, they went to the attached dining room, sat down at the large twenty-person mahogany table, and instructed their butler to fetch Tennly and Conner.

Tennly recognized the scent the minute they stepped into the dining room. The pungent yet sweet smell of sulfur indicated that cabbage was being baked. Along with the earthy, buttery aroma, it could only mean that colcannon was on the menu. Colcannon is an Irish potato dish made with mashed potatoes and cabbage, and Tennly loved it.

They spent the first hour getting to know each other over dinner. Nora shared how she met her husband, and in return, she asked Tennly and Conner about their story. Nora found their tale romantic, listening with tears in her eyes as they took turns recounting their experiences.

When dinner was finished, they departed to the den for after-dinner drinks to discuss what Keenan wanted to address. As they sat in carved wooden high back chairs with dark red cushions, facing each other, Keenan began to speak.

"I'm just going to get to it. I like you, Tennly. So, I'm going to be honest with you. You're going to be a great leader, but it isn't going to be easy. You will have resistance and outright defiance. If you handle it the way you did in the arena: firm, fair, merciful, and confident, you will win over more people than you lose. But you cannot hesitate to get rid of those that you know will not mold to your ways."

CHAPTER 10

Between the Donnybrook and her meeting with Keenan, Tennly kept replaying the individuals in her life that might become a problem. She pondered whom she could trust and whom she couldn't, and the person who occupied her thoughts the most was Riley. Over the past few weeks, Riley had been supportive of her family, which led her to believe he would continue to help. He had even spent several nights with her and Conner, sharing laughter and enjoying good times together. Yet she couldn't shake the feeling that his assistance was primarily due to Conner and that his loyalty might change if Conner's safety were at risk.

Thankfully, as soon as they returned from Ireland, she got assurance. She was in her bedroom, sitting at her vanity, brushing her hair, and preparing for bed when Conner walked in with Riley right behind him. Neither Conner nor Tennly realized it, but over the past few weeks, Riley had grown quite fond of her and made Conner promise to inform him the moment they returned to the mansion.

When Tennly saw Riley, she stood up, feeling confused as he approached; she stayed stiff-armed as he gave her a hug. Once he let go, she stared at him with bewilderment in her eyes, awaiting his words.

"I just thought the last time I saw you would be... well... the last."

"That doesn't inspire much confidence in me," she replied, smiling to break the tension.

Riley offered her a smile that she had never seen on him before. She had always thought he was cute, but their complicated feelings for each other made it difficult for her to fully appreciate him. However, as he stood in front of her wearing that charming and captivating expression, she finally understood what all the fuss about him being 'Untouchable' was all about.

"I'm glad you didn't die," Riley professed, a look in his eyes revealing that he truly cared for her. Then, with a mischievous grin on his face, he teased, "He's hard enough to deal with; he would have been unbearable if you had died."

Conner was eagerly anticipating his first Valentine's Day with Tennly. He had never celebrated the holiday before and had always considered it a silly occasion. However, this year, he found himself looking forward to it. After nearly a week of searching for the perfect idea, inspiration struck while they were at Benny's with their friends. He overheard her chatting with Josie about how she sometimes missed Prague.

That night, as soon as they got home, Conner snuck downstairs to find Daniel, locating him in the great room. As he approached the sitting area, he noticed Daniel lying on the couch to the left, listening to music. He had his arm resting over his eyes, and a rocks glass with remnants of whiskey sat on the coffee table beside him. He was still dressed in a suit, though his tie was loosened, his dress shirt was untucked, and his belt was unbuckled.

"Are you looking for me?" Daniel asked without moving.

"I was just going to ask you something," Conner answered.

Daniel removed his arm from over his head and sat up. "What is it?"

"I want to take Tennly to Prague for Valentine's Day. I know she misses it sometimes, and I thought that maybe it would be nice to surprise her and take her there. Valentine's Day is on a Thursday this year. I thought we could fly in that day and come back Sunday. We would miss two days of school. If that's okay?"

"That sounds nice. She'll love it. I'll set it up with the pilot and let you know when you need to be at the airport."

"Thank you." Conner sat there for a second. He was going to head to bed but couldn't leave Daniel in the state he was in. "You look like something's on your mind."

Daniel ran his hand over his chin, reached down, and picked up the glass of whiskey. He took a swig of the last bits that remained and set it back on the coffee table. Leaning back on the couch, he took a deep breath. "We have a lead on the intruders the night Marie and Tennly were here alone."

"That's great," Conner said enthusiastically, not understanding why Daniel was not as happy about it.

"Yeah," Daniel replied. "Problem is the person we need to speak to is an employee of ours."

"I'm not following."

"If any member of our syndicate knows who sent the intruders and didn't tell us, then that means they have betrayed us."

"And you don't want to just kill them because you need to find out what they know."

"Exactly," Daniel grabbed his rocks glass, walked over to the liquor cabinet, and poured two glasses of whiskey. After handing the second glass to Conner, he sat down and rested the glass on his knee, rubbing his middle finger around the rim.

"I'm beginning to think I may need to clean some house before Tennly takes over," Daniel implied. "It's bad enough I have clan chiefs trying to kill her. But now I have to worry about people sending intruders to find her."

"So, when are we leaving?"

"I don't want to ruin your Valentine's trip."

"That's like nine days away. Besides, you said the person who knows is an employee of yours. He'll recognize you or anyone else that works for you. Riley and I are your only choice."

"I don't know about using Riley. Being a couple hours away is one thing, but... if we have to go to New York, it won't be that easy to come back quickly if his mother starts asking questions."

"We'll find an excuse to tell his mom."

"I don't know, Conner."

"I promise you, his mom won't be a problem. She's used to him being away from the house from time to time."

"But days at a time?"

"Sometimes. So... do you want me to get Riley?"

"Yeah," Daniel responded, thinking back on the history that Riley's mother had with the O'Briens. "But I need to talk to his mother first."

Flashback:

Lexie had come over to see Daniel's sister, Janette, both of whom were 15 years old and in the ninth grade. They had not talked much in the past year, and Lexie had come over to find out what was going on between them.

Daniel had just settled down when he heard Janette's door slam shut, followed by Lexie crying as she darted past him and out of the house. Unable to stand the sight of her leaving so upset, Daniel decided to go after her. Over the years, Daniel had developed a secret attraction to her, and he couldn't bear to see her hurt.

"Lexie!" Daniel shouted after catching up to her on the sidewalk just past the porch steps.

Lexie turned around, tears in her eyes as she wailed, "What?"

"You shouldn't care about what my sister says. She's an asshole."

"I just don't understand... how can she just..."

"Because she's an asshole," Daniel repeated, trying to comfort her.

Lexie had always thought Daniel was good-looking and had a crush on him since she was eleven years old. So, when she saw him smiling at her and treating her kindly, she couldn't help but smile back. However, when he reached over and gently wiped her tears with his thumb, she could feel a spark developing between them.

"Ninth grade sucks. When you get into tenth next year, it'll be different. I promise."

As he stood there staring at her, he realized that he wasn't out there because he felt sorry for her; he was out there because he had feelings for her. Lexie had kissed boys before, but for some reason, when he kissed her, it felt different. Shivers raced through her body as her heart began to beat faster.

That kiss marked the beginning of a secret relationship that lasted throughout the summer, until one of Janette's new friends spotted them at the movies. It was a couple of weeks before the new school year started.

The next morning, she woke to the sound of her mother yelling outside the house. Someone had slashed all four tires on her car, leaving her unable to get to work. Lexie listened as her mother cried and begged her boss not to fire her, and it was devastating.

For someone like Janette, tires meant nothing. They had multiple vehicles, and even if they didn't, they could easily afford new tires. But for Lexie and her mother, those tires represented everything. They were their only means of income, and it would take two months to save enough to replace them.

Knowing who was behind the act, Lexie marched over to Janette's house to confront her. Her anger over what Janette had done was so strong that she wasn't sure how she would handle the situation upon arrival. Fortunately, after pounding on the door hard enough to hurt her hand, it was the O'Brien family's butler who answered. This gave her a moment to calm down before resorting to violence.

Upon hearing Lexie scream past the butler, Janette and three of her friends hurried down the stairs to see what was happening. When the girls reached the foyer and spotted Lexie, they began to laugh. In a burst of anger, Lexie darted past the butler and punched Janette in the face. Janette screamed as the other girls started yelling.

By then, everyone in the house had heard the commotion and rushed into the foyer to see what was going on. Janette's mother ran over to check on her daughter, while her father approached Lexie, who was being restrained by the butler.

"Get off me!" Screamed Lexie until she was released.

Daniel stood back, watching the scene unfold, unsure of what to do. He wanted to rush over to Lexie to find out why she had punched his sister, but he didn't want to jeopardize their secret. His parents were unaware of his relationship with Lexie, and he had no idea that his sister and her friends had discovered it.

"I think you need to go, Lexie," Mr. O'Brien said as he gestured for the butler to open the door.

Lexie wanted to tell everyone what Janette did, but as she looked around the foyer and saw all the wealthy people making accusations without knowing the facts, she realized that whatever she said, they wouldn't believe her.

What hurt her most was seeing Daniel standing there without defending her or even indicating that he was on her side. To her, it felt like he was embarrassed of her, as if he never wanted anyone to know about their relationship. So, without saying another word, Lexie stormed out of the house.

Daniel stood there, wanting to go after Lexie but unsure if he should. His parents were fair people who never looked down on those with less money, but he couldn't shake the feeling that, despite that, they would side with their daughter. He thought about telling them everything, how he had been dating Lexie all summer and how Janette had treated her, but he didn't. He just stood there, waiting for his parents to leave before running after her.

He soon spotted her on the next street over, about halfway to her house. He quickened his pace, and when he was just a few feet away, he called out her name. Despite his shouting, she continued walking, seemingly oblivious to him, so he shouted for her to stop.

"What?" Lexie fumed as she flailed around to look at him.

Seeing the tears roll down her cheeks caused his heart to break. He walked up to her and put her hands in his. "I don't care what they think... I don't care what any of them think. I love you."

It was the first time Daniel had said that to her, which made it even more difficult for her to take the action she needed to take. For Daniel, it was easy to avoid worrying about his sister, her friends, or anyone else at school. But for Lexie, it wasn't that simple.

She loved Daniel, but as she took his hand up to her mouth and kissed it, she cried, "It's just not me that I have to protect. They sliced my mom's tires, and she lost her job because of it."

Daniel had no idea, and his blood began to boil as thoughts of smacking his sister crossed his mind. "I'm going to kill her."

"I wish... Danny... I just..."

"I promise I'll make sure she never does anything like that again."

"You and I both know you can't control your sister."

"I can try." His smile made her almost forget everything and just melt away in his arms. She just about did until he added, "I'll buy you some new tires."

She pushed away as her heart shattered into tiny pieces and screamed, "I'm not your charity case! Just stay away from me!"

He grabbed her arm, keeping her from getting too far, and physically turned her around to face him. "You were never a charity case for me." He placed his hands on both of her shoulders and vowed, "And I promise I won't let anyone hurt you."

Lexie believed him, but she couldn't risk her mother becoming a casualty in her conflict with Janette. She placed her hands on his forearms, gently pushing them away.

"I know," she said as tears poured from her eyes. "But she lost her job, Danny. The last time she lost a job, we were evicted from our apartment. We lived in a car for three weeks until we got the house we're in now... My mom and I went hungry most nights... I love you. I do... but... I have another person I have to think about."

She kissed the back of his hand and then turned to walk away. He watched her for a moment, but as she walked farther away, his stomach began to churn, evident of how much he truly loved her.

"Please," he begged. "I won't let you live in a car. I won't let anythi..."

"Stop it!" She wept. "Stop! You may be able to keep anything from happening now... but what about when you leave for college? What will she do then?"

Daniel leaned in and gave her a big kiss to silence her. He knew she was right: his sister wouldn't stop. Even if he managed to keep Janette from hurting her for a little while, he would graduate at the end of the year and then be gone. As soon as he was away at college and no longer there to protect her, Janette, who held grudges, would finish what she had started.

He placed his hands on her cheeks and proclaimed, "I'll always love you."

She smiled at him and teased, "No, you won't. You'll graduate, go to college, and find some wealthy, beautiful girl who will sweep you off your feet." She started crying more as she continued. "And I will find out about it... because that's what this town does... and I will be so happy for you."

Daniel could feel his eyes become wet as he teased back. "And you will graduate; find a cute guy that sweeps you off your feet and treats you like a princess. Like you deserve to be treated. And I will find out about it... because that's what this town does... and I will be so happy for you."

Present:

Daniel didn't expect to feel as nervous as he did when he approached Lexie's front door and knocked. A part of him wanted to run away like a child, but a larger part was eager to talk to her. He had seen her around the neighborhood over the years but had never stopped to speak. To be honest, he often went out of his way to avoid passing her house. Each time he saw her, it never got any easier, and by avoiding her, he could keep his feelings hidden.

For Lexie, seeing him stand on her front porch was equally difficult. She, too, had noticed him over the years, but unlike him, she had longed for the day when he would come to confront her. She just never imagined that the day would actually arrive. So, when she opened the door and saw him standing there, it felt as if she had been hit by a strong gust of wind. Although her heart raced and her hand shook as she held on to the doorknob, she wasn't sure if she was ready for this moment.

"Do you want to come in?" She asked, giving him a smile, not sure what else to say.

"Yeah."

Once inside, she struggled to make eye contact, as she told him to take a seat and offered him a glass of hot tea. This brief moment allowed her some time to gather her composure before facing him.

She had just poured hot water into the kettle before Daniel arrived and knew it was about to whistle, so she stood by the stove until it did. After placing a tea bag into each mug, she walked over to the table and sat down. They stared at each other for a few moments, both feeling the remnants of the love they once shared. When the intensity became too overwhelming, she began adding sugar and creamer to her cup of tea. He watched her, finding all her little nuances adorable, but he said nothing. The way she poured the cream into her mug, barely holding out her pinky as if trying not to look prissy, her stirring of the sugar like she was churning butter, and how she dipped the tea bag in and out of the water as if washing a shirt in a bucket made him feel warm inside.

When she finally looked back up at him, she felt embarrassed. Covering her mouth with her hand in a shy gesture, she tried to look back down at her tea but instead smiled and shook her head, indicating that she couldn't believe he was there.

"You look good," he said, with yearning in his eyes.

"What are you doing here, Danny."

He smiled at the sound of his name being said like that. Most people called him Daniel, and only his closest friends referred to him as Dan. She was the only one who ever called him Danny. Not even his wife used that name, and it brought back so many memories and emotions. At first, it felt right, normal, and happy, but then those feelings turned into guilt. He considered leaving, but he reminded himself that he wasn't there to revisit an old relationship; he was there to do a job.

To lighten the atmosphere and cut the sexual tension between them, Lexie asked, "How's your sister?"

"Still an asshole," he chuckled.

"I heard she moved away."

"Yeah. You tick off enough people in a small town, and it's bound to run you out."

Lexie stopped laughing when she realized bringing up their relationship wasn't going to do either of them any good. "You didn't answer my question... Why are you here?"

"As I'm sure you're aware, Conner Marks is dating my daughter and now lives with us."

"I am... It's what this..."

"Town does," they both said simultaneously.

They chuckled as he continued. "Anyway, he also works for me. Odd jobs, mostly. But I could use another hand. He mentioned Riley."

"What would he be doing?"

He didn't want to lie to her. For some reason he had a strong desire to share everything about himself and the family he had married into, but after all these years, he wasn't sure if he could trust her. "My family deals with buying and selling a variety of things. Sometimes that requires a bit of brown-nosing. I have to... woo... potential clients and associates."

She smiled, thinking about how effortlessly he could charm anyone. Feeling a little embarrassed, he teasingly added, "I don't woo as well as I used to. That's why I need younger people. The youth are up to date with all the new lingo and trends that have become foreign to me. So, to answer your question, they would help me attract new clients or assist in merging with another business, if you will. Wooing..."

"Is it legal?" She asked, which caught him off guard.

He wished she hadn't asked that question and could see on her face that she had learned something about him. He wasn't sure if he should feel upset or relieved that he wouldn't have to lie to her.

"Do you know what I do?" She asked.

"You're a nurse."

"Yeah. It's funny how when people come into the ER they don't see nurses.

They say things that they assume no one hears. So, when I hear your name, I listen. I don't know exactly what you're into... and I don't want to know..."

"Lex..."

"Sh," she interrupted. "I haven't been able to tell my son what to do in years. He's a good kid, but he has a mind of his own. So, if he's already got his mind on working for you, there's nothing I can do about it. All I ask is that you promise me... swear to me, Danny, that you will keep him safe."

"I promise."

She took in a deep breath and said, "I know you will."

"Go on a date with me," he blurted out.

"What?" She giggled.

He abruptly stood up and demanded, "Yeah. I'm picking you up tonight. Be ready by 7."

"Danny... we can't... What would everyone say?"

"Be ready, Lex. I'll be here at 7. And wear something nice... I'm finally going to take you on a real date."

As soon as Daniel got home and stepped into the kitchen, he ran into Tennly, Conner, and Riley. They had been sitting at the island waiting for him to return, so when he got there, all three of them stood up to hear what the answer was going to be.

"She said it's fine," Daniel said as he walked past them.

They exchanged glances, each holding more questions than the original one. Then, all at once, they began to follow Daniel to his office. He sat down at his desk and observed as the three of them stopped in front of him.

"Don't you three have something more important to do?" He asked as he opened his laptop.

"She's just gonna let him go?" Conner asked.

"Yep," Daniel answered.

"What does she think we're doing?" Riley inquired.

"Get out of my office," Daniel ordered, giving them a look that told them he wasn't going to answer any more questions.

The three of them left and went back to the kitchen. While Tennly poured sweet tea, the boys sat at the bar and began talking.

"You know my mother," Riley mentioned. "She is and always has been super suspicious of the rich. She would never agree with me working for your father or going anywhere for him. It just doesn't seem right. Something's off."

"And why would he want to be the one to go ask her in the first place?" Conner added

"Wait a minute... remember... she used to be friends with my Aunt Janette," Tennly pointed out. "Maybe it's never been the rich she hated... Maybe it's always been just the O'Briens."

"Then that goes back to why would your father want to see her?" Conner asked.

Tennly thought back on the conversation she had with Lexie and the smile she got on her face when she spoke of Daniel. "I think I know."

"What?" The boys asked at the same time.

Tennly shook her head, not believing what she was about to say as she let out a sigh. "I think they liked each other."

"What?" The boys repeated, as their mouths flew open in disbelief.

Tennly gave them a look that told them to think about it. "No," Riley denied. "That goes against everything my mother ever taught me."

"You thought the same thing about Conner," Tennly reminded.

"She's got a point," Conner said.

"No way," Riley pressed. "She would never like someone like your dad."

Tennly and Conner both gave Riley a look that told him to look at them and think about what he said. "Again," Tennly reiterated. "You thought the same thing about Conner."

"Riley, come on," Conner pleaded.

"What?" Riley cringed, refusing to believe what he was hearing.

"It makes sense," Conner clarified. "The only way you can hate a whole group of people so much is if you were once hurt by someone or loved someone."

"Or both," Tennly added.

"Or both," Conner agreed.

"Well," Riley said, determination in his voice, "there's only one way to find out."

As soon as they arrived at Riley's house, Riley called out for his mother, to which she responded that she was in the laundry room.

As Tennly followed the boys down the hall, she noticed the differences between the two boys' houses. Although both homes were laid out similarly, Riley's house was slightly larger.

The living room and kitchen area were also more spacious and equipped with better appliances, including a dishwasher. Another noticeable difference was the overall atmosphere of the two homes. It was clear that a woman lived there; it was cutely decorated, much cleaner, and filled with a delightful rose fragrance.

"If you don't put your clothes back here," Lexie grumbled as they stepped into the laundry room, "they won't get done. You know today is my only day off this week."

They watched as she picked up the laundry basket full of clean clothes and walked down the hall without saying another word. She could sense their presence and understood they suspected something, hoping her silence would lead them to forget about it. She realized they hadn't given up when they stopped beside her at the kitchen table.

She started folding the clothes as she conceded, "Go ahead, ask."

"Why do you hate the O'Briens?" Riley responded.

She quietly folded the shirt she was holding, placed it on the table, and then looked at the three of them. "You might want to sit down."

CHAPTER II

Daniel stood in front of the full-length mirror in his dressing room, examining his reflection as he contemplated whether he was making a big mistake. Over the past several years, he had experienced a few one-night stands but had never been on an actual date. During that time, he had not met anyone he could envision loving more than his late wife, and the idea of going on a date felt like a betrayal. However, his business instincts told him he had no choice but to go out with Lexie. While he was somewhat looking forward to spending time with her, his primary concern was uncovering who had been discussing his illegal activities in public.

"You look so handsome," Marie complimented as she stood in the doorway to his closet.

"It's just business," Daniel replied as he continued to knot his tie.

"Most people may be blind, Daniel. But I see."

"It's just business, Marie," he repeated as if he were trying to convince himself.

"We'll see. Thomas is ready."

"Tell him I'll be right down."

Instead of leaving, Marie walked over to him and began straightening his tie. He had tied ties for so many years that he could do it in the dark, but for some reason, his fingers were shaking, and he just couldn't get it right.

"I remember doing this for you for your very first date," she reminded as she untied the tie to start over. "You were 15 years old. You asked me, how do I know if she likes me for me or because of my last name?"

"I remember. It was something I worried about every time I went out with someone. Until I met Leeny."

Marie smiled and said, "Aye, she was indeed special. But, Daniel, she wasn't the first one that liked you for you." Daniel gave her a look that asked her how she knew about Lexie. "I told you; I see things." Then she straightened his tie and patted him on the chest. "You might have asked her out for business this time, but it won't be for business the next."

After Marie left, he glanced at himself in the mirror once more, shaking his head in disbelief at what he was about to do. When he arrived at the garage, Thomas was standing beside the Mercedes, assuming Daniel would prefer that option to avoid appearing too formal.

"We're taking the limousine," Daniel said, walking toward it instead of the sedan.

Thomas looked confused by the choice of vehicle and raised an eyebrow in question as soon as they got into the limousine. "Don't," Daniel warned, as they drove off.

Daniel stood on Lexie's porch for a few seconds, taking deep breaths as he tried to understand why he felt so nervous. It didn't make any sense to him that he could confront the most dangerous criminals and even kill when necessary, yet he found it difficult to knock on his ex-girlfriend's door.

He waited long enough that he didn't need to knock. Just as he was about to turn away, the door opened, revealing Riley with a shit-eating grin on his face. "Do I need to go over the rules for dating my mother?"

Daniel returned his smile with a sarcastically threatening yet teasing one as he leaned in and whispered, "Do I need to find a secure location in which to bury your body?"

"Touche," Riley chuckled as he opened the door further and gestured for Daniel to go inside.

He was shocked to find Conner and Tennly there as well, and he wasn't sure how to feel about it. They were sitting on the couch with huge smiles on their faces, looking like they were at the zoo watching the monkeys. Daniel looked at Riley and added, "Make that three secure locations," loud enough for the other two to hear.

Laughter ensued as Tennly walked over to her father and gave him a hug. Hearing about her father's love story with Riley's mother made her see him in a new light. Ever since her mother's passing, all she could see was a man who had hardened his heart against any relationship. However, seeing the similarities between his relationship with Lexie and her relationship with Conner helped her understand a lot. He was heartbroken and didn't want her to suffer the same fate that had befallen him and Lexie.

"You look handsome," Tennly said.

He took her hands into his and asked, "If this bothers you in any..."

"No," she interrupted. "Not at all. I want you to go."

Before he could say anything, Lexie walked into the living room. Tennly had only seen her in casual clothes, usually with her hair in a ponytail or disheveled from a late night of work. But as she watched Lexie approach, she couldn't help but notice how much she resembled her mother.

She wore a sleek black, knee-length swing dress with spaghetti straps that flattered her tall, slender frame, paired with black pumps and a matching clutch. Diamond-studded barrettes pinned back her dark brown wavey hair allowing it to cascade behind her back and down to her shoulder blades. Her brown eyes were enhanced with eyeliner, mascara, and soft eyeshadow, which perfectly complemented her rosy cheeks. Whether the color was due to makeup or embarrassment was unclear.

As Daniel gazed at her, he kept reminding himself that this was just a business date. Yet, the longer he stared, the more he began to realize it was something more. After Lexie walked over to the coat rack and put on a long, wool, black button-up coat, Daniel extended his hand toward her and said, "Milexie."

With a shy and embarrassed expression, she gently placed her hand in his, and together they walked out of the house, hand in hand. Lexie couldn't believe that after all those years, he still remembered the nickname he had often used for her. It had originally started as a teasing blend of "milady" and her name, but over time it had become a term of endearment.

By the time they reached the limousine, the atmosphere was so awkwardly sexually charged that when Thomas opened the back door for them, he could practically feel it. Thomas found it difficult to watch the whole ordeal. He had always known Daniel to be a suave, confident man who carried himself with a commanding presence and spoke clearly without stumbling over his words.

After Lexie climbed inside, Daniel exchanged a glance with Thomas that conveyed his uncertainty, suggesting that he wasn't sure about the situation and perhaps regretted his choice. In response, Thomas's look urged him to gather his courage and get into the limousine. Reluctantly, Daniel shook his head and settled into the back seat next to Lexie.

"This one's different," Lexie noticed, breaking the silence.

"Yeah," Daniel replied. "I traded the old one in for this one a little over three years ago... when my oldest daughter was going to be around a lot more."

"Tara, right?"

"Yeah."

"Did she graduate? I haven't seen her around lately, and I thought she was a year older than Riley."

"She did. Last year. She's at college now."

"What is she studying?"

They talked the rest of the way to the restaurant about their families, engaging in light conversation to ease the tension. By the time they arrived, they were laughing about the funny things their kids had said or done when they were younger. However, her laughter gradually faded as she realized where they were: the best restaurant in Marinsburg, The Mountain Range.

The Mountain Range was a restaurant and lounge located inside one of the O'Brien hotels, The Mount Haven Appalachian Inn. This quaint inn, situated twenty miles from downtown on the old Mount Haven Plantation, was perched on the highest mountain and overlooked the valley below. Its design combined modern and traditional elements, showcasing the rich Appalachian culture.

The inn's rustic decor featured log furniture, homemade quilts, cast-iron light fixtures, and handwoven rugs, with antiques from centuries-old china to vintage farm tools scattered throughout. It offered eight guest rooms: four smaller ones with shared baths, two larger with private king suites, and two full suites with living areas. Guests also had access to modern amenities, including a pool house, game room, gym, computer lab, and services ranging from room service to limousine transport.

The restaurant, converted from the old kitchen, could seat 80 guests inside and 30 on the patio. It also had small stages for local bands and events such as weddings. The Appalachian-inspired menu highlighted locally sourced ingredients, featuring main dishes like chicken and dumplings, fried chicken, pork chops, and steak, along with sides like cornbread, biscuits, beans, carrots, potatoes, and corn prepared in various ways. Desserts changed daily and included pies, cakes, ice cream, and seasonal treats like cobblers, stuffed apples, and honey cake.

Lexie had never visited Mount Haven. She had grown up hearing about it and had talked about going with Janette, but their plans never materialized. After she was old enough to go on her own, she considered it, but she hesitated due to a fear of running into the O'Briens.

Upon her arrival, Lexie found the hotel even more beautiful than she had imagined. Hundreds of birch trees lined the driveway, creating a canopy overhead. To the left of the inn, rows of vineyards that were used by the O'Briens to create their own wines cascaded down a small incline, while a valley to the right housed the town of Marinsburg, backed by a distant mountain range.

In spring and summer, the hills and valley transformed into various shades of green, with a vibrant array of flowers resembling a Monet painting. While the beauty of spring and summer was undeniable, it was in the fall that the landscape became truly breathtaking. The changing leaves formed a natural mosaic that Tennly used to describe as looking like fruity pebbles.

But when Lexie first saw it, it was winter. The fresh white snow that had fallen that morning created a picturesque winter wonderland, blanketing each tree branch and vine, resembling cotton wrapped around a toothpick, while the ground was covered in a soft layer like a cloud.

It felt strange for Lexie to wait in the limousine while Thomas walked around to open the door for them. The seconds it took for him to do so seemed like several minutes, and the entire time she could feel her stomach churn.

"I'll be waiting in your office," Thomas said after they got out, and he shut the door behind them.

"Thank you," Daniel replied and then gestured for Lexie to follow him into the restaurant.

As they entered, Daniel placed his hand gently on her back, leading her past the front desk and down a long hallway, lined with doors that led to a banquet room, the restrooms, and his office. At the end of the hallway was the lounge, which housed the bar, and behind that was the restaurant.

As soon as they stepped into the restaurant, they were greeted by the hostess who showed them to their table which was in the far back right corner.

The table was large and round, with enough space for ten people. He had considered asking for a smaller, more intimate table but didn't want to create an awkward situation or send the wrong signals to Lexie. He pulled out two chairs and then asked to take her coat. She smiled as she handed it to him, letting her know she found his gesture funny.

"What?" He asked with a chuckle as he placed her coat on the back of her chair.

"Are we expecting company?"

"Shut up," he teased. "It's my table."

"I'm just messing," she teased back.

He enjoyed seeing the glimmer in her eyes, but it also brought back all the feelings he had once felt for her. Thankfully, the intense moment was interrupted by the waitress asking for their drink orders. They continued the casual conversation they had begun in the limousine during the first half of dinner. However, once they ran out of topics to discuss, a silence fell between them. They had both enjoyed the evening so far, but there were difficult topics each wanted to address. Daniel wanted to discuss the reason he had asked her out in the first place; he needed to find out who it was she had overheard talking about him at the hospital. It was challenging for him to voice his question, but before he could gather the courage, Lexie managed to ask hers.

"What do you need my son for?"

Daniel took a deep breath while he thought about how to answer. "How much do you know about me?"

"A question with a question is never good, Danny. Are you going to put my son in danger?"

"No more than I would put my own child in," he answered. "Now answer mine."

"How do I know that after I tell you what I know, you won't kill me?"

Hearing her say that stirred emotions within him that he had never experienced before. First, anger as he realized that she knew more than he had initially thought. Then he considered the fact that, despite her knowledge, she had never shared it with anyone. This realization brought forth a new feeling for him: shame.

"I can't do this," he snapped, and then left her there, sitting alone.

She sat there for a moment, contemplating how she would get home. If she called for a car, would the driver be one of his employees? If she stayed the night at the inn, would one of his employees be able to reach her while she slept? She couldn't call Riley because she didn't want to put him in further danger. Any decision she made could turn out to be the wrong one, and that sent shivers throughout her body. Resolute, she stood up and ran out of the restaurant, catching up with Daniel as he walked down the hall. Feeling her blood boiling, she pushed him, causing him to stumble back a couple of steps.

"Look at me!" She screamed. Then, in a whisper so not to be heard, she asked, "Are you going to kill me?"

He placed his hands on her upper arms and squeezed, giving her a harsh yet puzzled look. Fear gripped her as he pushed her away. She watched him turn and walk away again, all thoughts on her son and his safety.

"I need to know," she pressed as she started to cry. "If you do, please... please... don't hurt my son."

Daniel's heart began to break as he listened to her, but he couldn't bring himself to turn around. Instead, he kept walking. He found himself in an unfamiliar situation and didn't know what to do. His mind urged him to kill her before she could go to the police, but his heart wouldn't allow it. He had always trusted his logic and made rational decisions, never allowing his emotions to guide him. Since the death of his last love, he immersed himself in business and avoided any dilemma where following his heart was an option.

Out of fear for her son's life, Lexie ran in front of him and pleaded, "Please... please... If you ever cared for me..."

As he saw the scared look on her face, the feeling of shame washed over him once again. He gently ran the back of his right hand down her left cheek, trying to reassure her that he wasn't going to harm Riley. The gesture stirred mixed emotions in her that he could clearly see. She trembled in fear yet looked at him with love.

"It feels wrong," he confessed. "To still have feelings for you... It feels like I'm betraying my wife. I loved her so much. I miss her every day. But when I see you... other than my family, Lex..." At that moment, he found his answer. He loved her, and every part of him told him he could trust her. "Other than my family, there isn't anyone in this town safer than you. No one is going to harm you or Riley. Both of you are safe... I promise."

Before she could respond, he leaned down and began kissing her. Sensing that the kiss was leading to something more, she lowered her head, resting it on his chest. When she looked back up at him, a coy smile spread across her face.

"So," she said. "What does this mean... for us?"

He shook his head and replied, "I don't know. Why don't we just start with finishing dinner and getting to know each other again?"

They made their way back to the table and continued eating, occasionally glancing at each other with a smile. Although they were enjoying the moment of silence, they both knew that eventually they would have to return to the reason they were there.

"Riley's done a job for me before," he admitted, trying to find the best way to answer her question. "I needed Conner to do something, and he suggested Riley should be his wingman. He was never in any danger, and I had ears on them at all times."

"And this time?" She asked.

"It'll be similar, but I'm actually going to be using Tennly more."

"Your daughters know?"

"Just Tennly."

"It doesn't bother her? What you do?"

"What is it that you think I do?"

"I don't know. I... I hear things..."

"Like what?"

"People fear you."

"People respect me. There's a difference."

"Danny, I'm not stupid. I see you around, and I hear what people say. I can put two and two together. It's obvious that you're into something illegal. Is it drugs?"

"I'm going to ask you this question only one time. I will accept your answer no matter what. But think about it very carefully, because once you know, your life will never be the same. Do you understand?"

"You're going to have to be a little bit clearer."

He always admired her ability to stand up to him. It reminded him of his wife and was one of the reasons he fell in love with both women. He believed that this trait was essential for keeping him grounded and helping him make the right decisions. Because of this, he felt confident that she would be able to handle anything he shared with her.

"You'll basically be under my protection."

"You said I was safe already."

"It'll be different. Those who work for me will know, and you'll probably get special treatment wherever you go... but... your life will not be secret. I'll know where you are, who you're with, and what you do."

"Why?"

"Because of what I do, I need to know to keep everyone I love safe. I've strategically placed eyes and ears everywhere, and if any of them sense any dangers or betrayals, I'm told."

"You're speaking in riddles, Danny. Just tell me."

He nodded and then proceeded to explain what he did and how he got involved. Then he finished with, "What you know can be dangerous to me and my family. Not even those who work for me in this town know about the Connollys. All they know is that I have a lot of money and even more power. However, in this world, there are a lot of risks and dangers that will always be around us. But I promise you, I will do everything in my power to protect you both."

"Officer Taylor," she said, feeling that if he trusted her enough to tell her everything, then she should trust him. "A couple of years ago, he came into the ER for chest pains... While I was putting in his information in the computer, he made a call to someone. I heard him tell the other person that if you ever found out what he did, you would kill him. I couldn't believe what I heard, so I stopped what I was doing to listen. The next thing I heard was him saying that the person needed to come as quickly as he could to pick it up... I went out of the room to check on another patient, but when I got back, he was gone. I was torn between finding someone to report it to and running to you."

"Thank you," he said.

"What happens now?" She asked.

"We order dessert," he smiled, feeling relieved that it was an officer whom he had already disciplined for his loose lips.

Before they could order dessert, Thomas walked up and said, "I hate to interrupt, but we have a situation... with our missing associate."

Daniel didn't want his night with Lexie to end, and since he was going to use Riley in the case and had already shared details about his business with her, it seemed safe to take her back to the mansion, allowing them to spend more time together.

He took a sip from the wine glass, looked at Lexie, and asked, "Do you like pie?"

Daniel had called Tennly and told her that he needed her, Conner, and Riley to come to the mansion for a meeting and were sitting in the breakfast nook when Daniel, Lexie, and Thomas walked into the kitchen. Thomas placed the four whole pies he got from the restaurant on the counter while Daniel and Lexie sat down at the nook.

The three kids exchanged confused glances, wondering why Lexie was there. He took her hand, which made Tennly and Conner smile. However, Riley had mixed feelings. While it was nice to see his mother happy and he appreciated that Daniel could provide her with everything she deserved, he was also worried about the potential danger she might face.

As Thomas spoke, Marie sliced the pies and arranged small dessert plates and forks on the counter. Lexie found it odd that they could discuss something so criminally dangerous while someone prepared something as ordinary as dessert. However, observing how relaxed everyone was, along with Marie cutting the pie, gave her a sense of peace.

"He's left New York," Thomas finished regarding the employee who they believed knew something about the intruders. "To Pittsburgh of all places."

"Do we know where he's staying?" Daniel asked.

"Yeah," Thomas answered, "but it's too high traffic to just grab him there."

Daniel pressed his fingertips together and tapped his two pointer fingers back and forth on his lips as he thought of a way to approach his employee. He glanced between the boys and Tennly when an idea struck him. "Here's what we're going to do."

Thomas managed to secure a room at the same hotel where the employee, Chance Bennett, was staying. Chance was an average-looking guy; attractive and in his late twenties with brown eyes and sporting short dark hair and a small goatee. He was tall and thin, generally dressed in nice suits but occasionally wearing a stylish pair of jeans with a dress shirt.

For the first two nights, Conner and Riley lingered in the lobby and bar, watching Chance's comings and goings. By the third night, they noted his routine: leaving at 11:00 AM, returning by 3:00 PM, retreating to his room for two hours, then dining in the lounge. After dinner, he smoked on the patio, left for a couple of hours, and was always back by 7:30 PM. Each night around 8:00 PM, a different woman joined him for drinks before heading to his room.

The reports pleased Daniel. He had heard of Chance's habit of hiring escorts and hoped it would continue in Pittsburgh, since the plan hinged on Tennly taking on the role of one of the women.

At the safe house nearby, Conner and Riley confirmed the pattern to Daniel, Tennly, and the others. Tennly then transformed herself from a sixteen-year-old into a convincing escort: slick ponytail, smoky eyes, dark red lipstick, burgundy mini skirt with a plunging blouse, stiletto heels, and a black clutch concealing a Beretta and one of her throwing knives. Diamond studs hid her earpiece, a locket disguised her mic, and a thigh holster carried two more throwing knives.

Right on schedule, a woman entered the lobby at 8:00 PM. Riley intercepted her, pretending to be Chance, and walked her out. Daniel turned to Tennly, giving her a look that told her it was time. She hurried to the lounge, spotted Conner, and then approached Chance. He ordered drinks and spoke almost like he wanted a real connection, though before long his touches grew too familiar as he ran his fingers up and down her arm. Tennly played along convincingly, while Conner, gritting his teeth, reminded himself this was just a job.

After seeing Chance lead Tennly out of the lounge, Conner whispered into his microphone, "She's coming your way, Riley."

Riley had taken the real escort down the street, paid her four times what she would have earned, and instructed her not to return to that hotel for the night. Then he rushed back to the hotel and sat in the lobby, waiting for his cue.

"I see her," Riley said as Chance and Tennly walked into the lobby.

Together, they quickly made their way down the hall to a back door and opened it for Daniel. The three of them then sprinted to the stairwell, heading up the stairs to the fifth floor, where they knew Chance's room was located.

Inside the room, Chance started kissing Tennly harder and began to pull off her blouse, causing her to have to let go of her clutch. She went along with it until she could find the best time for him to be vulnerable enough for her to take over. She playfully sat him down on the bed, and then while he was preoccupied with kissing her neck, she reached down to her thigh and slowly grabbed one of her knives. Before he knew what was happening, she had him down on his back and the knife to his throat.

"Don't move," she threatened.

"What... what are you doing?" He asked with a quiver in his voice.

"I'm going to get up," she explained. "Get my clutch, and you're not going to move. Do you understand?"

"Who are you? What do you want?"

"Do you understand?" She repeated as she dug the knife harder into his neck, causing it to cut just enough to bleed a little.

"Yeah... yes."

Tennly slowly released the knife from his neck and scooted off the bed. But as soon as she reached for her clutch, he attempted to go after her. She gave him a disappointed look and threw the knife at him, hitting above his left clavicle about two inches down from his shoulder.

"I told you not to move," she scolded.

He screamed in pain but didn't do what she asked. Assuming that she only had the one knife, he believed he could take her since she was so tiny. When she saw that he was still coming after her, she reached down for her second knife and quickly threw it at him, lodging it directly on the opposite shoulder.

"Don't!" She screamed. "I'm not here to kill you. So, please don't make me."

Chance, writhing in pain, reluctantly sat back down on the bed. "Who are you?"

Ignoring his question, she retrieved the gun from her clutch, put on her shirt, and opened the door. Just then, Conner and Riley barged into the room. Conner went straight to Tennly, cupped her face in his hands, and asked her if she was okay, while Riley waited by the door.

When Conner noticed the two knives that were still in Chance's body, he started laughing. "Ouch. Looks like that hurts."

Thinking he was being robbed, Chance shuddered. "Just take whatever you want. My wallet is in my front pocket, and I have some cash in the top dra..."

"We're not here to rob you," Conner interrupted.

"We're here for some information," Tennly prodded as Daniel stood back by the door in the dark to see how the kids handled themselves.

"Rumor has it," Conner claimed, "you know who broke into the O'Brien estate a few weeks ago."

"Shit," Chance gulped. "Is that what this is about?"

"Answer the question," Tennly demanded.

"I only heard something about that, Chance fretted. "I don't know for sure."

"Then tell us what you know," Tennly urged.

"There's a bar in downtown New York," Chance explained, still moaning from the pain. "That I often go to. There's always this guy there, spending money like he owns a bank..."

Tennly made circles in the air with her finger as if to tell him to get to the point. "Anyway, he likes to talk. A couple of weeks ago, I overheard him talking with someone on the phone. He said that some estate in West Virginia would be hard to get into."

"Does this guy have a name?" Tennly asked.

"He never mentioned a name," Chance answered.

"Then I guess we no longer have any use for you," Tennly threatened as she pulled out the knife from his right shoulder, causing him to scream, and then held it up as if going to stab him.

"Whoa whoa," Chance panted. "Wait...
I don't have the guy's name, but... I
overheard him call the man over the phone,
something like... Mr. Blanc... or Banky...
I can't remember."

Even though it wasn't the exact name,
it was close enough to Bianchi that it sent
chills down Daniel's spine, as if a ghost
from his past had returned to haunt him.
The thought that someone from the Bianchi
family might be responsible for sending
intruders to their estate frightened him.
Before anyone could react, he stepped out
of the shadows and approached Chance. "You
need to think very carefully about what
you say from now on," Daniel warned.

"Mr. O'Brien," Chance shrieked, eyes
wide as his body began to tremble.

"Shut up," Daniel ordered. "Your life
depends on how you answer these next few
questions. Do I make myself clear?"

"Yes, sir."

"Was it Bianchi?" Daniel asked.

"Yeah, maybe... I'm sorry, I don't
know."

"Why didn't you report what you
heard?" Daniel inquired, upset that he
wasn't sure.

"I... I... swear I was about to," Chance stuttered. "It's not that... that easy to get a hold of one of you guys. You know there's a ladder... I was trying to find someone higher up when I... I got a call from my mom... That's why I'm here... in Pittsburgh. My grandmother is ill and doesn't have much time left... I swear."

"So," Daniel said lowering his voice "You're not here because you're hiding?"

Chance chuckled slightly through the pain and said, "If I were hiding from you, I wouldn't hide in a city where I know you have connections."

"Why not stay with your family?" Daniel inquired.

"There's not enough room in my mom's house, especially now that my grandmother is there. That... and believe it or not, they are religious. They don't allow smoking or drinking..."

"Or whoring," Conner added.

Chance gave Conner a look that told him he was right.

"What's she dying from?" Daniel asked.

"Cancer."

"What's her name?"

"Elenore Johnston."

"Did you get that, Thomas?" Daniel asked into his microphone.

"On it," Thomas said still sitting outside in the car. They only had to wait a few minutes before Thomas replied, "It's true."

Daniel pulled off a backpack that he had been carrying. Inside was a first aid kit that Daniel threw at Chance. "Just so we're clear, you're not out of the woods yet... but... so far, your story checks out. Don't... and I mean don't... keep something from me again. Understood?"

Mount
Haven
Appalachian
Inn

CHAPTER 12

Daniel felt relieved to discover that he didn't have a rogue employee. Chance had remained loyal to the family, and after speaking with Tennly, they realized he would continue to be loyal to her when she took over. However, the lingering concern about the identity of the mystery man still troubled them. Although Chance couldn't confirm that the last name was Bianchi, Daniel couldn't shake the feeling that it was a strong possibility.

"I still don't think it can be them," Jimmy said. "We killed all the men off."

"But there are still associates and other family members who could seek revenge," John reminded him.

Daniel recalled the night they killed everyone at the Bianchi restaurant, just as Jimmy added, "True, and don't forget about those two kids you let live."

Flashback:

After they had killed all the Bianchis in the restaurant following Eileen's funeral, Daniel ordered Jimmy to take John and Phillip outside and told them he would meet them back at their father's place.

Being overly cautious, Daniel wanted to take one more look around the restaurant to make sure they didn't leave anyone alive, who might have hidden when they heard the gunshots. He searched thoroughly, looking in and under everything that could conceal someone. Even the walk-in freezer was checked, but it was empty. As he was about to leave the kitchen, he stepped on a section of the floor that felt different. He tapped around the area and noticed the sound changed from solid to hollow.

Curious, he examined the floor closer and discovered a notch in one of the slats. Sliding his finger under it, he realized there was a secret door hidden in the floor. He hesitated to open it, for fear he might be met with gunfire. However, he couldn't risk leaving anyone behind.

Taking a deep breath, he leaned forward, quickly opened the door, and stepped back. He glanced down the hole a couple of times, and when no one shot at him, he began to climb down the ladder. His heart raced and sweat dripped into his eyes as he aimed his gun around the dimly lit room, scanning for any movement. Finally, he spotted two trembling young children, a 10-year-old girl and an 8-year-old boy, hunkered under a table in the center of the cellar, holding onto each other, their faces covered behind the red and white gingham table cloth as if that would keep them from being seen.

He had never killed children before, and he had no desire to start now. However, he also couldn't let them run through the restaurant, risking the chance of seeing their family members dead. He vacillated between whether he should kill them or not. Then he remembered Tennly waiting for him outside in the car.

"Shit!" Daniel screamed. Then he turned to the children and said, "If you come up that ladder, I will kill you. Do you understand?"

He watched their small chins move up and down, lips quivering as tears slid down their cheeks and fell onto their laps like fragile raindrops.

Present:

"I told you," Daniel said sternly, "I don't kill children. Do we know where they are today?"

"Last I heard," Jimmy replied, "they still live in New York with their paternal grandmother."

"Where's their mother?" Tennly asked, thinking about her own.

"Rumor has it," John answered, "she never liked the family business. She tried to take the kids a year after the boy was born. It didn't take."

"What do you mean it didn't take?" Riley asked, his concern evident.

"She was never seen or heard from again," Jimmy replied.

"Is that how this works?" Riley inquired, worried that his mother had gotten involved.

"In some families," Daniel answered, "yes."

"What about this one?" Riley pressed.

"We're not so black and white," Daniel answered, knowing that Riley was thinking of his mother. "Your mother is safe, Riley. I give you my word." Riley nodded, and Daniel continued, "Thomas, find out where they are."

"Yeah," Thomas affirmed and then walked out of the office.

"Jimmy and John, you two check with all the associates around New York and New Jersey to see if they may have heard anything else," Daniel ordered. "Whoever it is, knows where I live. They're either out for revenge or..." he looked over at his daughter and proposed, "they're out to get Tennly. Either way, we need to find out which and take care of it."

Conner was apprehensive about taking Tennly on a surprise Valentine's trip to Prague. However, Daniel believed that living in fear would not benefit any of them, so he encouraged Conner to go ahead with the plan. But when they boarded the jet, they noticed that in addition to the usual crew, there were four other men accompanying them. Tennly recognized these men as employees of her father, having seen them at various gatherings.

"Bodyguards?" Tennly pouted as she looked at Conner.

Conner shrugged his shoulders and replied, "I didn't know."

She approached one of the men and stated firmly, "Let's make something very clear. You are here solely to keep an eye out for danger and to ensure our safety, not to interfere with what we do. Understood?"

"Yes, boss," one of the men responded.

It was the first time someone had referred to her as 'boss.' It felt strange and somewhat intimidating to realize that in less than a year and a half, she would be the one in charge, controlling everything and everyone, including her father. She liked the thought; it made her feel powerful. Nodding at the man, she took her seat alongside Conner.

The airport in Prague they always used for their flights was a private one, exclusively for personal jets and helicopters. Tennly recognized it immediately and couldn't help but become all giddy.

"You brought me to Prague?" She asked, a heartfelt warmth flowing throughout her.

"I heard you talking about how much you miss it and your friends here," Conner answered. "Plus... I wanted to see where you spent all those years you were away from me."

She gave him a kiss and said, "You're amazing."

Tennly was excited to show Conner her favorite places, so they spent the afternoon touring the city. Their first stop was Letna Park, where clear winter skies let them enjoy the famous view. Next was Old Town Square, which still looked like the 10th century and was alive with restaurants, street performers, and artists. The highlight was the astronomical clock. Tennly timed their arrival for 2:00 PM, when the mechanical apostles appeared in procession above four figures of vanity, greed, death, and lust, followed by two chimes. Conner was amazed that such intricate mechanics had been built in the 15th century and wanted to stay for the next hour, but Tennly urged him on to Prague Castle. Too cold to walk across Charles Bridge, they took a taxi with the bodyguards trailing behind.

That evening, Daniel arranged a Valentine's dinner at one of Prague's best restaurants: a table for Conner and Tennly and another for their security. Unsure what to order, Conner let Tennly choose. She picked Pork Knuckle which was herb and beer marinated pork roasted and served with pickled vegetables, and Svickova, braised beef with vegetables in sweet sauce and dumplings. Conner enjoyed both, especially the pork, and for dessert they shared apple strudel and Medovnik, a honey cake that reminded Tennly of her father's local honey in Marinsburg.

The next morning, Conner's plan was to visit the school. Headmistress Novakova sent a limousine after breakfast, while the bodyguards stayed at the hotel since the school was more fortified than the O'Brien mansion. To Conner, the building looked more like an asylum or prison than a school, though the flowers and ivy spilling down its walls gave it an unexpected beauty. Inside felt surreal as they walked through the hallways, Conner having only imagined what it looked like from Tennly's letters. The ornate interior reminded him of Buckingham Palace, yet the silence was unsettling. He had expected to hear noise and see students, but the corridors were empty, leaving him with the feeling that he was being watched as he and Tennly made their way to the headmistress's office.

The headmistress noticed them as soon as they approached her office door. "There you are," Headmistress Novakova said, standing up from her desk and walking over to them. "Come in, come in." She embraced Tennly with a large hug and asked, "How was your trip?"

"It was good," Tennly replied. "This is Conner. Conner, this is Headmistress Novakova. She runs the place, like a mix of Marie and a principal."

"That's quite a compliment," Headmistress Novakova responded, knowing who Marie was. She then turned to Conner and extended her hand. "Nice to meet you."

"Nice to meet you, too," Conner responded.

"Come, have a seat," Headmistress Novakova gestured as she led them to the seating area. "I want to hear how things are going for you."

Tennly updated Headmistress Novakova on everything she had been doing since leaving the school, excluding anything related to her family's business. She was aware that Headmistress Novakova knew about her family and their activities, but she was uncertain about how much she truly understood. Instead, they focused mostly on her school, friends, and weekend activities. Tennly also shared that her father was in a new relationship with an old flame, who happened to be the mother of Conner's best friend.

"I'm so glad he has found someone," Headmistress Novakova said. "I always hated that he was alone." Her smile faded as her demeanor became serious. "Duncan tells me you're preparing to take over the business. How do you feel about that?"

"I don't know," Tennly replied, surprised by the question. "I'm excited... nervous... afraid that I won't be able to do it. What if I make a mistake and someone gets hurt?"

"Knowing Duncan, your father, and the head family in Ireland as I do, I can assure you they wouldn't put you in that position if they didn't believe you could handle it... Especially Keenan. Keenan is very smart and strategically places people under him whom he knows he can trust and who will be assets to the business."

Tennly became speechless as her squinting eyes revealed a curiosity at how well Headmistress Novakova knew her family. While Tennly knew that her mother attended school there, along with several other relatives, it didn't explain how the headmistress seemed to understand what Keenan would want, or how she knew him at all.

"Would you like a drink?" Headmistress Novakova asked as she stood. Tennly looked at her with a puzzled expression, wondering what kind of drink she meant. "Aye," Headmistress Novakova replied, using an Irish vernacular, nodding to indicate that she meant an alcoholic beverage.

"Sure," Tennly responded.

Headmistress Novakova walked over to her liquor cabinet, unlocked the section that held the expensive spirits, and pulled out a bottle of aged whiskey. Knowing what she was about to tell Tennly, she felt it deserved a choice drink. She returned to the seating area, setting down a tray with three glasses. After pouring an inch into each glass, she took one for herself and sat down across from them.

She took a sip, then a deep breath, and revealed, "I didn't always live in the Czech Republic. I was actually born in Ireland. In my early twenties, I traveled a lot and came to Prague when I was 22. It was here that I met the love of my life and married him. That's how I got my last name, Novakova. We moved to Ireland and were happy there for five years. He loved my family, and they adored him. He even worked for my family."

She got quiet while she tried to hold back tears as she thought about it. When she was able to gain her composure, she continued. "I became pregnant... but my husband died before I told him. He was killed... Within a month of his death, I had a miscarriage. I went into a deep depression and my family had me hospitalized. I was able to come out of it, but I just couldn't live in Ireland anymore. The only place that made me happy was being here, in Prague. I feel close to my husband here... I found this place on one of my outings. It wasn't in the best shape, but I knew immediately what I had to do with it. I mentioned it to my brother, and he bought it."

She took another sip as if what she was about to say was going to be shocking. "We worked for two years to get it ready. That first year, I only had eight girls. They were all relatives or friends' children, one of whom was your mother. She was just a small thing." A smile crossed her face as she went on. "I can still see the confusion on your face. Let me clarify... My name is Shannon O'Ceallaigh. I'm Keenan's younger sister."

Tennly's expression said it all; her original shocked expression intensified as she was completely surprised. "But your accent?"

"That's to keep my roots a secret," Headmistress Novakova replied. "Just in case anyone wanted to take revenge on the family, I kept my married name, shortened my first name to Anna on paper, and became Czeck. It was easy for me to pick up the language and accent after living here for so long and hearing it every day. Very few people know my truth."

Headmistress Novakova placed her glass on the coffee table, took a deep breath, and said, "I'm sure you have a lot of questions."

"Are all the students here children of family members?" Tennly asked.

"Not anymore. That's why it's kept more secretive than in the past. We have students here ranging from politicians' children to very wealthy individuals."

"Do you accept children from opposing families?" Tennly inquired.

"No. We discussed it, but it would be too risky. All it would take is for someone to recognize another, and this place would no longer be safe. When I receive an application, I conduct a thorough investigation."

"My father said he chose this school because it was the best place to train me."

"It is. Because of the family's connections, we can get the best trainers here. Not to mention, there's no other proper boarding school that allows for the extracurriculars we offer. You were sent here to learn from the best so you could become the best."

"Do you ever get back to Ireland?" Tennly asked, changing the subject.

"Sometimes." Then she began oscillating between her native Irish and adopted Czech accents, depending on which persona she was portraying. "I try to make it back a couple of times a year. But it's risky and takes a lot of effort. I have to remember which accent to use, what passport to carry, and what name to go by. I can't risk Anna flying into Ireland and Shannon coming back here. It would only take one mistake for our enemies to find me... and, in turn, find you and the other children."

"Are you lonely?" Tennly asked, thinking how sad it must be for her to have lost her husband.

"No, I have several children that I love, and many of our family members come visit. Duncan being the one who visits the most."

"Are we related?" Tennly asked.

"Distantly, aye. My grandfather and your grandfather's grandfather were siblings. That makes us 2nd cousins, twice removed."

"So, everyone in the families is related?" Tennly asked, thinking of the two young men she fought to gain her position.

"Out of the main families... somewhere along the line, aye. You're wondering how someone who is related to you can try to kill you."

"I was under the assumption that we weren't related," Tennly said surprised that she knew about the Donnybrook.

"Your ancestry traces back to two brothers who migrated to the United States over a hundred and fifty years ago. Approximately thirty years later, after they found success, the family sent two cousins from Ireland to join them. This is how your family lineage includes the four families you know: yours, the O'Gradys, the MacFaddens, and the Sweenys. At this point, the connections are quite distant, making it easy to forget how everyone is related."

"I suppose it's a good thing I didn't kill them, then," Tennly sighed, upset that her own blood could try and kill her.

Headmistress Novakova nodded in agreement with her and then informed, "Some in the families found your mercy to be a sign of weakness."

"It wasn't weakness," Tennly clarified. "I didn't kill them because I plan on using them as a reminder to anyone who tries to second guess me."

"And that is why my brother believes in you and your abilities to become one of the best bosses in the family." She stood up and added, "Let me show you to your room. I'm sure you want to settle in and have some time to show Conner around before lunch."

She guided Tennly and Conner to a room in the teachers' quarters and then left them to have some time alone. The room was twice the size of the students' rooms and had a private bathroom attached. It was decorated in soft yellow and tan hues with bright orange accents. Conner couldn't help but think it looked like a sunflower had exploded, and he chuckled under his breath as they walked further in. When they reached the king-size bed, they noticed their suitcases sitting in front of the dresser, so all they had to do was unpack the clothes they would need for the next two days.

"She seems like a very interesting person," Conner said as he hung a shirt in the closet.

"I can't believe that after all these years of knowing her, I had no idea we were related," Tennly lamented, closing the top drawer of the dresser. She turned to Conner and added, "Every time I think I know my family, someone says something that makes me realize I have so much more to learn."

"Maybe that's why she told you," Conner suggested, walking over to her.

"To remind me how clueless I am?"

"To make sure you know that as soon as we get home, you need to demand your father tell you everything you need to know to lead this family."

Tennly thought about his words, and knowing how Headmistress Novakova operated, it felt like her passive-aggressive way of offering help. She placed her hand on Conner's chest, gave him a kiss, and said, "Come on, I want to show you around."

After showing him the pool house, they walked back through the teachers' quarters and entered the part of the building that housed all the classrooms.

Tennly was excited to see that the door to the high school language arts room was open as they approached. She stopped just inside the doorway with Conner beside her and watched as the students performed a scene from *Macbeth*.

Her smile grew wide when she spotted her cousin, Victoria, playing the role of Lady Macbeth. As Victoria turned theatrically around the room and caught sight of Tennly in the doorway, she stopped, screamed in delight, and ran over to her. The other students and the teacher were momentarily startled until they realized Tennly was there. Victoria enveloped Tennly in a big hug, and the other students quickly gathered around them.

"What are you doing here?" Victoria asked as she released her grip.

"Conner brought me here as a Valentine's Day gift," Tennly replied.

"Hey, Conner," Victoria greeted. "Nice. Thanks for bringing her."

"She misses you," Conner explained. "So..."

"I do," Tennly admitted.

"Okay," the teacher said in English, her strong German accent noticeable. "Everyone, please return to your seats." She could see from the expressions on the students' faces that they were fascinated by Conner's presence, especially since they were not accustomed to having boys at the school.

As all the students except for Victoria returned to their desks, the teacher looked at Tennly and jokingly admitted, "It hasn't been the same here without your interruptions." She then gave Tennly a hug and added, "It's great to see you, but we'll have to catch up later. Right now, we have a class."

Tennly smiled and replied, "I understand. We'll talk later."

Next, Tennly took Conner to the students' dormitory wing of the school. They walked up the stairs straight to the third floor so she could show him the shared bathroom that all the students used. She peeked inside to ensure no one was in there and then gestured for him to follow her. Conner was pleasantly surprised by its appearance, which featured the same beautiful architecture and artwork as the rest of the school. However, he hadn't expected that the students, especially wealthy girls, would have to share one bathroom.

He laughed as he said, "Not very bougie, is it?"

"What?" She laughed as she playfully hit him on the shoulder. "I told you, we're not all stuck up."

"Yeah," he bantered. "This is some hard living."

"Shut up," she teased, punching him in the shoulder. "Come on."

She guided him back down the steps to the second floor and down the hallway. As they walked, she pointed out Victoria's room, explaining that she had stayed there during the month after she left Marinsburg before Thanksgiving. When they reached her old room, the door was closed. She hesitated before opening it, aware that it was no longer hers.

"It's just strange," she hesitated before going inside. "This was where I lived for ten years, and now it belongs to some other girl."

"Can you even get in?" he asked.

"Yeah, the doors don't have locks," she replied as she opened the door. "She changed the colors." The walls were newly painted a light sky blue with hot pink accessories, sheets, and curtains. She wandered around the room, touching everything as she went. "My walls used to be light pink... and I had black and white striped pillows and curtains."

Conner watched her glide through the room, moving between expressions of delight and sadness. He approached her as she disclosed, "Even my furniture is gone."

"What do they do with it?" he asked, wrapping his arm around her.

"They donate it to a local charity," she answered, approaching the desk. "The only thing that's the same is this desk."

He slowly leaned into her, reached around in a seductive manner, and placed his hand on the desk. "Is this the desk where you wrote my letters?"

She smiled and then licked her lips. "Yes."

He moved closer to her, kissing her neck softly. Gently, he picked her up and sat her down on the desktop. The heat radiated between them as their breathing became heavier. As he ran his hand along the front of her body, she leaned back, feeling his touch send shivers down her spine. She let out a sensual giggle as the thought of getting caught made the whole experience more erotic.

CHAPTER 13

Tennly and Conner were so focused on their training, eager to complete it before going out with their friends later that night, that they didn't notice Duncan standing just inside the door, watching their progress. He was pleased to see that Conner's initial hesitation about being too rough with her had disappeared. Although Conner won more than half of their matches, Duncan could see that Tennly was improving and becoming even better than she had been when she fought in Ireland.

"Very good," Duncan praised, clapping after she was able to knock Conner down on his back.

Hearing his voice, she became excited, but as soon as she saw the look on his face, she knew he wasn't there just to check on her progress.

"What are you doing here?" She asked.

"Why don't you both wash up and then meet me in your father's office?" Duncan suggested, dodging her question.

The fact that he didn't answer caused her alarm, which made them wash quickly and hurry to reunite. As soon as they arrived in Daniel's office, Duncan didn't hesitate to get down to the reason he was there. "The families are calling for a sit-down."

Daniel, knowing what that meant, got a worried look on his face as he took a drink. Tennly noticed her father's worry and asked, "What's a sit-down?"

"It's a meeting," Duncan answered. "Years ago, they used to happen twice a year. But when that became too risky, Keenan decided to only have them when it was necessary, or a skipper or clan chief requested it."

"Why was this one called?" Daniel asked.

"Redistricting," answered Duncan.

"That hasn't been done in over fifty years," Daniel stated with a concerned tone. Duncan nodded once to acknowledge that he was correct. "Who called for it?"

"Mikey MacFadden," Duncan replied. "Keenan agreed; he wants to redistrict Ireland as well."

"What are you talking about?" Tennly asked, growing frustrated that they were discussing something she didn't understand and hadn't explained to her.

"They're calling a meeting to discuss the reassignment of who will rule over what land," Duncan responded.

"What does that mean?" Tennly inquired. "Could they take my reign away?"

"They can," Daniel confirmed.

"They'll try," Duncan corrected.

"When is it?" Daniel inquired.

"Tomorrow evening at 5:00 PM," Duncan answered.

"That doesn't give us enough time to come up with a flight path," Daniel mentioned.

"That's why I'm here," Duncan assured. "I could have just called. Get packed. We leave in two hours."

Daniel called James before Duncan's jet departed because they didn't have time to pick him and John up on the way. James was worried about the situation and informed Daniel that he would arrange a flight as soon as possible. They both feared that their decision to appoint Tennly as their boss might jeopardize their leadership in the United States, and he felt they needed to be present to have a voice in the matter.

Duncan's jet arrived in Dublin at 9:30 AM the next morning where a limousine was waiting for them. Once at the O'Brien Estate, Duncan didn't stay long; he told them he would see them at the O'Ceallaigh Estate and then left them to rest before the meeting.

Daniel went to his office to handle some business, while Tennly and Conner remained in her bedroom. The thought of losing her reign before she even had the chance to rule weighed heavily on her mind, and Conner could sense her worry. In moments like this, he wished he were better at offering comfort. He wanted to say something to ease her feelings, but he wasn't sure if speaking would help or make things worse.

It wasn't until she sat up and looked at him with a disappointed smile that he knew he had to try and comfort her. "I'm sure everything will be fine."

"I just didn't know until now... when there's a possibility that I could lose it that I wanted it so badly. I think I could have been really good at it."

"I know you would... and you still might be. You don't know what's going to happen yet."

"I know. It's just... I'm only 16 and a girl... and as much as I think Keenan likes me, he's an old man... probably set in tradition and will probably listen to the other old men who are set in tradition." She let out a loud grunt as she leaned over and placed her forehead on his chest.

Upon arriving at the O'Ceallaigh Estate, they were greeted at the front door by the butler, who escorted them to a room featuring a long, antique-looking wooden table that could seat twenty-four people. The room was spacious, measuring 60 by 30 feet. A row of windows on the outer wall was adorned with ceiling-to-floor gold curtains. The chairs were leather, accented with gold and brown cushions on both the seat and backrest. A long gold lace runner stretched the entire length of the table, with three small candelabras evenly spaced on top. The walls, made of extremely expensive ebony wood, showcased priceless paintings placed every five feet. In the far-left corner, there was a liquor cabinet accompanied by a large humidor. Along the walls, black leather armchairs awaited those in attendance who weren't important enough to be seated at the table.

Keenan was already sitting at the head of the table, flanked by Seamus Connolly and Duncan on his right and four unfamiliar men on his left. The atmosphere was far more intimidating than Tennly had anticipated, prompting her to seek reassurance from Duncan. Although he smiled at her, she found it difficult to decipher whether it was a reassuring or a disappointing gesture.

"Come on in," Keenan said, signaling for them to enter the room.

Daniel motioned for Conner to take a seat in one of the leather chairs along the wall. As Conner settled in, Tennly started to sit next to him.

"Tennly," Keenan intervened, as Daniel took a seat at the table beside Seamus. "Please sit next to your father."

Tennly sat down at the table, feeling confused as she and her father puzzled over her placement as well as the absence of the underbosses from the other families from the United States. Her father initially assumed the other underbosses were simply running late and would arrive shortly. However, their confusion deepened when Keenan started to speak before the others had arrived.

"Since we're all here," Keenan began, "I have been thinking about how I want this organization to continue after I'm gone. I've considered who I want to take over in my place and how I envision things operating. As you know, I don't have any children. The closest thing I have to a child is Duncan."

Keenan gently patted Duncan's hand and declared, "That is why I have decided that, upon my death, I will pass my leadership responsibilities on to him."

Tennly couldn't contain her excitement at the thought of Duncan, her cousin and mentor, becoming the head of the entire organization. She looked at him, and when he caught her smiling, he winked at her, reassuring her that he would always support her.

"I was planning to wait a few more years before making this announcement," Keenan said. "However, given the demand for the Donnybrook and the recent request for redistricting from families in the States, I realize that the vultures have started to circle. I can't afford to wait any longer. You might notice that a few families are not represented here today, three from the States and ten from Ireland. I made this choice because I wanted to speak to all of you before our formal sit-down tomorrow."

Daniel, Tennly, and Conner were completely unaware that two sit-downs were planned; Duncan had never informed them. He wanted to share this information but was asked by Keenan to keep it a secret, wanting to ensure things went according to plan before the requested meeting.

"I called the leaders of the original five families together today, along with the main leader from the States, so we could discuss matters privately, without the others present," Keenan continued. "I want to go into tomorrow's sit-down already clear about my intentions, so there won't be any arguments, discussions, or confusion. There is no longer a need for fifteen individual clans in Ireland. I propose that we merge them into five groups, with either a concession or a Donnybrook to determine who will be in charge. Any thoughts on this?"

After extensive discussions, they agreed with Keenan and decided that the best way to merge the ten families was by their locations. The two families that were closest together would form one clan, with the leader being chosen either through one family conceding or by a fight to the death.

"Now, let's move on to the next topic," Keenan said. "When Duncan takes over for me, it will create a conflict of interest within the Connolly clan, since his father is the boss here in Ireland. However, Seamus has agreed to relinquish his position so that his son can take charge. Duncan has suggested, and I agree, that Tennly will become the boss over her family here in Ireland."

Tennly's mouth dropped open in disbelief as she processed what she was hearing. She glanced at her father, her mind racing with questions. She had arrived thinking she was about to lose her reign in the States, only to be told she was gaining more power.

Before she had a chance to ask any questions, Daniel spoke out, "How will that work? Will she have to move here?"

"She's more than welcome to if she wants," Keenan replied. "However, since she'll be the boss in the States, she can lead from there. It's not like it used to be years ago. With the internet, technology, and the ease of flying back and forth, staying in touch is much easier."

"That'll give her two families along with the sub-families to oversee," Daniel pointed out.

"Aye," Keenan nodded.

"I doubt the families in the States had this in mind when they requested the redistricting," Daniel remarked.

"They did not," Keenan confirmed.

"May I ask what they wanted?" Daniel inquired.

"The MacFaddens have requested to form their own faction alongside the O'Gradys," Keenan explained. "They want to remain in New York City, with the MacFaddens in charge there. They are also looking to force the Sweeneys to relocate to New Jersey, where the Connollys reside, and come under their authority, creating a New Jersey faction that Tennly will oversee."

Daniel could feel a fire burning inside him as he struggled to maintain his composure. He despised the disloyalty of two families under his authority, viewing it as a betrayal. Just as he was about to speak up, Tennly interjected.

"I risked my life," Tennly fumed. "I won fair and square. I could have killed their sons, but I chose to save them. And this is how they repay me? How can I trust them to be submissive if I can't even trust them not to betray me?"

"She's right," Daniel replied. "This is how feuds begin."

"I agree," Keenan added. "As you said, Tennly, you have proven yourself to be a skilled fighter and a fair leader. If I didn't believe you could handle this, I wouldn't leave you in charge."

"And you won't be alone," Duncan assured her. "I will be here for you..."

"As will we," said Thomas Lawlor, the man sitting across from her, and the boss of the Lawlor clan. She looked at him and noticed that the other three men also nodded in agreement.

"The main issue is," Keenan continued, "if we are reducing the number of clans in Ireland, why would we create more in the States? There is no need for more than one clan there, and Tennly is more than capable of managing it. It would be beneficial if she could fly here at least twice a year. The visits should be random, without specific dates or times, so they don't appear suspicious. You come for Thanksgiving every year; that would be a good time and wouldn't raise any alarms. Things like that."

"What do you think?" Daniel asked, a proud look on his face, as he looked at Tennly.

"I..." Tennly began, then glanced at the men across from her. "It doesn't bother you that I will be your equal?"

"I'll admit," Oliver O'Ceallaigh, the boss of the O'Ceallaigh clan, replied, "when we first heard that you were next in line for succession, we didn't like it. But then we saw the Donnybrook. We witnessed your capabilities. You were able to use your intelligence to secure your win, and you showed compassion, which we don't see much of, and let them live."

"The fact that you even asked us if it bothered us," Thomas Lawlor said, "tells us everything we need to know about you."

"You're the embodiment of the future we want for the next generation," Oliver added. "So, we are willing to give this a try."

Tennly smiled, nodded, and then turned to Keenan, assuring, "You will not be disappointed. I give you my word."

Keenan returned her smile and said, "Now we vote. All those in favor of the new redistricting plan say, 'aye.'"

For everyday matters or decisions, Keenan had the final say. However, when it came to anything that affected the organization as a whole, only the leaders of the original five clans voted. These clan leaders were Thomas Lawlor, Sean Moore, Colin Dowling, Oliver O'Ceallaigh, and Seamus Connolly.

Every vote had to pass with 100% approval for it to take effect, yet Keenan was not concerned that all five clan bosses would vote in favor of the new redistricting laws. After the vote passed, Keenan dismissed everyone except Tennly, needing to talk to her before the scheduled meeting the next day.

Tennly was confused about why he wanted to speak with her and hoped she hadn't disappointed him in any way. She sat quietly as she watched all the men leave the room and close the door behind them. She waited for Keenan to say something, but he just sat there, trying to find the right words without being direct. After a few moments of silence, she couldn't take it any longer.

"My headmistress told me that she's your sister."

"Hm," he replied with a smile. "Well, my sister has quite a big mouth."

"She's a brilliant woman," Tennly remarked. "Why didn't you ask her to take over after..."

"She is, but she's only a few years younger than I am. Not to mention she doesn't have any children. So, in a few short years after my death, we would find ourselves in the same position... She and Duncan are your biggest advocates. Duncan may have suggested that you take over the Connolly clan here in Ireland, but it was my sister who convinced me that it was the right decision.

"Now on to why I wanted to speak to you in private. I didn't want anyone else to hear. You will not only be the first female in that role, but also the youngest. I was 22 when I took over, and I faced many doubters, two of whom even tried to challenge me. I defeated them both in separate Donnybrooks... I wasn't as compassionate as you were."

He gave her a regretful smile and continued, "That's why you intrigue me. According to our rules, the two families had to obey me... and they still do. However, I spent years watching my back, afraid that they would find a way to kill me. Fortunately, they never succeeded... but it wasn't because they didn't want to; it was strictly due to our laws and the honor that goes with them."

"I've seen how people look at you," she mentioned. "It may have started out that way, but they like you now."

"Aye, maybe now. But I can't help but think that if I had done what you did, they might have liked me earlier. That brings me to why I wanted to talk to you. When you turn 18, you will have some important decisions to make. Regardless of whether I'm still in charge or not, you will take over leadership of your clans both in the States and here in Ireland. Duncan will only assume his role after I'm gone. This means you have less than a year and a half to choose who you want as your clan chiefs. Currently, under your father, you have your uncle James, and under Seamus, there's Duncan.

"For your clan in Ireland, you can choose to continue with Seamus or select someone else from your immediate family. In the States, you can stick with James or opt for someone from your other families, like the O'Gradys, Sweenys, or MacFaddens. Choose wisely, because you'll want someone you can trust. Who you choose for your chess pieces could be either a benefit or a downfall."

Tennly nodded and then said, "understood."

He took a sip from his glass and set it back down on the table. After a deep sigh, he became very serious. "I do not like the way Mikey MacFadden is handling the idea of you becoming his boss. He has always wanted the skipper position and believes that his family is the rightful line to rule in the United States and not yours. I'm giving him tomorrow to show me that he is going to stay obedient; if he doesn't, I'm stripping him of his title."

Seeing a confused look on her face, he explained, "The Irish Mafia is quite different from others. We aren't as structured, and most of the time, we operate individually rather than as a collective. Except for the power that the original five clans have, each of our families or clans is considered equal. This stands in contrast to other mafia organizations, where a head boss or godfather is often regarded as a deity. Blasphemy, if you ask me. There are certain matters where I have total control, but there are also areas where I do not. In some situations, our five original clans together wield more power than I do. This brings me to the second reason I needed to talk to you alone: what to do with Mikey.

"If I must demote him, he will need a replacement. Normally, that decision would go to the boss of his clan. However, since that role belongs to your father, who doesn't have the bloodline to make that call, this decision will come to you."

"I don't know enough about the MacFadden family to make that decision," she acknowledged, worried that she might reveal her inability to run anything.

He smiled at her and replied, "And that is why you will make the best choice."

"But I'm not even a boss yet," she countered.

"There's nothing in our laws or traditions that states you have to be. You are next in line. You have tonight to research and prepare to make your decision. You will also need to determine whether Mikey should be sentenced to death. One thing we can't afford in this business is traitors and people who don't respect the hierarchy. It poses a risk not only to the person they're betraying but to the entire organization. If someone is angry enough to turn against one of us, it's hard to predict their actions. Could they kill? Turn others against us? Or worse, become a whistleblower?"

"Why is that my decision and not yours?"

"Because it is your clan."

"You can strip a title, but you can't order a death?" she asked, a slight chuckle underneath her breath.

"I can, by law, do anything I want. However, that much power could destroy this organization. I learned a long time ago that power is only as strong as those who are willing to follow it. If you keep your followers believing they have a say in how things go, they will continue to grant you your power. Besides, like I said, each clan takes care of their own business. So, it is your call. Each family is responsible for its own. You must keep them in line, discipline them, and decide when it's time to let them go. By allowing each family to make those choices, you maintain law and order while fostering a sense of individual power."

"When should I let you know if I feel he needs... to be let go?"

"We don't hide things. I'll ask you in the meeting if it comes to that."

"Won't that just put a bigger target on me?"

"Tennly, this isn't a game. This is how things are done. You will have to make these decisions for the rest of your life, and with each choice, there are two possible outcomes. Your clan will either learn to respect you, allowing you to maintain your power, or they won't. Now, let's move on to the second reason I needed to speak to you alone."

Tennly sat there, struggling to move on to the second subject. She found it difficult to focus on anything else, as the thought that she might have to make her first decision the very next day weighed heavily on her mind. It wasn't going to be an easy choice. The idea that her initial act as a future boss, before she was even old enough to be officially recognized, could involve ordering the death of an underboss was almost too much to comprehend.

"When you turn 18 and are coronated, and once you become a skipper, a boss, for the first time in our history, you will hold more power than anyone else. You will rule over two clans and in two countries. That means you have twice the decisions, appointments, anything that comes up, and you will have the power of being a boss over one of the five original clans, which also means twice the voting power."

"Then why would you do it?" she asked. "Doesn't putting me ahead of two clans pose a significant risk to the stability of this organization? If they sense a weakness, won't it be like wolves to a kill?"

"It does, and it could," he replied. She looked at him with a questioning expression, so she didn't have to repeat her concern. He smiled and added, "I'm curious to see how it will turn out. Consider it a social experiment."

"With my life on the line?"

"Do you not think you can handle it?"

"Simply asking me that question puts me in a precarious position."

"Exactly why we are having this conversation alone. You have a year and a half, Tennly, to decide if you want to accept this position."

"And if I don't... who takes it?"

"Your father has done an excellent job, but it has always been temporary. Once you come of age, he will no longer be eligible to continue as the skipper. The position will either pass to you, or there will be another Donnybrook. As for the position here in Ireland, it will remain with Seamus until I pass away."

"Who will have to fight in the Donnybrook?" she asked.

"Whoever wants it," he replied. "But you could also risk your family's reign. Either way, you're risking the chance that your family back in the States could be overthrown. You need to decide which option offers you a better chance of success."

"Is it possible for me to take control of the States while denying the position in Ireland?" Tennly asked.

"Aye, that's an option. But if I were a betting man, Tennly, I would place my bets on you. No one has ever faced the challenges you will encounter, and no one has had to face them at such a young age. I understand it's a lot to consider, but if you embrace this opportunity and succeed in earning the respect and love of all the families, you could one day find yourself sitting in my chair."

"Duncan isn't that old," she pointed out, not sure how she felt about being the head boss someday.

"Duncan is only taking it so he can resign it to you when the time comes."

"What?" She gasped. "Why?"

"Duncan, as much as I believe he will excel at it, and as much as I care for him like a son, he doesn't truly want it. He's a soldier; he can't sit still long enough to be in charge."

"And yet you are giving it to him?"

Keenan smiled and insinuated, "What does that tell you?"

Tennly quickly realized that Keenan shared Duncan's opinion about making her the head boss as soon as possible. They believed that this would prepare her to eventually lead the entire organization. The younger a captain is when they take over, the longer they can reign and the more successful the organization becomes.

"That you hope he will eventually settle into the position," she teased, incredulously, as she slightly winked. It was one thing to take on the role of skipper, but the thought of being the captain, the leader of the entire syndicate, gave her pause. The responsibility that came with being a skipper was significant enough, let alone the added duties of the head boss position.

"Perhaps. Now go. You have a lot to think about tonight. My suggestion is to keep it to yourself. Find a place where you can be alone tonight and without distractions. You'll have plenty of advice tomorrow. You need to know what you want before then." Tennly got three steps away when Keenan added, "Tennly, you have all night to think about what I told you. Learn what you need to... know everything before you come back here tomorrow. You have a library at your place. I highly suggest you use that as your quiet space. There's a lot of inspiration in a library. I wish I could tell you more, but I cannot."

The library in the O'Brien mansion in Ireland featured dark wood floors and ceilings, accented with deep red and gold. Three soaring walls were lined with two-story bookshelves filled with a vast array of books, while the far wall showcased a Palladian window draped in red sheers, accompanied by a liquor table in front.

In the corners, straight-backed chairs with red cushions and lamps provided additional seating. A massive

Persian rug spread across the floor, and at the front of the rug, four plush red armchairs surrounded a coffee table. At the back of the room, an eight-seat wooden table held a desktop computer and a small printer.

Keenan's cryptic message to her suggested that there was something in the library that could help her make her decisions. Why else would he have recommended the library instead of just using her laptop in her bedroom? It had to be more than simply wanting to avoid distractions, and something she just couldn't find on the internet, so she surveyed the room for clues. Eventually, she noticed something she had overlooked many times before: twenty books, bound in black leather with gold lettering, sitting on the top shelf of the left wall, two stories high.

She positioned the sliding ladder and climbed up to reach them. The books were larger than they appeared from the floor, each about three inches thick. She pulled out the first book and opened it. As she skimmed through the initial pages, it became evident that it was dedicated to the history of how Ireland was settled, covering the years from 300 AD to 1100 AD.

During her investigation, she discovered that the first six books chronicled various eras of Irish history, while the seventh detailed Ireland's struggle for independence, spanning from the 1st century through the Anglo-Saxon invasion, right up to its recognition as an independent nation in 1937.

Books eight through ten focused on Irish royals, describing their lives, reigns, residences, deaths, and the battles or contributions that shaped the nation. Though Tennly longed to read these books, she didn't have time at that moment. The eleventh book, which covered the origins of the Irish Mafia, revealed a narrative that contradicted the commonly held belief that the Mafia began in the U.S. during the 19th century and only reached Ireland in the 1960s.

The text indicated that the Norman invasion of England in 1066 coincided with Irish clans fighting for dominance. Ireland was divided into seven tribes: O'Mordha, O'Deevy, O'Deoradhain, O'Lalor, O'Dunlaing, O'Conghaile, and O'Ceallaigh, all ruled by clan kings under a high king, who could be dethroned in battle. By the mid-1100s, the O'Deevy king had allied with Norman soldiers, uniting Ireland under one ruler by 1166. The loyal

O'Deoradhains merged with them to form the Devoy clan, while the other five clans banded together as an organized family.

As Tennly read, she recognized Keenan's table companions among the descendants of these clans: the O'Conghailes (Connollys), O'Ceallaighs, O'Lalors (Lawlors), O'Mordhas (Moores), and O'Dunlaings (Dowlings). Some O'Ceallaighs had become O'Kellys, although Keenan's line chose to keep the original name. The five clans lacked the strength to defeat the Normans and gradually faded into secrecy while assisting the oppressed, inspiring tales some linked to Robin Hood.

By the 1600s, their legends had vanished, but they continued quietly, maintaining kingships and the competition for high king—later renamed skipper and captain. She skimmed ahead to where the clans spread into New York's five boroughs, then turned to the laws and traditions in book fifteen, followed by the betrayals and Donnybrooks discussed in books sixteen through eighteen.

Books nineteen and twenty shocked her: both were blank, except for ten pages in the nineteenth book. On page four, she found details about her mother's murder and her family's retaliation. What stunned her the most the mention of her first Donnybrook victory and the possibility for becoming the first female boss. Pride swelled at the realization that she, too, had been woven into history. Pride swelled at the thought that she, too, had been written into history. Smiling, she set the nineteenth and twentieth books back, took the four books she needed, and returned to the table to finalize her plan for the next day.

CHAPTER 14

The Connolly jet made it to Dublin just in time for Jimmy and John to meet Daniel, Tennly, and Conner as they were heading to the O'Ceallaigh Estate. When they stepped into the conference room, everyone was already gathered and waiting. Keenan, Duncan, and the five bosses she had met with the day before were seated in the same spots as if their places were assigned. In addition to them, there were ten bosses from Ireland who hadn't attended the previous meeting, along with Mikey MacFadden, Peter O'Grady, and Tyler Sweeny from the States.

The leader in the United States held the same level of power as the five original bosses in Ireland. Below them, the ten Irish bosses and three U.S. bosses under Daniel were considered equals. This structure enabled Daniel's three subordinates to have seats at the table, despite being the lowest-ranking bosses in the hierarchy.

Mitchell MacFadden and Petey O'Grady were seated along the wall with the underbosses and a few other men. Among them was Grady Connolly, her mother's cousin and Seamus's younger brother. All the men sitting along the wall were close family members from each clan who had a direct lineage to eventually become clan chiefs. Although they were allowed to attend the meeting, they had no say and were not allowed to speak.

When Mikey MacFadden, sitting at the other end of the table with Peter O'Grady and Tyler Sweeny, noticed Tennly walk in, a smug expression spread across his face, as if to say he had finally succeeded in getting rid of her. However, his smile faded when Conner and John took a seat with the other family members along the wall, while Tennly followed Daniel to his seat at the table.

Unaware of the prior meeting, Mikey assumed that Tennly didn't know the protocol and mistakenly believed she had a right to sit at the table. "Your seat is back there," Mikey rasped, gesturing toward the chairs along the wall. "You're not a boss yet."

Tennly shot him a defiant smile that seemed to say he should have thought twice before crossing her and continued sitting beside her father. Mikey's irritation was evident on his face, but before he could say anything further, Keenan called the meeting to order.

"I have asked you all here today," Keenan began. "Under the request that we discuss the redistricting of our families. I gave it much thought, and I agree it is time. However, with the world shrinking and the use of technology making it easier to communicate, I don't see the need for districts to get smaller, but the opposite."

Keenan specifically looked at Mikey and explained, "With there only being four families represented in the States, there is no need to divide them. Tennly *will* take over when she turns 18."

Mikey wasn't even trying to hide his feelings, evident by his scowl and pursed lips. Everyone could see his anger as he sat there, struggling to stay quiet. Tennly, on the other hand, tried to maintain her composure but struggled to conceal her true emotions. It wasn't easy; she desperately wanted to stick her tongue out at Mikey or flip him off. To keep herself in check, she focused her attention on Keenan to avoid acting out.

"The five original clans," Keenan continued. "Will remain the same, but the other ten here will merge." The bosses of the ten families began to look around confused and upset at the possibility they would lose their power. Keenan allowed them to voice their opinions and whisper amongst themselves for a few seconds before saying, "Quiet! This is not going to be a negotiation. Centuries ago, the original five clans called upon your families to help, due to the vast land and inconvenience of travel. And it worked for many years. But there is no need for that many anymore. One boss can rule over two families. So, the ten will become five."

He went on to disclose which families would merge and that it was decided by location. Then he explained, "You will have a say in who the boss will be. The two families can either pick a new boss or keep a current boss, which will be determined by one conceding or a Donnybrook. Your choice. If you choose a new boss altogether, that boss will need to choose a clan chief. If there is a conceding, the boss that gives up their title will become the clan chief. If there is a Donnybrook, it will be to the death, and the winning boss will choose their clan chief. You will have enough time to discuss amongst your combined clans and put your affairs in order... I will give you a week to get me your decisions."

"Any questions?" Keenan asked before proceeding when the room was silent. "Now to move... Upon my passing, I have chosen Duncan to replace me as the captain. Due to the conflict of interest, his father has agreed to step down, which will create a vacancy in the Connolly faction here in Ireland. The Connolly Clan has requested that Tennly be appointed as their leader."

Keenan paused, knowing that either Mikey or one of the other bosses from the States would have some qualms about that decision. Sure enough, as soon as he stopped talking, negative whispers and discussions went out over the whole table.

"Ruling over two countries and two families is ludicrous!" Mikey shouted.

"It has been voted on and approved," Keenan stated firmly. "There will be no discussion!"

"Well," Mikey began, "I believe it's time for the laws to change! We have been following outdated regulations for too long, and there are enough of us to hold a legitimate vote!" He glanced around at the other bosses, seeking their support, and added, "Who's with me? We don't have to tolerate this any longer."

Despite the fact that the ten bosses from Ireland disagreed with the new plan, they remained rooted in tradition and honor. Having come from Ireland, they understood the potential consequences of defying the original five. They bowed their heads to avoid making eye contact with Mikey, silently signaling that he was on his own.

Mikey then turned to Peter and Tyler and pleaded, "Come on. I know you don't agree with this nonsense."

As Mikey voiced his disapproval of the situation, Keenan glanced at Tennly, silently asking if she was prepared to do what needed to be done. She nodded in response, affirming her readiness, and then Keenan looked back at Mikey, who was still babbling.

Once Mikey was quiet, Keenan declared, "I have given you a chance to obey and respect our laws and traditions, but it is clear that you cannot. Therefore, as of today, you are stripped of your title."

Mikey opened his mouth to respond, but before he could speak, Keenan warned, "Be very careful with your next move! It may not just be your title that I take." Mikey sank back into his chair as Keenan composed himself as he sat in silence for a moment.

"If I may continue," Keenan said, not bothering to wait for a response. "Since Daniel is not of Connolly blood, he cannot choose a new boss. And since there is no law stating that an emerging boss cannot make that decision, Tennly will determine who will take over the MacFadden clan or if the MacFaddens should merge with another family." He looked at Tennly and asked, "Have you made that decision?"

"I have," Tennly answered.

"And what say you?" Keenan asked.

"I spent over eight hours reading and researching our laws, traditions, and history last night. I understand that it is common practice to pass leadership to a son if one is available. In this case, we have an eligible son, Mitchell. However, our laws state that if betrayal is a concern, that direct descendant can be passed over. I want to believe I can trust Mitchell since I spared his life, but I worry that my future decisions might jeopardize that trust. Therefore, I recommend merging the MacFaddens with the O'Gradys."

Keenan nodded and replied, "It is done. As of today, the MacFadden family will report to the O'Gradys. Peter, you and your clan chief will remain in power, but I warn you: do not think of going against Tennly's wishes. What's done is done. Mikey's title has been stripped. That decision has been made and voted on, but what to do with him is again up to Tennly."

She looked at Mikey and took a deep breath, knowing that what she was about to say would upset Conner and her father. "I could demand that you be punished for your betrayal. However, after studying our history and traditions, laws, and consequences, and considering the many battles and Donnybrooks fought to secure the top positions, I am going to give you a chance to fight me for your life."

Everyone in the room gasped and began whispering at her decision. Daniel closed his eyes as Conner hung his head, both fully understanding why she had refused to talk to them earlier. If she had confided in them, they would have tried to talk her out of it. They had barely survived the stress and worry of the first Donnybrook, and neither could bear the thought of watching her fight in a second one.

"Silence!" Keenan commanded, quieting the room. He felt a sense of pride in Tennly. She not only read the books but also remembered what he had told her the day before when they were alone. He was pleased that she paid attention when he explained how many times he had to fight to maintain his position, earning the respect needed to lead the entire organization.

"Are you sure?" Keenan asked.

"Everyone deserves the chance to fight for their life," she replied. "And I still have a lot to prove. So, yes... I'm sure."

"Whoa," Mikey wavered, his voice trembling. "Wait a minute. That's not necessary. I'll step down, and I swear I won't cause any problems."

"You would do that to your family? You're more of a spineless snake than I originally thought." Keenan said, which made Tennly realize that what she had read about their fate was true. She hadn't suggested the Donnybrook for Mikey, but for his family.

"It's not right," Mikey insisted. "There's no..."

"I said enough!" Keenan shouted, cutting him off and silencing everyone else who had been engaged in their own conversations. "It's done! The redistricting in the States will take effect immediately. The ten families here have one week to inform me of their decision... and Tennly, you and Mikey have the rest of the day to prepare for the Donnybrook. Be at the church by 7:00 AM tomorrow morning. The same rules apply as the last one."

Keenan fixed a stern gaze on Mikey and threatened, "If any weapons are found hidden in the church, I strongly advise against using them. If you do, I kill you, your son, and then the rest of your family. Do I make myself clear?"

"Yes, sir," Mikey replied, a mix of anger and worry in his voice.

"You don't show up at 7 in the morning," Keenan added. "You'll go home to a houseful of dead family members... and you will live out the rest of your life looking over your shoulder. Understood?"

"Yes, sir." Mikey repeated.

"Very well," Keenan said, and then dismissed everyone except for Duncan. Once the two men were alone, Keenan remarked, "She's impressive. Not many people would take on what she's about to do, especially for a family she doesn't know very well."

"She knows she'll win," Duncan implied confidently. "He's old and out of shape. It won't take much for her to defeat him."

"That's my concern," Keenan replied. "If he's that easy to beat, she might consider letting him live as a sign of compassion."

Duncan paused, taking a deep breath as he pondered that possibility. "Aye, she might."

"If she does that, she'll lose all the respect she has," Keenan warned. "Showing mercy to two young men who didn't want to fight her in the first place is one thing. But showing mercy to a veteran boss who tried to take her title, and what he could do to his own family would be her downfall."

"I understand," Duncan replied.

"Then I suppose this is also your first trial," Keenan noted.

"How so?" Duncan asked.

"There are two reasons," Keenan explained. "First, if she loses the respect of the other bosses, they'll also lose respect for you since you vouched for her. Secondly, if you tell her she can't show mercy, you might always question whether she is the right person to take over my position one day."

As they drove back to the O'Brien Estate, Tennly could sense Conner and Daniel's frustration. She sat in silence, waiting for one of them to speak, but halfway home, she realized they weren't going to.

She turned around and looked at Conner, who was sitting behind her and staring out the window, his hand over his mouth as if he were covering his quivering lips. When he refused to meet her gaze, she turned back around, and they continued their drive home in silence. Once they arrived, they quietly walked into the mansion. She allowed them to take a few steps through the foyer before she could no longer hold back.

"Stop!" She screamed, which made them both freeze. She walked around to face them and tried to justify her decision. "I know you don't like it, but I didn't have a choice. Dad, you know how this works. A boss that isn't respected won't live long. I'm a girl... I'm young... and all of them are going to be watching every single thing I do. They will be waiting for me to make one mistake and if I do, they will pounce like a tiger in wait. This isn't something I can just hope away and wait until I'm older. This is a decision I must make now. They need to know right away that I'm not going to be someone they can push around, or worse."

Daniel listened, each word she spoke striking a truth he didn't want to face. Deep down, he knew she was right, but didn't want to admit it. Conner on the other hand, new to the brutal world of organized crime couldn't didn't understand, and his confusion showed in the tight furrow of his brow and the sharp, angry glare in his eyes.

"How did you think this was going to work?" she asked. "Me being the first female boss? Hm? Did you expect that I would just take over like you did? With no one opposing me? Everyone happy that I'm in charge of two families? You knew this wasn't going to be easy, yet you trained me for it, anyway, causing me to have no choice."

"I know," Daniel finally accepted, which made Conner so angry that he stormed out of the foyer and up to his room.

The thud of a slamming door off in the distance, prompted Daniel to say, "You better go to him. As upset as I am about it, I understand and know underneath you are making the right decision."

"Maybe you should talk to him," she sighed. "I don't think he wants to see me right now."

"As angry as he is with you, he's more worried and will want to see you. But you're probably right about this as well. Maybe I can help soften it a little."

She gave her father a kiss on the cheek and thanked him. "I love you," he said as he grabbed her hands into his. "And

I'm very proud of you. Especially since I know the real reason you're fighting."

Daniel made his way to Conner's room and knocked on the door. When he received no response, he opened it and stepped inside. The floor was scattered with shards of glass from a broken mirror that had fallen off the wall, right in front of the door. As he ventured further into the room, he heard water running from the bathroom that connected to another guest room.

"Go away!" Conner yelled from the other side, after hearing the knock.

Not heeding his order, Daniel slowly opened the door and saw Conner standing at the sink, rinsing his hands under the water. Blood dripped from his knuckles into the basin as he used soap to disinfect his wounds.

"How bad is it?" Daniel asked.

"I'm fine," Conner replied tersely.

"I didn't ask that," Daniel said as he walked over and took Conner's hand. He examined the cuts and noticed that at least two were deep enough to require stitches. "I'll call for a doctor."

"I said I'm fine," Conner replied, pulling his hand away. He grabbed a towel hanging next to the sink and wrapped it around his hand. After turning off the water, he walked out of the bathroom and into the bedroom.

"You're not the only one who hates what she's doing," Daniel said as he sat down across from him. "It kills me too. But you knew about this family... And before you say it, yes, I'm her father, but I don't have the same authority over my daughter that most father's do... But you know that... And she's right... if she doesn't prove herself now... gain their respect... it will end her. This isn't a game, Conner. You can't just choose when to play it. It's every day. You can either stay by her side and support her for however long we have with her... or you need to let her go. She can't go into a Donnybrook... to the death... thinking about you."

As soon as Daniel left the room, Conner let out a long growl and pounded his good fist into the bed. He knew Daniel was right, but he hated it anyway. Running his hand through his hair, he took a deep sigh and then went to see Tennly.

She had changed out of the dress pants and blouse she had been wearing and into a pair of pajamas. He approached her from behind, as she sat at her vanity, brushing her hair, and wrapped his arms around her. "I'm sorry."

She placed her hands on his wrists and replied, "Me too."

"You don't have to apologize to me. I have no right to tell you what you can or cannot do when it comes to your family."

She turned around and stood up. "If I saw another way, I would have taken it, but there isn't. Keenan warned me when we spoke alone that the vultures are already beginning to circle. Look at me, Conner..." She let go of him and held out her arms so he could get a good look. "When they see me... all they see is a small little girl. If I don't make a name for myself right now... If I don't show them that I am a boss... strong... smart... fearless... merciless... they will not hesitate to try and take not only my title but overtake my family. I can't let that happen."

"I know," he responded, giving her a hug. "I don't like it... but... I get it. It's sort of like that on the streets. Respect... if you have it... for the most part you are left alone."

She smiled and assured, "He's fat and slow. I will beat him."

"I have no doubt."

"So, then let's go make a name for myself."

There were more people in attendance than during her first Donnybrook. The choir seats were filled, forcing some to sit on the steps or stand on the stage. Word had spread that she was fighting, and everyone who could make it had shown up. Although it was a bit overwhelming to realize that so many people had come just for her, it filled her with confidence rather than making her nervous.

As soon as Mikey and his group entered the church, they stopped beside Tennly in an attempt to intimidate her before settling to watch the fight.

She remained silent and focused as Mikey whispered, "You still have time to change your mind."

She laughed but said nothing, aware that engaging in a verbal fight with him would be pointless. He was clearly trying to get into her head, and it was evident that he was scared. She was on the brink of making her mark in front of everyone in the organization, so all she wanted to do was get it over with. The waiting was the hardest part, but she used that time to observe her surroundings, locating anything that could help her win. Once Keenan instructed them to separate into opposite sides of the church, she found a better vantage point. As she looked up and down every row between the pews, the best plan came to her; all she had to do was wait for Keenan to give the signal to begin.

As soon as she heard Keenan yell, "Dul," she dashed between two rows of pews toward Mikey. When she was just a few feet away from him, she jumped over the back of a pew as if she were fleeing. She ran down the row with Mikey in hot pursuit.

The moment she reached the end of the pew, she quickly darted into the next row. At first glance, it appeared as though she was scared and trying to evade him. However, after her fourth run down a row, it became clear to everyone watching what her strategy was.

"She's wearing him out," Duncan whispered with a smile on his face.

Although Mikey was overweight and out of shape, he was still bigger and stronger than she was. As a boss, he had received training, so she knew he could easily overpower her if placed in the right situation. She realized that the best strategy to defeat him was to tire him out first. Once that was accomplished, she would be able to launch her attack.

She made her way to the front of the church, stopping at the front row right before the stage. Pausing for a moment, pretending to be out of breath. When he came within three feet of her, she jumped onto the pew seat, pulled a ribbon from her hair, and wrapped it around his neck.

She then jumped behind the pew, while simultaneously she slammed his head against the back of the seat. The petrified wood shattered as he let out a loud scream. She didn't want to give him any opportunity to fight her off, so she slammed his head again. As his body went limp, he reached up to his neck to try and release the ribbon, but he was unable to make any progress due to her pulling with her whole body.

She sat down on the pew behind him and pulled his head back, cutting off his circulation. However, he managed to gather enough strength to stand up, which took away her leverage. He took a step forward, gasping for air, as she held tightly to the ribbon and was pulled off the seat onto the back of the pew. Realizing that she needed to act quickly, or he would turn around and gain the advantage, she let go, causing him to fall to the ground due to his momentum.

She jumped the pew, ran over to him as he was on his hands and knees and kicked him across the face, causing him to fall back down. However, when she went to kick him again, he grabbed her foot and pulled. She fell on her back, knocking the breath out of her.

As she scooted away from him, she noticed a long shard of glass a few feet directly behind him. She performed a kip-up to get back on her feet and ran toward him as if she were about to attack. Instead, as he attempted to hit her, she slid onto the floor, grabbed the glass, and then jumped back up to her feet. His swing caused him to rotate just right, to the point where she was able to get her arm around his neck and place the sharp end of the glass into the left side of his throat. She pushed the glass in just deep enough to scare him into not moving, for fear that if he did it would cut his artery. She felt him slowly raise his arms as if to swat them away.

"I wouldn't," she warned as she twisted the glass in a little further. "Walk." She commanded as she pushed him toward the stage.

As they approached the front row of men seated in the choir section, she came to a halt just a few feet away. For a few seconds, she remained silent, scanning the faces of each man. Trying to steady her breathing, she realized that all the men were wide-eyed and filled with anticipation.

"I know many of you don't like the fact that I'll be a boss," she addressed, anger coming through her tone. "And to be honest... I don't give a fuck!" She leaned down to make sure that Mikey knew she was talking to him, as sighs of disbelief could be heard throughout. "You tried to kill me twice... You won't get a third." Without warning, she forcefully jammed the glass into his throat and then immediately sliced it across the front of his neck.

Blood sprayed in every direction, drenching the front of her. She dropped Mikey's lifeless body onto the floor, keeping her eyes fixed on the men on the stage. As she surveyed the faces in the crowd again, she noticed a range of emotions. Some looked shocked, while others appeared relieved or even proud. Regardless of their feelings, one thing was clear: they were all impressed by her ability to accomplish what she had just done.

Keenan nodded at her to express his approval, and she nodded back to show that she understood. He then said, "Traditions guide us and keep us in line. However, we sometimes encounter traditions that are so outdated they become a hindrance. The unspoken rule against allowing women to be leaders is one such tradition. I understand that this change is new and may be frightening for all of us. But I would hate to think that our pride would prevent us from progressing and potentially missing out on something great.

"With that said, a formal Ceilidh will be held at the O'Ceallaigh Estate. Tonight, we will grieve our losses and remember their contributions; we will celebrate our victories, and we will move forward into the future!"

Conner entered Tennly's bedroom wearing a simple yet elegant black tuxedo. The outfit consisted of black pants, a collarless black silk dress shirt, a jacket with silk black lapels, and flat black dress shoes. He sat on the edge of her bed and asked what the name of the party was that they were about to attend as she finished with the final touches of her appearance.

"Wow!" she exclaimed as she turned to look at him. "Rich looks good on you."

"Well, don't get used to it."

She smiled and said, "It's a Ceilidh," pronouncing it like cay-lee. "It's an old Gaelic word basically meaning a large gathering... or formal party." She tied off the last braid and then stood and asked, "How do I look?"

To honor her Irish roots, she wore a long, floor-length, princess-cut designer gown in rich forest green. The gown featured intricate lace that accentuated her shoulders and extended down the first half of the bodice. Attached to the shoulders was a built-in capelet that wrapped around her arms and flowed to the floor behind her. The outside of the capelet matched the dress in color, while the inside showcased an Irish-inspired plaid of green, blue, and gold. Her shoes complemented the gown perfectly; they were designer forest green high-heeled pumps adorned with the same plaid pattern on the soles.

She decided to style her hair like a female Irish warrior. On either side, she wore two cornrow braids, each threaded with green ribbon. The lower braid was smaller, about half an inch thick, while the thicker braid above it measured a full inch. Atop her head, she had one large, puffy French braid that cascaded down the back and merged with the four braids on the sides. The hair beneath the five braids was left loose in messy waves that flowed down to her waist.

She didn't stop at her hairstyle; she wanted her makeup to reflect the essence of an Irish warrior as well. Her eyes were styled with a dark shadow, creating a smoky eye effect. Along the bridge of her nose, she drew a thin black line that stretched from one side to the other, finished with tiny arrows at each end. Her lips were adorned with light pink lipstick, highlighted by a dark burgundy line that was a centimeter wide down the center of her lower lip, extending onto her chin. In the middle of her forehead, she etched an old Irish bind rune symbol for strength, which took the form of a one-inch line straight down with a small 'X' in the center.

"You're gorgeous," he said, mesmerized by her beauty, then teasingly added, "Slightly terrifying..."

She smiled and said, "Good."

Tennly wasn't the only one in an old Irish-inspired outfit. Several women wore similar gowns in plaid or gold, while many men donned traditional saffron kilts paired with Irish jackets. Even Daniel sported a black and tan plaid flat cap that complemented his tuxedo vest.

Before entering the ballroom, they could hear music from an Irish quintet playing in the far-right corner. The walls were adorned in various shades of blue and ivory, accented by large windows draped with blue sheer curtains from ceiling to floor. The ceiling was a light gold, except for a twenty-by-twenty-foot mural in the center depicting the Battle of Aughrim in 1691.

The battle is considered one of the bloodiest in Irish history, with estimates of casualties ranging from 6,000 to 9,000 people. It was fought primarily between the Jacobite Army, loyal to King James II, and those supporting William III. The Jacobites fought for the English King, while the five original clans seeking Irish independence and going against the sixth and seventh clans sided with William III. These clans played a crucial behind-the-scenes role, helping William III achieve victory at the Battle of Aughrim.

Inside the ballroom, fifteen round tables, each seating eight people, were spaced adequately apart. Each table was adorned with an ivory tablecloth and featured a six-foot-tall floral arrangement as a centerpiece, along with place settings at each chair. The walls were lined with high-back, intricately carved wooden chairs upholstered in gold, paired with matching wooden side tables that held lamps.

The floor was made of ivory and gold marble, accented by three large Persian rugs placed four feet apart. On one side of the room, adjacent to the band, was a small dance floor measuring twenty by fifteen feet, where four couples were already dancing slowly to the music.

Before they could reach their destination, they were stopped by Thomas Lawlor. He was dressed in the formal attire of their Celtic ancestors, wearing an azure blue tunic cinched with a brown leather belt, a brown cloak fastened at his left shoulder with a brooch displaying his family coat of arms, and a pair of brown trousers. Unlike the other men who wore more modernized kilts, Thomas and the other five original family leaders opted for the trousers that were typical in earlier centuries.

Thomas Lawlor extended his hand toward Daniel and said, "I want to be the first to congratulate you on raising such an astonishing young woman."

"Thank you," Daniel replied. "I wish I could take the credit, but she's just like her mother."

"I would agree," Thomas Lawlor said, then turned to Tennly. "I knew your mother, and I see her in you. You've done well.

But remember this: don't ever become complacent. Stand guard, for the wolves will come." He kissed the back of her hand and then walked away.

Thomas Lawlor wasn't the only one who approached Tennly that evening. Before she reached Duncan's table, three more people came up to her, and several more approached throughout the night. They all wanted to either congratulate her or meet the girl who had won two Donnybrooks, including taking down a boss. By the end of the night, Tennly felt as if she had been caught in a whirlwind and was eager to return to her estate. While she enjoyed mingling with the elite and spending time with Duncan and Keenan, as well as getting to know the heads of the original clans, she had reached her limit. All she wanted was a good night's rest and to get back to Marinsburg.

As the evening ended, Tennly said goodbye to everyone and informed her father that she and Conner were going to meet him in the car. Daniel was engaged in conversation with Seamus and a few other relatives of his wife's and told Tennly he would be there shortly. As they made their way through the ballroom, she was taken by surprise when Mitchell MacFadden confronted them.

"I loved my father," Mitchell said, sadness in his voice. "But he wasn't a good man. When your grandfather died and he realized that your father would be the interim leader until you were old enough, he became furious. He called the other two families together, hoping to turn them against you. It didn't work... I didn't want to fight... neither did Petey... and we both thank you for sparing our lives."

"Whose idea was it to plant the knife?" Tennly asked, sternly but with slight compassion.

"My father told us where it was and said that if, by some slim chance, you were winning, whoever could get to it should use it to protect our family's pride. The thought of a girl beating his son was something he couldn't fathom; something he didn't let me live down."

"Do you expect me to feel sorry for you?" she asked.

"No, I don't expect you to feel sorry for me, but..." Mitchell lifted his bangs on the right side and showed her an inch-long scar. "He beat me as soon as we got home for embarrassing him." He chuckled slightly as he added, "I was still healing from the wound you gave me." Then his expression turned somber as he continued,

"When my mom tried to stop him, he beat her too."

Tennly reflected on how the women had been treated within the families, recalling what Mitchell's mother had told her after her first Donnybrook. The entire experience stirred something within her; despite Keenan advising her not to make any major changes right from the start, she felt a strong urge to take action to support the women.

"Is your mother here?" Tennly asked. "I didn't see her."

"No," Mitchell replied. "We didn't know there was going to be a Donnybrook, so I had to call her this afternoon."

"I would like to speak with her," Tennly requested. "Can you arrange that?"

"Yeah," Mitchell confirmed.

Tennly nodded and said, "Then set it up."

Mitchell nodded in agreement and then said, "I will. I'm truly sorry for what my father tried to do to you."

"Thank you," Tennly replied. "And I'm sorry for your loss."

"Tennly," Mitchell said, stopping her from walking away. "I wanted to let you know that my family, and those loyal to us, won't be a problem for you." He smiled and added, "Truth be told, I never wanted to be in this business. So, in a roundabout way, thank you."

CHAPTER 15

Transitioning from the thrill of the underworld to the routines of ordinary teenage life was the hardest part of Tennly and Conner's days. In class, Tennly often drifted into thoughts of what it would mean to lead her family, while Conner quietly mapped out ways to sharpen her training and keep her strong.

Teachers had to call Tennly back to attention more than once, a reminder that unless they found a way to balance both worlds, she would never truly adjust. After only a few days back at school, the two decided that inviting their friends over the following weekend might help ease the transition.

Josie and Abby were the first to arrive at the mansion, greeted at the door by Marie, who directed them to the game room where Tennly and Conner waited. A short while later, Dougy and Rick showed up. Conner hadn't seen much of his brother outside of a few hurried conversations at lunch, so when Dougy stepped into the room, he immediately rose from where he had been sitting with the girls and crossed the space to meet him.

"Hey," Conner said as they watched Rick sit down with the girls.

"Hey," Dougy replied.

"I'm glad you came," Conner continued.

"Thanks."

"How have you been?"

"Good. And you?"

"Good."

The brothers had never had trouble talking to each other, but ever since Conner moved in with Tennly, their conversations felt different. Conner wasn't sure if it was because they didn't have as much time together or if it was guilt over leaving Dougy with their father.

"Is Dad still... I mean, he isn't..." Conner started.

"No," Dougy answered. "He leaves me alone. Where have you guys been?"

"Living with the wealthy is definitely different," Conner replied, trying to think of a lie that was partly true. "It seems like every other month, some relative from another state or country has something going on that we have to fly out to."

"Sounds terrible," Dougy said sarcastically, but with a smile.

Conner put his arm around hi, gave him a gentle squeeze, and then led him over to the sitting area where the others were gathered. Although hugging wasn't something the boys typically did, Dougy found comfort in the embrace. He appreciated the new side of Conner, even if it felt strange after seeing him behave differently for the past three years. Dougy took a seat, hoping that this newfound closeness signaled the start of the bond he had longed for with his brother ever since their mother left.

About ten minutes later, Lucy arrived, followed quickly by Tina. Conner's three friends had barely settled in when Marie wheeled in a cart of catered food from an O'Brien-owned restaurant—mini beef tourtières, pork skewers, bruschetta, pot stickers, shrimp skewers, pâtés with crackers, and an array of desserts from beignet bites to baklava tartlets.

Everyone lined up, filling plates while Tennly took drink orders from the mocktail-and-soda menu.

"One thing's for sure," Sam said, biting into a tourtière. "You rich people have the best food."

Laughter followed as they moved to the sitting area. Tennly was pleased to see how easily her and Conner's friends were getting along. It was so different from the tense New Year's Eve gathering. However, there was one relationship that caught her attention the most; Sam and Tina were sitting unusually close. At first, she brushed it off as Sam's usual playboy behavior, but when he finished the last bite off Tina's plate, then offered her his hand and led her back to the bar for more food, Tennly realized she wasn't imagining things.

"Okay," Tennly said, motioning toward Sam and Tina. "How long has that been going on?"

Everyone turned to look at Sam and Tina before glancing back at Tennly. They had debated how to tell Tennly and Conner about Sam and Tina, uncertain of how they would react.

"Since New Year's," Josie answered.

"Why didn't anyone tell me?" Tennly asked.

"We didn't find out until around Valentine's Day," Josie explained.

"By then, we hadn't seen much of you," Abby added.

Tennly felt a surge of protectiveness for her friend. She cared for Sam but was aware of his reputation and how he viewed most women. She couldn't shake the feeling that he might end up hurting Tina. However, at the same time, she felt happy for them and somewhat hypocritical. Conner shared similar feelings. He didn't know Tina well, so he was indifferent to the potential for Sam to hurt her. His primary concern was how it would affect his relationship with Tennly if that happened. He wanted to avoid any negative feelings between his friends and his girlfriend. Still, he had never seen Sam so happy with a girl as he appeared to be with Tina, and he couldn't help but feel glad for him.

"How did this happen?" Tennly asked, half concerned, half intrigued.

"She said Sam saw her walking down the street, upset about something," Josie answered.

"Sam asked if she was okay," Lucy added. "Then he offered her a ride."

"They ended up going out to dinner," Abby chimed in. "The rest is history."

Just as Abby finished speaking, Tina and Sam returned. Noticing the sudden quiet, Sam exchanged a glance with Tina, indicating that Tennly and Conner must have found out about them.

"A game of pool?" Sam asked, seeing the look on Conner's face that he wanted to talk.

"Yeah," Conner replied.

They made their way to the pool table and as Sam racked the balls into the triangle, Conner picked up a cue stick and positioned himself at the opposite end, ready to break.

"I like her," Sam stated as he removed the triangle.

"She's not really your type," Conner declared while applying chalk to his cue stick.

"She doesn't talk much," Sam responded, stepping aside for Conner to break.

"You like her because she doesn't talk a lot?" Conner asked after taking his first shot and walking around to line up his next one.

"It's a redeeming factor," Sam replied.

"I'll give you that," Conner said. "But she..."

"I like her," Sam insisted, giving Conner a serious look.

Conner let out a sigh and warned, "She's fragile, Sam. Not like the girls you're used to."

"I know," Sam acknowledged, even though Conner thought his tone was nonchalant.

"What if this doesn't end well?" Conner asked, wanting to believe his friend.

Hating the hypocrisy, Sam set his cue stick down on the pool table and stepped closer to Conner. With a puffed chest, he reminded him, "Not long ago, people thought the same about you and Tennly. You need to be careful. This money is changing you."

Conner narrowed the space between them in a confrontational manner and replied, "You need to watch your fucking mouth."

At that point, it became clear to everyone that what started as a friendly game of pool had escalated into a heated discussion. They all watched as Riley braced himself to intervene if necessary.

"Why?" Sam goaded, their faces inches apart. "Ask anyone. You've changed. You talk like them. You act like them. Hell, you even dress like them now."

As Riley saw Conner tighten his fist, he rushed over and positioned himself between the two boys. "Okay!" Riley yelled, holding his arms out to push them apart. "That's enough." Conner and Sam lowered their guard as the others let out huge sighs of relief. "We just miss you," Riley said, looking at Conner. Then he turned to Sam and added, "But we knew this day would come. You know that."

"What are you saying?" Conner asked, confused.

Riley lowered his arms and replied, "The three of us always knew you were different. That you would... someday... leave."

"That's not true," Conner protested.

Riley gave him a look that conveyed the truth of his statement. "You and I both know you are meant for something bigger than this town. Tennly... her family... is your way out." When Conner didn't respond, the room completely silent, Riley continued, "It's not a bad thing. You fit in here. That's why it was so easy for you to, as Sam said, dress like them and act like them. You were meant for this world."

Conner glanced over at his brother, silently asking if what Riley said was true, while at the same time his eyes portrayed that he hoped it wasn't. Dougy nodded in agreement, but instead of feeling reassured, Conner felt worse. He felt like he was betraying everything he knew and believed. He knew Riley was right, but he didn't want to confront it. In frustration, he slammed his fists down on the pool table and quickly walked out of the game room. Everyone exchanged uncertain looks, unsure of what to do next as Riley signaled to his friends that it was time to go.

Conner tended to sabotage difficult situations in order to avoid them, making it easier to move on or simply pretend they didn't exist at all. This was the first tactic he had employed in his relationship with Tennly, and she could see him applying the same approach with his friends. That's how she realized it was only a matter of time before keeping her family's secrets from Sam and Joel would inevitably end badly. Therefore, she knew she had to find a way to resolve the situation before it destroyed him.

"You, okay?" she asked as she walked inside Conner's bedroom.

He muted the television, sat up straight, and confessed, "They're not wrong. I have changed. I can feel it. And the scary thing is... I like the new me. I'm just afraid they won't understand. It feels like I'm two different people...

I've never kept anything from them, and it's killing me."

"You kept me from them for years," she smiled, trying to get him to see it was okay.

"And I was miserable. I was angry all the time. I can't keep lying to them. It's either going to kill our friendship or suffocate me."

"Then tell them."

Conner's face lit up with hope, but it quickly faded as he considered the possible consequences. "Your father will never allow it."

"My father isn't the boss."

"He is for another year and a half."

"He's never really been the boss, Conner. I finally realized that when we were in Ireland. He was just a placeholder. But if it makes you feel better, a respect thing between men, we can talk to him about it tomorrow."

Conner had always followed the unwritten rule among men regarding respect, but he had never felt it as strongly as he did after joining the Connolly family. Despite Tennly ranking higher than her father in terms of the family business, he was still her father and believed he deserved a deeper respect. So, he liked the idea of speaking with Daniel before letting his friends know about the Connollys.

They got up early the next morning to ensure they had time to talk with Daniel before he got busy and wouldn't want to be interrupted. They found him in the kitchen, seated at the breakfast nook. He was working on his laptop and sipping a cup of coffee when they approached and sat down across from him.

Marie came over before they began speaking, placed two mugs of coffee and a plate of sugar and cream in front of them, and then said, "I made a meat and cheese quiche if you two would like a slice."

"That would be great," Tennly replied. "Thank you."

"What's on your mind?" Daniel asked, closing his laptop as he looked at them.

"We need to talk to you about something," Tennly said as Marie set the plates of quiche in front of them and then exited the kitchen.

Tennly started to speak, but Conner stopped her by placing his hand on her arm and saying, "There's nothing I can do or say that will ever express how grateful I am for everything you've done for me. So, I don't want you to think that I'm ungrateful for what I'm about to say."

"Go ahead," Daniel said after Conner paused.

"Before I was welcomed into your family, I only had my friends. Other than Dougy, they were my family. They kept me grounded... out of trouble, as much as they could... we watched out for each other, kept each other safe. Since we've been traveling a lot lately, I feel a distance growing between us. I can tell Riley the truth, but most of the time I don't, because I know how hard it is for him to keep our secret from them as well."

"You want to tell Sam and Joel?" Daniel asked.

"I do," Conner replied.

"Absolutely not," Daniel insisted. "It's bad enough that Riley knows. It's just too much of a risk to tell anyone else."

"Dad," Tennly began to speak.

No," Conner interrupted her, feeling his heart sink to his stomach. "It's okay. Thanks anyway." Conner walked out of the kitchen, leaving Tennly staring angrily at her father.

"You knew this wasn't going to be easy," Daniel said once he was sure Conner was far enough away.

"Conner would never go against you out of respect, but that won't stop me from telling them..."

"Tenn..."

"No!" Tennly interrupted. "Over the last few years, you and I have had our ups and downs. I know a lot of that was due to Conner, but I can't help but think that some of it was your fear of me growing up and eventually taking on the biggest responsibility of my life. That must be incredibly difficult for you, knowing the dangers I will always face."

Daniel let out a relaxed sigh, feeling a sense of calm after hearing her understanding words, and with his eyes, he told her he was listening. "Conner never had unconditional love from a parent. Riley, Sam, and Joel became his family. Tonight, he and Sam got into an argument. Sam told him he was changing and that he could feel the distance growing between them. If Conner can't share his life with them, we will lose him; maybe not physically, but emotionally. So, if you don't give him permission to tell them, I will go behind your back and do it anyway."

She took a deep breath as she completed her thoughts. "I've heard their relationship described like this: the four of them are like one person. They move as one, make decisions as one, and feel as one. When something is wrong with one of them, the others can sense it. It's only a matter of time before they figure it out or start questioning. At least if we tell them, we can control the situation. So, I'm begging you... and you know I don't technically need your permission... please... please let him tell them."

Daniel ran his hand over his mouth as he thought about what she said and then took a drink before saying, "I'll talk with him and make my decision. If the decision is to let them know, you will be responsible for them and everything they do. They aren't known for making the best choices. Things can turn bad really quickly if they're not careful."

Tennly agreed and then watched as he walked out of the kitchen, hoping she had made the right choice. When Daniel entered Conner's room, he found him sitting on his bed, staring at a blank television screen. As Conner saw Daniel standing at the door, he felt his face flush with embarrassment and his chest tighten in fear of why Daniel was there. He watched Daniel walk through the room and sit down in a chair, wishing he could crawl under the bed to escape the situation.

"You trust these boys?" Daniel asked.

"With my life," Conner answered, hope evident in his voice.

"You've already put one friend at risk. Are you prepared to do the same thing to the other two?"

"I don't see it as a risk."

"Then enlighten me."

"We're better together. We always have been. When one of us is at our worst, the rest of us step in to pull them back up."

"Okay," Daniel nodded. "But before you tell them, you need to make sure they understand how risky and dangerous what you're about to share is. If they agree, bring them to me immediately. Understood?"

"Understood." Conner spun around, excited, placed his feet on the floor, and said, "Thank you."

"I'm trusting you, Conner."

"I know."

Conner waited until Daniel left before he called Riley, hoping he could bring Sam and Joel to the mansion. However, when he heard Sam yelling in the background that he didn't want to talk to him, Conner insisted that Riley keep them at his house, stating that he would be there right away.

Not wanting to do it by himself, he grabbed Tennly along the way. When they arrived at Riley's, the boys were sitting in the living room, covered with blankets, having spent the night there. Sam huffed and shot Conner a nasty glare, but didn't move as he waited for him to speak.

"You're right," Conner said, causing Sam to lower his defense. "I have changed. And I'm sorry. But it's not just because of living with Tennly. I've been keeping a huge secret from you, but I had no choice... it wasn't mine to tell. So, it was easier for me to stay away from you... to avoid your questions about where we've been... what we've been doing. I was just given permission to tell you, but before I do, I have to warn you that this secret is a matter of life and death. Once you know, your life will never be the same, and you could possibly be in continuous danger."

"Well," Sam said with a jovial smile, "how can I say no to that?"

"I'm serious, Sam," Conner warned. "There will be no more shenanigans or breaking rules. If the police catch you doing anything illegal, your life may be over. You will have to constantly monitor your behavior."

"Will that fix the distance that's starting to form between you two?" Joel asked.

"I hope so," Conner answered.

"Then I'm in," Joel said, frustrated over the whole situation.

"Yeah," Sam agreed. "Me too. Whatever you're into, we're into... remember?"

Once they felt they had explained everything to the boys, Conner mentioned that they had one more thing to do: meet with Daniel. Tennly was surprised when Conner revealed her father's request, as he was never one for meeting with teenagers, let alone discussing family business, and felt nervous about what he might tell them.

"Come on in," Daniel gestured. "Take a seat. I'm just ordering some supplies for the restaurants. Tennly, can you get them a drink?"

Riley, Sam, and Joel sat side by side on the couch closest to the window, while Conner took a chair facing Daniel's desk. Tennly poured five rocks glasses of whiskey, arranged them on a tray, and carried it over to the boys, handing each one a glass, and then sat down on the chair opposite them.

The boys glanced at their glasses, surprised that she had given them alcohol. Unsure whether to drink it, they exchanged looks with Conner, silently asking if it was okay.

"It's not a test," Conner reassured them.

Daniel overheard the conversation and found their fear amusing. He chuckled to himself, picked up his glass of whiskey, and walked over, settling into the adjacent to Conner.

"Since you're here, I'm assuming you've been informed about our family's secret and agree to the terms."

"Yes," Sam and Joel replied simultaneously.

"Did Conner also mention that I was against this?" Daniel asked.

"Yes," Sam answered.

"Then," Daniel said, trying to sound as menacing as possible, successfully achieving his goal. "Reassure me that this wasn't a mistake."

Sam and Joel exchanged glances, trying to determine who would respond. Sam noticed Joel's legs bouncing, realizing he likely wouldn't be able to speak. Sam shot him a look that conveyed he owed him before turning back to Daniel.

"I don't think there's anything we can say that will reassure you," Sam said. "Only time will tell. But I can assure you this: we're as close as anyone can be. Conner is not just my friend; he's my brother, closer than any family I've ever had. There's no way we would ever betray each other. We would die first."

Daniel clasped his hands together, feeling a sense of déjà vu as Sam's response mirrored what Conner had said when he questioned why he should allow him to date his daughter. The fact that they reacted in the same way made Tennly's comment about them thinking as one seem more understandable, and it was reassuring.

However, wanting to stay terrifying in order to emphasize the seriousness of the situation, he cautioned, "In this business, you might just have to do that."

"Dad," Tennly interjected.

"They need to understand what they're getting into," Daniel persisted.

"They're aware," Conner responded.

"Okay," Daniel conceded, and then hit them with something they weren't expecting. "As long as you remain our employees, you will be on retainer, which means you will receive $2,000 a month, being on call for whatever we need, day or night. In addition to the monthly salary, if you undertake specific jobs, you will receive additional payment."

Daniel noticed the astonishment on Sam and Joel's faces; it looked like their eyeballs were about to pop out of their heads. Ignoring their visible shock, he continued explaining what he had shared with Conner and Riley regarding how to manage the money they receive.

"Use your common sense," Daniel instructed. "And if I ever feel you're getting out of control, I'll revoke your finances and privileges. Is that understood?"

"Yes," they responded in unison.

"Good," Daniel said. Then he stood up and added, "One more thing. Follow me."

He walked out of the office, with Tennly and the boys trailing behind him, curious about where he was taking them and what he planned to do. They eventually arrived at the gym, and as he walked inside, Conner and Tennly exchanged puzzled looks.

She hadn't seen her father in a gym since before she became a teenager; as far as she was concerned, he never worked out. This made his presence there quite confusing for her.

They followed Daniel to the boxing ring and watched as he hopped inside the ropes. "Which one of you three is the strongest?"

"Me," Sam said as Riley and Joel pointed at him.

"Get in," Daniel ordered.

Sam looked at Conner, questioning what to do next. Conner nodded, encouraging him to proceed with the task. Taking a deep breath, Sam jumped into the ring. Although Tennly, Conner, and Riley had an idea of what Daniel was planning, they still felt uncertain and were anxious to see what would happen next.

"Take me down," Daniel asked.

"What?" Sam responded, not believing what he heard.

"You're young and strong," Daniel said smiling. "I'm much older than you. Surely you can take me down."

"Um," Sam faltered as he just stood there, a little leery of hitting a mob boss.

Without warning, Daniel sucker-punched Sam on the left side of the face.

"Shit!" Sam shouted after he stumbled back and held his hand up to his cheek. "Okay, old man."

That was all it took for Sam to go all out against Daniel. He swung twice but missed both times due to Daniel's evasive dodging. Then, Daniel countered by kicking Sam in the back, causing him to stumble again. However, Sam managed to regain his balance and ducked just in time when Daniel swung at him, avoiding the hit.

The missed punch threw Daniel off balance, giving Sam the opportunity to land a punch in Daniel's stomach, followed by a strike to his face. But just as Sam got too cocky and attempted to hit him again, Daniel quickly maneuvered behind him and wrapped his arm around his neck. Squeezing tightly until Sam tapped out, Daniel let go, causing Sam to drop to the floor, taking deep breaths and wondering what the purpose of the exercise had been.

Daniel reached down and offered his hand to Sam, helping him up. After giving Sam a pat on the shoulder, he gestured for Sam to leave the ring and called out, "Conner," motioning for him to step in.

As soon as Conner entered the ring, Daniel instructed, "Take me down."

The fight between Daniel and Conner was longer and more engaging than Daniel's bout with Sam. Conner had the advantage of months of training that Sam hadn't had, but Daniel still emerged victorious. Tennly was in awe at watching her father fight. He moved with the agility of a twenty-year-old, and it filled her with pride.

They both unleashed their full training and went at it with intensity. In the end, Daniel ended up with a busted lip and a black eye, while Conner had a bloody nose and several bruises on his stomach and sides. Conner would have continued, but Daniel managed to get him down on his stomach and held his arm back to the point of breaking. Conner tapped out when he realized Daniel wasn't going to relent.

Riley had watched Conner and Tennly fight before, so he wasn't surprised to see that their fights were real and not staged. However, Sam and Joel were completely shocked. As Conner stood up, wiped the blood from his nose, and slung it on the floor, he looked at his friends. In that moment, they realized how serious the predicament they had gotten themselves into really was.

Daniel glanced at the boys and asked, "Why could I beat both of you?"

"You're stronger," Sam replied.

"Hm," Daniel hesitated. "Tennly... get in."

Sam and Joel exchanged worried looks, uncertain about what Daniel had in mind for her. They couldn't believe he would allow her to fight, especially after he had been so adamant about keeping her safe. They had seen her fight another girl before and knew she was tough and skilled, but she was still a girl.

Daniel climbed out of the ring and told Tennly and Conner to fight. Tennly began to dance around the ring, skillfully maneuvering to avoid every swing that Conner attempted. After Conner missed five times, he finally landed a punch in the stomach, causing her to bend over in pain.

Sam and Joel gasped loudly enough for Daniel and Riley to hear them. They couldn't believe that Conner would actually punch her that hard; moreover, they were shocked that Daniel not only allowed it but also instigated it. While Tennly was bent over, Conner wrapped his arms around her chest, trying to lift her to throw her down on the floor. However, she wrapped her legs around his waist and squeezed. With her hand on the floor, she gained enough leverage to pull her right leg back and kick him in the chest, causing him to release her and stumble backward.

"Nice," Conner chuckled, smiling at her.

"Thank you. If you liked that, then you'll love this."

She ran toward him, but instead of throwing a punch at his stomach or face, she tackled him. He wrapped his arms around her waist as she pushed him into the ropes. Climbing up on the bottom rope, she used its elasticity to knee him in the chest and then immediately in the mouth. Blood spattered down Conner's chin and onto the floor. As he stood up. Daniel stopped the fight by shouting, "Enough!"

Daniel realized that without using Tennly's knives, Conner would eventually win the fight. He didn't want anyone to get seriously hurt; he was just trying to prove a point. He looked at the boys and asked, "Why was Tennly able to do so well? She's not stronger or bigger."

"It doesn't matter," Sam replied. "If you hadn't stopped it, she would have lost. And if it were a real fight, the guy wouldn't have gone easy on her."

"Really?" Daniel asked. "Then get in the ring."

"What?" Sam said, unsure of what Daniel was suggesting.

"Get... in... the... ring," Daniel repeated, emphasizing each word.

As Sam was climbing in, Daniel told Conner to step out of the ring and then looked at Sam, saying, "Take her down."

Sam glanced at Tennly, who said, "Don't take it easy on me." Then he looked at Conner, as if to ask for approval to fight her. Conner nodded, and then, still hesitant, Sam turned back to Tennly.

"Alright," Sam said, and then took the first swing.

Tennly anticipated the throw and was able to block it with her right arm. Then she blocked the second, but when he threw the third, she grabbed his arm and twisted it behind his back. He used the weight of his upper body to break free from her, causing her to stumble enough for him to punch her across the left side of the face. He hit her again on the other side, which was exactly what she hoped he would do. It gave him enough confidence to think that he had her. So, when he went to punch her again, she turned around and rammed her back into his chest.

Again, thinking he had her where he wanted her, he put his arms around her and squeezed. When she realized she had him convinced that she was about to tap out, she brought her arms back and wrapped them around his head. Then, she lifted her legs and suddenly fell to the floor, taking him down with her.

She rolled out of the way and then did a quick kip up onto her feet, immediately kicking him on the side of the stomach. When she went to kick him a second time, he grabbed her foot and pulled her back to the floor as she kicked him on the right cheek, allowing her to be able to get away. She managed to get up and quickly ran back to the corner of the ropes, climbing up to the top. Then, she jumped, executing a front flip over his head and landing skillfully behind him. He was so amazed by her maneuvering that he didn't notice she was behind him until she had a knife to his throat.

"Sh," she warned. "I wouldn't move if I were you."

"Holy shit!" Sam exclaimed, raising his arms in surrender. "I give."

"That's enough," Daniel said.

Tennly lowered the knife and stepped away from Sam as he said, impressed, "That's sneaky."

"All is fair," Tennly replied, giving him a wink.

"Again," Daniel chimed in. "Why did Tennly win?"

"She had a freaking knife," Sam pointed out. "If I had a knife..."

"Oh my God," Riley interrupted. "Sam... just stop..."

"No," Daniel interjected. "He makes a valid point." He turned to Tennly and added, "Give him a knife."

"Dad," she questioned, unsure if she wanted to continue the game.

"Give... him... a knife," Daniel repeated firmly.

Reluctantly, she handed Sam the knife while the other boys watched, afraid of what might happen next. They all felt the situation was spiraling out of control but didn't dare question it.

"Take her down," Daniel instructed, giving Sam a pressured glare.

"But she doesn't have a knife now," Sam protested.

Tennly took a deep breath as she agreed with her father. "Go ahead, Sam. It's okay."

"I can't," Sam replied. "I won't."

"Tennly," Daniel warned, his tone serious.

"I'll do it," Conner offered.

"No," Daniel ordered. "Take her down, Sam."

Sam looked at Conner with a scared expression, silently asking for permission. Conner nodded and encouraged him, saying, "It's okay, just do it."

Taking a deep breath, Sam turned back to Tennly and then lunged toward her with the knife as if he were going to stab her in the left shoulder. She swatted it away with her left arm and then took a step back to give him another try.

"Again," Tennly instructed, as if she were training him. It was then that she realized what her father was trying to do. "If you go after a shoulder, you will lose."

Daniel grinned, pleased that his daughter had finally grasped his intentions. Upon seeing Daniel's reaction, Conner and Riley also began to understand. Joel, however, remained very confused as they all continued to watch.

Sam lunged toward her again, only going more toward her stomach. She jumped backwards out of the way and said, "It might seem easier to fight with a knife, but it's completely different. It is easier to anticipate the blows. You have to do something that the other person isn't going to expect."

"Distract them somehow," she continued as she walked slowly around, luring him into the far corner of the ring. Sam stood there, contemplating how to distract her. With a smile, he lunged at her with the knife, pretending to follow through as he had before. But when she slapped his arm away, he swiftly punched her in the face with his other fist. That allowed him to get behind her and place the knife up to her throat.

"I wouldn't move if I were you," he said repeating what she had said to him.

The only issue was that, due to her training, she knew exactly how to escape the situation. She slowly raised her arms, placing her hands flat on her chest, right beneath her neck. Then she quickly pushed her hands up in between her shoulders and his arms. At the same time, she reared her head back as hard as she could. The move caused him to drop the knife as he stumbled backward due to the hit he took in the chest.

She quickly reached down, picked up the knife, and threw it toward Sam, landing on the floor in between his feet.

"Jesus!" Sam screamed as he jumped back. He bent down and picked up the knife, but when he stood back up, he noticed that she had another knife in her hand. "Okay, Legolas," Sam teased, making a reference to 'Lord of the Rings', referring to how the elf never seemed to run out of arrows.

"Okay!" Daniel shouted. "Tennly, why didn't you hit his foot?"

"I wasn't going to actually hurt him," she answered calmly.

Daniel looked at Sam and explained, "You see Sam, Tennly could have killed you within seconds of the first fight. Can anyone tell me why?"

"She's trained," Conner stated.

"She's disciplined," Riley added. "And smart."

"Indeed," Daniel said. He then gestured for Sam to leave the ring as he went on, "Since she was five, Tennly has been training. She has had the best trainers money can buy: Olympians, government agents, spies, and anyone else needed. Being the first female boss will require her to be tough, so much so that she has been transformed into a weapon." He then turned to his daughter and said, "Cut the rope."

Tennly nodded and then threw the knife toward the boxing ring, landing it in the top rope and slicing it in half.

"Shit," Sam said, while Joel wasn't sure if he was impressed, scared, or both.

"If you're going to work for me, you need to be as prepared as I can make you. It's obvious you all are tough and good fighters, but street fighting is one thing... fighting trained assassins and soldiers is another. I will not have one of you killed on my watch. If you are to protect my daughter, I expect you to be at your peak fighting abilities. You will train every day until instructed otherwise. If you miss a single day without a legitimate reason, you will no longer be an employee of this family."

CHAPTER 16

The next day, as soon as they entered the gym, Tennly immediately spotted Duncan near the boxing ring. She let out a scream and ran towards him, giving him a big embrace. "Donut. What are you doing here?"

"I happened to be in the States when your father called asking for help," Duncan explained.

As Tennly introduced the guys to Duncan, Daniel interjected, "Okay, okay... Enough with the formalities. I called Duncan to help you all get started on your training. Listen to him and do everything he tells you to do. And... dinner is at 6:00 PM. Plan on staying; Marie made enough for everyone and is insisting."

With that, Daniel walked away, and Tennly whispered to the boys, "You think my dad is scary? Just wait."

Sam and Joel's faces turned white as they hoped her teasing smile was telling them she was kidding. Conner's laughter eased their worries a little, but they still anxiously awaited to hear what Duncan had planned for them. The first thing he had the boys do was take turns sparring with each other. He wanted to assess how they fought and identify their strengths and weaknesses.

On the second day of Duncan's visit, he analyzed what they had learned the day before, discussing how they could use this knowledge to become better fighters. And for the third day, he outlined a daily routine for them to follow every day until his return in two weeks.

By the time the two weeks were over, the five of them had become like a well-oiled machine. When they fought together, they had learned to predict each other's actions in any situation. They surpassed all of Duncan's expectations, and he had never seen a group so closely aligned.

"Their training is complete," Duncan said to Daniel as they sat in Daniel's office. "There's nothing more I can teach them."

"What do you think?" Daniel asked.

"I've never seen anything like it," Duncan replied. "It's as if someone has choreographed their fighting style."

"Is that a bad thing?"

"As long as they fight together and not against each other, it's the best scenario. It's truly amazing and a bit scary... like they share a brain."

"The way Tennly talks about them, it seems like they do," Daniel noted.

Duncan pondered this, a smile spreading across his face as he considered whether Tennly had planned it that way.

"What?" Daniel asked.

"They move like her," Duncan answered. "They think like her. They care about her... but most importantly, they listen to her."

"All employees listen to their boss," Daniel pointed out.

"Most do so out of fear, which carries its own risks. But with Conner and the boys, they love her. They are her. Opposing her would be like opposing themselves. I genuinely believe they would die for her."

If Duncan believed that Conner and his friends were the ideal employees to protect Tennly, then he was going to give them the opportunity to prove it.

Their first assignment began when Tennly received a call to meet with Mrs. MacFadden in New York. Daniel suggested using their family restaurant, The Buzzin' Fella, as the meeting place. Since it didn't open until noon, Tennly had ample time to discuss matters with Mrs. MacFadden before the employees arrived. However, for her safety, Tennly decided to have Mrs. MacFadden go to a nearby coffee shop first. She wanted to ensure that no one was following her and that she hadn't reported anything to the police. Therefore, while she and Sam stayed at The Buzzin' Fella Conner, Riley, and Joel went to meet Mrs. MacFadden.

When they arrived at the coffee shop. Joel got a coffee and went back outside to sit, while Conner and Riley walked around to ensure everything looked safe. Once satisfied, Conner approached the table where he saw Mrs. MacFadden sitting as Riley stood behind him.

She was an attractive woman in her late fifties with straight gray hair, brown eyes, and a pink designer skirt suit. Polished and professional, she wore diamond hoop earrings, gold bangles, and left red lipstick on her coffee cup.

"Mrs. MacFadden?" Conner asked after he sat down across from her.

"Yes?" she replied, placing her coffee cup down.

"I work for the Connollys," Conner stated.

"I know," she answered. "I recognize you from Ireland. Where's Tennly?"

"If you agree to our terms," Conner replied, "I'll take you to her."

Mrs. MacFadden nodded, clearly understanding how things worked in this business. Conner took her phone and placed it in a Faraday Bag to ensure it couldn't be traced or used for recording. He then asked her if she was being followed or if she had told anyone about their meeting. She admitted that Mitchell knew, but no one else did. After that, he went over all the rules she needed to follow during the meeting, including handing over her gun, which she said she carried in her purse.

When he felt that everything was safe, he instructed her to follow them.

Once inside The Buzzin' Fella, Riley handed the purse to Joel and then began patting Mrs. MacFadden down for any hidden weapons. Before he had the chance to do much, they heard Tennly say, "That's enough," as she approached them.

"Ten…" Conner said, a concerned look on his face.

"It's okay," she reassured him. She held out her hand toward the seat opposite the one she had been in and asked, "Would you like something to drink?"

"Water would be fine," Mrs. MacFadden replied.

Tennly nodded to Sam, who was standing behind the bar, signaling him to get a couple of glasses of water.

"Thank you for meeting with me," Tennly said. "I know I don't deserve it, so I'll get to the point. I understand that when a patriarch is demoted, for lack of a better word, his income is significantly reduced. If he is killed due to betrayal, the family no longer receives any of his income. As you know, your family is merging with the O'Gradys, which would have meant a demotion under normal circumstances.

However, that was never going to happen."

"I know my family," Tennly continued as Sam placed two glasses of water on the table. "They were never going to let your husband live. He expressed his opinions and blatant disobedience; he could never be trusted. We cannot have that in this line of business. But I have studied everything I can about the laws and traditions we follow. I've read and re-read every book I could find to ensure I understand everything before taking over, which is why I wanted to speak with you."

"If a patriarch is killed in a Donnybrook," Tennly explained, "it is considered honorable, and therefore the family retains the income. I could have done nothing and let him be killed, branding him a traitor, which would mean your family would lose everything. Alternatively, I chose to fight him, risking my life to save your livelihood."

Conner had no idea that this was the main reason Tennly chose to confront Mikey in the Donnybrook. It made sense why Keenan and Daniel were disgusted with Mikey when he begged not to have to fight. The realization that Tennly risked her life to ensure that another family wouldn't lose their income made him believe in her even more. The other boys shared this sentiment, impressed by how much a wealthy person could genuinely care for others.

"So," Tennly concluded, "while you will not be receiving what you have been accustomed to, you will still have an income from your merger with the O'Gradys and the honorable death of your husband. With that said, I am here to make you an offer: a way for you to supplement your income."

"Why would you trust me?" Mrs. MacFadden asked, surprised that Tennly would want her to work for her.

"Because the job I need you for requires your trust in me," Tennly replied. "I need a liaison between me and the women of the families; a person who can report any concerns, ideas, or suggestions that the women might have to improve their lives. I understand how women are treated in this business, and one of my primary goals is to change that. I refuse to keep women in the background, and I will not tolerate any abuse directed at women under my leadership. I don't expect you to answer now. Take..."

"I'll do it," Mrs. MacFadden interrupted. "Pardon me, I'm sorry, but yes, I'll do it. But not for the money. I love my son very much, but my daughter was raised to think her only duty was to her future husband and family. And we're not the only family like this."

"Thank you." Tennly gestured for Riley to come over to the table. When he arrived, he handed Mrs. MacFadden's phone back to her. "We've added a contact number on here," Tennly informed. "It's listed under gynecologist, but it's actually my phone number. Only call me, no texting, and only if it's an emergency or you have new information or concerns. I'll be back here sometime around St. Patrick's Day if you need anything."

As Riley walked Mrs. MacFadden to the front door, Conner sat down at the table; his heart was full of pride. "You never cease to amaze me. There's more to this women's thing than you let on, isn't there?"

"There's nothing more formidable than a group of women with a shared agenda," Tennly revealed.

Indeed, Tennly had a plan. She aimed to empower the women who had been overlooked or mistreated, demonstrating that they were valuable in the business. If everything went as she hoped, she would cultivate the most loyal and dedicated employees the family had ever seen.

When the Irish settled in large numbers in the United States, they brought with them their traditions and celebrations associated with St. Patrick's Day. These festivities were widely accepted, causing what was once a religious holiday in Ireland to transform into a secular celebration.

The first St. Patrick's Day parade in the New World was held in Boston in 1737, paving the way for celebrations across the country over the next three hundred years. Even though the Connollys participated in parades and other modern festivities, they never stopped viewing St. Patrick's Day as the Irish religious holiday their ancestors had originally created.

Every year the Connollys held a large gathering for all the families in the syndicate to celebrate their heritage. It took place on the Saturday closest to St. Patrick's Day, in a different hotel ballroom in Manhattan every year.

That year, Daniel invited Lexie and Riley to travel to New York with them, where they met up with Tara and her boyfriend, Joey. This was the first time Tennly had been in the same room with all the families from the United States since she had killed Mikey MacFadden. She understood that the eyes watching her that night were filled with a mix of fear, respect, admiration, or a combination of all three.

Halfway through the gathering, she received a message from Mrs. MacFadden, along with a hotel key card, informing her that she and some women were waiting in the pool room to see her. There were eight women sitting around a table at a balcony overlooking the pool: Among them were Fiona MacFadden and her daughter Gracie, and Katherine O'Grady.

Tennly couldn't help but notice that all the women looked and dressed like Mrs. MacFadden. They all wore matching suit dresses with jackets, flaunted plenty of jewelry, and carried similar handbags. It was as if the Irish-American mafia had a cookie-cutter recipe for how the wives were supposed to look and act. The only variation among them was their hair; despite similar styles, the lengths and colors differed.

As Tennly walked over to the table, she casually scanned the room, looking for any signs of an ambush and mentally noting anything she could potentially use as a weapon if needed. In addition to searching for weapons, she observed a woman and her toddler son swimming in the pool, along with two younger girls in the hot tub to her left. Tennly realized the reason they chose the balcony: it provided a clear view of who was entering the pool room, giving them ample time to exit before being seen.

When they reached the table, Katherine O'Grady stood and asked, "Fiona said we can trust you?"

"You can," Tennly replied.

"And that you will help us?" Katherine asked.

"I will," Tennly answered as Fiona MacFadden pulled up a chair and gestured for her to sit down. Tennly looked at Mrs. MacFadden with concern about the vulnerable position. "Thank you, but I'll stand," she said, gesturing for Mrs. MacFadden to sit instead.

"You're not trusting by nature, are you?" Katherine inquired.

"When you're in my position," Tennly answered, "you can't afford to be."

"We will not harm you," Katherine assured her.

"That remains to be seen," Tennly replied, taking one more look around the room.

"They just wanted to formally meet you, Tennly," Fiona assured. "They mean you no harm."

"It's okay, Fiona," Katherine said to Mrs. MacFadden. "She has every right to be cautious."

"Well," one of the women Tennly didn't know, interrupted as she stood up, "I have no time to wait for her to decide if we're worth helping. My husband will soon be wondering where we are."

"Sit," Tennly said firmly, yet with an undertone of compassion. When Caitlyn complied, Tennly asked, "Who are you?"

"My name is Caitlyn Sullivan. This is my daughter, Maeve."

"They work under us," Katherine added.

"You're afraid of your husband?" Tennly questioned, looking directly at Caitlyn.

"That's why we're here," Caitlyn informed. "I married my husband without knowing anything about his family or their business. I fell in love with him; he was so sweet and handsome. But as soon as we returned from our honeymoon, everything changed. He became distant. I thought it was just the stress of his job; he told me he was a stockbroker. Then I got pregnant, and after Maeve was born, things got worse. He became abusive, as if it were my fault we had a daughter instead of a son. When I threatened to leave, he finally revealed the truth about his family... Said he would have me killed if I left him and that he would take our daughter to use her however his family needed. So, I stayed. That was twenty-four years ago."

"My father," Maeve added, "has never treated me like a daughter. He ignores me and only uses me to threaten my mother. I tried to leave, but he found me and..."

"He brought her home," Caitlyn finished, tears forming in her eyes. "And beat her in front of me... Then beat me for not training her better. We live every

453

day in fear. So, when Fiona said that you were here to help, we had to meet you."

Tennly knew the situation was serious, but she had no idea just how severe until she heard Caitlyn's story. The anger she felt overpowered the heaviness in her heart, and she had to keep her legs from marching out to the ballroom and stabbing Mr. Sullivan in the face. Despite her feelings about it, she realized that she still needed to consider the organization as a whole.

"Why didn't you ever go to the police?" Tennly asked.

"He told me there are officers on the family's payroll," Caitlyn replied. "He said that if I ever went to the police, he would find out, and we would be killed. I didn't know how far your family's reach extended, so..."

"Pretty far," Tennly answered, warning them as well. "You were smart not to go to the police. If you had, we wouldn't be speaking right now. How serious are you about getting my help?"

"We can't do this anymore," Maeve replied, speaking for her mother.

"Are you prepared for any consequences?" Tennly queried. "You may not like what I do or the outcome."

"Are you going to kill him?" Maeve asked.

"Not if he heeds my advice," Tennly answered.

"We're ready," Caitlyn said.

"Good," Tennly replied as she pulled out her phone. She opened the memo app and slid it over to Caitlyn. "Type in your address."

"Leave your front door open tonight," Tennly instructed after getting her phone back. "Make sure all systems are shut down: alarm, video, everything."

Caitlyn nodded.

Tennly then looked at all the women and said, "I will do everything in my power to keep you safe. But remember, my main job is to protect the entire family and keep it secret. So, I need you to trust me and come to me. Please do not go to the police... I would hate to have to do something I really don't want to do."

While they waited for everyone in Jimmy's mansion to fall asleep, Tennly, Conner, and Riley changed out of their formal attire and into black pants and black shirts. Once the coast was clear, they made their way to the guest room where Daniel and Lexie were staying. Tennly knew they would still be awake since she had informed her father earlier that she needed to speak with him after everyone had settled for the night.

"I'm assuming this is something your sister can't know about," Daniel presumed.

"It is," Tennly replied. "I've sort of started something, and before you get upset, hear me out." Daniel remained silent, despite a heavy tongue. "I will no longer let any woman under my charge be mistreated. I have offered to help them..."

"Tennly," Daniel interrupted, unable to stay quiet. "you're stirring up something that's none of your business.

You're not even old enough to be in charge yet, and several people are still unsure if you'll make a good leader."

Tennly smiled to keep from yelling at her father and calmly said, "You mean men?"

"What?" Daniel asked, taken aback.

"The people you're talking about are all men," Tennly explained as Lexie moved from the vanity to sit on the edge of the bed. "Even though men run everything, they only make up half of this organization, and not all of them think that way. If I get the women on my side, I'll have the majority."

Tennly always had multiple motives for her actions, and her desire to help women was no exception. While she genuinely wanted to prevent any woman from being abused, she also recognized that by becoming their advocate, she would gain a loyal group of supporters.

Daniel turned to Lexie, the only other woman present, seeking her opinion. "Women can be unpredictable," Lexie stated. "Anger them, and you create an enemy for life. But if you protect them and their families, you have an army."

Daniel smiled at Lexie, nodded, and then turned back to Tennly. "Why tell me this tonight..."

"Well..." Tennly hesitated, dreading the conversation. "Because... I told one of the women I would speak with her husband... tonight."

"Are you insane?" Daniel shouted. "How do you know it's not a trap?"

"I thought about that," Tennly replied, her response sparking anger in Conner for her willingness to risk her safety. "But it's worth the risk."

"You're playing a very dangerous game," Daniel growled. "I assume you're going to this person's house?"

"Yes."

"Where they will have the advantage," Daniel pointed out.

"If I don't show the women that I trust them," she explained, "then they'll never trust me, and I'll never win them over. I don't have a choice."

Daniel ran his hands through his hair and bowed his head in thought. He realized there was no convincing her otherwise and that he wouldn't be able to stop her from going. Conner watched, biting his lower lip, hoping Daniel would come up with a solution.

"You two are a part of this?" Daniel asked, directing his question at Conner and Riley. Conner tilted his head, suggesting that while they didn't agree with Tennly, they also couldn't talk her out of it. "Fine," Daniel conceded. "But you're also taking Thomas and Phillip." He reached for the landline phone on the end table beside the bed, pushed a button, and said, "Call Phillip. Have him get ready and then get the car and pull around front." He then instructed the three of them to follow him.

Before they left the room, Lexie rushed over to Riley, embracing him in a tight hug. "I love you. Be careful."

The three followed Daniel through the mansion to the downstairs living room, a spacious area with two hallway doors about thirty feet apart. Entering, they found two sitting areas furnished with couches, a loveseat, and high-back chairs. A piano stood in the far-right corner, while a small bar lined the opposite wall between a row of windows. In the center, beneath a crystal chandelier, an eight-foot table displayed a vase of roses, while large area rugs covered the Brazilian cherry wood floors. Light yellow walls with ivory trim, dark brown and gold accents, floor-to-ceiling curtains, and paintings, along with mirrors, and sconces that adorned the walls, gave the room an inviting atmosphere.

Tennly told her father her plans, hoping he would give them weapons, and watched as he moved toward the left wall. He pulled a sconce beside a painting, revealing a hidden door. Inside, a secret room mirrored the one in his office: computer monitors to the right, another door to the left, and directly ahead, a cache of guns. Daniel took five pistols with magazines, handing two each to Conner and Riley before turning to Tennly.

"Do you have your knives?" he asked as he handed her the last gun and magazine.

"Yeah," Tennly replied, placing the gun behind her back.

"You only use the guns if your lives are in danger," Daniel cautioned. "It's hard to explain the sound of gunshots. Come on."

They followed Daniel through the mansion to the front door and quietly opened it, revealing a parked black

Mercedes sedan. Thomas stood beside the running vehicle, waiting for their arrival. He opened the back door as the four of them approached.

"Tennly will tell you where to go," Daniel said. "Pick up Phillip. I want one of you to go inside with her..."

"Dad, I don't need..."

"I want one of you to go inside with her," Daniel interrupted, ignoring his daughter's request. "And one of you needs to stay by the car. She's in charge, so do what she says once you're inside, and keep an eye out for anything suspicious or dangerous."

Thomas gave Daniel his word and then gestured for Tennly and the boys to get into the car. Before Tennly got in, Daniel grabbed her arm and turned her to face him.

"Be careful," Daniel said seriously, hoping she couldn't see his heart beating out of his chest. "If you sense anything, you get out of there."

"I will," she assured him.

Tennly felt relieved to see that the Sullivan house was down a secluded driveway, making it easier to get in and out without being noticed. However, the seclusion also heightened her sense of danger, increasing the chance of a setup.

Tennly asked Thomas to park the car a few feet away from the house to ensure it couldn't be heard or seen from inside. Knowing Tennly better than Phillip did, Thomas accompanied her and the two boys, while Phillip stayed with the car. They snuck down the driveway, tiptoed up the front steps, and onto the wraparound porch.

Tennly reached the door first, and as she placed her hand on the doorknob, she closed her eyes and took a deep breath, hoping the door would be unlocked. When she opened her eyes and turned the knob, she let out a quiet sigh of relief upon discovering it opened.

Once they entered the house, they moved quietly around the first floor, checking every nook and cranny to ensure no one was hiding to ambush them. Feeling confident it was clear, Tennly told Thomas to stay downstairs to keep a lookout.

They continued their cautious approach on the second floor, ensuring there were no hidden threats before finally arriving at the master bedroom. Tennly knew it was the last door on the left down the hallway because Caitlyn had provided the exact location, including which side of the door the bed was on. As they got closer, they noticed the door was open and the light was on.

Tennly raised her hand to signal the boys to stop and mouthed, "On three." After the boys nodded, she raised her pointer finger, then two fingers, and as the third finger went up, they walked quickly into the room, looking to the left. Caitlyn, who was sitting on the left side of the bed, reading a book, let out a slight scream, backing up as if trying to get far away from them. Mr. Sullivan, who was on the right, dropped his phone and reached for his gun, which was in the drawer of the end table to his left.

Before anyone could react, Tennly threw one of her knives at the end table. It landed squarely in the center of the drawer, narrowly missing Mr. Sullivan's hand. "I wouldn't do that," Tennly warned as Conner approached the end table and aimed his gun two feet from Mr. Sullivan's head while Riley stayed back at the bedroom door.

All three of them felt relieved by how easy it was to enter the room and reach Mr. Sullivan without any problems. This ease made Tennly believe she could trust Caitlyn, and she realized that to keep her safe, she had to ensure her husband never discovered her betrayal.

"Do you know who I am?" Tennly asked.

"You're Daniel O'Brien's daughter," Mr. Sullivan replied, with a smug undertone. "The one who killed Mikey MacFadden."

"More importantly," Tennly corrected, "I'm James Connolly's granddaughter. I'm the one who is going to be your boss someday."

"We'll see," Mr. Sullivan retorted.

As if Conner could read Tennly's mind, without hesitation, he pistol-whipped Mr. Sullivan across his left temple. Even though Caitlyn had requested their presence, the violence startled her, and she jumped, pulling her covers up as if they would protect her.

"Oh," Tennly maniacally giggled as blood rolled down the side of Mr. Sullivan's face. "Okay, I see. You don't want to be under a woman's rule. That's fine. What is your name?"

"Kevin," Mr. Sullivan answered, having no fear in his voice.

"You see, Kevin," Tennly continued. "What you don't realize is that as an employee with no blood relation to the founding families, you have no legal rights. I could just as easily make your wife my employee instead of you."

"I'm hired by Peter O'Grady," Kevin refuted.

"Who reports to me," Tennly emphasized with a harsh tone. "Unlike you, Peter understands the hierarchy. He knows he has no choice but to follow my lead."

"Are you..." Kevin started.

"Shut up!" Tennly demanded, as Conner pushed his gun harder into his temple. "I am in control, and from now on, if I hear that you have laid a finger on your wife or daughter, someone will come back here, and make sure you can't ever again. Do you understand?"

"Yeah," Kevin said, his indifferent tone indicating he wasn't taking her seriously.

Tennly smiled in frustration, knowing that Kevin had no intention of abiding by her rules. So, without another word, she threw another knife at him, lodging into his right shoulder just above his pectoral muscle. He let out a loud scream as he instinctively reached over with his left hand toward the end table.

"Don't," Tennly warned as Conner cocked his gun. She took a few steps closer to the foot of the bed in a threatening manner. "I'm not playing around. My word is law. Disobey it, and you dig your own grave. Start a rebellion, and you dig your own grave. Go to the police, and you dig your own grave. Do I make myself clear?"

"Yes," Kevin shuddered as he grimaced from the pain.

"Good," Tennly said as Conner lowered his gun and took out the knife from Kevin's shoulder. The bloodcurdling scream made Tennly shake her head at how much of a wimp he was. To keep from throwing another knife into his chest to shut him up, she looked at Caitlyn. "Your name?"

"Caitlyn," she replied, her body shaking despite knowing that Tennly was pretending to conceal that she knew her.

"If you need me, call my Uncle James. He'll get in touch with me."

"Okay," Caitlyn whispered, barely able to get it out.

Tennly looked back at Kevin and warned, "If anything happens to your wife, your daughter, or... any woman for that matter, I will blame you. And then our next encounter will not end well for you."

The three of them left that night, unaware that Daniel had followed them. He met up with Thomas downstairs and waited in the living room for them to leave. After they departed, he quickly made his way to the master bedroom. When he arrived, he found Kevin sitting sideways on the bed, while Caitlyn was next to him, wiping blood from his face with a wet washcloth.

"Have you called the doctor yet?" Daniel asked.

"Daniel?" Kevin whimpered, worried as to why he was there.

"Have you?" Daniel pressed.

"Yes," Kevin responded as he took the washcloth from his wife and turned to face Daniel.

"Good," Daniel said, strolling around the room and examining the Americana decorations, as if he were out for a Sunday stroll. "Then I won't keep you long. I'm just here to make sure you completely understand my daughter. You are disposable. The fact that she left here with you still breathing tells me she has a specific plan. But don't let her mercy tonight fool you; she will kill you if you betray her, and she will have the backing of the five original families. So, it would behoove you to do as she asks."

CHAPTER 17

Conner's birthday was on the Thursday before Easter, and since this was the first time they would be celebrating it together, Tennly wanted to make it special. He was turning 18 that year and had never been to the beach. To create a memorable experience, she arranged for them to fly to their estate in Yucatan, Mexico. To make it even more special, she enlisted her father to talk to the parents of all their friends about joining them. Since they would only miss three days of school that week, Thursday being a teacher workday and Friday being Good Friday, all the parents granted permission for their children to go.

Tennly also wanted to keep the trip a surprise for Conner. She didn't want him to know where they were heading or that their friends would be joining them. She had Marie buy several birthday decorations and balloons, which she had delivered to the Connolly jet, where they spent all day Sunday decorating while Tennly and Daniel kept Conner occupied.

Conner had no idea what Monday had in store for him. He did his normal morning routine before meeting Tennly in the kitchen for breakfast. The pancakes, syrup, and sausage patties were already plated at the breakfast nook, where Tennly was sitting, drinking a cup of coffee.

"Isn't today the day everyone thinks is your birthday?" Tennly asked.

He chuckled and said, "Yeah. Where's Marie?"

There hadn't been a morning since he moved in that Marie wasn't in the kitchen during breakfast. Knowing this, Tennly needed to come up with a credible excuse for her absence. She was with the others on the jet, waiting for them to get there and finalizing any last-minute decorations.

"She has her yearly checkup today," Tennly lied. "Including her mammogram."

"Is she okay?" Conner asked, unaware of female healthcare.

"She's fine," Tennly reassured him, sensing his concern. "It's just something women have to do every year after they reach a certain age."

"You guys ready?" Thomas asked, interrupting their breakfast.

"For what?" Conner questioned.

"Today is the day that Daniel gets all the cars inspected," Thomas explained, continuing the facade that Tennly had started. "You live here now, so your car too."

"Are you serious?" Conner asked, surprised.

"He's a man with many routines," Thomas declared. "I don't question it."

Conner didn't suspect anything as they got into the limousine and started driving toward the school. However, when Thomas passed it, Conner looked at Tennly with question. Being April Fool's Day, he thought maybe she had planned a trick to play on him, so he gave her a suspicious smile.

"What are you up to?" he asked.

"Nothing," she responded with a shrug.

"Are you planning an April Fool's joke?" When she remained quiet, only shrugging her shoulders, he asked, "You're doing something for my birthday, aren't you?"

"Maybe."

"Ten, you know my birthday isn't actually today."

"I know." What he said gave her more ideas about how to keep the trip a secret. "But there are still some people who think it is, and I thought it would be fun to play along. So, happy fake birthday."

He leaned over to her, believing what she said, and gave her a kiss. "If you're going out of your way to do this much for my fake birthday, I expect a lot for my real one."

She smiled and replied, "I guess you'll just have to wait and see."

Normally, the regional county airport didn't handle large jets, but at Daniel's request, an exception was made that day. Since the jet required so much runway space, it was the only plane on the airfield, leaving the terminal empty of other passengers. As they ascended the steps up to the entrance of the jet, Tennly moved ahead of Conner, ensuring she would already be inside by the time he caught sight of everyone waiting.

"Surprise!" everyone shouted as soon as they saw Conner.

The inside was decorated with colorful streamers, balloons, and a large banner that read, 'Happy 18th Birthday.' Conner looked at the decorations and then around to see who was there, shocked to see his brother.

As happy as he was to see everyone, none filled his heart with joy more than seeing Dougy. He gave him a hug, then placed his hands on his shoulders, giving him a look that told him he loved him.

Shortly after the jet took off, Daniel stood in front of everyone to get their attention. "I've been told that our guest of honor has two birthdays... Today is the first... Happy fake birthday, Conner."

Daniel's mansion in Mexico was situated on a 20-acre beachfront property. The house itself was close to 18,000 square feet and was designed in a traditional two-story hacienda architectural style.

The estate featured not only the main house but also three separate buildings: a garage, servant quarters, and a pool house that included an attached four-bedroom apartment. All exteriors were painted a bright yellow, and the main house was accented with white pillars that formed a wraparound porch. A yellow stone wall, positioned fifty feet from the house, enclosed the back and sides of the property while leaving the front open to the ocean.

The inside of the mansion had an open design with lofty ceilings and vibrant Mexican décor. At the center of the home was a sixty-by-seventy-foot courtyard, surrounded by the same white pillars that supported the second-floor porch. The courtyard was filled with trees, plants, bright flowers, statues, tiled walkways, seating areas, and a large central fountain.

The mansion contained ten bedrooms, four community bathrooms, and private baths for Daniel, Tara, and Tennly. It also featured three living rooms, two dining rooms, a music room, a game room, a ballroom, and a kitchen that was larger than most commercial kitchens.

The veranda stretched the width of the house and extended fifty feet toward the beach. Its dark orange tile floors were accented with Talavera designs. To the left was an outdoor kitchen equipped with a rotisserie and brick oven, along with two Talavera-topped wooden tables that seated twenty each, paired with brightly painted chairs. To the right was a fully stocked bar featuring a matching Talavera counter, ten colorful barstools, and four bar-style tables with six stools each.

Centered in front of the front door was a sunken seating area that extended toward the beach, furnished with two U-shaped couches upholstered in red cushions and adorned with teal, orange, and yellow pillows, all surrounding a fire pit.

The pool house located to the right contained a four-bedroom apartment, along with a pool that overlooked the ocean and was divided into indoor and outdoor sections. A concrete patio framed the pool, which was furnished with lounge chairs and two tables seating six each.

For beachside security, a ten-foot white iron fence replaced the stone wall, featuring spiked rungs set six inches apart. A double gate in the middle opened to a stone walkway leading to the shore. At the back of the property, there was a coded gate that allowed vehicle access, leading to a long driveway that forked left toward the servant quarters and right toward the four-stall garage.

The limousine, driven by the Mexican chauffeur and carrying all the kids, pulled into the garage first. Following behind was Thomas in a black sedan, accompanied by Marie, Daniel, and Lexie.

The kids quickly exited their vehicle and followed Tennly through the garage and into the main house. They wandered around, exploring every corner and commenting on the beauty of the surroundings as if they were in a museum. They finally made it out to the veranda, and when Conner and the other boys saw the ocean, they stopped in their tracks. All the girls had been to the beach several times, but none of the boys had. Their childlike excitement faded, replaced by a sense of melancholy as they walked slowly to the edge of the veranda. When they reached the gate, Conner looked at Tennly, silently asking for permission to go out onto the beach.

"It's Paraiso," Tennly said giving him the code. "Spanish for Paradise... 7272476."

The beach was even more magnificent than Conner had expected. The water was crystal clear, unlike the muddy, dark brownish-green, and the sand was not the tan color he had seen in pictures; it was white and felt smooth like silk beneath his feet, rather than coarse like sandpaper he had heard in descriptions. He walked right up to where the waves lapped at the shore and gazed out across the water. It was so clear that he could see fish swimming in the distance. He rolled up his pants legs to let the water wash over his feet and laughed surprisingly, not expecting to sink as the water receded.

Several palm trees lined the beach, providing shade closer to the mansion. Under the shade, there was a cabana with four water-resistant couches arranged around a firepit. Straight in front of the cabana, across the sand, was a long wooden dock with a yacht anchored slightly beyond it. The yacht was twice the size of the one in Marinsburg, with three times as many amenities, including radar that allowed it to travel overseas.

"You have another yacht?" Abby asked as the kids stood on the shore, looking toward the dock.

Hesitantly, Tennly replied, "We have four. This is the biggest."

"Kids," Marie called out as she stood by the gate, "we need to get ready for dinner." They walked back across the beach to where Marie was waiting. "Daniel wants you to pick out your rooms." She then smiled at The Untouchables and added, "You might want to check out the pool house. Once you're done finding your rooms, wash up and be out on the veranda for dinner. Martinique is preparing something special for us."

As soon as they stepped inside the pool house, The Untouchables claimed it for their stay. All four bedrooms were the same size, and none had windows facing the ocean, so there was no need for any fights over them. The living room and kitchen were open to each other and featured floor-to-ceiling windows that offered an excellent view of the beach.

"It's like it was made just for us," Sam said, falling back onto the couch in the living room.

"Yes," Tennly teased. "You were exactly what my mother had in mind when she asked my father to build it."

"I knew I would have loved that woman," Sam said with a smile, giving Tennly a wink.

"She would have loved you, too, Sam," Tennly said, reciprocating his gesture.

They didn't stay long in the pool house, as the others needed to get to the main house to find their rooms. The Untouchables walked with them to explore the rest of the house and to see where everyone would be sleeping.

Once all the bedrooms were settled, they spent the next hour unpacking and freshening up for dinner. It was nice to have everyone sitting at the same table to eat. Even Marie and Thomas joined them as guests rather than employees. It was hard for Marie not to get up and help serve, but Martinique insisted that she stay seated.

Throughout the entire dinner, the boys fidgeted, struggling to control their excitement about getting into the ocean. Not wanting to prolong their anticipation any longer, Daniel dismissed them. They quickly rushed to the pool house to change into their swim trunks and headed to the beach ahead of the others.

Although the temperature was a cool 69 degrees Fahrenheit, the boys were determined not to let that stop them from enjoying their first time in the ocean. The coolness of the water created some hesitation, but their determination won over.

The others made it just in time to see the boys venture out for the very first time. The waves reached nearly four feet, and it was quite windy that night. As the boys walked further out, Rick was knocked down by a wave and rolled back onto the shore. The girls laughed as Dougy picked him up, and they continued out with The Untouchables.

The boys were having fun in the ocean, but they didn't swim for long. By the time they dried off, it was nearly 10:00 PM, and since they had to wake up early the next day, everyone decided it would be best to head to bed.

The next morning, they boarded Daniel's 15-seat passenger van to avoid taking multiple vehicles and were on the road by 7:30 AM headed to Chichen Itza. Daniel had arranged a private tour of two ruins: El Castillo, a 79-foot Mayan step pyramid built between the 8th and 12th centuries, and El Caracol, an observatory from 906 AD used for astronomical studies. After three hours of exploration, they stopped for lunch before heading to Cenote Ik Kil, arriving two hours before closing time.

They walked along the pathway around the sinkhole, gazing into the crystal-blue water framed by plants and hanging vines. At the visitor center, they showered and removed any deodorant, perfume, or makeup before entering. A long staircase led them to a viewing platform covered in vines, resembling a waterfall, and then further down to the water itself. Sunlight streamed through the opening above, creating a beautiful shimmer on the blue surface. Swimmers could cross on a tightrope, enter from the lower platform, or climb to a higher ledge twenty feet above to enter the water. They swam until closing time before returning to the mansion, where Martinique was preparing dinner on the veranda.

The following morning, they gathered at 6:00 AM and then followed Tennly and Daniel to the yacht. On the fourth deck, they entered a glass-enclosed dining room with a 360-degree view, where Thomas and Marie were chatting with Martinique. Two crew members assisted in serving breakfast, and excitement grew as the yacht began to move.

During the voyage, they toured the six-story yacht before settling on the third deck, which featured a pool and lounge areas. After a swim, snacks were served until they reached Cancun, just in time for parasailing. They chose to parasail in pairs, starting with Tennly and Conner. Sam and Tina went second followed by Dougy and Rick. Since Daniel had been parasailing many times before but Lexie had not, he suggested that she go with her son. Joel and Josie went next and finally Lucy and Abby. Each pair enjoyed two rounds before the next adventure: snorkeling.

A quick training session preceded their trip to the underwater museum, which they viewed first through the boat's glass bottom. The museum, run by a nonprofit dedicated to sea life conservation, housed three galleries with over 500 sculptures placed 19 feet deep. The works ranged from human figures to a Volkswagen Beetle with a curled woman on the windshield. Sea life thrived among the sculptures: fish wove through the crevices, coral and barnacles clung to their bases, an eel peeked from behind a statue, and a sea turtle glided past.

As stunning as it was, it couldn't compare to Tennly's next surprise. The boat sailed twelve miles farther into open water, where land was no longer visible, and only three distant boats dotted the horizon.

"You guys are going to love this," Tennly said as she jumped off the side of the boat. When she surfaced, she saw everyone looking at her as if she were crazy. "Come on!" she encouraged.

"We're pretty far out, Ten," Josie said.

"It's perfectly safe," Daniel reassured them. "You'll just be swimming with sharks."

"Dad!" Tennly exclaimed.

"Sharks?" they all echoed almost in unison.

"They're whale sharks," Tennly clarified. "They won't hurt you. Come on!"

"I'm in!" Sam said, leaping into the water.

Conner took a deep breath and jumped in right after Sam, followed by the rest of the boys. The girls stayed on the boat, looking over the edge and through the glass bottom, curious about what they might see.

"Suit yourselves," Tennly said before diving under the water.

The boys followed her, swimming down five feet until they spotted a large gray mass beneath them. Riley and Joel moved closer to Tennly as if she could protect them, watching in awe as the enormous creature swam to the surface. It approached them, coming within ten feet, allowing them to see its impressive size.

The creature had a white underbelly, and a gray top scattered with white spots, measuring at least thirty feet long. Its mouth was wide open as it glided past, taking in small shrimp, plankton, and fish. Intrigued, it circled back and swam close enough for them to touch its side. Its teeth-like scales felt like sandpaper as the kids rubbed their hands across it before it swam out of their view.

From the boat, the girls watched as the giant approached their friends. Its gentle nature compelled them all to jump in and experience it. It wasn't long before they spotted several whale sharks in the distance, and soon another one came within a good viewing distance. The magnificent creature swam about twenty feet from them, circling before finally closing the gap for them to touch it as well. As if sensing it was time to go, the whale shark made one last lap around the group and slowly swam away.

Their excitement made it nearly impossible for them to stay seated during the return trip to Cancun. The boys paced around, acting out what they had just experienced, finding it difficult to relax. They couldn't stop talking about the incredible adventure, and their conversation continued even after they reached the shore and arrived at the restaurant where they had dinner reservations.

Once they arrived, they were taken to the top-floor deck, which Daniel had reserved for their private dining experience. They had just ordered their drinks and appetizers when the sun began to set over the ocean. Oranges and pinks painted the sky as the bright yellow disk touched the surface of the water and then disappeared, leaving a dark purple sky dotted with navy blue clouds. It was the perfect ending to a perfect day. As Conner watched the setting sun, he glanced over at Tennly and saw her face beaming, which warmed his soul.

They arrived back at the yacht by 10:00 PM, where they gathered in the sitting area on the fourth floor. The adults bid the group goodnight and left for their rooms. Tennly requested two bottles of champagne as a nightcap and made a toast to their delightful day as the yacht began to sail away.

When they finally got tired enough to go to bed, Tennly went from room to room, being a gracious hostess, saying goodnight to all her guests before heading to her cabin. Seeing Conner sitting on her bed, facing the door, with a peaceful look on his face, she walked over, positioning herself between his legs, as he buried his head into her stomach. She ran her fingers through his hair, prompting him to look up at her.

He wrapped his arms around her, placing his hands on her back, and gently lifted her onto his lap. He leaned back as her legs fell to either side of his waist, and she helped him remove her shirt.

"I love you," he said.

The yacht returned to the mansion by 6:00 AM the next morning, but Daniel instructed the crew to set the alarms for 8:00 AM for breakfast. Everyone, except Tennly and Conner, was up and gathered on the main dining deck by 8:30 AM. Tennly and Conner finally arrived closer to 9:00 AM, just as everyone else was nearly done eating.

"It's his birthday," Tennly blushed, noticing the confused looks they were receiving for arriving late together.

"I don't want to know," Daniel replied as he approached them. He hugged his daughter and turned to Conner, saying, "Happy birthday."

"Thanks," Conner replied.

After a few fun-filled days, all Conner wanted to do on his actual birthday was spend the rest of the day at the beach. They enjoyed a clam bake for lunch, then played volleyball, bocce ball, surfed, and swam in the ocean all afternoon.

By the time dinner arrived, they were exhausted and decided to stay home to eat on the veranda. As the night progressed, they relaxed, enjoyed drinks, and reminisced about their trip. Marie and Martinique surprised Conner with a birthday cake, which they brought out along with the cards everyone had given him.

His face turned beet red as everyone showered him with affection. Although he never expected to enjoy so much attention, he could feel the love on everyone's faces and realized that all these years, he had been craving it.

"Thanks, everyone," Conner said after finishing reading the last card.

"So," Abby began, "today is really your actual birthday?"

"Yeah," Conner replied with a mischievous grin.

"You know everyone thinks it's on the 1st, right?" Abby continued.

"Yeah," Conner confirmed, giving her a wink.

CHAPTER 18

On Easter Day, Daniel's mother hosted a gathering at her home. She had arranged for catering that included 18 one-pound hams, five large bowls of mashed potatoes, ham gravy, and homemade rolls. The O'Brien wives brought various side dishes, while the Connolly women contributed desserts.

After lunch, they held an Easter egg hunt. The groundskeepers hid over 500 eggs, each containing a monetary amount on a slip of paper, in the backyard before the guests arrived. The older kids walked more slowly than the younger ones to give them a better chance of finding more eggs. Despite this, Conner still felt guilty about keeping any of the eggs. He discreetly walked past the younger kids and placed all but five of his eggs on the ground where they could see them and then watched as they enthusiastically discovered the eggs.

Once all the planned activities were finished, the kids stayed in the great room while the adults moved to separate areas of the house. Just like during Christmas, the younger boys couldn't get enough of Conner. He played video games with them, engaged in hide-and-seek, and even helped them build a Lego set toward the end of the evening.

Conner couldn't help but notice that one person wasn't having as good a time as the others: Joey. He seemed restless, shifting in his seat as if he were extremely uncomfortable and constantly glancing at his watch.

"Do you have somewhere you need to be?" Conner asked, briefly looking at Joey before returning his focus to the scattered Lego pieces.

"No, why?" Joey replied, sounding defensive.

"You keep looking at your watch," Conner pointed out.

"It's just a habit," Joey said, shooting Conner a glare that clearly communicated he should mind his own business.

Conner clenched his teeth and then spotted the Lego piece they were searching for. He knew that if he looked at Joey again, it would be hard to resist the urge to hit him. So, he handed the piece to Seamus and continued his search for the next one.

"Do you have a problem with me?" Joey taunted, determined not to let Conner ignore him.

Conner chuckled, "Not here... not now."

"Why not?" Joey pressed. "It's just a question."

"It's disrespectful," Conner replied, noticing the girls starting to look uneasy. "We can talk about it when we get home."

"Your home?" Joey laughed. "Oh, that's right... you mean Tennly's home."

Conner dug his fingernails into his palms to restrain the urge to jump up and punch him. Taking a deep breath, he looked Joey in the eye and said, "Do you want to fight me, Joey? We can do it in the ring."

"Sounds good to..."

"Joey," Tara interrupted, gripping his arm. "Please, stop."

"He insulted me first," Joey protested.

"I was just asking a question," Conner said defensively. "A simple question... unless it wasn't?"

Joey didn't respond, prompting Conner to stop playing with the boys and stand up. Tennly had been watching quietly, curious about how the situation would unfold, but when she saw Conner's jaw tighten as he took a step toward Joey, she knew she had to step in. If Conner did something disrespectful in her grandmother's home, he would never forgive himself.

Tennly extended her arm to prevent Conner from getting too close to Joey and said, "Okay, I'm sure Joey doesn't mean anything by it." She glanced at Tara, silently urging her to help keep Joey under control before Conner reached his breaking point. "Right, Joey?"

Tara looked at Joey with pleading eyes, prompting him to respond, "Right."

"Yeah," Conner replied, then turned to the boys and tousled Jack's hair. "I'll be back, okay?"

"Okay," the boys replied in unison, completely ignoring the tension of the confrontation.

Conner felt thankful that they left shortly after, arriving back at the O'Brien Estate just before 8:00 PM. As soon as they walked into the great room, they found eight additional Easter baskets placed neatly on the coffee table in the far seating area. The three younger boys eagerly rushed over to the baskets, each excited to grab the one with their name on it.

It was nearly 11:00 PM when everyone decided to head to bed. Upon an earlier request, Tennly and Conner stayed behind with Daniel and the two uncles, having understood that Daniel wanted to discuss something privately. Daniel poured each of them a shot of whiskey and gestured for them to move closer together.

"It was a nice day," Jimmy said as Daniel handed them their drinks. "Make sure to tell your mother we appreciate her hospitality."

"It was," Daniel replied as he sat down. "And I will." He then turned to Conner and said, "You were quiet this evening."

"Just keeping my mouth shut before it gets me into trouble," Conner replied.

"What do you mean?" Daniel asked.

"In case you haven't noticed," Tennly interjected, "Conner and Joey don't get along."

"Did something happen today?" Daniel asked.

"No," answered Conner. "But if he says one more damn thing about my pedigree, I'm going to kick his ass."

"He is a big turd," Jimmy implied, which caused them all to laugh.

"Yeah," John agreed with a questionable undertone. "What is it about him? I can't quite put my finger on it."

"Whatever it is," Jimmy replied, "I don't like him either."

"Okay," Daniel said. "He's my daughter's boyfriend, so we're going to have to learn to accept him."

"He could have an accident," John suggested.

They all fell silent and exchanged wide-eyed glances, as if considering it. Then, in unison, they burst into laughter when they realized it was probably not a good idea.

"No one is going to have any accidents," Daniel demanded, trying to silence his chuckling, getting them to quiet down. "So... now that we're alone, I have something for the two of you." He reached behind his seat and pulled out two gift bags. Handing the first one to Tennly, he said, "Open it."

Tennly removed the crepe paper from the bag and looked inside. She pulled out a small box, measuring three inches by five inches.

"I saw this on my last trip and knew you had to have it," Daniel said as she opened the box.

Inside was a hidden knife hairpin, four and a half inches long, with a two-inch blue and green gem-studded clip to hold it in place. The blade was half an inch thick, tapering to a sharp point at the tip. The handle, measuring two inches, was adorned with the same gems as the clip, helping to conceal the blade.

"It's beautiful," Tennly admired, pulling the knife out of the clip and resting the blade against the inside of her middle · finger. "It's perfectly balanced."

"I thought you would like it," Daniel replied.

"I love it," Tennly exclaimed. "Thank you." She placed the gift back in the bag and then turned to Conner. "Open yours." She was eager to see what her father had chosen for him.

Inside his bag was an envelope that had three pages inside that were folded into thirds. As he unfolded the papers, he realized they contained a legal document. "Holy..." Conner gasped, taking a deep breath. He looked at Daniel while Tennly lowered his hand so she could see what it said. "It's a deed."

"It is," Daniel confirmed. "Tennly told me about your grandfather's property and that it was eventually going to become yours. I went to the courthouse to check it out, and it turns out the paperwork still has your grandfather leaving it to your mother, with no mention of you on it anywhere. Anyway, I pulled some strings and got a judge to sign it over to you.

This is the deed; it's officially your land; all of it."

"I don't know what to say," Conner replied, a lump forming in his throat as he could feel the corners of his eyes becoming wet. "I can't imagine what I would have done if I hadn't gotten it. Thank you so much."

"You're more than welcome," Daniel said. "You'll notice on the second page there's a place where you can sign a portion over to Dougy if you want. I figured you'd want him to have some of the land."

"I do," Conner said as he looked at the second page. "Thank you..." He folded the deed and placed it back into the envelope. "I'm going to go put this in my room... somewhere safe so it doesn't get misplaced."

Conner and Tennly quietly slipped up to his room, not only to avoid waking anyone but also to give him a moment to steady himself. He had left to secure the deed, though the real reason was that he didn't want the men see him cry.

At the corner desk, he slid open the top drawer and tucked the deed safely inside, finding the perfect hiding place.

Turning to Tennly, his voice was thick with disbelief. "I can't believe he did this... Now I can finally build my house."

"Yeah," she whispered, her eyes shining as a happy tear traced down her cheek.

"I will never be able to repay your father for everything he's done for me."

"Happy Easter, Marks," she said, giving him a kiss, to which he returned the gesture.

They left his room, dropped her gift off at the vanity in her bedroom, and then continued down the hall. When they reached the top of the foyer stairs, they heard whispering. They stopped, peered down the stairs, and saw two men standing in the foyer, each holding a gun. Silently, they backed away around the corner and exchanged worried glances.

"Joey," mouthed Conner.

"Tara!" Tennly frightfully whispered, her eyes filled with fear. She ran toward Tara's room, with Conner following closely behind her.

As they entered Tara's bedroom, they found her sleeping soundly and unharmed, but Joey was missing. Conner told Tennly that he would go warn her father while she got Tara and the others to safety. After giving her a kiss and reminding one another to be careful, Tennly watched him leave. She then approached her sister and quietly began to wake her.

"What?" Tara mumbled, sluggishly.

"Get up," Tennly softly spoke, trying not to sound afraid so as to not scare her. "There are intruders in the house, and we need to find the others."

"Where's Joey?" Tara asked, glancing around, as if she didn't quite understand what Tennly had said.

"I don't know," Tennly replied. "Conner is going to warn Dad; he'll probably find Joey along the way. We need to go now."

"Not without Joey," Tara insisted.

Tennly placed her hands on Tara's shoulders and, as patiently as she could, said, "Tara... we have to get to the aunts and the boys... Vicki... I'm sure Joey is fine. But if we don't leave now, we won't be safe. Okay?"

"Okay," Tara responded, her voice trembling.

Tennly quietly approached the door and peeked outside. Just as she was about to lead them out, she spotted a man stepping into the hallway from the foyer stairs, walking in their direction. Quickly, she pulled back into the room and pressed her back against the wall beside the door. She put a finger to her lips, signaling Tara to be quiet and hide.

Tennly pulled a knife from her belt, straining to hear the man's footsteps growing closer. When she heard him just outside the door, she darted out of the room, throwing her knife at the man and striking him directly between the ribs. He screamed and fell to the floor as bullets shot toward the ceiling. As soon as the gun stopped firing, Tennly rushed over to him and twisted the knife to make sure he was dead before pulling it out of his chest. Just then she spotted another man entering the hallway from the foyer stairs, prompting her to hide behind the dead body to avoid the bullets sprayed her way.

She scooted closer to her bedroom door, using the dead man as a shield until she was close enough to roll into her room. She slammed the door shut and quickly jumped to her feet. Realizing she had dropped her knife while using the human shield, she grabbed the scarf hanging on a hook behind the door. She considered making a move toward her vanity, where some weapons were kept, but feared she wouldn't make it in time and would leave her back exposed.

It was fortunate that she had waited, for within a few seconds, the door slowly creaked open. As soon as she spotted the man's arm aiming a gun around the room, she took a deep breath, swung the scarf around his elbow, and twisted it until he dropped the weapon. She swiftly circled around him, kicking the gun with enough force to send it sliding under her bed. Then, she managed to wrap the scarf around the man's neck. She squeezed as hard as she could, but he was much larger.

While he held on to her as tight as he could, he slammed her back against the wall, causing her to fall to the floor. Before she could get up, he kicked her twice in the stomach, then lifted her by the shoulders and held her against the wall. There was only one way she knew she could get free, so despite the pain she was in, she kneed the man as hard as she could in between his legs. He let out a loud moan, loosening his grip just enough for her to break free. She dashed over to her vanity, but before she could open the drawer to grab the pistol hidden in the back of the top compartment, she felt her body being yanked away.

In that moment, she seized the new hairpin her father had given her just as the man pulled her from the vanity. Despite that his grip was clamped hard around her arms, keeping her from striking anywhere fatal, she gathered every ounce of energy she had and drove the knife deep into his stomach. He screamed as he stumbled backwards, allowing her to run back to her vanity.

She was just about to open the drawer when she felt him grab her by the hair of her head and violently slam her head onto her vanity mirror. The shattered glass caused a large cut on her forehead, and as the blood trickled down into her eyes, she heard a scream from behind her. At first, she thought it was herself, about to dose out of consciousness, but as she gasped for air, she knew it wasn't. Tara!

Using all her strength, she reached toward the vanity, searching for anything she could use as a weapon. She managed to open the drawer just enough to grab the pistol. Fearing that she might hit her sister, if she shot backwards, she fell to the ground, twisting her body and pulling the man on top of her as she pulled the trigger.

Blood splattered all over her face, and the weight of the dead man felt as though a building had collapsed onto her. The ringing in her ears from the loud bang was not enough to silence Tara's screams in the background, which reminded Tennly she had to act quickly.

She pushed the body off, tucked the pistol into the back of her pants, grabbed a couple of throwing knives from the top drawer, and stuffed them into the holsters on her belt.

The only thing Tara could do was watch her sister as if what had just happened was something Tennly encountered regularly. She didn't know whether to be in awe of her sister or scared of her. Thoughts formed on her tongue; questions she wanted to ask, but when she tried to speak, no words came out. When Tennly finally walked over to her, Tara was shaking so violently that she feared she might be sick.

"Sh," Tennly consoled, trying to keep Tara calm. "We've got to get Vicki and the boys. Okay?"

"You... you..." Tara stammered, doing everything she could to keep from throwing up.

"Tara, we have to go." Tennly didn't have time to soothe her sister; instead, she went to her bed, bent down, and retrieved the man's gun.

Grabbing Tara's hand, Tennly led her down the hallway and around the corner to the guest rooms where the others were sleeping. Upon reaching the first room on the right, where Vicki was supposed to be, they discovered it was empty. They quickly moved to the adjacent guest room where Jimmy and Valerie were staying but found that room deserted as well.

Continuing on, they approached the guest room where John and Stella always slept, just as they heard more gunshots in the distance. Tennly could feel Tara wince with each shot as she felt her own muscles tense, hoping Conner and the other men were safe. They burst into John's room to find Valeria standing in the middle, aiming a gun at the door, with a dead man lying just inside it.

"Aunt Val!" Tennly called out.

"Tennly," Valerie exclaimed, lowering her weapon as she ran over to the girls, hugging them both.

"Where are the others?" Tennly asked.

"We heard the gunshots," Valerie shuddered. "We got to the boys... Stella took them to the panic room, and I came back to find Vicki."

"She's not in her room," Tennly informed.

"Oh my gosh," Valerie gasped. "We have to find her!"

"I will," Tennly assured. "But you need to get Tara to the panic room. Please."

"I can't leave Vicki," Valerie insisted. "I have to..."

"I'll find her," Tennly promised. "But please, get Tara to safety."

Valerie cupped Tennly's face in her hands and gently wiped away the blood running down from the cut on her forehead with her thumb. "You have to find her," she said firmly.

"I promise," Tennly replied.

Valerie kissed Tennly on the cheek and then led Tara toward the door. Tennly made sure the hallway was clear before watching them head down the corridor to the panic room. Once she was certain her sister was safe, she began checking every room, whispering for Victoria. When she couldn't find her in any of the bedrooms, it occurred to her that there was only one other place she could be: the bathroom across from the upstairs living room. Carefully, she peeked around the corner to ensure there were no intruders before running to the bathroom.

"Vicki," Tennly whispered as soon as she stepped inside, looking around anxiously.

Hearing her cousin, Victoria opened the linen closet door and stepped out. Tears rolled down her face as she trembled in fear. "What's happening?"

"Several men have somehow managed to get into the mansion," Tennly replied.

"I was using the bathroom when I heard..." Victoria started but broke down in tears, unable to finish her sentence.

"Sh," Tennly soothed gently. "I know. It's okay. You did the smart thing."

"What about Mom... and Seamus?" Victoria asked, her voice shaking.

"They're safe," Tennly reassured her.

Tennly wanted to take Victoria to the panic room, not only to ensure her safety but also because having someone with her would make it more difficult to focus on killing the intruders. However, as gunshots rang out in the distance, Tennly peeked her head into the hallway and spotted a man approaching from the direction of the panic room. "Shit," she whispered, quickly pulling herself back into the room.

"Stay here," Tennly demanded, gesturing with her hands for her to hunker down.

Taking a deep breath, she gripped the commandeered gun and crouched down, rolling out of the bathroom and into the hallway. As bullets whizzed over her head, missing her by about two feet, she took aim at the man's chest and fired twice, hitting him perfectly in the heart and causing him to fall, dead. Just then, another man emerged from around the corner and began shooting toward her, unexpectedly hitting her on the left shoulder. Startled, she screamed out in pain, then quickly aimed her gun at him and shot three times, hitting him dead center in the head. Afterward, she called for Victoria to come out, and the two girls ran down the hall, stopping at the corner.

As they crept down the hallway, Victoria clung to Tennly's shirt as they stepped around the bodies and stopped just before the stairs. Peering down the staircase, Tennly noticed two men lying lifeless on the foyer floor. Thinking it was safe to go down, she grabbed Victoria's hand and led her toward the foyer. They were halfway down the steps when Tennly heard voices coming from the kitchen. She tugged on Victoria's arm, urging her to hurry, and then ran down the remaining steps.

Once they reached the foyer, they quickly scurried behind the right staircase to hide. One man went down the left hall, which led to Daniel's office, while the other took the right hall, coming directly toward them. Tennly felt Victoria squeeze her hand in fear, as she quietly slung the gun strap over her right shoulder and replaced it with one of her throwing knives. She waited until the man walked around the right staircase, and as soon as he came into her line of sight, she threw the knife, hitting him directly in the temple. The man dropped the gun and collapsed to the floor, dead.

When they reached the great hall, they found three dead men lying just inside the entryway. They quietly walked over to the sitting areas where they saw a lot of blood on the couch where Tennly's uncles had been sitting.

Tennly paused for a moment, trying to give Victoria the most reassuring look she could while she thought about the best location for her family to go that would give them the advantage: the atrium.

Instead of rushing to the atrium, Tennly guided Victoria back through the foyer and up to the library. The library had a balcony that overlooked the atrium, providing the perfect vantage point. Tennly instructed Victoria to hide under the desk in the far corner and then approached one of the bookshelves. Behind a concealed set of fake books, she retrieved a sniper rifle, an extra magazine, and two pistols. She grabbed the magazine, tucked it into her back pocket before taking the loaded rifle, and carefully walked to the balcony.

Lying down, she propped the rifle up with her arm and aimed, scanning the atrium for any signs of the intruders. She spotted one walking next to the gazebo and fired, hitting the target just before he could shoot Conner. She let out a long sigh as she reflected on how close Conner had come to being killed. Her shot resonated through the atrium, and as the intruders looked up to identify the source, Daniel and Conner seized the opportunity to take out two more of them.

Tennly shot and killed another man just before he was able to get a shot off at her father. She felt a moment of relief, but it was short-lived when she heard someone enter the library. Rolling onto her back, she aimed the rifle at the balcony door and waited. It wasn't the best situation for her, especially since Victoria was still hiding under the desk. She couldn't let the intruder find Victoria, so she yelled for him to come and get her. Just as she prepared to fire, she heard a gunshot and saw the man collapse to the floor. Standing behind him was Victoria, holding a gun. Quickly, Tennly got up and rushed back into the library to her cousin.

"Are you okay?" Tennly asked, caressing her shoulders to calm her.

"Yeah," Victoria shuddered.

"I told you to stay under the desk," Tennly smiled, pride evident in her tone.

"Good thing I didn't," Victoria shot back after she was able to catch her breath.

Tennly had always felt a closer connection to Victoria than to Tara, which made it easier for her to confide in Victoria. She believed that if Tara had been in the room instead of Victoria, the outcome might have been different. So, she nodded to her cousin in appreciation and indicated that she would explain what had happened once they were in the clear.

As soon as the two girls stepped out of the library, Thomas came running toward them. "Are you girls okay?"

"Yeah," Tennly replied.

"It's over," Thomas hurriedly declared. "Come on." As the girls walked down the steps of the foyer, they noticed that Thomas had shot and killed two more men on his way to the library.

When they entered the kitchen, they saw Conner sitting on the bench in the nook. His left leg was extended outward, revealing blood on his jeans from a gunshot wound in his upper thigh. Daniel was seated in a chair facing two intruders who were tied to chairs, still alive. Their hands were tied behind their backs, and their ankles were secured to the front legs of their chairs. The man on the right had been shot in the stomach and the right side of his chest and looked like he had very little time left, as blood gurgled out of his mouth. The other man had been shot three times, but none of the wounds were fatal.

"You're shot," Daniel said as Conner started to stand up.

"Ten?" Conner asked, concern heavy in his voice.

"I'm fine," Tennly responded, touching her forehead. "I had a confrontation with my vanity mirror." She smiled and continued, "The bullet went through. It hurts like a son of a bitch, but I'm fine." Then she turned to Conner and asked, "Are you okay?"

"Yeah," Conner replied. "I'll live."

"Dr. Pratt should be here soon," Daniel mentioned. Then he looked at Victoria and added, "I'm going to have to do some things that might be hard to watch. If you need to leave..."

"I'm good," Victoria said, appearing more stable than expected.

Daniel nodded and gestured for Thomas to approach the intruders, while the two girls moved back. The first question Daniel asked was how they managed to enter without triggering the alarm. To his surprise, the intruders responded quickly. They explained that during the last invasion, they had concealed jamming devices underground around the mansion. All they needed to do was activate those devices when they were outside the gate.

Out of shear anger, Daniel shot the man on the right in the head and then turned the gun on the other man. "Who sent you?!" Daniel exploded.

"Pauly," the intruder blurted out, begging with his eyes to let him live. "Pauly Bianchi."

Daniel, Thomas, Conner, and Tennly could hear their breaths escaping as a wave of sickness washed over them. They exchanged glances of disbelief, struggling to comprehend how they had overlooked the situation. Daniel fixed his fierce stare on the man before him. After a few tense seconds, Daniel finally said, "If you want to live, I strongly suggest you answer each of my questions. If I don't like what I hear... if I don't believe you... do you understand?"

"Yes..." the man replied, nodding his head as he trembled in fear.

Daniel turned away for a moment to compose his emotions before facing the man again. "Do you know Pauly personally?" Daniel asked.

"No, I work for someone who works for him... his family."

"Where?" Daniel pressed.

"Florida."

"How does he know where I live?"

"I don't know."

Without hesitation, Daniel shot the man in the right knee.

After the man screamed, he stuttered, "S... s... some... I heard... he knows someone..." He began to breathe heavier as he continued, "... in your family... or something... I swear... that's all I know... I swear..."

"Where does he know them from?" Daniel demanded.

"School... college or somewhere... I think..."

Instantly, Daniel and the others thought of Tara. Throughout the entire invasion, they had completely forgotten about Joey. Daniel glanced at Thomas, who returned a look that showed he was thinking the same thing. Then he turned to Tennly. She didn't want to believe it, and it showed on her face, but deep down, she knew it to be true. It was the only conclusion that made sense.

Daniel turned back to Thomas and demanded, "Get Tara!"

Thomas nodded and left without saying another word. On the way back from fetching Tara, she continued to ask where Joey was and what was happening. They stopped at her bedroom, where Thomas grabbed her phone from the nightstand beside her bed. Tara didn't understand why Thomas needed her phone but was hesitant to ask.

As they walked through the mansion, Tara screamed at the sight of all the dead bodies, struggling to breathe as she spoke through short, rasping exhales. By the time they entered the kitchen, Tara's confusion and fear grew stronger when she spotted the two men, blood covering their bodies, as her father stood next to them holding a gun. She glanced at her father and sister, once more asking what was happening, but they remained silent, watching as Thomas walked through the kitchen and handed Daniel Tara's phone.

Tara pressed her back against the counter, trying to suppress her fear, while Daniel examined her phone. She watched him with mounting anticipation as he scrolled through the pictures until he found what he was searching for. She couldn't understand what could possibly be on her phone that was connected to the intruders. Her confusion deepened when he held up the phone for the man to see the picture.

"Is this Pauly?" Daniel asked.

"Yes," the man replied.

"Is who...?" Tara asked, taking a few steps toward her father. However, Thomas stopped her before she could get too close.

Tennly closed her eyes and then slowly reopened them as Daniel signaled for Thomas to let Tara approach him. Tennly knew who was in the picture on Tara's phone, and she felt a deep sense of sorrow for her sister. Tara cautiously walked to her father, as if entering a dangerous situation.

Tara glanced at the picture and realized it was Joey. "What...? This isn't someone named Pauly... This is Joey..." Tara insisted, frantically showing the man the picture again. "Tell him he's wrong. His name isn't Pauly."

The man remained silent as Daniel walked over to the island and sat down on a bar stool. He felt torn between anger and disappointment that his daughter had brought someone like Pauly Bianchi into their home, alongside a deep concern and sadness for her. However, the anger he felt at that moment was more powerful, and he knew he needed to take a step back to think before saying or doing something he might regret.

Tara glanced at her father, hoping for an answer, but when he refused to meet her gaze, she turned her attention to Tennly.

"I'm so sorry," Tennly mouthed, a regretful sadness in her eyes.

"What...? I don't understand," Tara responded, tears rolling down her cheeks.

Just as Tennly was about to answer, Dr. Pratt entered through the door from the garage. "Well, you guys have made quite a mess in here."

Before they realized what was happening that night, the intruders opened fire as soon as they entered the great room. One shot struck John in the right shoulder, while three shots hit Jimmy; one in the stomach, one in the right shoulder, and one in the lower back. Conner emerged from the elevator too late to warn them, but he was able to help neutralize the three men from behind, shooting two of them in the back while Daniel took out the third.

Recognizing that Jimmy was unable to walk, they carefully placed him on a rolling serving table and pushed him toward the secret door that led to the tunnels. John then rolled Jimmy down through the tunnel that led to the front turret, where they waited for the doctor to call them back and confirm that it was safe to come out before they met him outside the gate.

Dr. Pratt drove them to the local veterinarian's office, which was owned by Daniel's employees. Since it was not possible to go to a hospital, Dr. Pratt did his best to treat both Jimmy and John at the veterinarian hospital.

"John's fine," Dr. Pratt said. "I got the bullet out and sewn up. Jimmy, on the other hand... the one in the shoulder went through with no damage. One of the bullets hit his lower intestine... I was able to repair that... but the third one hit his lower back. It ricocheted around and severed his spinal cord."

Victoria let out a loud wail, followed by short breaths. Tennly placed her hand on her cousin's shoulder while they continued to listen to the doctor.

"He's stable," Dr. Pratt continued, "but more than likely, he will be paralyzed from the waist down."

Victoria's sobs grew stronger as Tennly and Tara let out sorrowful sighs.

"He's alive," Tennly comforted, looking at Victoria. "Okay... He's alive."

Daniel turned from his family back to the intruder. He would have to deal with Tara and what was happening to Jimmy later; right now, there were still a couple of answers they needed, and he had to focus on that.

"You said you work for Pauly?" Daniel asked.

"Yeah," the man panted, still in agony.

"But you also mentioned his family," Daniel reminded him. "What did you mean by that?"

"The Bianchis," the man answered, looking confused.

"The Bianchi men were all killed eleven years ago in New York," Daniel reported.

"The New York Bianchis, yes," the man replied. "But over thirty years ago, the family split. One brother, Paul Bianchi, stayed in New York, while the other brother, Joseph Bianchi, moved his family to Florida."

Daniel looked at Thomas, as if asking whether he remembered anything about that. Thomas shrugged, took out his phone, and walked out of the kitchen to call John.

"How did Jo... Pauly come to live with his great uncle?" Daniel asked while he waited for Thomas to return.

"When their grandmother died, Joseph took them in," the man answered.

"Where's the girl?" Daniel asked.

"She's estranged from the family," answered the man. "Wants nothing to do with them or the business."

"Paul's brother... did he send Pauly to do this?"

"No. Joseph could have cared less about getting revenge. He hated his brother."

Before Daniel could ask another question, Thomas walked back in. "John said there is a brother, Joseph, that lives in Florida. He said that your father-in-law had a truce with him... He's telling the truth."

Daniel nodded, looked back at the man, and surmised, "I'm assuming Pauly is waiting for a phone call... to say it's over?"

"Yeah."

"Good," Daniel said and then gestured for Thomas to search in the man's pockets for a phone. As if Thomas understood what Daniel wanted next, he untied the man's hands and handed him his phone. "Call him."

"What?" Asked the man, confused.

"Give him a call," Daniel clarified. "Tell him it's over. Tell him that you lost some people but that we're all dead... and put it on speaker."

After only two rings, Pauly was heard saying, "Yeah."

"It's done."

"And?" Pauly asked.

"We lost some men, but we got them."

"They're all dead?"

"Yeah."

"Tara?"

"Yeah."

After a small pause, Pauly asked, "Even the kids?"

"Yeah."

"Good," Pauly remarked with a low sense of gloom detected. "You know what to do?"

"Yeah."

Without saying another word, Pauly hung up the phone. Although Tara didn't know the name Pauly, she recognized his voice; it was the voice of her boyfriend. Hearing Pauly say he wanted her dead, along with her entire family, including the little ones, was incredibly difficult and painful for Tara to process.

Daniel glanced at Tara, having no intention of her finding out about the family this way, and he wasn't sure whether to be angry at Pauly or at himself. All he knew at that moment was that he didn't have time to dwell.

"Where is he now?" Daniel asked.

"I don't know," the man replied. Daniel aimed the gun at the man's good knee. Trembling, the man informed, "I know he's flying out from somewhere." Once more, Daniel gave him a look that indicated he expected more details. "He hates to fly commercial. He'll probably have a private plane ready somewhere."

Thomas quickly picked up the phone to check every airport within a few hours' drive from Marinsburg. Aside from a few whimpers from Victoria about her father, occasional cries from Tara, who still didn't understand what was happening, and some moans of pain from the man, there was silence. After ten minutes, Thomas finally reported that Pauly had a private plane reserved for him at the county airport outside Pittsburgh.

"It leaves in three and a half hours," Thomas added.

"That doesn't give us much time," Daniel fretted.

"It gives us enough," Thomas assured him.

"Then set it up," Daniel commanded, his tone leaving no room for argument. He then shifted his gaze to Tennly.

She recognized that look immediately. When he called her name, she understood what he was asking. Allowing the man to live was not in the family's best interest. As far as they knew, only the man and Pauly were aware of their location. Although her father had told the man that he would let him live if he complied and answered all his questions, doing so would continue to put their entire family in danger.

"Kill him," Tennly ordered.

CHAPTER 19

Everyone was aware of the negative reputation that came with being part of an organized crime family, but few understood that behind every bad quality was an even greater positive attribute: honor. Honor was what allowed opposing family bosses to meet without bloodshed. It prevented families from encroaching on each other's territories, and it was the reason Daniel was able to meet the Bianchis in Florida.

This would be Daniel's first encounter with Joseph Bianchi and any of his descendants. The prospect of meeting the former Don's younger brother was stressful enough, but the uncertainty surrounding why his father-in-law had kept

Joseph Bianchi and their truce a secret made Daniel even more anxious.

The secret pact that James Connolly had made with Joseph Bianchi had put Daniel in an impossible situation. They had located Pauly, and as much as Daniel wanted to kill him, he knew that keeping Pauly alive was essential to demonstrating to the Bianchis that the pact was still in effect. This decision would ultimately be better for his family in the long run.

As Conner, along with his friends and a few of Daniel's trusted local cleaners, tidied up the mansion, Daniel, Thomas, and Tennly drove to retrieve Pauly at the airport just in time for the pilot, who was a trusted colleague of the Connollys, to secretly allow Daniel, Tennly, and Thomas onto the jet.

When Pauly finally boarded, he let out a confused, yet petrified moan as he saw Daniel aiming a gun at him. He turned to head back down the ramp, but blocking his exit was Thomas.

"Have a seat," Daniel demanded, gesturing toward the chair across from him.

Are you going to kill me?" Pauly asked, as he slowly did as he was ordered.

"I should," Daniel answered.

"Did you care for her at all?" Tennly inquired. "Or was it solely to get to us?"

"I could have killed her," Pauly stressed, hoping to gain some sympathy. "But I didn't."

"No," Tennly spat. "You're too much of a coward for that."

The pilot came over and informed them that they were preparing for takeoff and instructed them to take their seats. Pauly glanced over at Thomas, hoping he would sit down, giving him a chance to reach the door, but Thomas remained standing, only taking a seat once the jet was in the air.

Aside from an occasional conversation between Daniel and Tennly, the flight was mostly quiet. The palpable tension stemming from their desire to kill Pauly and the stress of not knowing what awaited them in Florida, created a suffocating atmosphere.

Things got more intense as they approached the Bianchi Estate. Before entering, the chauffeur requested that all weapons be handed over. Daniel understood the risks involved but chose to trust in the old ways and the honor of Joseph

Bianchi. He nodded to Thomas and Tennly, signaling them to relinquish their weapons.

When Tennly only handed over the pistol she had in her hand and a second gun from an ankle holster, Daniel gestured for her to also surrender the knife he suspected she had tucked in her belt, as well as the hair comb he noticed in her hair. Not comprehending why her father would allow them to enter the home of their enemy without some means of defending themselves, she gave him a questioning look, as she handed over what she hoped he thought were her last two weapons.

"Tennly," Daniel pressed. Then, he mouthed, "Trust me," so that only she could see.

Reluctantly, she handed over a second knife she had concealed in a holster behind her back, a third knife tucked up her left sleeve, and a small pistol wedged between the front of her bra.

The driveway was lined with white sand, adorned with islands of flower gardens and circles of palm trees alongside the path. Even though a high stone wall blocked the view of the ocean, the smell of salt and sea life hinted that the beach was nearby. The sky was a clear light blue, with not a cloud in sight, as the sun shone down through the trees.

As soon as they entered the foyer, inside the mansion, they were confronted by five large men, each aiming guns at them. The biggest man lowered his weapon and walked up to Daniel.

"Arms out," the man instructed.

Daniel complied, allowing the man to pat him down. He shot a glance at Tennly that conveyed the message: This was why she needed to get rid of all her weapons. After finishing with Daniel, the man proceeded to check Thomas and then Tennly. It was the first time she had been patted down, and she was pretty sure the man took liberties that weren't necessary. When he spent a little too much time between the inside of her thighs, she could feel her blood boiling.

Just as she was about to knee the man in the nose, they heard a voice say, "That's enough," in the strongest Italian accent Tennly had ever heard.

Standing there was Joseph Bianchi, an older man in his late seventies. He had thick white hair and a clean-shaven face. Despite being fit, he had a small stomach that was hidden beneath an expensively tailored shirt and dress pants.

Tennly found it odd that while everything about the man was well-groomed, he was wearing suede house slippers that matched the color of his trousers: dark blue. Even more odd, than Joseph's footwear was when he walked over to the man that had patted them down and without warning took the cane he had in his hand and beat it across the man's head.

"These are our guests," Joseph scolded. "And you treat them like common whores?"

"I'm sorry, boss," the man winced as he held his head where the cane had struck.

"Get out of here," Joseph commanded. "Clean up." He then turned to Daniel and extended his hand. "I apologize for his behavior. I'm Joseph."

"I appreciate that," Daniel said as they shook hands. "I'm Daniel, and this is Thomas, and my daughter, Tennly."

Joseph approached Tennly and held out his hand. "Please accept my apology."

She took his hand and smiled. "Of course. No harm done."

"Come," Joseph said, leading everyone down a long hallway to an open-air courtyard in the center of the mansion.

The courtyard was surrounded by large, round white columns and filled with bright, colorful plants and exotic trees. Cobblestone walkways meandered throughout, leading to various benches, ponds, and a central sitting area. Joseph gestured for everyone to sit down, but Pauly remained standing with the other men, as if he were part of his uncle's entourage.

Joseph called for drinks from a male servant, dressed in a flowing all-white suit, who approached them. He then turned to Daniel and disclosed, "I was shocked to hear from you."

"I'm sorry it was under these circumstances," Daniel apologized.

"Me too," Joseph agreed. "How did you find out about the truce? It was supposed to be between James and me."

Daniel understood that he needed to be extremely careful with his response; one wrong answer could lead to disaster. "It was," he confirmed. "I knew nothing of it. James informed his two sons just before he died and swore them to secrecy. I only found out after your great-nephew broke that truce."

"It wasn't my truce to break!" Pauly shouted from behind them.

Joseph nodded to one of his men, who walked over to Pauly and punched him in the stomach. He then turned back to Daniel and asked, "Was anyone killed?"

"Thanks to the trained eye of my daughter and her boyfriend, no, but my brother-in-law Jimmy will most likely be paralyzed from the waist down."

"I apologize. This was never meant to happen."

"Thank you."

"If you don't mind my asking, why are you doing all the talking?" Joseph inquired, looking at Daniel. Then he turned to Tennly and said, "I heard you're the boss."

Out of everything they could have prepared for that day, the fact that Joseph knew Tennly was going to become a boss was not one of them. Tennly looked at her father for guidance, uncertain whether she should speak up or wait for him to answer Joseph's question.

"I'm not asking your father," Joseph continued. "I'm asking you."

Tennly could have responded in many ways; she was young, she was still learning, and she needed protection. However, she knew those answers were wrong. It was a test. There was a reason Joseph had a truce with her grandfather: respect. And just like when she was fighting for respect in the Donnybrooks, she understood that her own respect was on the line yet again.

"Because if I were the one giving the orders right now," Tennly said, staring directly into Joseph's eyes with as much confidence as someone who had been a boss in the business for years, "Your nephew wouldn't have made it down here, and I would still have all my weapons."

Only the rustling of the slight spring breeze could be heard throughout the courtyard as the men looked from one to another, waiting to see what would happen.

Joseph glanced over at his chauffeur, who informed him, "She had an arsenal on her person."

Joseph let out a long, loud laugh, catching everyone off guard, believing that he wouldn't let her get away with her threat. Daniel felt his shoulders tense as they waited to see if the laughter was just the calm before the storm.

"Keenan warned me about you," Joseph responded, surprising them by even knowing who Keenan was. "He said you were... how did he put it... aigeanta."

Aigeanta was an old Irish word for high-spirited. The fact that an Italian mobster not only knew that word but knew about Keenan told Daniel and Tennly there was a lot more to the truce than even Jimmy and John knew.

Without missing a beat, Tennly said, "Well, he is an old, stubborn man," in Old Irish. Always being one step ahead, she wanted to see how much of the old language Joseph knew, giving her an idea of how much she could trust him.

Joseph laughed, impressed with her, and, in Old Irish, responded, "He is indeed."

The man who had been sent to get drinks returned, and, as he handed them out, Joseph continued the conversation in English. "That stubborn old man is one of my longest and dearest friends. We met in college years ago, and it was then that I decided I would not partake in the age-old

Bianchi and Connolly feud. When I told my family, they exiled me and wrote me out of everything. It is because of Keenan that I have what I have today. And because of him, I agreed to the truce with James."

As everyone listened, Joseph continued, "I stayed out of your feud; I wanted nothing to do with it. Then one day, I found myself facing a dilemma. My brother had been murdered, and I was being asked by his entire organization to take over: to avenge him. It would have been easier to simply do that; believe me, I thought about it... But my love for Keenan was stronger than my love for my brother. So, where do you think we should go from here?"

"I believe Keenan knew what he was doing when he asked for the truce," Tennly replied. "And that if we handle this correctly, we can reach a mutual agreement that would be very beneficial for both of our families."

"What do you have in mind?" Joseph asked as Pauly began to squirm, not hearing what he wanted.

"If we can put aside this feud," Tennly proposed, "and get our two families to collaborate, it could be profitable. You have the south, and I'm sure there are parts of Italy... while we have the north and Ireland."

As Pauly noticed that his great uncle was considering the offer, he grew angry. "You can't be serious about this, Uncle," he said, walking over to them. "They killed my father and your brother..."

"And they killed her mother," Joseph snapped back to keep him quiet.

Pauly's rage inside him was so strong that he could no longer control himself. He pushed the closest man next to him as hard as he could as he grabbed the gun from the man's side holster. Then, as he yelled, "I won't allow it," he aimed the gun at Tennly.

A loud shot rang out through the courtyard, which caused everyone to jump. Daniel leaned over toward Tennly as she looked down at her chest, her heart stopping as she expected to see red. After two heavy breaths, she realized she wasn't shot and looked back at Pauly. Pain came over Pauly's eyes as small tears began to form and roll down his cheeks. The gray-colored t-shirt he was wearing slowly radiated out in a bright red, like someone had dropped food coloring in a glass of water. He blinked once, dropped the gun to the ground, and fell dead.

Behind Pauly's body stood the man who had brought them their drinks, aiming his firearm in the direction where Pauly once stood, his gaze fixed on Joseph. For a split second, Daniel, Tennly, and Thomas believed they were going to be next, perhaps driven by anger. Joseph gestured for the man to lower his gun and then turned back to Tennly and Daniel.

"I was hoping it wouldn't come to this," Joseph mumbled solemnly. After a few moments of collecting himself, he took a napkin from the table beside him and wiped his eyes, as if struggling to hide any tears. Once he felt ready to continue, he looked at Tennly and Daniel, saying, "I loved my great-nephew very much... but his need for vengeance overshadowed any common sense. I was hoping he would realize the feud was over, but..."

Joseph stood and added, "Come up with some proposals, and I'll consider working with you."

"We will," Tennly replied as she stood and extended her hand to Joseph. "Thank you."

Joseph took her hand, kissed the back of it, and then patted her wrist. "It was nice to meet you, Tennly. Learn everything you can... and remember that sometimes you have to make hard decisions... decisions you may not want to make."

"I will," Tennly responded. "I'm sorry for your loss."

He appreciated her condolences and, with a sullen tone, said, "Tell your family the feud is over... and in its place, a new friendship."

Tara wasn't ready to talk to anyone. She was angry that her family had kept secrets from her and devastated that her boyfriend had betrayed her and was killed. However, she wasn't sure whether she was more upset about his actions or the fact that she had been so easily deceived. Above all, she worried that what had happened that night might happen again. Every time she closed her eyes, fear crept in, waking her up. Even though she had been reassured that they were safe, she couldn't shake the feeling that at any moment, someone might burst through her door.

Her mind raced as she tried to piece together everything that had happened, making it impossible to focus on the television playing in the background. She shifted back and forth between crying and screaming into her pillow. When she heard a knock on her door, it startled her. Sitting up and shaking, she grabbed a pillow and hugged it to her chest as if it were a bulletproof vest. It wasn't until she heard Victoria call out her name that she finally put the pillow down.

"Go away!" Tara shouted.

"I'm not going to," Victoria countered. "I'm staying out here until you let me in."

Tara considered not letting her in but remembered that it wasn't her cousin's fault; she, too, was unaware about their family. Reluctantly, she walked to the door, and as soon as she opened it, she saw Victoria holding a plate of food.

"I thought maybe you might be hungry."

Tara gestured for her to come inside as she took the plate. "Thanks," she muttered.

"Are you doing, okay?"

"Not really. You?"

"I don't know. A lot of things now make sense."

"I just can't stop thinking that if I had known about our family... maybe I would have been a little more skeptical..."

"Well," Victoria said, giving her a hug. "Maybe that was the point. Maybe our family didn't want us to have a childhood of skepticism, always worried something might happen, afraid to go out, meet people." Seeing that Tara wasn't going to respond, she added, "I'm here if you need me," and then left to let her eat in peace.

Tara reflected on her cousin's words, and although she didn't feel significantly better by the time she finished eating, she did gain a bit more understanding. With that thought in mind, she gathered her plate and left her bedroom to return it to the kitchen. When she arrived, she found Conner sitting at the bar, snacking on a sandwich. She knew he could provide her with a lot of answers, but she wasn't sure if she was ready to talk to him. Conner respected her silence as he watched her place the plate in the dishwasher and then start to walk back toward the kitchen door. He took a sip from his water glass, thinking she would leave, but was surprised when she turned back around.

"How's your leg?" she asked.

"It's okay," he replied as he put his glass down.

"Is what my father does the reason he accepted you so easily?" Tara inquired as she walked back toward him.

Conner nearly choked on the bite of food as he let out a slight chuckle.

"What?" she asked, both perturbed and curious.

"I wouldn't say your father accepted me that easily. He kept us apart, tried to pay me off, and at one point, threatened my life."

"I wasn't aware. I'm sorry."

"She wanted to tell you," he said, regarding the family.

"Then why didn't she? Because of Daddy?"

"Yeah, he wanted you to have a carefree college experience. If even for the first year. It really weighed heavy on her... but in the end she agreed, wanting to give you something she would never have."

Tara felt bad for being so angry with her sister. She had been so wrapped up in her own feelings that she hadn't considered what her sister had been going through.

"How long has she known?" she asked.

"She suspected years ago that something was off, but she only truly found out this past year."

"Do you work for them?"

"Yeah... that's one reason your dad moved me in here."

"Which, by the way," she smiled, letting him know she was feeling a little better, "is still weird."

"Tell me about it," he replied, giving her a wink.

Tara spent the rest of the afternoon contemplating what her family did for a living and trying to understand who her sister really was. Although she remained uncertain about her feelings, one thing was clear: she loved them, and she needed her sister to know that. So later that evening, after dinner, she searched the mansion until she finally found her in the gym.

Peeking inside, Tara spotted her sister sparring with Riley in the ring, while Conner was sitting on the sidelines, giving her instructions like a coach. It was strange seeing Riley there, and she wondered if he knew about her family.

She stayed back and watched in awe at how well her sister held her own against two of the toughest boys in the city, and she was doing it with her left arm tightly wrapped against her body, making it immobile. She grimaced as she saw Tennly skillfully avoid a jab to her stomach and maneuver around behind Riley. However, before she could get a grip on him, he flipped her over and slammed her down onto the mat, landing her on her back.

Tennly let out a loud moan and grunted, "This would be easier with my other arm."

"The doctor said you can't use that arm for at least two weeks," Riley reminded her as he helped her up.

"Besides," Conner added, "you rely too much on both arms. There may come a time when you can only use one."

Tara continued to watch as they started back up, feeling a sense of pride when Tennly kicked Riley in the chest, causing him to stumble. It was then that

Tennly noticed her standing there. Tennly raised her hand, stopping Riley from advancing, and locked eyes with her sister.

"Hey, Ten," Tara said with a regretful tone.

Tennly stepped out of the ring, unwrapping her arm as she approached her sister. "I'm so sorry."

"No," Tara replied. "I'm sorry. I..." She hesitated before changing her demeanor and asking, "Can you teach me to do that?"

"Fight?" Tennly asked, excited that her sister was interested in their family's activities rather than being upset about them.

"Yeah."

Tennly smiled. "I think we can teach you a few things."

Tennly instructed Riley to show Tara some basic self-defense moves to start with. It took Tara a few attempts before she felt comfortable being touched by an Untouchable, and the first time she punched him in the face with her elbow, she quickly apologized.

Riley laughed, rubbing his upper lip. "Don't be sorry; that's how you do it. Let's go again."

Life gradually settled into a semblance of normalcy for Tennly and her family over the next couple of months. Pauly's death had closed one chapter of danger, and Tennly's unexpected but growing relationship with Joseph Bianchi had opened a safer one. With the threat seemingly behind them, Daniel finally felt it was safe enough for his daughters to resume their lives, which meant sending them back to school.

For Tennly, Conner, and their circle of friends, school quickly became less about academics and more about being together. They were nearly inseparable. Each morning, they met in the parking lot and walked in as a group; those who had the same lunch ate together, and after school, they waited for one another at their cars before heading home. Evenings consisted of gathering at the mansion, meeting on the yacht, or venturing into town to restaurants, movie theaters, or arcades.

No matter where they were or what they were doing, one thing became clear: The Untouchables had become touchable. Once infamous for their reputation as unapproachable bad boys, they were now viewed as being more human. The mystery that had once surrounded them dissolved, replaced with a surprising sense of normalcy. Conner's growing closeness with Tennly and Sam's steady relationship with Tina drew admiration from nearly everyone; Everyone except Shelby.

Shelby remained in the background, watching and waiting for an opportunity to seek revenge. Her past failures to best Tennly had taught her caution, prompting her to mask her bitterness beneath a careful façade while she watched, waiting for the precise moment to strike back.

But Shelby wasn't the only one biding her time. Unbeknownst to Daniel and the rest of the Connolly family, another storm was brewing; One far more dangerous, deliberate, and capable. Someone had been watching from a distance, gathering information, and studying their routines.

Someone who had the training, background, and financial resources to aid in their quest for vengeance. Someone who possessed the patience and capability to attain whatever they desired.

Most chilling of all, this someone had personal reasons for wanting Daniel and his family to pay, and it was someone the Connollys would never have expected:

Sofia Bianchi.

IRISH MAFIA HIERARCHY

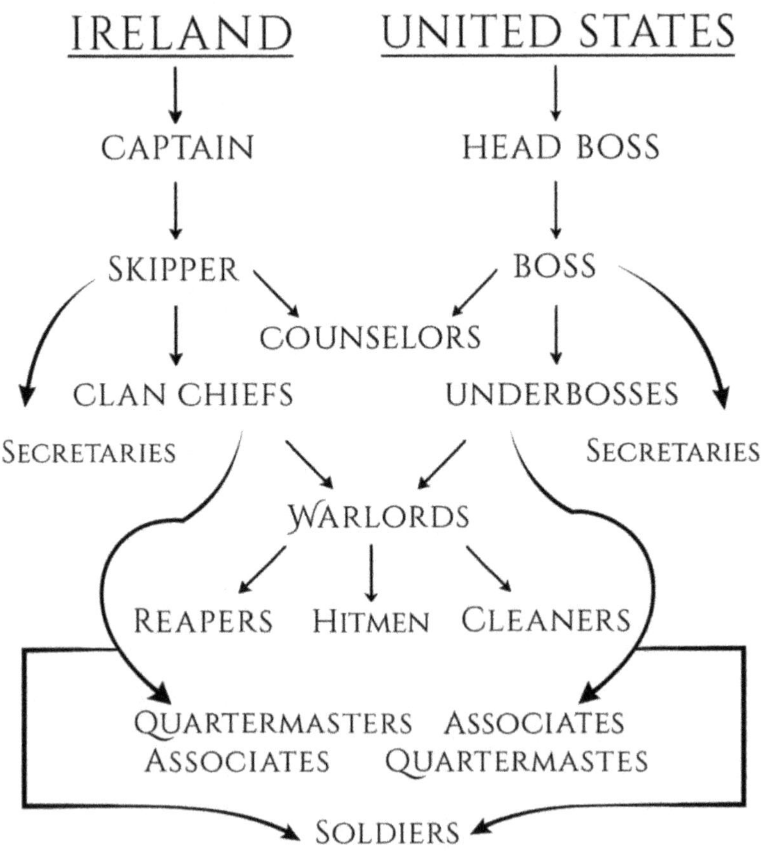

CONNOLLY FAMILY HIERARCHY

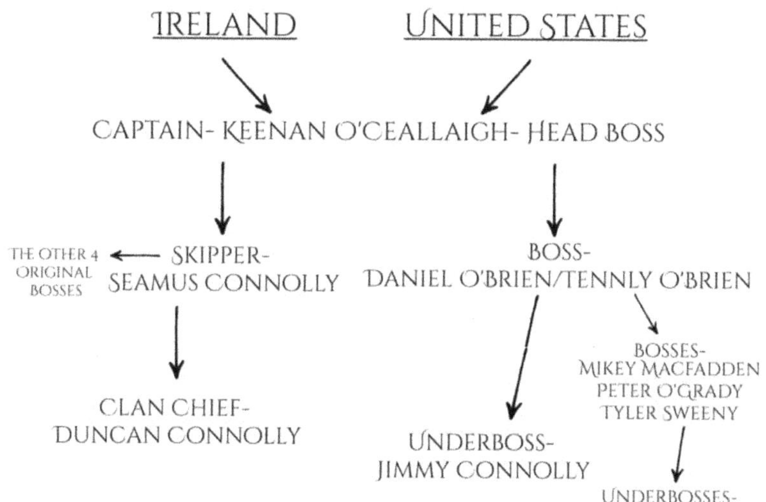

To be concluded in...

Scan QR Code to link to my webpage to get 'Worlds Unite' as well as future books.

If you enjoyed 'Worlds Collide,' please consider leaving an honest review on Amazon or your preferred media platforms. I would greatly appreciate it. Thank you for entering my world! I hope you found it enjoyable!

9 798999 405616